The Lure of Illusions
a tale of intrigue and tragedy in war-torn Syria

Yannis Andricopoulos is a Greek ex-journalist, author of eight non-fiction books and co-founder of the legendary Skyros Holidays. In this book, his first fictional book, he tells the story of Ari, UNRWA's chief information officer in the Syrian capital, and Laura, the BBC journalist, whose love for each other is hit by the horrors of the war and the illusions of its protagonists which threaten to turn the conflict into the-end-of-the-world final battle.

By the same Author –

In Bed With Madness
Trying to make sense inboxed a World that Doesn't
Imprint Academic, London, 2008

The Greek Inheritance
Ancient Greek wisdom for the Digital Era
Imprint Acadenic, London, 2008

The Future of the Past
From the Culture of Profit to the Culture of Joy
Imprint Academic, London, 2008

History, Politics and Dreams
Grosvenor House Publishing Ltd., London, 2015

1944 Κρισιμη Χρονια
Διογενης, Αθηνα, 1974

Οι Ριζες του Ελληνικου Φασισμου
Διογενης, Αθηνα, 1977

Το Ευρωπαικο Αδιεξοδο
Διογενης, Αθηνα, 1978

Η Δημοκρατια του Μεσοπολεμου
Φυτρακης, Αθηνα, 1987

The Lure of Illusions

a tale of intrigue and tragedy in war-torn Syria

Yannis Andricopoulos

Arena Books

First published in 2017 by Arena Books

Arena Books
6 Southgate Green
Bury St. Edmunds
IP33 2BL

www.arenabooks.co.uk

Distributed in America by Ingram International, One Ingram Blvd., PO Box
3006, La Vergne, TN 37086-1985, USA.

Danuta Gray
The Lure of Illusions a tale of intrigue and tragedy in war-torn Syria

British Library cataloguing in Publication Data. A Catalogue record
for this book is available from the British Library.

ISBN-13   978-1-911593-17-1

BIC classifications:- FA, FHP, FJM, FRD.

Printed and bound by Lightning Source UK

Cover design
By Jason Anscomb

Typeset in
Times New Roman

Contents

Chapter 1
Nothing To Worry About

The Cham Wings Airlines 747 SP went into a sudden yet imperceptible circular path in the endless blue of the Damascus sky. Mentally in the Syrian capital or perhaps still back in Kuwait, the passengers remained unaware of the forced course change for a few minutes. The picture changed dramatically, however, as soon as several Syrian military aeroplanes, MiG-25s, appeared flying close to the airliner. Everybody's eyes instantly recovered their mobility, hitherto lost in the boredom of the journey, and anxiety licked its tongue into all corners of their existence.

'What the hell...?' a heavily overweight man entering the final phase of his middle life shouted out loud. Leaping out of his seat, he knocked his water bottle and glass, their contents spraying over his black, baggy suit trousers. Knowing that the appearance of these military planes did not bode well, other passengers also yelled, many of them silently. A few of them bombarded the flight attendants with questions to which no coherent reply could possibly yet be given. Others tried their iPhones, albeit without success.

Laura, an engaging young woman with bright brown eyes and long, dark shining hair, who was on her way to Damascus as the BBC's Syrian correspondent, surveyed the turbulence around her. She kept her cool but, edgy like everyone else, wondered what exactly was going on.

Hypotheses of one kind or another were already flying through the cabin's thick air. Perhaps, as some passengers suggested, the rebels were once again attacking the capital's airport – maybe they had taken it over, or, much worse, rebel groups with access to ground-to-air missiles were trying to take down the planes? In the prevailing uncertainty the danger seemed only to grow, and anxiety, visible on so many faces, obliterated all concerns and thoughts not associated with the animal instinct of survival.

Of course, the danger did not appear out of the blue. Everybody knew that Damascus International Airport should be avoided if at all possible. Many airlines had actually stopped flying there as soon as civil war broke out in Syria.

'Emergencies in this part of the world are part of our everyday routines,' someone suggested humourlessly.

'Good to know,' a co-passenger sitting close to him grumbled sarcastically. The man was clearly in no mood for this sort of drollery. Another passenger with a hoarse voice and a vicious disposition mumbled, 'Piss off' under his breath. His eyes were wide and fat with fear.

Meanwhile, anxious and rather agitated, two burly male passengers had risen from their seats and started moving menacingly towards the pilots' cabin.

'Where are you going?' a pudgy, middle-aged and bearded man with harassed eyes asked them loudly. Judging from his white keffiyeh with black aghals, he was probably from the UAE. 'You want to force them to give us information that the flying attendants can't or won't give us? Or to force them to do what?'

Laura silently agreed with him while her anxiety, tucked away neatly, was beginning to flutter noisily its wings.

An Arab man with a face that age had corrugated joined the clamour. His medical condition, he peevishly told the flight attendant, required immediate attention. A clot had apparently formed in a deep vein in his leg causing him pain and swelling. 'I need to get off the plane right now!' he demanded. His twitching agony gave his words a geometric precision. 'I cannot wait…'

'I can hear you,' was the only answer that the flight attendant was prepared to provide. The baleful look she gave him conveyed the true meaning of her response. In times like this, the man should, obviously, not have made such a 'preposterous' request.

The prevailing state of suspense had, meanwhile, introduced the threat of physical violence. Some passengers could barely suppress their eagerness to force the captain to tell them what was going on, and a number of them had already started moving menacingly towards his cabin. But nothing happened as the captain pre-empted any such action by announcing that landing would be delayed 'for just a while'. Some unspecified emergency on the ground had to be dealt with first. His explanation, which in itself needed explaining, was followed by the reassurance that the passengers had nothing to worry about.

'Lovely,' one of them mockingly said. Others responded to the announcement with acid smiles, their faces white as a codfish belly. The smiles disappeared as soon as the plane's wings dipped enough for explosions and fires on the ground near the landing area to be visible through the windows. Rising plumes of thick black smoke were all over it.

'Welcome to Damascus International Airport,' someone shouted from the back of the airbus. The airport had been dubbed by some the 'Highway of Death'.

Landing eventually took place uneventfully some twenty minutes later, to everybody's relief. Happy to have the soil back under their feet, the passengers moved to the airport's reception where they had strong drinks or coffees, every bit as essential, in that moment, as the sky is for the stars. The smokers among them were desperate for a drag. One of them, a woman with dark circles beneath her eyes, ignored the 'No Smoking' signs all around her and lit-up.

Instantly a uniformed official was next to her, berating her for disregarding the airport regulations. 'No smoking here,' he shouted at her.

The woman looked at him with an ironical emotional detachment before telling him bluntly to 'Go to hell'. The words came out of her mouth with the viciousness of a hissing snake. Looking at him provocatively, she then continued to smoke until she quietly finished her cigarette and flicked the butt into the Bird of Paradise pot plant on duty in the corner.

The ongoing emergency had, of course, gained total priority. A glimpse into what had happened came from some visibly disturbed uniformed staff.

'Targets at or near the airport were hit by an Israeli air strike,' a tall uniformed policeman informed them in a voice as bitter as his life. Apparently determined to make sure any potential attackers would be dead before they could act, his eyes kept darting anxiously left and right.

'Bloody Israelis...' another one with an old-fashioned nose, like Girolamo Savonarola's, and bushy eyebrows, who was standing next to him, explained. Neither of them seemed to know exactly what was going on. All they could say was that loud explosions were heard, followed by a power outage and the temporary suspension of all flights.

The Israelis had already stated they would make sure that sophisticated weapons did not reach Hezbollah, the Lebanon-based Shi'ite militant group that had been active in Syria on the side of president Bashar al-Assad. Their target, Laura heard later, had been some advanced weapons shipments from Iran. It was not the first time such an attack had occurred. In other air raids carried out since the civil war in Syria began, or at least since January 2013, Israel had bombed many other military-related targets in the Syrian capital, across Syria's porous frontier with Lebanon or in the Syrian-controlled part of the Golan Heights.

As one would expect, the air raid had heavily disrupted the airport's routines. Armed military units were positioning and re-positioning themselves between its various sections, secret police officers were visually interrogating every passenger, and people were instructed through loudspeakers to conform fully to the security personnel's orders.

'We'd better stay here until we know what's going on outside the airport,' a middle-aged Mediterranean-looking woman mumbled. With terror-gnawed bewilderment, she was now queuing with Laura in front of passport control. 'That would be much safer.'

'Don't worry!' Laura reassured her. 'If the roads to town aren't safe, we won't be able to go anywhere anyway.' The woman continued mumbling, oblivious to her words. Laura, meanwhile, calm on the outside like a swan, but paddling frantically underneath, was anything but sure that what she had said was actually true.

The turmoil and the chaotic conditions the emergency had engendered had not surprised her. It was more or less what she expected to see in a country tormented by a most destructive civil strife, now in its fifth year. Yet, the terror of the moment had hit a nerve. 'When will we escape it all?' she wondered as she was waiting to get through the passport control. 'Probably never,' was her answer to her own question. 'Ambition, greed, envy, pride, stupidity – all this ensures we'll always be in tune with the "sad music of humanity".'

Laura Heineken, born in Buckinghamshire in 1986, studied politics at Queen Mary College, University of London. After completing the BBC journalism training programme, she started her broadcasting career with Radio 5 Live and then BBC Breakfast. Later on, she joined the BBC news channel. A flair for languages and her taste for adventure had ensured that, as time went on, foreign assignments came her way including postings to Tunisia, Egypt and Libya during the 'Arab Spring'. Her last short appointment before moving on to Damascus had been in Jerusalem where she had produced a documentary on the Golan Heights. Her appointment in Damascus as the BBC's Syrian correspondent both thrilled but also frightened her as never before in her professional life. This little adventure at the airport only strengthened her apprehension.

The airport facilities in Damascus in the middle of the long civil war were rather spartan. This did not bother her though. All she cared about now was getting through passport control as quickly as possible and reaching the exit where Ari Boletis waited patiently for her. The two of them had met at Conway Hall in London's Red Lion Square while she was interviewing pro-Palestinian supporters on the military operation launched by Israel in the summer of 2014 on the Gaza strip. They had instantly bonded and became very good friends in no time. Their friendship was cemented in the summer of 2015, when together with a few friends they had spent a week on the Greek island of Hydra. She could not wait to see him again.

Ari had arrived in Damascus one month earlier, in the early part of September 2015 as the chief information officer of UNRWA, the United Nations Relief and Works Agency for Palestine Refugees. He was an Arabic-speaking Greek with family roots in Alexandria. In 2001, when he was 16, he had moved with his parents to Athens where soon after, he had entered university and got a degree in law. Later he had moved to London. The research he did at the LSE on the relationship between civil society and the media earned him a PhD which helped him get a job in Brussels with UNRWA.

Ari spotted Laura, and waved his arms to catch her attention. As happy to see him as a sunflower in sunshine, she waved back and rushed to meet him with open arms and an incandescent smile. She had missed his reassuring presence, his warmth, his support and his smile, which was always reflected in his bright eyes. Although neither of them had ever acknowledged such feelings, she was as attracted to him as she believed he was to her.

Ari, too, was delighted to see her. 'I need to be close to her ... whether it's in London, Athens, Rome or Timbuktu,' he kept thinking. 'But here in Damascus, away from the comforting certainties of life, in a place where times are stressful and friendship is rarely extended to foreigners, her arrival is a blessing to me.' Laura was the one person he could talk honestly with, share his worries with, and bring some sanity into his deranged daily life. But more than that, she was a lovely woman who could effortlessly nourish his spirit and his heart. He realised that she was the only person that he felt totally at home with.

'I'm in love with her,' he thought to himself almost blushing in embarrassment. As the words were flowing in his mind, he became suddenly aware that he had crossed the threshold from reality into reverie that the ineffable joy of her arrival had generated. Yes, he was in love with this woman.

They kissed each other on the cheek and then walked together to the airport coffee shop. On its wall there was a 'No Smoking' sign. Someone had added, 'No Suicides Either'.

'You look great,' he said to her lovingly.

'So do you,' she replied appreciatively. That was certainly the case as Laura knew, after all, that Ari was related to Antigone Boletis, a woman who had been crowned Miss Egypt and then Miss World in 1954. The genes had made their mark.

He ordered a double espresso for himself and a cappuccino for Laura. Though he knew what had happened, he asked her how her journey had been.

'Colourful,' she answered with a taut smile. 'So was the grilling I was subjected to soon after we landed,' she added, flexing her long slim fingers with grace. 'All my bags and the pockets inside them have been assiduously inspected by the polite but meticulous security. They examined everything, even my toothpaste and cosmetics.'

'Well, life would be boring without a little drama,' Ari joked. 'Like airport novels.'

She parted her lips, usually moist and peachy, but at that moment as dry as the biscuit that came with her coffee, smiled cheerily and then asked Ari about his time in Damascus. An elderly man, infatuated with her legs, was staring at her with a senile, cackling laugh. She looked back at him with an expression of reproachful sorrow and then re-focused on Ari's dark and soulful eyes.

'Not as bad as I thought,' Ari said. 'Damascus isn't as bad as Yarmouk or Al-Raqqah. But on the other hand, the city has many faces. One face here and another only fifty meters away. This isn't just the case in Damascus either. The whole country has become a patchwork of zones.'

'Hmm,' Laura responded, thoughtfully, wrapped up in her own reflections.

'In the parts of Damascus that are heavily guarded by government troops,' Ari carried on, 'almost everything functions as if there is no war raging all around. This doesn't mean that the locals aren't affected by the war. Yet...they still go out to smoke their shisha, play backgammon and relax. But then, in other parts of the city, life is pure terror.'

Damascus was not, of course, as familiar to Laura as the neighbourhood she had grown up in, but she knew what Ari was talking about. His words helped to calm her still-frayed nerve, but anxiety forced one more question.

'The journey to the Old City is pretty safe though, isn't it?' she asked. She knew Damascus was under siege and that any kind of movement was risky.

'Well, rebels do sometimes like to party and have fun,' Ari answered light-heartedly. 'They shoot at passing cars and sometimes they take hostages.'

It was not quite the response she was looking for. She gave him a vague smile that resisted its movement to the precision of the final form as she was not sure how exactly to interpret his comment. Ari looked at her, captivated by her sparkling eyes and the smile that lingered on her lips.

'Any trip along this road,' he added, aware of her discomfort and more seriously this time, 'is inevitably a flirtation with death. But things have improved a lot lately and a few major routes are now fairly safe, including the road to and from the airport.'

'And the Old City itself?' Laura persisted.

'Well, the Old City is even safer. You can easily move around by foot or by taxi.' Ari usually travelled around on a Honda VFR motorbike that he had bought in Damascus, but it was not what he had used to get to the airport. Instead, he had booked a cab driven by a short, stocky man with a round face and plump cheeks, who was now waiting for them in the car park. Despite the turmoil, tired of waiting for his customer to come back, the man had fallen asleep in his seat. He woke up the moment Ari opened the door of his vehicle.

'So sorry,' he apologised. 'Long hours...'

Ari asked him to take them to the Sheraton hotel in the centre of Damascus. He started the engine and then, as if they were about to enter London's North Circular Road, reminded them to wear their seat belts.

'So weird,' Laura whispered to Ari. 'We can easily get killed by a rocket, and he wants us to wear our seat belts!'

'Their sense of order,' Ari replied.

Neither of them were really into small talk, yet words were endlessly flowing from their lips, while their eyes were sending out different messages: the flowering messages of love. Their scent tinged the air and engulfed them in a fragrant cloud that kept them apart from the malodorous environment the war had generated.

Driving across a broken lane, all they could see was the tormented skin of a town disfigured by the bombing – deserted, squalid arrays of crumpled buildings. The minaret of a mosque, veined by the dispassionate midday sun, was now twisted metal and crumbling stone, tattered and bullet-riddled. Huge haulage trucks sounded their horns as they squeezed past yellow taxis and minibuses on the cracked tarmac. A white pickup truck with eight people, each with their AK-47 hanging loosely by their sides, overtook Ari and Laura's cab and moved speedily ahead.

Soon they reached Jeramana, a town 8 km from the capital and once a frontline in the battle for Damascus. As Laura recalled, the town was in a predominantly Druze-Christian area, home to a large number of Iraqi Assyrian Christian refugees who had moved there since 2003. There were also Palestinian refugees who had moved into the area in 1948 and then again in 1967, and now, the town was also home to many displaced families who had fled the war in neighbouring suburbs, mainly Eastern Ghouta.

The pre-prepared background notes she had made on her laptop in London that she was now consulting in the taxi, told her that the city had been heavily damaged at the end of 2012 by rockets and suicide bombers. The government was now in control of its streets, but safety was a very relative term. Just one week before, rebels had ambushed volunteers at a checkpoint close to the highway and killed many of them. The danger was still evident in later days, too, when an Israeli air-to-surface missile had destroyed a six-storey residential building in the area, killing eight people, including several Hezbollah field commanders.

Laura suggested that they drive through the town. 'I'd like to see what daily life is like,' she said.

Ari instructed the taxi driver accordingly. Crossing its 'borders', they passed a number of military checkpoints manned by armed men who were not part of the Syrian army, but 'shabeeha', a militia formed by local men to protect their community. Drivers were stopped by them, questioned and asked to produce an ID, if necessary. Some had their trunks checked and all were subjected to a check that electronically detected the presence of explosives. Similar militias guarded other towns and neighbourhoods, aiding Bashar al-Assad's overstretched army. Though helpful, this very strict security could not prevent the occasional smuggling of car bombs into the city centre.

The checkpoint volunteers seemed quite relaxed. They let the taxi through without any excessive checks and even wished Ari and Laura 'an enjoyable holiday break'.

When in town, Ari told the driver, who identified himself as Wael Sharabi and had mentioned in passing that he had to deal with 'an uninvited toothache', to wait for a while so that they could take a short walk along the market. The street was busy, with shops, often offering seasonal discounts, serving customers, and people were moving around on buses, taxes or bicycles. Pictures of Bashar al-Assad in civilian or military outfits were everywhere, accusingly pointing his finger, posing with a smile of eternal reassurance or even in a meditative pose with his chin resting in his hand and his eyes scanning the horizon.

'His dysfunctional conscience is nowhere to be seen,' remarked Laura.

Flags hanging from the top of a few poles, limp and crumpled, seemed entirely disinterested in what was going on beneath them. So, too, was the constant, growling soundtrack of generators supplying electricity to a town that enjoyed just six hours of mains electricity per day. With Isis, the 'Islamic State', controlling the oil fields, prolonged electricity cuts were now part of the normal abnormality of life.

'We have to live with these restrictions,' explained a barefoot female shopkeeper who, though she carried her weight at her hips and stomach, still possessed elements of grace.

Keen to hear the real life stories of people in the midst of this war, Laura wanted to hear more. The journalist in her had taken the upper hand. 'How are you getting on?' she enquired. The growling of the diesel generator out on the pavement drowned out their conversation and they had to shout to make themselves heard.

'On sweltering days,' the woman replied, 'we have no air conditioning and we routinely use the lights in our mobile phones to navigate through the streets at night. To do the laundry while there's power, I had to get up at 3am last night. Often, food rots in the fridge and has to be thrown out.' She paused for a minute. 'No chocolate ice-cream these days,' she added jokingly as she would have done in 'the good old days', when shopping in the high street was the day's priority. Despite the catastrophic impact of the war, Laura became aware that emotions were kept firmly under control and spirits remained unconquerable.

'The promise of a better future rests on this indomitable spirit,' Ari remarked when the woman had gone to collect her shoes.

'You know, my father, always told me to put my right shoe on first while pronouncing the name of God. I still do it. Old habits die hard,' the woman said, when she returned with her shoes on.

For a second, Ari thought of his aunt back in Athens. The only discomfort in life she had experienced was when she had to deal with her fashionable new shoes which were too tight. The injustice did not escape him.

As they talked, the deep roar of a jet engine filled their ears as a Syrian Air Force MiG flew over, swooping through the cerulean sky to attack. Soon after, a single building in the distance was burning. A man with a back that had hunched at an early age, climbed up onto the roof of a building. Ducking between the forest of satellite dishes, he tried to get a better look at what was happening.

Ari wondered why he bothered. Explosions and billowing smoke were now routine. So was the thud of the shelling from Mount Qasioun, the mountain overlooking Damascus, and the distant roar of air force jets.

'Only birds and visitors jump at the sound of bombings and artillery fire these days,' a helpful Damascene had told him not all that long ago. Most Damascenes, hardened by the war, had been ignoring the bombs, not even looking at where they had landed or what they might have hit. 'When a shell landed nearby and a man fell in front of me,' a dentist with more years behind her than in front had told him in Damascus, 'I never knew whether he was wounded or dead. I just stepped over him and carried on,' she recalled with bovine indifference.

Her reaction was extreme and Ari felt nauseated, so much so, that he actually told her so, but she excused herself. 'I've turned into a nervous wreck,' she said. 'I've got nobody to take care of my cat.'

Back in the taxi, Laura and Ari drove towards the Old City of Damascus. The neighbourhood, on the other side of the highway just a few hundred metres to the west, seemed to be floating on an abyss like so many others. Rendered barren by mortar fire, barrel bombs and airstrikes, it had turned into an eerie and desolate urban landscape. Its utter silence was only broken by the barking of a dog standing next to the burnt-out wreckage of an armoured military vehicle. The country had been converted into a desert and a graveyard. One could almost see the maundering spirits of the dead in the battered landscape.

Engrossed in the apocalypse's aura, Laura, in particular, was numb with horror. Her face summed up feelings that she found impossible to articulate. Words seemed to be superfluous. If anything deserved to be said, it was the inexpressible. But words would only disturb the sacred rest of the dead.

Meanwhile, the closer they were getting to the Old City, the more cumbersome the traffic was becoming. The streets were clogged with cars and Sharabi had to deal with endless traffic jams whilst also making way for long convoys that carried military hardware. Though mostly covered by tarps, the lorries could not conceal the outline of the artillery, machine-guns and rocket launchers they carried.

'Brand new equipment, a gift from the Russians,' Wael Sharabi suggested helpfully.

While they were waiting for the convoy to pass, he then told them about his brother, a man who had lived in Sakba, a suburb of Damascus. 'He was determined not to join the army because he'd experienced a premonition that he would be killed in a battle against the rebels on the outskirts of Aleppo. I told him that premonitions were a fantasy, and advised him to stop hiding and join the army like everyone else. He didn't listen. Instead, he hid in our aunt's house just outside the city. But one day, when he tried to repair the electrics that had been damaged when a rocket hit the neighbourhood, the power suddenly surged back. He died instantly. Electrocuted.'

'Appointment in Samarra,' Ari said. 'Death had an appointment with him in your aunt's house. Not in the battlefield.'

Sharabi had not heard Somerset Maugham's version of the story or of John O'Hara's novel, but he knew the old story of the merchant's servant who went from Baghdad to Samarra to run away from Death only to discover that Death was instead waiting for him there.

The driver was not poor in sorrows. Despite the tragedy that had hit his family, he was nevertheless feeling more 'relaxed' and 'not afraid anymore'. 'Things are looking up,' he added with a dogged, unflinching spirit and a broad smile. To emphasise his optimism, he explained that last year he would work afternoons and then go home. 'But just yesterday, I picked up my last fare at two in the morning.'

'I hope I won't have to work until two in the morning. I've already done it a few times in Egypt and Libya. It's really not something I would look forward to,' mused Laura.

'I hope not too,' Ari said. 'But as I said, abnormal is the new normal now.'

As if additional evidence in support of his statement were needed, the Syrian military provided it. Armed men stopped the taxi 'just for a while' because, at a nearby checkpoint, a grenade detonated by Islamists in the inspection room had killed the checkpoint officer.

'That's Syria for you,' Ari whispered, barely moving his lips, just to break the nerve-racking silence fed by the tragic incident.

Chapter 2
In Front of the Astral Gates

Located in the 'Green Zone' of Damascus, the Sheraton hotel, home to many of the UN personnel dealing with the country's crisis, had been anything but immune to the effects of the war. During the summer, a rocket fired by the rebels had landed in its swimming pool while earlier bombing had left other marks on the site. Still, regularly engulfed by music and flowers, the hotel hosted vast weddings with grinning new husbands, smiling brides and ladies in outrageous dresses.

Soon after her arrival, Laura checked into her room. She found it rather dated, but was happy nonetheless as it faced the mountains whose bewitching beauty filled her with a breathless, inarticulate excitement. After dumping her bags and freshening up from the long journey, she then joined Ari downstairs for a bite to eat. On their way to the hotel's Italian-style restaurant, they came across groups of ubiquitous security guards in camouflage trousers hanging around in the corridors, some elderly smokers in the bar and sleepy UN officers.

Dizzy with exhaustion, Laura barely touched her food, and before too long, she excused herself and left the comfort of Ari's company for the comfort of her bed. Back in her room, she bade a goodnight kiss to the moon, whose light was bouncing off the garden leaves, and she was in bed in no time. Yet rest did not come easily. Neither the air-conditioners nor the lighting worked. The room was so stifling that she felt tempted to spend the night on the balcony. Some people, she heard later, were sleeping in the Old City's parks for exactly this reason. But sleeping outdoors, on the balcony, offered little protection from shells or mosquitoes.

And then as darkness fully descended, the artillery barrages intensified. Not all that far away, rockets were being fired and explosions shattered the antediluvian tranquillity of the night. Shells arched across the vast ocean of the darkness and lit up stricken buildings where the yellow lines of tracer bullets criss-crossed them. She had an almost sleepless night, but jet-lag finally overtook her in the small hours, and consequently, she overslept the following morning. Breakfast was already over by the time she made it to the restaurant. While cursing her bad luck, her iPhone rang. It was Ari warning her about taxis.

'Their drivers don't make much so they can easily be tempted to deliver their passenger to a district controlled by the rebels. The front line between rebels and government forces is often only marked by a single street or a stretch of wasteland,' he said, repeating his words from the day before.

'Not very reassuring,' she reflected.

'But even without the 'help' of taxi drivers,' Ari carried on, 'it's anything but difficult to find yourself in areas you don't want to be in. You walk down one street with children, cars and coffee shops only to find you're suddenly in a parallel world of sandbags, look-out posts, armed men and bunkers.'

Somewhat subdued by Ari's cautionary advice, Laura thanked him and left for the Four Seasons hotel in the centre of the city, where she was to meet Lyse Webb, the BBC's chief Middle Eastern correspondent. Army and militia checkpoints were everywhere, controlling access to government offices, the big hotels and the main shopping centre. Heavy barriers surrounded government buildings, all painted in the red, black and white of the Syrian flag.

Portraits of Bashar al-Assad dominated the city: as a soldier, a businessman and a father. Beneath them, vehicles were thoroughly searched by soldiers or scruffy militiamen in camouflage trousers and T-shirts. Cars in some central areas were stopped and searched every two blocks. Those with special passes issued by government security ministries were waived through express lanes at each checkpoint. The checking exacerbated the already bad traffic that rumbled up and down the streets, sometimes causing the windows at the front of the buildings to vibrate. Right now, it was at its demented worst.

'The fastest way to move around,' the taxi driver told Laura, 'is by bicycle.' Laura could see many of them around. 'People, are encouraged by the government to bike. Its campaign even has a name of its own: "Yalla, let's bike!"' he said. 'The rising price of fuel sends us the same message,' he added rather bitterly.

The Four Seasons hotel, also part of the so-called Green Zone, was used by both the United Nations and the international media. Laura and

Lyse chatted for a while about the difficulties a journalist should expect in this part of the world, including the surveillance of his or her work by the security services, and the threats each one's life was constantly under.

'Many journalists have been murdered by thugs or jihadists,' Lyse warned Laura.

Laura knew that Lyse was determined to see the end of the Bashar al-Assad regime and its leaders in The Hague, charged for war crimes committed against their own people. Her views were expressed with considerable animation, as though she was born with them. Laura, as solemn as an owl, chose to keep her own opinions to herself.

Their discussion was carried on against the background thuds produced by the growl of warplanes, government guns and the rolling explosions of bombs being dropped every few minutes. Still, people looked quite calm and reassured as all of this was taking place relatively 'far away', in the rebel-held suburb of Daraya. Plumes of smoke mushrooming up from shells that were landing among houses and homes, could occasionally be seen from the hotel roof.

Ari met Laura later in the day and took her out for a walk in the Old City. It was a beautiful, bright day with islands of white clouds winking playfully at them. 'These streets must still look pretty much like they did when Agatha Christie visited them in the 1930s?' Laura mused. Their antiquated, mellow quality was reinforced at times when they could smell the rich and pungent incense that was still used in Damascus. Nonetheless, Laura wondered how safe their walk was.

'What are our chances of being hit by a rocket?' she asked, chuckling yet at the same time annoyed at herself for unearthing her subterranean anxiety.

'You can never be certain of anything,' Ari replied. 'Anyway,' he added, disinclined to let doubts interfere with the bliss of their meeting, 'you don't need to worry. It's unlikely that something will happen as very few mortars reach the heart of the city these days.'

Being a journalist, she knew, of course, that it is not unusual for things to happen contrary to probability, yet his reassurance dispelled her anxiety the same way the sun dissipates the morning mist.

'Things were worse in the spring,' Ari added, 'when the rebels, trying to force people out of Damascus, were shelling the city daily. Their bombs fell on Sunni Muslim as well as Christian or Alawite areas and were often lethal because of the high population density.'

However, as they both knew, the picture had been changing since September, when Russia launched targeted airstrikes against both the Islamic State and Jabhat al-Nusra, the al-Qaeda affiliate army. Hundreds of sorties by more than 50 jets and helicopters had been ruthlessly destroying dozens of ammunition depots, explosives production plants and command posts primarily in the parts of Northern Syria controlled by Isis, Jabhat al-Nusra and Ahrar al-Sham, the jihadi group backed by Turkey and Qatar. It was what had turned the momentum in Bashar al-Assad's favour, indicating that the war might soon be over.

Greeting this possibility with joy, people often loudly cheered at the news. As Ari was told, in the peaceful past, only football would capture the Damascenes' interest to such an extent.

At the same time, weakened by the air bombardment and without the heavy equipment of Bashar al-Assad's army, Jaysh al-Islam, the jihadi group backed up by Saudi Arabia, and other rebel groups active in the suburbs of Damascus, had practically abandoned the targeting of the capital. As a result, the Damascenes felt less embattled than they had even a few months earlier. But as nothing could guarantee safety, people were still at the mercy of their fears. Survival, they knew, was only a matter of luck. Still, people had somehow adjusted to it. It was their reality.

In any case, despite all the horrors, life in Damascus was not altogether intolerable. Government departments, while scrappy, still functioned. Employees received their salaries even if the value of the local currency kept falling. Electricity and water were available, though shortages were part of the daily routine. And health care was still available, although several doctors had become refugees seeking a home in other parts of the world.

Walking on, Ari and Laura passed the famous Damascene sword, the monument in the Umayyad square that stood as a symbol of the victories, strength and achievements of the Syrian people. They carried on into the ancient city whose heart kept beating on. Its streets, Ari said, had been designed by Hippodamus, the first urban planner whose principles were later adopted in many important cities such as Halicarnassus, Alexandria and Antioch. Walking through them was a delight.

The Old City was packed with people shopping or just wandering around. Women were trying on clothes at the al-Hamidia market or looking at paintings for sale. People at the al-Bzoria market were smoking their shishas in downtown coffee houses, which many customers had turned into their own personal office or lounge. The youngsters, in particular, seemed absorbed by their iPhones – Tweeting, Facebooking or Instagramming. Some were nodding their heads to a YouTube tune.

The famous ice-cream shop Baghdash, in the middle of Hamideh market, was not short of customers. Ari and Laura joined the queue, bought their vanilla ice cream and chatted for a minute or two about the man with the Yul Brynner looks who was observing Laura from a distance. Demonstrating his 'inner animal', he was greedily devouring her with his eyes. She was probably to him what the wildebeest is to a lion.

As the day still had summer blood in its veins, other people, both young and old, were sitting on the grass in the nearby parks under the umbriferous bougainvillea and jacaranda trees. Many of them were from all over Syria, displaced people who had probably left their houses in ruins. On a footbridge, a Syrian soldier and a girl were talking on their phones. Children, a whole fleet of them, on tour with a young man from their church, were positioning themselves for photos.

As soon as they passed the East Gate, Laura's attention was caught by a row of shoe shops. Her old and threadbare sandals needed urgent replacement. She walked into one of them and tried on a pair while Ari's eyes surveyed her slim fingers and shapely ankles, that distinctive toss of her hair and the half smile she rewarded herself with in the mirror.

'This woman,' he thought, 'certainly doesn't need to take a course in feminine graces.'

While trying on another pair of sandals, Laura's attention was caught by a woman on the bench desperate to look a generation younger than her age. She was trying on a pair of Louboutins. Puzzled, Ari focused on her for a minute, too.

'I think these shoes would look best with my Dolce & Gabanna dress, Tiffany necklace and Fendi handbag,' the woman told the assistant rather too loudly, flicking a smile full of charm like a teenager. 'My son's engagement is coming up soon. I think these will be a good choice.'

'How strange,' Laura said, after she had bought her sandals and they had walked out of the shop. 'The war has destroyed her entire country and she still clings to the latest fashion.' Her eyes were drawn, for a moment, to another woman talking to herself. Bent by time and probably homeless, she was removing the wrapper of a half-eaten burger she had found outside a nearby takeaway. Ari was not sure she was mentally stable. Many people in her situation were both physically and psychologically shattered.

While he was looking at her, she moved closer and addressed him in a querulous voice. 'I don't want men around me anymore. Men are useless. Good for nothing.'

Soon after, they ended up in the Abu al-Abd restaurant, where a crowd was waiting to taste its famous lamb shawarma and Syrian kebab. Business seemed to be so good that more restaurants and coffee houses, along with new bars, were opening in the richer areas of Damascus. Some bars even had karaoke. The Old City of Damascus itself, nicknamed the City of Jasmine, looked like it did in times past, buzzing like a bee hive.

This became much more evident to Laura on her first Friday in Damascus, "the best day in the sight of God, the day of congregation". In the evening, Ari took her for a walk in the Old City beyond the Abu Rummaneh air-conditioned bubble. It was alive with hooting and jostling cars. Women in short skirts were resting beside their friends in hijabs or chatting in numerous restaurants and coffee houses. The latter buzzed with life even though many customers could only afford a cup of tea. In other places, they could see elderly people hooked in front of their television screens watching a popular soap opera. They all seemed determined to stay alive at least until the next episode. The brutal civil war ravaging the country did not seem like it existed.

'Though its oars are broken,' Ari told Laura, 'Damascus' middle class is sailing out into the open sea once again.'

'Bizarre,' said Laura.

'Indeed,' Ari responded, 'especially if you take into account that living standards have collapsed since the start of the conflict. The Syrian pound has catastrophically dropped against the dollar, you know, and purchasing power has plummeted as prices have shot up seven or eight-fold. Poorer people are facing malnutrition and hunger.'

As if they intended to document the penuriousness of their condition, the owners of the antique shops on their route, who used to have a steady flow of cash from tourists, were now lazily dusting their precious collections. The tourist trade, on which Syria banked in the good old days, had collapsed.

'How do ordinary Damascenes manage to survive in such circumstances?' Laura asked. 'It's a mystery to me. None of it seems to make sense.'

It was not the reporter in her asking these questions. It was instead a human being trying to enter the unfathomable depths of the human psyche and uncover the inexhaustible inner reserves it takes to look the abyss straight in the eye. It was her effort to discover the secret of survival when the spring of life seemed to be giving away.

'What saves humanity from such unintelligent brutality and mortal agony?' she asked Ari.

'Good question,' he replied. 'I've been thinking about it constantly. My answer is that people carry on because they are fighting for their lives and they need to win – and winning requires something that resembles normality. Their subliminal understanding of the situation gives them no other choice.'

Robert Forester, the veteran British journalist, had mentioned something to him on the subject some weeks back, which had set him thinking. Forester had told him of a young man in the Alawite mountains who had to bury his wife. She had died of complications from an infection caught at local hospital. Jabhat al-Nusra forces were just four miles down the road, yet the villagers who had turned up for the funeral wore spotless clothes and well-shined shoes. They walked past the gardens of roses and vines as they had done for generations. It was their way of clinging to normality.

'Perhaps,' Ari told Laura who looked rather puzzled, 'this is how people tell themselves that, whatever happens in the country, life still goes on in tune with their values, feelings, and traditions. The past, gone but still around, ensures that their self-respect and pride remain unimpaired.'

A young waitress who Ari had been speaking with a couple of weeks earlier had given him a different perspective. 'People go out to enjoy themselves because they don't know what will happen next. Or they're just trying to forget what's happening outside. They say "Live today, and don't worry about tomorrow". Tomorrow is totally unscripted.'

As if life wanted to make the point crystal clear, all hell broke loose almost the very second Ari had finished his sentence. Men, violently pushing through the crowd, were trying to catch a bearded and wild-eyed young man, who was himself pushing everyone aside to run away from his pursuers. There was a lot of screaming and shouting, particularly by mothers who were trying to protect their children and, like everyone else, were desperate to flee the scene.

All of a sudden, the beautiful day had run out of colour. The centre of life's meaning had moved to the periphery.

Very soon, the chased man became fully aware that escape was not possible. The Mukhabarat security men outnumbered even the coins in the pockets of the crowd. Knowing that he had reached life's exit door, the man stopped running. Motionless for a moment as if he was having some kind of 'out-of-body' experience, he stretched his arms wide, perhaps to the outer reaches of non-being, and, with a look of defiance on his face, he stared straight into the eye of his approaching pursuers. The latter's eyes were likewise riveted upon him.

'Down!' Ari screamed, grabbing Laura and dragging her to the pavement, protecting her with his own body.

'What?' she tried to say, but the words that were forming on her lips remained unspoken as a huge blast silenced her.

The youngster had acted with noxious efficacy which had, for sure, conferred upon his soul eternal immortality. Splinters of brick, glass, tarmac and shrapnel from cars hit walls and people indiscriminately. The area which a second earlier was crowded with families had now turned into a ravaged wasteground featuring piles of debris, wrecked shops, amputated trees, dangling electricity cables, mangled cars and plumes of black smoke. On the pavement, body-like shapes slumped in the debris, amid pools of blood.

Dumbstruck, Laura looked at Ari with horror in her eyes. She had experienced the savagery of the Middle East strife, but she had never before come face to face with death like this. She was trembling. 'Thank you,' she said, grateful for the protection Ari had offered her. She was indeed grateful, but she was also shell-shocked. Her face looked as if she was craving for air underwater.

Ari responded as if he had not heard her. 'A suicide bomber,' he muttered. 'A bloody suicide bomber. He was being chased by members of the Mukhabarat security who must've spotted him acting suspiciously, and wanted to arrest him. Rather than surrender, he chose to blow himself up…'

'But how did you know what was coming?'

'Sixth sense,' Ari replied, trying to drive the chill of death away with his nervous laughter. 'C'mon – let's see if we can help,' he added a moment later as he started moving towards the injured in the crowd.

Lying in the street, next to the suicide bomber's marred body were a couple of unquestionably dead and scores of critically injured people. Those that survived the onslaught intact were tending to their bleeding friends or relatives, often sobbing over their bodies. Others were helping victims trapped in a burning car. The fire-fighters who were quickly on the scene, struggled to extinguish the flames that engulfed a shop, whilst medical personnel in ambulances were looking after the injured. Paramedics, helped by volunteers, were carrying them on stretchers.

Laura watched, as Ari helped a young man to cover his bleeding head with a T-shirt, but she was unable to do anything herself. Rooted to the spot, she was staring in shock at the grisly scene of another man close to Ari, who was beyond help. His head was blown off by the force of the blast. The paramedics wrapped him in a white sheet and he was laid alongside an ambulance. 'God won't forgive the criminal perpetrators of this atrocity,' a woman close to them cried, tears streaming down her face. An elderly man standing next to her, someone who looked both kind and useless, offered her a tissue.

Ari looked in Laura's direction. Her face was the colour of white marble.

Despite the shock, Laura's enquiring mind was trying to make some sense of what had just happened. 'I wonder if he intended to detonate the bomb here?' she told Ari as he returned to her side, unable to do anything further to help. 'He probably intended to blow up a public building – right? – but he didn't manage to get there?'

'You're probably right,' Ari said.

As they were surveying the gaping earth, which seemed to be leaking blood, they saw that the Mukhabarat had made an arrest. Another bearded young man in handcuffs was being led to the white police van that was parked nearby.

'He's probably a partner of the jihadi suicide bomber,' Laura speculated. 'I wonder what his fate will be?'

'They'll interrogate him, torture him to get what they want, and then they'll take him to Sednaya, the military prison north of Damascus,' Ari answered.

'I've heard of the place,' Laura said. Her voice sounded mechanical, disconnected from her inner self. 'Amnesty International has highlighted the horrors of the inhumane conditions and the use of torture…not to mention the extrajudicial execution of thousands of detainees.'

'It's exactly as you say,' Ari said, nodding his head in agreement, albeit absentmindedly. 'The cruelty is unbelievable. You know, by the way, that among others, Zahran Alloush, leader of Jaysh al-Islam, Abu Yahia al-Hamawi, leader of Ahrar ash-Sham, and other prominent jihadis were held there.'

'Where exactly is this prison?'

'It's about thirty kilometers north of Damascus, close to the Aramaic-speaking village of Sednaya. It was built in 1987, and it's one of the country's largest prison establishments administered by the military police. Do you want to know more?' he asked.

'Yes,' she said.

'Well, it has two wings, the White wing for offenders of one kind or another and the Red wing for terrorists. The Red Jail, as it is known, is called "the prison of death". Few survive it.'

Talking about Sednaya at the moment was, as they both knew, a flight from the cage of reality they were trapped in. But coming to terms with such a reality, the truth of things previously unseen, was a huge task and one which was at that moment beyond their power. The sheer horror of what they had witnessed seemed to poison their blood, its crudity clouded their thinking, its inanity blotted out their vision. The impact of such heinousness was just overwhelming. It invaded every bit of their quintessence.

'Let's get out of here,' Ari eventually said, the grimace on his face full of anguish. 'We've had more than enough of this.' They both needed to distance themselves from the new centre of gravity the suicide had created.

Yet, several blocks away, where they soon found themselves, the picture was entirely different. The dismal world they had just left behind had disappeared. Its place had been taken by crowds enjoying life, and the mellow air of the autumnal sunshine. The flight from reason and the cult of violence, both of which thrilled the Islamists, was nowhere in evidence. It was not what the crowds here identified with.

'Isn't it interesting,' Laura observed, giving voice to her relief, 'that people don't identify 'normality' with the zealotry of the jihadis, but actually, with their refusal to plunge into the Islamist religious gloom? Look at how life goes on here... Their behaviour, their actions are anything but guided by religious convictions, extreme or otherwise.'

'Look at these people and think,' Ari said, following his own thoughts on the subject.

'Think what?' Laura asked, not understanding what he meant. After the horrors they had witnessed, his thoughts had obviously lost their usual fluorescent accessibility.

'The revolt against Bashar al-Assad, started because the minority Alawite Shi'ites ruled Syria dictatorially, protecting their own people but also the Christians and other minorities from the fury of the majority Sunnis. But most of Damascus' population and, indeed, most of Syria's army and its generals are Sunni. Even so, they've backed Bashar al-Assad because they know what to expect if Jabhat al-Nusra or Isis were to take over. Religion for the insane is not what they want.'

'Religion for the insane – yes, that's what it was.' Laura knew the Islamist rebellion was dominated by Sunnis, and yet the Syrian Sunnis were actually Bashar al-Assad's chief power base.

'If supported only by the minorities – Alawites, Shi'ites and Christians – the regime would never be able to survive,' Ari added.

Laura nodded in agreement. 'Even when people thought otherwise, the emergence of Isis and Jabhat al-Nusra, the al-Qaeda affiliate in Syria, changed the picture radically. Why? Because,' she answered her own question, 'while both Bashar al-Assad and the jihadis don't want anyone to challenge their authority, the dictator still lets people do what they want to do – they can still go shopping or listen to music. But the jihadis, on the other hand, *force* people to do what *they* want them to do.'

'That's a very good way of describing the choices people have,' Ari said.

'Yes,' she carried on, now fully engaged with the subject, 'Bashar al-Assad will say, "Don't you ever dare to stand against me" – which is what Isis say too – but he won't say, "Don't listen to music, don't read any books, don't go to the movies, don't make yourself look good, don't have any sex, wine or fun. Fun for the jihadis is an anathema. Pleasure is a sin. Beauty is immoral. Their bodies no longer know how to love...'

'They have nothing but religion to amuse themselves,' Ari added to reinforce the point she was making. 'Privately or publicly.'

But Laura was on a roll. 'The dictator,' she continued, ignoring him, 'won't force you to cover yourself in black or to pray sixteen times a day either.'

'Indeed!'

'So, Ari,' she said, turning to him, having finished making her point, 'how would you define the difference in two words?'

'Sorry, Laura,' he smiled, 'unlike you, I'm not all that good at epigrammatic witticisms... But what you've said is true, and makes the difference very clear.'

Chapter 3
Stunning as a Russian Bullet

Back at his office the next day, Ari was still struggling to recover from the dreadful experience he had gone through the day before and its traumatic effects on his and Laura's lives. He felt utterly drained, overwhelmed by circumstances beyond his control, and he yearned for some peace. Getting away from it all for a while – even having just a couple of days of sweet idleness, what the Romans cutely called *dolce far niente* – would be of great help.

But, it was not to be. Instead, he reluctantly dived into the great pile of paperwork that had been impatiently waiting for him. It was a job he did not particularly fancy. But routines, and the lumpy, enervating burden of the mundane, had to be observed, though he knew some people loved the comfortable protection they offered.

Despite her emotional distress, Laura had also returned to her own daily routines. In her search for good stories, she had decided to investigate what was going on in Sednaya, the military prison. She told Ari so over the phone. He urged her not to get involved, partly because he was sure she was not going to get anything of interest out of those in charge, and partly because she could easily get in trouble with the regime. She did not take his advice.

'Colleagues have told me that reporting in Syria isn't as difficult as it was in Saddam Hussein's Baghdad or in Colonel Gaddafi's Tripoli,' she told him. 'Bashar al-Assad has imposed fewer restrictions on reporters.'

'Whatever,' Ari argued back, slightly alarmed that she was ignoring his advice, 'but you'll get up their noses and they won't leave you alone from then on.'

'Don't worry, Ari! Bye-bye,' she said and then disappeared for the day.

Ari finished some of the most urgent things on his desk and then left for the town of Husseiniyeh, just south of Damascus. UNRWA had just opened a new school there, close to the Qabr Essit refugee camp, home to some 40,000 Palestinian refugees. The 'guide' he was given, Sayid, was an eleven-year old boy, whose family had fled the town for the protective shelter of Jeramana where they lived in a rented, unfinished flat. Having missed three years of education, Sayid was now proud and happy to be back at school where other children were now singing and clapping.

At the solemn ceremony that started soon after, Ari graciously accepted the parents' silent gratitude and the school Head's formal appreciation of the contribution UNRWA was making to their welfare, on behalf of his organisation. He listened to a couple of speeches, often disrupted by the thunder of military jets flying above the heavily damaged town, and enjoyed the children's songs and dances. The sight of the delicious pistachio baklava that local ladies had prepared for the occasion made his tongue tingle in anticipation.

It all made him feel that he and the organisation he represented were doing something useful, which justified all the risks they were taking. Many of his colleagues had actually been killed on the job.

'Still, it's better than working for a bank,' he told himself almost self-indulgently, nodding his head in agreement with himself.

The event and the children's laughter had brightened his day, though he knew that some five thousand Syrian schools had stopped functioning altogether. They had either been destroyed, were being used by military forces or were close to the front lines, which everyone was trying to get away from. Rather than attending schools in their neat blue uniforms, now destitute and hopeless, disavowed by the future, hundreds of thousands of children, mostly from rebel-held lands, had been left to their fate.

Laura contacted Ari that evening. She phoned to tell him that she had gone to see the prison governor, but she had not succeeded and would try a different route the next day, by attempting to meet the deputy Minister of the Interior instead. Ari could not help but admire her fearless determination.

The following day was a Saturday, and Ari arranged with James Garrahan, his Irish colleague with that inscrutable West Cork accent, to spend the morning in the gym. They chose the one in Chafeek Jabri Street, in the Old City.

'Our goal today,' Ari emphasized to Garrahan when they met, 'is to work on having stronger bones, bigger muscles, increased strength.' For reasons that Ari could not work out immediately, Garrahan's smile was as wide as O'Connell Street.

'My task,' the Irishman said, 'is also to get to know the Swedish woman I met last time I was there.' That had been a month earlier, and the Swedish woman he was talking about was working for a Non-Governmental Organisation. He had a gym-buddy relationship with her, but they had never really talked about their lives outside the gym. They did not even know each other's names.

'How come you let her slip through your fingers?' Ari asked as if he could hardly believe Garrahan's failure to act. 'You're usually so garrulous.'

'I'm a failure,' Garrahan answered with a self-depreciating laugh.

They arrived in the gym and did a five-minute warm up on a stationary bike. While Ari moved onto a few pull-ups, Garrahan fiddled with his phone, telling someone how wonderful being in the gym was. The Swedish woman who he had looked for was sadly not there. Having lifted some light weights, and feigning exhaustion, Garrahan suggested they'd done enough for one day.

'I must start work at the gym at least two or three times a week,' he added with a total absence of conviction.

'I'm sure your secretary can do it for you.' Ari retorted. 'Just ask her.'

On their way back to the market, they passed the Damascus Opera House, a potent symbol of the Assad family's rule over Syria. It was opened in 2004 by Bashar al-Assad himself and his British-born wife, Asma, amidst great fanfare and fireworks. The sprawling complex included a large opera hall, two smaller theatres along with acting, singing and ballet schools, offering classical concerts and works by Arab playwrights.

At the building's entrance, by the huge photo of an actress whose face was beaming as if she had just emerged from a mountain spa retreat, Garrahan came across a young woman, whom, as one might expect, he knew. He stopped to exchange a few niceties with her. The woman, a petite 24-year-old drama student with chestnut-brown eyes, was limping. Ari asked what had happened.

'I was on my way to my classes,' she said, 'and a mortar shell fired from rebel positions struck the pavement, just five meters away from me. All I'd heard was a deafening bang and I fell to the ground, bleeding. I didn't feel any pain. And then everything went black.'

Flying shrapnel had pierced her right leg. Another five of her classmates were also wounded, and two others had died in the explosion.

'Bloody hell, I'm so sorry...' was all Ari could say, but the girl's story had drained the day of its languorous autumn splendour.

As they walked on, Ari asked Garrahan how he knew this girl.

'Took her and a few other volunteer students to distribute winter clothes to Palestinian refugees in Jeramana.'

Later, Ari met Laura in the Old City. The sun, still fiery red in a cloudless sky, forced them to seek shade on a bench under a tree. Ari was wondering whether Laura had recovered from the shock of the suicide bomber's attack.

'How are you feeling?' he asked, trying to hide his apprehension.

'Fine,' she answered. 'I'm okay. Mind you, what we experienced is not something that will fade away. It's not something I'll ever forget. Such inhuman cruelty... It's just so horrible. I don't know if you can heal from that kind of trauma.' Her face was marked by a deep sadness and her gaze was unfocused.

'Yes, such inhuman cruelty,' Ari said, repeating what she had just said, 'but it is so *humanly* inhuman.'

Laura looked at him in an absent way. 'Perhaps,' she said with pure sadness in her voice when she re-focused, 'we've forgotten how to be humane. Or perhaps cruelty is our true nature.' 'It probably is,' Ari answered, getting up from the bench they were sitting. 'Except that we, in the West, have given cruelty a better education.'

Unwilling to succumb to depression, they made a move to the Old City's maze of alleys, a labyrinth of small arched streets and aged houses that take people to the distant past. They stopped and had a black tea, served in sturdy glass tumblers by a waiter who delivered them on an engraved brass tray. Next to them was a man and his wife, a woman in a black hijab with gorgeous kohl-rimmed eyes, holding her wriggling toddler. The man was smoking his pipe.

'Do you know,' Ari said, 'that the UN Health Agency has insisted that, notwithstanding the current crisis in this country, Syrian officials should collaborate with the UN to cut down on the use of tobacco?'

'Yes! Crazy isn't it?' Laura answered. 'It's like telling the passengers on the Titanic to help the staff to tidy away the deckchairs, whilst the ship's sinking.'

Having emerged from the hole of their earlier depressing thoughts where the chill of futility had settled, Laura, as Ari discovered, was quite excited about something. But she was keeping it to herself.

'Well,' he prompted her, 'you seem to be up to something. What is it?'

'I've found out about something that's very, very interesting,' she said, animatedly. Then, lowering her voice she said, 'Weapons worth millions of dollars shipped into Jordan by the Central Intelligence Agency and Saudi Arabia for the benefit of Syrian rebels, are being systematically stolen by Jordanian intelligence operatives. They're then being sold to arms merchants on the black market.'

'Oh, my…' was Ari's first reaction.

'Some of these weapons,' Laura carried on, 'were used in the recent killing of two Americans and three others at a police training facility in Amman.'

'And don't the Americans know about it?' Ari asked. 'They've got numerous spy units in Jordan, working alongside other units such as British, French and whatever else. They're also recruiting agents out of Jordanian refugee camps whom they train to supply the intelligence they need. They must know.'

'I'm sure they do,' Laura answered. 'But nothing has come to light, and the stolen weapons still find their way to the jihadis.'

Then another thought hit Ari. 'This information, if accurate, is bound to bring down the American plan to train and equip "moderate" Syrian rebels for good.'

Laura nodded in agreement.

'But how on earth did you find out about it?' was Ari's next question. He could not believe that she had managed to contact important informants and get hold of such startling information so quickly.

'It was good luck,' she answered modestly. 'Like I told you yesterday on the phone, I went to the Ministry of Interior to ask some questions about the Sednaya prison and, while waiting to see him, I was befriended by a Jordanian. He wanted the Syrian Minister to release his brother, held in custody in Damascus for unspecified offences, in return for another favour he could arrange for the Syrians in Amman. He was obviously a man of some influence.'

'And...?'

'Well, we met later on for a coffee, and it was there that he told me about his brother's "alleged" involvement with the black-market arms business. "It's a ridiculous allegation", he said, "as everybody is involved in this kind of business. Even officials in both of our countries". Then, he mentioned a few Syrian names, who I'll interview as soon as possible, to get hopefully the full picture about this Jordanian business.'

'Oh my...' Ari gasped, but his wave of excitement disappeared from view the moment a sudden spasm of apprehension hit his vitals. He could hardly speak it aloud. 'Laura, if they find out what you're up to, they'll chop your head off.'

Laura stared at him for a moment, her eyes registering the concern on his handsome face. Concern hovered visibly on her face, too, as the same danger had already entered the chamber of her consciousness. But she did not answer him.

Death, until a few days ago, was something that happened silently, the way the clock stops ticking. Now, particularly after the death of the suicide bomber they had both witnessed, death was the gush of blood from a ruptured body, a head sliced from a torso. The picture was unutterably gloomy as was her subliminal sense of foreboding, yet nothing was enough to force Laura to abandon her commitment to the truth to which Ari, she knew, remained as committed. The Godly fire that kept them going would not allow pathetic compromises which would only too happily deliver them to the comfortable arms of self-deception.

Leaving behind the excitement and the fears that Laura's discovery had produced, they went for a drink at one of the locals' favourite spots, the Abu Abdou's fruit cocktail bar. They ordered cold drinks and fruit salads and enjoyed them in the honey-gold quietness of the late afternoon hours. As they talked, a shell fired by the army at rebel areas, whiffled over Damascus. A MiG jet howled into a bombing run and Jabhat al-Nusra's mortars meekly responded.

But no-one around interrupted their conversation or stopped enjoying their smoothies. A woman next to them, who, rather oddly, reminded Ari of Wayne Rooney, continued talking to her friend about how to cure a wart, a soldier snapped a selfie with his friends, and another woman with a bunch of keys suspended around her waist continued to restock the vending machine. 'The same thing day in, day out,' she grumbled, addressing a couple of middle-aged men who were playing backgammon. She was referring to the bombing. 'We'll soon die of boredom before our time.'

If the shelling was indicative of something serious, they could find out on the Internet or YouTube, later. Life was going on because people had grown used to the turbulence, even though they knew they might be returning home in a box or as scattered body parts gathered in a bag. Death was never far away.

'What a life,' Laura murmured while squinting up at the kind November sun, which caressed her glowing face with affection.

Once, Ari had asked a brigadier of Bashar al-Assad's army what he would tell his children about the war when they grew up. His answer was, 'I don't think I'll tell them anything.' Ari's first thought was that he would want to avoid talking to them about the war as he would not want to relive its horrors. But then it dawned on him that this was not what the man had in mind. He would not tell them anything because he would not be around to tell them anything. He would be dead before the war was over. Whatever they were doing, people seemed to have accepted that death was just around the corner. Unfenced, their fate was in the hands of their destiny.

Others were on a different wavelength. Haya, a young girl at the Abu Abdou's fruit bar, told them that her father had been killed and that her family lived with relatives. 'I want to have a better life. My father wanted me to study and achieve good things.' She was twenty summers old and was studying economics at Damascus university.

After taking a sip of a frozen concoction, tall, fruity and delicious, the girl offered them a glowing smile before giving them her Facebook name because she wanted them to be her friends. A minute later, she got up, moved to the exit, waved goodbye and left in a hurry to catch the capital's only surviving railway train.

'The journey will bring back good memories,' she said just before leaving.

'What memories?'

'It's the train of my childhood... I want to ride it again to bring back those beautiful days.'

Memories, such as picnics in the nearby idyllic villages which were now destroyed by heavy shelling, helped many people in their personal struggle for survival. The rail route, which had closed in 2011, had been re-opened in May 2015 and was now viewed as a family treat.

'Do you fancy a little trip on the train?' Ari asked Laura impulsively.

The following day, they were on their way to the railway station near the Umayyad Mosque, on Ari's motorbike. The bright yellow one-carriage train was waiting there to take them on a short trip to the greener parts of Damascus. They both felt so cheered up at the thought of the romantic journey that their bodies tingled with pleasure.

On the platform, there were dozens of shrieking Syrian children, some of them who knew nothing but war, and many young men and women. All of them were waiting to get on board for the four-kilometre journey to the outskirts of the city. The large yellow leather-seated wagon, which could hold one hundred people, was from Hungary, a tiny remnant of Syria's state railways. Its engine was a German diesel shunter.

Ari and Laura almost failed to find a seat, but they were helped by the train's driver, a man who sported a glorious white moustache and shiny hair. 'He dips his comb in lemon juice to make it shine,' Ari told Laura. The friendly driver then danced and chatted in the carriage with the other passengers, mostly Christian and Druze.

A young man wearing a decade-old Manchester United shirt who, thanks to the driver had offered Laura his seat, had meanwhile been paying her much more attention than mere civility demanded. 'How chatting with a beautiful lady can civilise a wild young man,' Ari reflected with a smile on his face.

Once inside, the loudspeaker started playing a popular song, 'The Russian Bullet'. It was about a young man who is telling his girlfriend that she is as stunning as a Russian bullet. This was a reference to the AK-47 rifle. Soon after, chugging the distance up the gorge of the river Barada, the train rumbled at 15 miles an hour to the end of the line. Beyond it was Jabhat al-Nusra territory.

During the journey, people ate, sang and danced the dabka, an Arab folk circle dance. Pop music, piped over the car's PA system, often blasted through the carriage. People were, or seemed to be, indifferent to what was going on in the world outside their wagon. They did not seem to care about Isis' ban of all musical instruments and singing because they 'distract from remembering God and the Quran' either. It was as if the war was just a bad dream.

Of course, the brief pleasures of the train trip did not alter the reality on the ground. They all knew what that reality was. But they wanted to distance themselves from it for at least a while. Hence their displays of joy, their glistening dance routines in the packed carriage were nothing less than a show of defiance, their resistance to the debilitating spirit of their time, a puff of hope to a city in the arms of self-destruction.

Laura and Ari let themselves slide into the euphoria of the day, and at the end of what had been a most enjoyable, albeit brief trip, Ari invited Laura to his place for dinner as it was getting pretty late.

'What a good idea,' she said. 'What are we having?'

'Just something I prepared earlier,' he said rather enigmatically. Ari was a good cook and his butter beans in sweet and sour sauce were particularly delicious. They both enjoyed the meal and chatted about the old times in London, the stressful times they were experiencing now, and their need for some sort of a 'balanced life'. Ari put Berlioz's *Symphonie Fantastique* on his mini DV deck. Berlioz had, he told Laura, composed it under the influence of opium.

Ensconcing themselves on the couch, they felt elated by the spontaneous warmth of the occasion and each other's presence. Ari touched Laura's hand and she responded by squeezing his.

'Do you know,' he said, in a confidential whisper, 'what words Paris traced in wine on the table top when he met Helen?'

'No, tell me.'

'I'll show you instead.' He took a piece of paper from the coffee table in front of them and wrote, 'I love you, Laura.'

They had both known for quite a while that they had crossed the mystical bridge of love and that this moment was coming. 'It takes time for the grapes to ripen,' Ari told Laura later. Even so, he could see her outside his future's open window from the very first moment they had met.

Their connection, growing in intimacy and friendship, had developed effortlessly. They had a good understanding of each other, and almost subconsciously knew what the other was experiencing or feeling. 'Like two branches of the same tree,' as Laura had put it. But more importantly, both of them knew they could lean on each other whatever the circumstances. Undaunted by difficulties or trials, their relationship did indeed feed the fire of life inside each other and blessed all four corners of their existence. Meeting each other was like sunshine after rain.

With eyes dewy with emotion, Laura lovingly gazed at Ari and whispered the words, 'I love you, too.' Overpowered by emotion, she fell into his arms. 'I love you, too,' she said again with a canorous voice as she was both laughing and crying. 'I've loved you since the first day we met.'

His lips touched hers again. The passion of the moment and the soothing promises of eternal happiness flowed through their bodies and intensified the naked fluidity of their emotions. It transfigured them. Lost in the timeless present, they were both on fire.

It was an evening that Ari was never going to forget. Its fragrance would linger in his memory forever.

But the next evening, Laura came back to him with some more information about 'the Jordanian business', and a knot of anxiety tied itself in Ari's gut. She had interviewed a couple of arms merchants. She explained to Ari that the rebels' 'arming programme', code-named Timber Sycamore, had been authorised by President Barack Obama back in April 2013. That was after more than a year's debate inside the administration about the wisdom of using the CIA for the purpose. The venture had already turned into an outstanding failure whose ghost kept haunting the Americans.

'Sixty to eighty percent of the arms that the US has shovelled into Syria and Iraq ended up in the jihadis' hands,' she said. 'And then, in another devastating blow to the US efforts, rebels trained by CIA paramilitary operatives in the use of Kalashnikovs, mortars, antitank guided missiles and other weapons had also either been captured by Isis or joined it. The operation had been so mismanaged that its abandonment by the Obama administration seems to be only a matter of time.'

'But how did you hear about all this?' a curious Ari asked.

'Arms dealers can't keep their mouths shut,' she said. 'They've been bragging to their customers about the large stocks of US and Saudi-provided weapons in their possession for sale.'

'Fear or shame come in very short supply,' Ari said.

His winged thoughts once again focused on Laura. 'You must be very careful who you talk to, and what you say,' he told her. Make sure you're not shadowed. What you're doing is bloody dangerous.'

He was sure that she was fully aware of it.

Chapter 4
Syrial blunders

The following day Ari was back at work. The usual routines were there waiting for him like a bus stop waits for the bus. He went through the pile of papers in front of him, receiving in return huge appreciation from those stuck at the bottom.

In the evening, he had to go to a lecture. The speaker was Karl Beyer, a Berlin Humboldt-Universität professor, and the theme was Europe's responsibilities for the Syrian crisis. He had no desire to listen to any lecture – he would rather spend the evening in Laura's company at home or in one of the city's attractive restaurants. But the lecture, to be given in the multipurpose hall of the newly built Damascus Opera House, was expected to attract the members of the capital's establishment. He had to be there.

He arrived in the elegant building on time, successfully passed the security checks, greeted the receptionist who flashed a quick smile copied from Glamour magazine and, for a moment afterwards, felt lost in a sea of well-dressed men and women. They were all chatting about their children, their holidays or the ongoing market uncertainties.

'If they run out of topics,' Ari thought, 'they might even talk about the higher cost of bribing.'

If you did not know that battles were raging just a few kilometres away, the war did not exist. Or if it did, it was only an excuse for a gathering like this.

He met a few people he knew, journalists from a number of European countries, diplomats from the few embassies that remained open in Damascus and officials of government departments. He took a seat and was very soon joined by a man who looked like someone you would meet in McDonald's. 'Definitely not one with recorded ancestors,' Ari thought and smiled. 'Do you know the professor?' the man asked as soon as he sat next to him.

'He was a member of the East German communist party as a young man,' Ari answered. 'Then he escaped to West Germany where he joined the Greens and won a seat in the Bundestag.'

The man looked puzzled as if Ari had tried to explain to him something about Greek irregular verbs. A few minutes later, he disappeared. His seat was instantly taken by a young man of intellectual persuasion. He identified himself as Thiago. He was Spanish and was working in Syria for Médecins Sans Frontières.

The professor, a soft-spoken man in his late fifties, dealt with the rise and fall of Arab nationalism. Dormant for four centuries, when the Ottoman Empire ruled the Arab lands, he said, it awoke and gathered pace during World War I. It was when the British promised the Hashemite dynast Hussein ibn Alf, Sharif of Mecca, an independent Arab state if the Arabs joined their war against the Ottoman Empire.

The promised Arab state was to stretch from the Taurus Mountains in south eastern Turkey to the Red Sea and from the Mediterranean to the Iranian border. It included Palestine. The Sharif, a loyal Ottoman official who spoke better Turkish than Arabic, accepted the proposal. But the professor did not mention that his call to arms addressed to his fellow Arab Muslims, whom he looked down upon as backward, ignorant people whom he was 'destined' to rule, was not made in the name of an Arab nation waiting to be born. He instead called the Arab Muslims to a sacred rebellion against the 'impious' Ottoman government, which was violating the sacred tenets of Islam.

'Perhaps,' Thiago whispered to Ari, 'he believed that God wanted him to be the caliph just as George W. Bush believed that God wanted him to be the President.'

'How do you know that He didn't?' Ari asked with all the false seriousness his voice could command.

'Well, I don't actually know what God did or didn't want,' Thiago answered in the same tone. 'Honestly! But if He did, all you see around us is the work of people He has presumably given the moral right to kill their fellow human beings. In such a case, God may not have the virtues attributed to Him...'

The bitterness in his voice was as plain as the miserable face of the security man standing by the door.

'Man,' Thiago added, 'has just created God in his own image.'

He then carried on striking a different note. 'The Sharif did so because he had learnt that Istanbul was planning his replacement!'

'Oh well! You do have a point here,' Ari agreed with him. 'He was indeed falling out with his masters in Istanbul when they embarked upon a policy of centralization. He didn't like it. It was taking away his power.'

'The Sharif was ready to join the British,' the German professor continued, 'because the Arabs were treated like dogs. The dogs of the Turkish nation.'

'Well, well, well!' Ari thought. 'That's quite a statement. The Ottomans were certainly oppressive, but their rule wasn't heavy-handed. The Arabs, after all, saw themselves as Muslims rather than Arabs and they were, as such, loyal to the Ottoman Empire and the Sultan who claimed to be the caliph. Apart from this, all they cared about was their own families, clans, and tribes. They weren't, therefore, eager to revolt. A few intellectuals had, of course, called upon the Arabs in the 19th century to throw off the yoke of the Turks. But nationalism hadn't penetrated their heart as it had penetrated the heart of the peoples of the Balkans or of the Armenians.'

He nevertheless kept his thoughts to himself while the professor carried on talking about Arab nationalism, which, he said, 'is rooted in history'.

'Apparently,' Thiago whispered to Ari, 'he's recalling details of events that never happened.'

'The same promises made to the Sharif,' professor Beyer continued, 'were also delivered to the Arabs by Lawrence of Arabia, the British archaeologist and secret agent, who later on contributed significantly to the success of the Arab revolt.'

'Mind you,' the professor added, 'Lawrence did also reassure his own government at the same time that the British had nothing to be apprehensive about if they supported the Arabs. "They would be harmless to ourselves",' he wrote. "If properly handled, they would remain in a state of political mosaic, a tissue of small jealous principalities incapable of cohesion".'

'How right he was…' Thiago whispered again to Ari.

Though the majority of the Ottoman Arabs stayed loyal to the Sultan, the revolt began in June 1916, supported initially by Bedouins and other nomadic desert tribes. The professor did not mention that none of them would fight unless paid in advance with gold coins that both the British and the French had happily supplied. The revolt did nevertheless succeed in pinning down tens of thousands of Turkish troops which would have otherwise been used in different fronts.

His listeners did, of course, know all about it, but they were still looking forward to hearing about the great betrayal that demonstrated the perfidy and duplicity of the British on account of which they could never be trusted or forgiven.

'The commitment to the Arab cause,' the professor continued by going into an emotional peronation, 'was, however, totally deceitful. Only a month earlier, in May 1916, the British, together with the French, had signed the secret Sykes – Picot agreement. Rather than grant the Arabs their promised independence against the Ottomans, the accord carved the latter's vast area stretching from Persia to the Mediterranean into British and French spheres of influence.

'They carved among themselves the skin of a bear that was still alive,' someone from the audience loudly said. The comment was met with widespread approval. A few at the back of the hall rose up from their seats, and, climbing on angry words, denounced 'colonialism, imperialism and the British interferences in the Middle East'. Something fiery and unrestrainable seemed to be dizzily coursing through their arteries.

The Syrian litoral and much of modern-day Lebanon were, as a result, placed under French administration. Britain, for its part, was to take direct control over central and southern Mesopotamia, around the Baghdad and Basra provinces and also over the Mediterranean port of Haifa. The rest of the territory in question – a huge area including modern-day Syria, Mosul in northern Iraq, and Jordan – would have local Arab chiefs under French supervision in the north and British in the south.

Maps and photos, displayed on a high-quality screen behind the speaker from a projector on a table close to him, intended to highlight his point. But the professor absentmindedly walked and stood directly in front of the screen. His face started to glow and weird shapes and shadows started moving across his body and the screen behind him. The audience tried as discreetly as possible to draw his attention to the problem, but he persistently remained unaware of it. The problem was solved when a technician approached him and whispered something in his ear.

'I'm so sorry,' the professor said, addressing his audience with a nervous laugh and carried on with his story.

'Incidentally, Egypt,' he said, 'was already a British Protectorate since 1882, and Algeria and Tunisia were already under French control. In 1911, the Italians had also established a bridgehead in Libya.'

Talking about the Europeans' interest in the Middle East, the professor did not fail to remind everybody that oil was already an important factor in the European Powers imperial designs and also in the fierce rivalries that subsequently developed between them. Oil was first extracted in Iran in 1908. By 1911, Winston Churchill, First Lord of the Admiralty at the time, had ordered the conversion of all Royal Navy ships to oil.

'A year later, in November 1917,' the professor carried on, 'the Balfour declaration, again in denial of the agreement reached with the Sharif of Mecca, committed the British to the establishment of a national home in Palestine for Jewish people. The Jews were only a small minority in the Holy Land at the time. This declaration was incorporated into the British Mandate to administer Palestine.'

Without discretion, a man in the audience at that point embarked on an ill-timed cough. The professor kindly gave him a minute to recover.

'The Anglo-French "arrangement",' he then proceeded to add for the benefit of the vulnerably ignorant, 'ratified by the League of Nations, which drew up the borders we see on modern political maps of the Middle East, divided the Middle East into countries. And this was done without paying any attention to the existing ethnic, tribal, geographic and confessional boundaries or to linguistic diversities. Reality had never been of much use out in their quarters. The division was truly arbitrary, so arbitrary,' the professor continued, 'that even today the legend lives on that the borderlines were drawn as a result of someone accidentally bumping the elbow of Colonial Secretary Winston Churchill.'

Religious entities such Sunni Arabs, Shi'ite Arabs, Christian Orthodox, Maronites, Alawites, Druze or Jewish were split between different states and Turkomen, Circassians, Assyrians, Yazidis, and Chaldeans were isolated throughout. The Kurds, who had been denied statehood by the colonisers, were dispersed to four different countries – Turkey, Iran, Iraq and Syria – and were denied their rights.

The reference to the Kurds created a haze of disapproval in the air. But this did not disturb the proceedings and the professor carried on. Statehood was also denied to the Armenians who were trying to recover, if that was possible, from the 1915 – 1916 genocide orchestrated by the Turks with murderous ferocity. This ended up with the death of around one million of them.

'As in Europe, where the main result of the First World War was to prepare the ground for the Second World War,' Ari told Thiago later on when the lecture had finished, 'the Middle East had to live with its consequences too. The accord had driven ashore the prejudices of history. The area was in a shambles.'

'But,' Thiago wondered, 'would the state that the British had promised the Sharif of Mecca have been possible? Or viable?'

'You can never tell,' was Ari's answer. 'In theory, the views that Faisal ibn al-Hussein, Sharif's son and "King of Greater Syria", voiced in Aleppo in 1918 did promise a happier future.'

Faisal did acknowledge that the Arabs were diverse peoples living in different regions. 'An Aleppan,' he had said, 'is not the same as the Hijazi, nor is the Damascene the same as the Yemeni. That's why my father had pursued a state of affairs in which each party follows its own special laws in tune with its own circumstances and people. The Arabs,' he added, 'were Arabs before Moses, Christ and Mohammed. Anyone who sows discord between Muslim, Christian and Jew is not an Arab. And I am an Arab before all else ...'

'That was a call for a pan-Arab nationalism,' Thiago said, 'if he meant what he said and said what he meant. Perhaps what he had in mind was something like the US Federal system. But anyway, that wasn't what the British and the French had in mind.'

'Of course not!'

Though it did not draw the borders of Arab states – that came later, the Sykes – Picot agreement, constructed with more devoutness to imperial interests than thinking, left a legacy of trouble. This was manifested as early as 1920, when a major revolt broke out in Syria, which was savagely crushed by the French. Faisal lost his 'throne' and Greater Syria was divided into several client states under the French mandate of Syria and Lebanon.

In the same year, another revolt, against British occupation this time, broke out in Iraq, part of the British mandate for Mesopotamia. It was suppressed with thousands of casualties. In response, the British changed tactics. They co-opted the existing élite, the Hashemite monarchy, which, in return for Britain's support, ensured the country's control by the imperial Power.

'Thankfully,' Ari said, 'the British did not use chemical weapons against the Iraqis as Churchill, Secretary of State for War, had advocated on the 12th of May, 1919. He was "strongly in favour of using poisonous gas against uncivilized tribes". Unfortunately for him, poisonous gas wasn't readily available.'

But Iraq, an artificial state, cobbled together by Britain out of three ex-Ottoman provinces, and bereft of any ethnic or religious rationale, remained a severely fragmented country.

Soon after, the Kurds also revolted against the British, but they were also militarily crushed. In the meantime, following the Third Anglo-Afghan war, the British were forced in 1919 to recognise the independence of Afghanistan. In the same year, wide-scale revolts also broke out in Egypt. The Egyptians' demand for independence was 'granted' in 1922. Britain retained, however, control over all the country's essential institutions and also over the 'Anglo-Egyptian' Sudan, a part of the British Empire since 1896.

'How interesting developments have been,' Thiago said with a voice indicating great surprise as if he had never before thought of what he was thinking now. 'Centuries of Ottoman rule and no Arab revolts against it. But as soon as the British and the French step in, the roof is coming down.'

'Muslims…' Ari said, mentally weighing up Thiago's statement, but without finishing his sentence. 'Mind you,' he said after a while, 'what the European "protectors" offered the Arabs was cruel dictatorships, utterly corrupt governments or fake democracies.'

"You're not telling me they revolted because they couldn't stand authoritarianism, are you?'

Ari did not respond. Meanwhile, the professor was carrying on with his lecture. 'As importantly,' he said, 'the élite in the new, fabricated states often appropriated existing tribal identities, semblances of such identities or, as in the case of Jordan, contrived nationhood to produce regional nationalist ideologies designed to sustain the status quo and their privileges. The élite was helped in this by conflicting loyalties to tribe, sect and religion and also by the tension between Iraqi, Syrian, Egyptian and other regional identities. They all ensured that the Arab state the British had promised the Sharif of Mecca would never become reality.'

'Yes,' Ari thought, 'but if pan-Arab nationalism was a force to be reckoned with, they wouldn't have succeeded.' He knew his thinking was strolling into a world that needed to be imagined. 'Just like Marx's egalitarian society!'

Still, revolts against the foreign rule continued. In 1925, Sunnis, Druze, Shi'ites and many Christians fought together for independence in Syria against the French and died side by side. It was the largest, longest and most destructive of the Arab Middle Eastern revolts against the Mandates.

At that point, the lights in the lecture hall started to flicker as if they were fighting for their life like a man after a heart attack. Wondering what was going on, everybody started talking loudly.

'Jihadis' was the word on everybody's lips. The assumption was that a rocket had hit the network. Despite the factual mist, people did not panic as they were used to this sort of attack. While several got up and started moving to the exits, the majority remained seated in the expectation that it would all be over very soon. It was.

Caught by the long arm of his anxieties, Ari had meanwhile been temporarily transported to his own world, dominated by his concern for Laura. 'What is she up to right now,' he wondered. 'I hope she's not swimming too far from shore. I hope she doesn't expose herself to dangers she won't even be given the time to regret.' The situation in the hall had retreated to the back of his awareness. His anxiety, though overlaid with a thick carapace of outer calm, had taken over for the moment.

As soon as order was re-established, the professor, who seemed to be the only person urgently in need of priming himself with a drink with some body in it to overcome his edginess, continued with his lecture.

'But the tide,' he said emphatically, 'changed in the post-World War II period. Rather than accept its colonial status, the Iranian government under Mohammad Mosaddegh, a leading champion of secular democracy, nationalised Iran's oil industry. But the 1953 coup, conceived and approved at the highest levels of the US government, replaced him with a monarchy. The latter was overthrown in 1979 by the Iranian revolution.

'Further, in 1952, a nationalist revolution in Egypt brought to power Gamal Abdel Nasser and led to the 1956 nationalisation of the Suez Canal, the joint invasion of his country by Britain, France and Israel and, with the comminatory prospect of a Soviet intervention hanging up in the air, their subsequent forced withdrawal. Their invasion, which was opposed by the US, too, and had caused outrage even in Britain itself, had ended up in disaster. Humiliated, Britain could no longer claim a role as one of the world's major powers.'

Arab nationalism at that point, as everyone knew, invaded every corner of the Arab world. Excavating their future, the Arabs discovered that they had missed something substantial. They questioned, as a result, their division into twenty-two states and strove for some sort of unity. But in opposition to it, Saudi Arabia, the Power the US chose as the counterweight to Nasser's Egypt, raised the flag of pan-Islamism.'

The nationalist movement seemed to be unstoppable at the moment. Early in 1958 the short-lived United Arab Republic was established by the merger of Syria and Egypt, and in July of the same year a nationalist revolution swept away the monarchy in Iraq and transformed the country into a radical republic. In 1961, after a very long guerrilla war against France, Algeria managed to win its independence, and in 1963 the Ba'athists seized power in Syria. Then Muammar Gaddafi's 1969 revolution ended the rule of his country by foreigners. The pro-western regimes in Jordan and Lebanon teetered on the brink of collapse.

'That was the time,' Ari thought, 'that the jubilant masses believed that Arab nationalism was about to triumph. But it was all a dream that was recklessly de-petalled.'

Time had opened, but it had also closed the gates to the fulfilment of their dream. Regionalism and vested interests made sure of it. The professor could have mentioned here the Syrian Ba'ath party's denunciation of Nasser's 'patronizing, bullying tone' and his insistence on a single centralized party structure under his leadership. He could have also acknowledged the failed 1963 Nasserite coup d'état in Syria that ended with hundreds of deaths and the denunciation by Nasser of the Syrian Ba'athists as 'fascists and murderers'. But he chose not to.

'Who wants absolute truth?' Ari wondered. 'Truth, supposedly a ravishing beauty, usually has hair on her lips.'

But the tide again changed after the crushing defeat of the Arab coalition by Israel in the 1967 Six-Day War. It was the battle that Nasser had dubbed the battle of destiny – *al-Ma'raka al-Masiriya*. With their territories occupied, their economies ruined and the Palestinians badly let down, disillusionment and despair replaced the dream in the Arab psyche. Abjectly humiliated, the nationalist movement was almost instantly marginalised. Tribalism and sectarianism, which had for a while retreated into the recesses of people's consciousness, resurfaced.

Thwarted by foreign Powers, undermined by Islamism and local nationalism and debilitated by inherent religious, cultural and linguistic rivalries, nationalism had just failed to establish the single, secular Arab state. Spoon-fed, the morrow had ended by not resembling a morrow.

'Modernity, such as western clothing,' Ari told Thiago later on in the bar, 'simply camouflaged the deeply-ingrained tribal values, the traditions of all the dead generations which weighed on the minds of the living like a mountain.'

'And one would have thought,' Thiago said, as if he meant it, 'that the dead cast no shadows.'

'Oh yes, they do,' Ari answered. 'They do through their values. And these values,' he carried on, 'were chimed in with authoritarian traits which made sure that workable democratic institutional structures were never developed or even pursued. Countries such as Syria, Egypt and Iraq took no time to descend into dictatorships, which brutally suppressed all opposition. Freedom, Nasser had said, meant only freedom from Western domination. It had nothing to do with democracy, which he only disdained.

'The separation of powers,' he once said, 'is nothing but a big deception. There really is no such thing as a separation of powers.'

'Being able to ruin anybody they wished to ruin,' Thiago interrupted him, 'must have given them the kicks...'

Ari did not know whether to take Thiago's comment seriously – perhaps he was just talking. He, thus, carried on.

'Unwilling to create the democratic institutions, the authoritarianism's custodians instead focused on the control of a system whose credibility depended only on their own credibility. When such an authoritarian leader failed, his system's ideology and values also inevitably went down the drain. The authoritarian states' nationalist ideology couldn't survive political setbacks, which democracy could have resuscitated in moments of crisis. But, unfortunately, the absence of democracy was the very way Arab nationalism was defined.'

The German professor had not mentioned anything of the above as he had avoided mentioning the 'Arab Spring' of 2011.

'If he had, he would, or rather should, have said,' Ari said, 'that the Nassers, the Sadats, the Saddams, the Mubaraks, the Assads or the Gaddafis had just failed their people. But perhaps that is what happens with revolutions. The most unscrupulous always rise to the top. Britain, France and also the US later on did also treat the Arab people as nothing but the eternal outsiders to their own land. But equally contributing to the Arab misery was the rampant failure of the Arab nationalists to grab the opportunities given to build up institutions which would empower their people. They relied, instead, on brutal force to perpetuate their own rule, depriving people of their rights.

'Woken from a deep sleep and helped by the power of social media,' Ari continued, 'the latter had at last decided in 2011, the year of the big wind, to take their destiny into their own hands. They wanted to own their world. But they were crushed. And it all ended in another tragedy – wars, authoritarianism, jihadism. It is, some say, as if democracy is not in the blood of the Muslim theocratic world.'

The time for radical Islam to enter the scene had arrived. The dictators had made sure of it by blocking the democratic development of their countries and turning religious militancy into the default option for many of their aggrieved citizens. For the Islamists, the ties that would knit the Arab nation into one state were religious rather than cultural, linguistic or historical. The existence of separate Arab states, as far as they were concerned, served only the interests of the imperialists. In this spirit, they had already challenged Arab governments throughout the Middle East. Most notable of these challenges were those faced by the Ba'athist government in Iraq in the late 1970s, the Ba'athists in Syria in the 1980s, the Algerian secular leaderships in the 1990s, and successive Egyptian governments during all three decades.

Meanwhile, the West got engaged in new military interventions – in Iraq in 2003, in Libya in 2011 and in Syria soon after. The ensuing chaos could only be predicted.

'These foreign interventions,' the German professor said, 'have only strengthened the Arabs' determination to put an end to the imperialist era initiated with the conclusion of the Sykes – Picot agreement.'

'Really?' Ari whispered.

The US-led overthrow of Saddam Hussein's minority Sunni regime in Iraq in particular was, indeed, a pivotal moment in the modern Middle East. Majority Shi'ite rule returned to Baghdad for the first time since the 17th century, raising the hopes of beleaguered Shi'ite Arab populations in Kuwait, Bahrain, Yemen and eastern Saudi Arabia.

But the Sykes – Picot agreement was not being challenged by the 'Arab Spring' forces, those striving for the dignity and justice that had been denied to the Arabs for as long as anyone alive could remember. It was challenged by the jihadis.

Ari was talking about it at the end of the lecture with a French journalist, Jean-Claude. Squinting slightly, the Frenchman did not answer him immediately. He was focusing on something else. 'Yes,' he said, eventually turning back from where he was to meet his colloquist's eyes. 'The Arabs themselves have given fate a hand in the completion of its task.'

'Fate, of course, is not absolute. It confronts man with a choice and the choice is his,' Ari told himself. His soliloquy was unvoiced. 'No point in being "too clever"?' another part of him had convincingly argued.

Frustrated and with a scarcely perceptible nod in agreement with the above, he left for a cool drink. He felt quite parched.

Chapter 5
Not like a Swiss tennis court

Queuing for a refreshment, Ari found himself standing next to a youngish-looking guy, quite pleasant and alert to what was going on around him. The two of them exchanged some trivialities about queuing in the heat and the clarity with which the professor had expressed his thoughts. But in the process, Ari discovered that the man was the Russian cultural attaché. His other thoughts vaporised and his approach to him did, as a result, change. The Russians were heavily involved in the war on the side of the Syrian President, and anything that could help to throw light on the state of their mind would be more than useful.

His attempt to draw the man, Sergei, to some meaningful conversation was nevertheless hampered – too many people around, too much noise, too much demand for his attention.

'He's being treated as if he were an imam,' a local businessman, aware of what was going on, told Ari with a laugh. Assaulted by circumstances, Ari gave up, but before doing so he got Sergei's details and his promise that they would meet for a drink sometime in the near future.

By the time he returned home, his mind had once again focused on Laura. He was in seventh heaven that their relationship met both his dreams and expectations, and he was looking forward to feeling the warmth of her presence again now and in the future. But Laura's investigation into the Jordanian arm dealers' schemes was quite alarming. The moment that the smugglers became aware that they were being investigated, they were bound to act. And action could only mean one thing: Making sure she was silenced. For good.

'Can I tell her to drop the story?' he wondered. The question could not be answered. 'For one thing, she wouldn't listen to me – no decent journalist would. But even if she were prepared to listen, would I be right pushing her in that direction? If what she's discovered came out into the open, it could change the nature of this conflict. Perhaps just shorten it. And shortening it meant sparing the lives of several thousand Syrians. Would I be right in trying to stop her doing it?'

He reflected on it for a while.

'No,' he decided. 'There's no way I can do such a thing. No way. All I can do is tell her again and again to be very careful. But this would guarantee absolutely nothing.'

The two of them met the next day, exchanged a couple of kisses, which attracted the attention of bystanders, and visited the great Umayyad Mosque. The building with three minarets is an architectural wonder. Originally an Assyrian temple and then a Roman temple to Jupiter, it was converted by Theodosius, the Byzantine Emperor, to a Byzantine cathedral in 706 AD. A few years later, it was transformed into a mosque. Its mosaics, created by Byzantine Greeks, were still visible.

'That was the time,' Ari told Laura, 'that the Umayyad caliph, Abd al-Malik, banned the Greek language from all public administrative documents. It was also the time the long modus vivendi by which Christians and Muslims lived in mutual tolerance had ended.'

Its museum houses a shrine which is said to contain the head of John the Baptist, considered a prophet by both Christians and Muslims alike. It had actually been built on the Christian basilica dedicated to him. The tomb of Saladin, the first Sultan of Egypt and Syria who led the Muslim military campaign against the crusaders, is also in a small garden adjoining the mosque.

Although hit by the rebels several times in the past, the Mosque was still well preserved. No severe damage had been inflicted to it or, as was the case, to any sites of cultural heritage within Damascus. But this was not the case in the rest of Syria where the mark of over 5,000 years or more made by the flourishing civilisations of the Babylonians, the Assyrians and the Hittites and then the Greeks, the Sasanians, the Persians, the Romans, the Byzantines and the Arabs was being steadily buried under rubble. The case was the same with the most impressive castles the European Crusaders had left and everything the Ottoman Empire had made its mark. Nothing was intrinsically valued any longer.

'All these cultures,' Ari said as they were walking, 'co-existed and conflicted, forming something new and special that was unique in the world. The six sites on the Unesco World Heritage List represent at least two thousand years of Syrian history. Sitting on the shorelines of this history, we can see its splendour. But, miserably, we can also see the damage inflicted on it by history's own makers. Shelling, shooting and major looting have been the leading causes of destruction.'

The picture changed at the corner of Souk al-Hamidiyeh, close to the Umayyad Mosque, where traders of the most important bazaar in the city were looking for customers. After almost five years of war, the well-off tourists who used to visit their shops were just a distant memory. The opposite shore, the good times, had vanished. Some thought it had never existed. Still, though bucketed with vinegar, hope had not been lost.

'I hope that a new sun will rise soon,' a juice man told Ari whilst taking a break from slinging cups of tamarind juice from a magic lantern-style brass cooler. He was decked out in a red fez and ballooned pants, a throwback to a time when tourists thronged the storied souk and posed for snapshots with the Ottoman-era-like figure.

'Each day,' he added, 'I get the feeling more and more that people think the worst is behind us.'

'Is it?' Ari wondered. His eye had just caught someone who he would have never noticed if he was not intensely staring at Laura from some distance. He was a man who could easily have won the 'Mr Most Average-Looking Person in Damascus' contest. Once seen, he could never be remembered. Ari's inner anxiety was instantly dilated and his eyes were again filled with his uninvited and unwelcome fears. The man could be seen through at a glance. He was there for a purpose.

'But who could have sent him?' was the next question. 'Was it Bashar al-Assad's Mukhabarat or the arms traders' agents?' Meanwhile, the man, though he now knew that Ari had spotted him, did not even bother to conceal his interest in Laura's movements. Ari's fears grew to awesome proportions just like the genitalia of this Stasi agent, the hero of a Thomas Brussig story, after his participation in a secret medical experiment.

Still, he said nothing to Laura as, in the meantime, in the shade of the Umayyad Mosque, an imam with a long beard and thinning hair on his head engaged them in a stimulating discussion.

'Muslim scholars and religious figures from all over the world,' he said, distancing himself completely from the jihadis, 'had slammed Isis because the group's practices have nothing to do with Islam. Our Prophet,' he fiercely argued on the marble floor of the Mosque whose mosaic walls incorporate a history of battles and bloody occupations, 'said that a Muslim cannot kill a person for practicing a different religion. By killing people, the extremists violate our Prophet's commandments. They are not true Muslims. Extremism,' he added, 'contains within it the seeds of destruction.'

Emotionally intense, he was ready to carry on, but their discussion had to end at that point as noon prayers were called for and visitors were requested to speak only in a low voice.

Powerful convictions, Ari thought, are not the prerogative of the Muslims. The apostle Paul, who, according to the New Testament, was blinded when a bright light from heaven flashed around him, had demonstrated this most convincingly. Converted to Christianity after his sight was 'miraculously' restored near the place they were chatting, he had turned into a righteous Christian fanatic, who, by reverting to the crudities of the wrathful Old Testament God, happily veered away from the concept of the loving God. Christianity in the Dark Ages turned into the ideology of terror.

'In old Ireland,' he told Laura, 'epilepsy was known as Saint Paul's disease.'

'What are you talking about?' she asked, wondering if she had missed a crucial point in their conversation.

''God, darkness and light...' he answered. 'I'm talking about Saint Paul. He lost his sight when he'd had a fit.'

'You don't make sense. What does Saint Paul have to do with anything?'

'Sorry, you're right. Forget it. I was in my own world. I was thinking about Saint Paul and his conversion to Christianity after the sudden loss of his sight. I've read somewhere that sight impediment, including temporary blindness, is a symptom or result of an epileptic seizure.'

'So what?' said Laura.

'Never mind,' he answered. 'Sometimes my mind flies to outer space. Sorry.'

'Why on earth do I have to burden myself with such thoughts,' he caught himself wondering a minute later. 'They never take me anywhere.' He instantly put all of them to the basement of his mind and kissed her tenderly. This was real. Tactile. Worth dying for. He then took her for a fruit cocktail at the nearby bar. The man, whose stare could easily give St Paul's statue a heart attack, was still around, following Laura's movements. He now looked as permanent as the Umayyad Mosque.

The atmosphere in the bar was quite cheerful. 'People obviously aren't talking about Apostle Paul and his convictions,' he said once again talking to himself. 'There are more important matters to talk about, like where to go for dinner.'

And this was the topic he raised with Laura, who however told him that she had made other arrangements. 'I need to meet with Lyse again.'

While still talking, she jumped and then ran towards a man approaching her with a big smile on his face. His graciously friendly gestures, an Englishman would think, belonged to ancient times. 'It's an Italian journalist, Pierro,' she whispered to Ari before giving her colleague a hug.

'How long have you been here?'

'Just two weeks,' the Italian answered. 'I was previously in Beirut for two weeks.'

'And how long do you intend to stay?'

'Perhaps one more week,' Pierro said, 'though I must say I don't like my accommodation.'

'Really? Where are you staying?'

'Dar al-Yasmin,' he said. 'It's a hotel in the old walled city.' Dar al-Yasmin, Ari knew, is a beautiful hotel several centuries old which was always full of tourists before the war. Now it was practically uninhabitable. 'We've got a spluttering tap,' the Italian said, 'and mostly there's no electricity. Most nights I've gone to bed by the light of my mobile phone.' There was, of course, nothing unusual to all this.

Laura had in the meantime introduced Pierro to Ari, who, upon hearing him address the waiter in Arabic, asked how he had managed to speak that language.

'Oh, I was born in Alexandria,' Ari said.

'Really?'

He could not say more as Laura stepped in to tell Ari that she would rather make the move back to her flat as she was rather tired. Besides, the next day was a big day and she had to prepare for it mentally. They were going to Eastern Ghouta. Laura wanted to go there to get a feeling of what it was like to live in the war zones.

'Let's see,' she had said, 'what the situation on the ground is.'

'It's nothing like the Swiss tennis courts at the Gstaad Palace,' Ari had warned her as if she did not know.

'Let's go,' she had insisted, only to regret her decision later. It was a decision taken against the wishes of her will, and Ari had most reluctantly accepted it.

At that point, having again been offered Ari's advice to watch her movements, she left. In his sinewy style, so did Pierro.

The journey to the rebel-held Ayn Tarba suburb of Eastern Ghouta, just three kilometres east of Damascus, was made on Ari's motorbike. Going there by taxi was at the moment an impossibility. At the crossing point, a street in which all houses on both its sides were almost totally destroyed, an army officer warned them against moving on.

'You're not safe. Don't go. But if you're determined to, do at least leave it for another day.'

They carried on.

They drove down the road, were stopped by rebels and, allowed to proceed, they continued the journey to the city's centre a few blocks away. The picture here was as similar to what Laura had as yet experienced in the Old City of Damascus as day is to night. The district, a working class area, had been subjected to earlier chemical attacks by the Bashar al-Assad regime and was still being bombarded by its air force and tanks. Those who had not fled to other parts of Syria remained trapped in their destroyed homes or in the massive network of tunnels that linked Eastern Ghouta to other parts of the country.

As humanitarian aid was largely blocked by the government, the needs of the locals were often met in the flourishing black market active in those tunnels in which Jaysh al-Islam had also established a number of prisons. Government and opposition fighters alike were only too happy to take their cuts from bribes for smuggling whatever was absolutely necessary. Some rebels were acting as warlords, enriching themselves and cracking down on dissent.

The shooting started as soon as they had stopped to look at a young boy who was seated on a pile of bricks, timber and stones on the side of the road.

'What are you doing here? Go home,' Ari told the boy, whose legs, he had noticed, looked as skinny as a spider's.

'I've no home,' the boy said.

'Go to your parents.'

'I've got no parents. They've been killed.'

An old man sitting a little further away was watching them.

'What are you doing here?' Ari asked him.

'I'm growing older,' he replied. The man seemed ready to quit a life he was thoroughly weary of. Nothing before him held any promise. The vision of a decent future had totally disappeared from his horizon. Talking to either of them soon became impossible as the roar of warplanes overhead was followed by the loud blasts of their strikes. More charred vehicles soon littered the streets. Smoke welled and rolled from one of them, a bus.

Having cover-fire, regime troops soon after stormed the rebel stronghold and positioned themselves near a petrol station in the southwest corner of the town. Tanks kept pounding it, while the rebels, fighting back behind burning barricades, were firing rocket-propelled grenades. The battle continued amid heavy tank fire, machine gun fire, mortar shells and sniper fire.

'Watch out,' Ari shouted, grabbing Laura's arm and pulling her towards him.

A tank shell had slammed into a wall just above them, sending chunks of plaster and concrete onto their heads. Amid flying debris and shrapnel, the very few people around were sprinting forward across the street, looking for cover in a building still standing among the neighbourhood's rubble.

The boy they had talked to had not moved from the rubble on which he was seated.

'Move out of there!' Ari shouted at him.

The boy did not move. Another rocket hit the ground close to him and fragments of plaster fell over his head. Still, he did not move.

'Wait here,' Ari told Laura. He rushed to the boy, grabbed him and, while bullets pierced the space all around them, took him to the relative safety of their hideout.

'You just stay here,' he ordered the boy. The boy stared at him and said nothing. Laura's cheeks and lips had, meanwhile, been drained of their colour.

The two sides continued shooting at one another, unleashing sustained volleys of automatic fire from behind sandbagged positions. At some point, one of the rebels was hit by a Syrian army sniper, who had managed to find a hole in between the sandbags behind which the rebel had sought cover. Shot in the chest, he said goodbye to his misery and died instantly. Another rebel, close to the dead man, was sobbing disconsolately over the body. A minute later, shot too by sniper fire, he was dragged close to a wall by fellow fighters where he died. The last image the dying man's bleary eyes had received would certainly be engraved in his memory forever.

Another man was carrying an injured, haemorrhaging child, who was pulled from underneath debris. The child was taken to a local field hospital which operated without anaesthetic or sterile supplies. Shortages could, of course, be deadly. One woman, Ari heard, had died waiting for a blood bag to arrive. 'Or,' he thought, 'she had died of disgust.'

The rebels seemed to move easily from building to building, through holes they had made in the walls. Most of the time these buildings were abandoned as the families had sought refuge elsewhere. It was through such buildings that rebels were recovering the bodies of their comrades. With a long stick on which they had attached a hook, they dragged the bodies a few meters off the street and then passed them to one another through holes in the buildings. The bodies were to be sent back to their families.

At some point, the firing died down, but a building had caught fire. Smoke and flames belched from its shattered windows, spewing through gaps in its ruined roof. But the rebels ignored it. They were busy wrapping up the bodies of two dead fighters, loyal to the Syrian President Bashar al-Assad that laid in the vicinity.

Ari looked at Laura. 'Are you okay?' he asked, a bit unsure.

She blinked, but instantly broke the confluence of her thoughts and reassured him she was fine. They both stayed there for a while until the firing and the sound of the explosions had completely died down. Laura's eye had meanwhile caught the action of the rebels who collected the bodies of the regime soldiers and wondered why they were doing it.

'I would expect them to collect the bodies of their own people rather than the bodies of those they were fighting against,' she said, rather puzzled.

Ari told her that they did so in order to exchange them later on for their own fallen comrades in the government's hands. The process had started a few years earlier, following negotiations which, fraught with suspicion, had led to some rebel leaders wearing suicide vests primed to explode if they were killed. That was in order to head off the danger of ambush.

'The dread,' one of them had told Ari, 'is so great that the vests contain a special sensor causing it to explode if they stop breathing.'

The exchange of bodies was, however, carried out now in the more congenial spirit of routine.

When some calm was established, Ari and Laura stopped about a hundred metres behind the nearest frontline position to chat with a group of women. They were seated next to a heavily damaged small van advertising the services of an electrician. The air was thick with a sickly smell – a combination of high explosives and blood, but the women were enjoying a cup of tea in the shade of a damaged tree.

The oldest of them, Amali, a woman whose skin was darkened by as many creases as her years, but who must have been strikingly beautiful in her early years, invited them to join her group. To start the conversation, she mentioned how difficult it was even to get water for their tea – 'difficult,' she said, 'as getting a rope through the eye of a needle.' Her own water tank had been hit by a sniper's bullet and her water supply had given up the ghost.

'I hope I'll fix it soon,' she added, but the problems remained. The building's outside walls were pockmarked with bullets and shrapnel-packed barrel bombs. The neighbourhood had to live with three hours of electricity a day, enough to charge her battery lamps, and suffered in cold weather as there was no heating. Some had to live without any running water or sewage facilities. That was the case not just in Eastern Ghouta, but across Syria as all sides had placed thousands of people in danger of starving to death to gain an advantage on the battlefield.

It was what had led to an international outcry over the use of siege tactics by all sides in the war.

Amali then took them to her house to show them the damage. A chilly breeze, coming through the cracks in the walls, immediately hit them. The hallway was pitch-black, but a dim light coming in through the windows enabled them to see their way. In the kitchen, a deep crack ran across its dingy yellow walls and the cheap, battered wooden table was cracked and held together by stitches. On it, there were some stone cold baked potatoes. In what passed for the bedroom, the thin mattresses on the concrete floor were torn. Mousetraps were laid all over the infested building.

Neither Amali nor her neighbours could ever climb the stairs to the second floor of their houses for fear of being shot. Climbing up her staircase was not easy anyway. The lower steps were missing.

'Lots of our people are killed,' she said while taking out her curlers to run her comb through her grey hair. 'My cousin. My nephew. My cousin's son. Living here is gambling with our lives. We don't know whether we'll wake up dead or alive.'

'Don't worry,' Ari reassured her with a smile. 'You'll never wake up dead.'

'Right,' she conceded laughingly. 'Still,' she carried on, 'I'm not leaving this place or my country as so many Palestinians have. I've lived here for 40 years and I won't leave.'

Another woman wondered loudly, 'where can we go in any case? We're destined to die one day, and it's better to die at home than in exile.'

'Except,' Laura told Ari later, 'they no longer expect to die peacefully in bed.'

Although Amali had not put it this way, exhausted as they were, many people just did not want to run away and be refugees. They preferred to hang on for as long as they could. To earn some money, she herself knitted jumpers. Ari and Laura got ready to go, but on their way out Ari asked the woman if she had any children. The question was rhetorical as he was sure she honoured the old tradition of having children.

'Yes, I do,' she answered.

'How many?'

'Sixteen. Many of them female.'

Laura, stunned, looked at Ari before addressing Amali. 'You must have been born pregnant.'

'You make me laugh,' Amali giggled, unable to stop the shaking of her breasts. 'I haven't laughed for ages.'

The conversation ended there as the mother of the sixteen children ran to welcome some of her boys back home who had gone to work to pay for the essentials. Ari and Laura left the place struck by the distress of the locals, enough to last them a hundred lifetimes, but also overwhelmed by their spirit of resilience.

'Who said that hell comes after death?' Ari said after they had walked away. Laura did not answer.

'Wouldn't you rather be back on Hydra's beach, enjoying the azure sea with a glass of pineapple sangria and an Isabella Allende book in your hand?' he mumbled a minute later.

It was something he said to ease the excruciating pain of the moment, too intense for the mind to accommodate. But embarrassed by it, he almost did not finish the sentence. The idea seemed so irreverent in the place they were that words faded as if the wind had picked them up and carried them away.

'Perhaps she didn't hear me,' Ari thought.

He was certain she had not when he heard her voice again. 'Let's get back "home",' she said with a voice heavily accented by tiredness. Back 'home', in the Old City, she felt much better. While there, they sat in a café bar, ordered a strong coffee and remained silent for a while in an effort to absorb what they had experienced.

'How things have changed since the early days,' Laura eventually said. 'How the "Arab Spring" has turned into a spring of blood... But perhaps,' reflecting on what she had just said, 'there's nothing strange about it all. The peaceful protests against the oppressive Syrian government had the overwhelming backing of the population. But the jihadis instantly turned these protests into an armed insurrection. The government, in turn, instead of trying to win over the peaceful demonstrators, resorted to brutal force. But silencing the voice of discontent was just not possible.'

They both knew exactly what followed. Supported by the US, which had been secretly supplying the rebels with weapons from Libyan arms depots and also by Saudi Arabia, Turkey and Qatar, the Islamists soon established a formidable fighting force. By December 2011, the Jabhat al-Nusra deadly car bombs were exploding in the centre of Damascus. Soon after, its fighters were active in eleven of Syria's fourteen provinces, particularly in Idlib, Aleppo and Deir al-Zour.

Responsible for dozens of suicide bombings in major city centres, the group had in no time turned into a disciplined and well-armed force that began to take part in major offensives against the government before expanding its operations to Lebanon. To the delight of the Israelis, its attacks on Lebanese soil were directed against both the Lebanese military and the Iranian-backed Hezbollah.

In November 2012, Jabhat al-Nusra, the most formidable opposition group outside Isis, was designated a terrorist entity by the Americans. The West had put its money on the Free Syrian Army, the 'moderate' opposition to Bashar al-Assad. But the FSA was subsequently marginalised and the spirit of the Arab spring was turned into a memory nobody could or wanted to discuss. Actually the US Defence Intelligence Agency knew as early as August 2012 that 'the Salafists, the Muslim Brotherhood and al-Qaeda in Iraq' were 'the major forces driving the insurgency' in Syria.

But for some reason, which the Americans prefer to forget, it all made no difference. By 2013, external involvement in Syria against Bashar al-Assad was at the same level as that against the Soviet Union, following the latter's intervention in Afghanistan. In addition to the arms supplied to extremist groups, the CIA had also trained and equipped thousands of fighters who, paid monthly stipends, were sent into Syria to fight against the regime. Disastrously for everybody, many of them defected to Isis or Jabhat al-Nusra, turning the weapons the US had supplied them with against the 'moderate' rebels.

'What a failure,' Laura cried with a trace of exasperation in her voice. 'It's as if nothing can teach us anything. The failure of our interventionist policy in Afghanistan, followed by the failure of the same policy in Iraq and Libya, taught us nothing. Nothing at all. It's as though failure didn't matter. And here we are again, following the same old, worn and bent policy in Syria. "We're like a dog",' she added quoting a British diplomat, "returning to its vomit". How can we explain it?

'The excuse for the failure they offered,' she continued, 'was that the US government didn't have sufficient control over its policies – whom to arm and whom to fund. And it had also failed to monitor properly the massive help it offered to the rebels. But that's really only a fragment of the truth.

'The other major part was the unmentioned fact that the US-led coalition, honouring its traditional incompetence, had actually sponsored violent Islamist insurgents to get rid of Bashar al-Assad, and together with him, the Russian presence in Syria. They did this in the full knowledge that this was a very dangerous game. Yet, despite different signals emanating from sections of the West's intelligence agencies, the coalition ploughed ahead anyway. According to the prevailing view that nonetheless lacked any visible means of support, the jihadi groups were "a strategic asset".'

'Yes,' Ari agreed. 'The jihadis did not seem like an obstacle to the realisation of the aims the Americans, the British and the French had set. Bashar al-Assad had to go.'

'But this was never acknowledged,' Laura carried on. 'Instead, a concerted effort was made to present a different picture through a highly misleading campaign. The rebellion was credited to "moderates", the "liberal, secular and democratic" forces of Syria, and as such it of course deserved the West's support. When the West woke up, it was already too late. The blunders it had made could not be rectified.'

'It was too late in Libya too,' Ari said, 'where in playing a similar game the Western intervention, that "shit show" as Barak Obama called it, produced only a failed state run by gangs.'

'The alternative,' Laura suggested, 'would have been open Western involvement. But this was, of course, out of the question. The West couldn't just interfere militarily into the affairs of a sovereign country without a UN resolution authorizing it to do so. The dogged self-assertion of imperialism is not fashionable these days. Besides, a direct military intervention could easily lead to World War III. Apart from this, any military intervention requires ground troops which neither the US nor any other Western nation are eager to provide. The previous military interventions and the chaos their failure engendered has drained public support for such entanglements. It could easily turn Syria into the graveyard of thousands of Western soldiers. And the West has no stomach for it.'

'I'll tell you a joke,' Ari said.

Laura looked at him, uncertain as to what he had in mind.

'It's about a Bedouin. A Bedouin, with huge eyelashes to protect his eyes against the strong sunlight, who lived near a river. He wanted to take a bath, but not in cold water as the evening was already pretty cold. He searched for his bucket in which he could heat the water up, but he could not find it. It was on the other side of the river. To fetch it, he took off his clothes and swam to the other side of the cold river and then returned with the bucket in which he warmed the water to have his bath.'

'Funny,' Laura said.

'It's more than funny,' Ari answered. 'It's what the Americans are doing. They want a hot bath in the warm waters of a Syria without Bashar al-Assad, but to get it they're stupidly crossing the cold jihadi river. The hot bath, even if they get it, won't compensate them for all they've gone through.'

'Two things are infinite,' Laura said. 'The universe and human stupidity. And I'm not sure about the universe.' She was quoting Einstein. 'Stupidity,' she added, 'ought to be outlawed.'

They both had a good laugh. They needed it after the tormenting experiences they had been through. But the moment only underlined the algedonic polarity of existence. That was particularly the case when Ari told Laura that she had been shadowed in the Umayyad Mosque.

'Someone, I don't know who, is after you, and I'm scared to death. You seem to have been targeted. And this, I'm afraid, means only one thing. You'll probably have to move on to Beirut.'

She said nothing. And the void was instantly filled with the tenebrous shadows of angst.

Chapter 6
Up for sale in the black market

In an UNRWA gathering the next day, Ari again came face to face with all the uncertainties of the current situation. As it was now obvious, the peaceful anti-authoritarian protests were now a thing of the past. The jihadis had made sure of it. No-one in the government-controlled, or much less in the rebel-controlled, areas believed in the 'Arab Spring' revolution any more. 'To do so,' Ari had been told time and again, 'would just be naïve at this stage.' What had also changed was the momentum of the peace process. It looked more promising following the advances of the government forces and also the changes in the attitude of many people.

'I hate Bashar al-Assad,' a bespectacled Druze intellectual had said to Ari during this UNRWA gathering. 'But I want to stop the killing. If the regime is defeated, it'll be a catastrophe.'

It was after all only very recently that Jabhat al-Nusra troops had 'spontaneously' massacred at least thirty Druze in Idlib, the town in north-western Syria. In Qalb Lawza, one of the Druze villages in the same area, they had forced inhabitants to renounce their faith and accept Sunni Islam earlier in the year. In the process, they had destroyed Druze shrines and made the residents abide by their regulations, such as gender segregation.

It was the same man, the Druze, who bitterly recalled how the proposed peace deal submitted by Russia on the 30th of January 2012, providing among other things for the 'elegant' replacement of Bashar al-Assad from the scene, had been ignored by the US, Britain and France. Living in their fantasy world and guided by their pompous certainties, they were all convinced that the Syrian dictator 'would be thrown out of office in a few weeks'. The political compromise that would have ended the conflict was, therefore, never pursued.

None of the countries involved in the conflict, the Druze concluded, 'had the interest of the Syrian people as their first priority.'

'Surprise, surprise...' Ari reflected, but did not say anything.

He listened to the Druze fellow attentively, but in response, he confined himself to trivialities of the kind that frustrated his companion.

'Sorry,' the Druze said at the end, 'there's an urgent call I need to make.' He had obviously not learned to revel in trite confabulations.

'Sorry,' Ari said too. At the same time, he reproached himself for not having come up with some refreshing new platitudes.

But representing a UN organisation meant that, when talking to Syrians, he had to make sure he stayed out of the conflict's politics. This was not an easy task as the UN aid agencies were already under attack from the rebels for prioritising cooperation with the Syrian government over aid deliveries to areas beyond government control.

'It's what enables the government,' one of them, a Yarmouk resident waving his finger, had accusingly told Ari a few weeks earlier, 'to use starvation as a weapon of war.'

'Strictly speaking,' Ari had reassured him, 'this isn't absolutely true. The Syrian government had allowed aid into, for example, the besieged rebel-held village of Madaya, near Damascus, whose residents were starving to death.' The reassurance was received with a sound of frustration that rolled down the street before turning into thin air.

Ari knew, however, that starvation was a weapon both sides in the conflict were still using extensively.

To ease the tension that the Eastern Ghouta experience had created, Ari took Laura to a karaoke club the next evening. DJs played songs in praise of President Bashar al-Assad, or his ally, the Hezbollah leader Hassan Nasrallah, and a crazy selection of songs, from the Beatles to Big Sean and Drake's latest hits. Some filled the dance floors, but others remained seated and carried on drinking. It looked as if dancing was an act of loyalty and seating a sign of dissent.

When the DJ put on a different song – 'I'll Survive' – everyone danced along. These youngsters were the survivors of the war, or at least the ones who had managed, at least so far, to escape its damage. They kept their head down and stayed clear of politics.

But no matter how jubilant their spirit, Laura could not recover from the Eastern Ghouta experience. She looked as if she was carrying an invisible burden, responding to questions and greetings rather impatiently and with a grudging voice. 'Having crossed such a very rough sea of suffering,' Ari thought, 'she needed some time to recover from that painful experience.'

'No matter what,' he told her in an effort to help, 'their spirits are not beaten and life carries on. When it's all over, they'll be able to dream again.' He knew, of course, that what he was talking about was the distant, imponderable future. As long as current circumstances persisted, spirits seemed destined to orbit only the lifeless shadows of their broken dreams.

They went back to his flat and, whispering like the breathing of the trees, fell into each other's arms. The happiness of the moment whose language has no alphabet, pushed all else to the background. It revived their thirst for life. But they both needed, Ari decided, a bit more time to relax away from all the pressing needs of their work. So, the next day they visited the Arabic Cultural Centre, where a marble mosaics exhibition was being held. However, Laura found it difficult to concentrate on the exhibits as her mind was preoccupied with the 'numerous illegal arms sales' she had heard about, particularly those in Jordan.

'I've got to see some arms dealers,' she said, 'and work out how the arms delivered to "moderate" rebels often fall into the hands of the jihadis.'

'Well,' Ari thought ruefully, 'she has at least recovered from the gut-wrenching Eastern Ghouta experience.' But more than that, she had also made significant in-roads into investigating the illegal arms trafficking business.

'Many of these weapons,' Laura said, 'up for sale in the black market, were bought in bulk in the Balkans and elsewhere around Eastern Europe. At least one of the guns used in a Paris attack, an M92 pistol,' she added, 'was imported from Serbia to the United States by Century International Arms, a Florida-based online firearms dealer, and then re-exported back to Europe.' Century Arms had close ties to the CIA. Weapons could not be re-exported without reams of paperwork and approval by numerous federal agencies. But they could be re-exported illegally.

'Take another firm, Purple Shovel LLC, a Delaware-based company,' she carried on. 'Two months ago, this company was authorised by the State Department to buy arms from Belarus, Europe's last dictatorship, and hand them over to US-trained rebels in Syria.' Belarus was a country internationally prohibited to sell arms.

'Other equipment, including rocket-propelled grenades, was bought by the same company in Bulgaria. Way past their shelf life, one of them had exploded in the hands of an American contractor and killed him. Croatia had come into the picture too, as had Romania, countries from Central Asia and also the Ukraine from where a stockpile of Soviet arms was passed onto Syria.

'Weapon shipments,' she said, 'are coordinated by several other European countries including Britain, which had said it would provide only "non-lethal assistance" to the rebels. All the West needs to do,' she added sarcastically, 'is ensure that the arms from Eastern Europe are transported to Syria without alerting the international authorities or the media.'

Though happy to hear her talk, Ari was not familiar with the arms deals Laura was talking about. And at the moment, neither Laura nor himself of course knew that the arms purchases in Eastern Europe were connected with the original Obama programme to arm the 'moderate' Syrian rebels. Nor did they know that similar weapons had also been bought in those countries by Qatar, Saudi Arabia, Abu Dhabi or the Emirates — at the US's request. None of them were expected to buy the Bulgarian, mainly Soviet-style, weapons for themselves. Their destination was either Syria, Yemen or both.

Looking at her lovingly, all Ari could say was just a few words. 'I don't like what you're doing. You're sailing too close to the wind and you're bound to end up in trouble.' The spasm of apprehension he felt was only too evident.

'Yes,' she answered. 'I know that anything connected with such issues is fraught with danger. But I can't stop. I've got to get through.'

'Why? Do you have to?'

He did not mean to corner her. In asking, all he really wanted was an answer. One that would at least dissuade him from urging her not to pursue her story. He knew that what she was doing was the right thing – it was exactly what he would do in her position. But he wanted to hear the answer from her.

'It's my work,' she said. 'It's my mission as a journalist to search for the truth in all its hiding places, expose the wrongdoings of people in power, contribute to the creation of something better than what we have today. Journalism for me is not about entertainment or celebrity gossip. The journalist is a fighter for truth, decency, humanity, the principles and the values of the civilised world. Not sticking to these values is a betrayal of the trust placed on me, a betrayal of myself. And I won't do that. I would hate myself if I did.'

Ari did not feel he could say anything else. She had made up her mind and was impervious to discouragement. But she looked like a moth cruising over a flame.

'Be bloody careful,' he advised her once again, quite apprehensively. 'Be careful.'

'And you calm down,' she urged him.

'Calmness is not an end in itself,' he responded with undisguised resignation. His reaction, though full of quiet energy, betrayed his surrender.

The next day was not Ari's day. With members of the National Defence Force, the pro-government militia, he had driven down to the industrial suburb of al-Qadam in southwest Damascus to assess the locals' requests for help. It was a normal Monday with nothing unusual going on in the area, other than the usual long queues to buy petrol which lined the streets. Women were buying goods, children playing, men enjoying their coffee.

This superficial tranquillity was suddenly interrupted by a loud mortar explosion, followed by sniper fire from rooftops – all terrifyingly close. People started screaming. The sound of it rolled down the shadowed streets, echoing in the canyons of the buildings. Ari's motorbike was thrown to the pavement by the blast. His shoulder was dislocated and deep scratches there left him bleeding. His torn shirt was gradually turning red. Chaos reigned. No one was sure who began firing or why. A few people received shrapnel wounds and dust covered everyone.

'It could have been much worse,' he thought afterwards. 'If the traffic light had not changed to green, I would have been exactly where the bomb had landed.' The issue suddenly became a puzzle. 'Being there and getting injured,' he wondered, 'was all due to my bad luck or did getting out of it alive mark the luckiest day of my life?' He opted for the latter.

A passing taxi took him to the nearby Shami Hospital in al-Malky Street, the hospital used by Syria's political and military elite. On the way, he could not stop thinking about how chance determines our fate, how something totally unimportant could fully metamorphose our life. 'The most important things in life happen by chance,' he recalled a childhood friend telling him when he was still in Alexandria. A traffic accident had left his friend with only one leg.

He stopped moving into the cloisters of his memories the moment he arrived at the hospital. He was helped inside, taken to its makeshift clinic and offered the first aid that he needed. The doctor was to see him soon. TV cameras were hooked up everywhere.

Lying next to him was a young boy, probably a student, recovering from severe injuries to his abdomen and thorax. Another slightly younger boy with dark skin and big eyes, who had lost both legs when a bomb had blown up a lorry, was in another room. That boy grabbed Ari's attention, but only when his father launched into a cursing of Isis. 'Those cowards who do things like this. He's just a boy,' he yelled fiercely. 'He wasn't doing anything. He was just waiting to cross the road.' He then pulled back the sheet to display his son's disfigured body and shouted again. 'We are not afraid of whatever the Turks, the Saudis and any of Syria's enemies do.'

A man next to the boy, bandaged from the chest down, had, he said, only just survived an explosion. He was a van driver who had been transporting empty gas cylinders when a rocket had struck his vehicle.

'The pain is unbearable,' he said with trembling lips. 'Whatever way I turn I'm in agony. And I worry about my children now that their breadwinner has more than forty per cent of his body burnt.'

As they were talking, someone Ari knew but could not remember where from, approached him to say hello. He was working there as a nurse. Sensing Ari's difficulty, he reminded him that he was Sharif, a Palestinian from Yemen, and that they had met when Ari had attended a meeting of Palestinians from Jeramana. He asked how he was doing and Ari, trying to ignore the pain which travelled up and down the injured part of his body like a rheumatic disorder, reassured him he was fine.

Then he joked. 'You're still as tall as you were last time we met.'

'A totally accidental development,' Sharif answered in the same tone and with a big smile which gave a new shape to what looked like the map of Japan, the birthmark that figured on his face.

Ari proceeded to ask him how things were in Yemen.

'Pretty bad,' the man answered. 'The Saudi-led bombardment that started last March continues to be widespread and barbaric. They use US-made cluster bombs and attack everything. Hospitals, schools, factories, marketplaces, whole neighbourhoods, ancient sites, funerals and wedding parties, everything. My brother was killed in one of those attacks.'

'I'm so sorry,' Ari said. 'Their air attacks are indeed reckless and horrible. Quite incompetent and stupid, too, as they don't take them anywhere. The rebellious Houthis, their target, still in control of the capital, have stretched their influence to the Saudi border. In the meantime, thousands of lives are lost, most victims of airstrikes.'

'Not just of airstrikes,' Sharif said. 'The naval, air and land blockade imposed by the Saudi-led coalition since August, particularly the blockade of Hudaydah, the main point of entry for most goods into the north, is bringing the country on the brink of a humanitarian catastrophe. More than 14 million Yemenis – more than half of the population of the country – now desperately need food, water, vital medical supplies and fuel.

Ari said nothing in response. He chose instead to focus on his pain, which, he said, seemed to be getting worse.

Yemen, he knew, had for some time been the centre of a proxy war between the region's biggest powers, Saudi Arabia, a country with a majority of Sunni Arabs, and Iran, a country with a majority of Shi'a Muslims. Iranian-backed rebels had seized the Yemeni capital and a Saudi coalition of Arab states had been trying in vain to defeat them in order to restore the previous client regime.

The war had inflamed anti-Saudi sentiment and created a coarse military and political quagmire for the Saudi government. Things got worse for them when many Western Powers expressed their disapproval of their 'impulsive policy of intervention' or, in other instances, of their intolerant forms of Islam. Yet, though uncomfortable about it, the US, Britain and France continued to provide Riyadh with intelligence, targeting assistance, aerial refuelling and hardware to replenish its munition stockpiles.

'How the Americans can claim the moral high ground,' Sharif continued as if Ari had not indicated that the conversation on the subject was over, 'is totally beyond my comprehension. The Saudis massacre the population and the West is only there to give them a hand. Even the media ignores what's going on.'

'Perhaps their sources of information,' Ari answered with a tone of resignation in his voice, 'fail to provide the necessary information.'

It was the Palestinian's turn to say nothing.

At that point, the doctor, Hussein, stepped in and took a look at Ari's injury. He reassured him that he would be fine in a few days and then apologised for not being able to take care of him himself immediately. 'Long hours of work,' he said. 'We have to deal with numerous casualties on a daily basis, while improvising treatments as even basic medicines are unavailable. Still,' he added, 'the greatest difficulty is the maintenance of sophisticated machinery like scanners and also adequate reserves of diesel and water.'

'Staff-wise?' Ari asked.

'We're doing all right, but many doctors have left the country. The brain drain is more evident in the examining rooms, which are manned by youngsters who lack the experience.'

He sucked the Marlboro Red he had just lit, narrowing his eyes as the smoke stung them. His own job, he added, was easier as he primarily had to take care of the 'important' people who needed hospitalisation. The ashtray next to his chair, Ari noticed, needed emptying. The man looked as if he was smoking himself to death.

In the meantime, Laura, who Ari had texted, appeared at the door, looking for him with a terrified look on her face. When her eyes caught him, she took a deep breath, a sign of relief that he was all in one piece. He had told her it was only a very minor injury, but she would not believe it until she had seen for herself. Happy he was alive and kicking, she gave him a light kiss before she was introduced to Hussein, who had reappeared to check his bandages.

Together with him this time was a nurse, Aniya. She was, Hussein told Ari, a Yazidi living in Sinjar, the Iraqi town mainly populated by Yazidis, an ancient religious minority regarded by Isis as heretics. In August 2014 Sinjar had been taken over by the Isis jihadis. When they had moved in 'no leaf was spared because of its beauty, no flower because of its fragrance'. 'They killed,' Aniya said, 'thousands of Yazidi men and took away all the women and children as war booty to be sold and bartered as chattels or used as sex slaves.'

Reacting to the Sinjar massacre, the US launched its first airstrikes against Isis in northern Iraq. They were joined by several other countries.

Interestingly, however, and as Hussein explained, a State Department memorandum dated August 2014 and leaked later did acknowledge that both the Isis forces that were butchering the Yazidi and other Iraqi and

Syrian villagers, along with other jihadi groups, were being provided 'clandestine financial and logistic support by the governments of Qatar and Saudi Arabia'. This was never openly admitted as the US was reluctant to antagonise Saudi Arabia, the Gulf monarchies and also Turkey and Pakistan. Doing so, it believed, would fatally undermine US power in the Middle East and South Asia.

'Aniya was used as a sex slave by the jihadis for eight months,' Hussein's voice explained to Ari. 'But about eight months ago, she and other Yazidi women were rescued by smugglers who had infiltrated the terrorist organization. After that, she was taken to a hospital for medical examination, including tests for sexually transmitted diseases.'

Aniya, sitting very straight with her knees closed together and her body stiffly erect like an Egyptian goddess, kept her head down while Hussein was speaking. But soon after, despite her understandable tendency to block out completely the horrors she had experienced, she made just a very brief reference to them. 'The way the sex slaves are treated,' she said, 'is absolutely horrific. Even worse, the jihadis are proud of it.'

'What do you mean? Laura asked.

'Well, take their own pamphlet, printed by Isis' publishing house, Al-Himma Library,' Aniya explained. Ari had not seen it, but he had heard about it. As Aniya explicated, 'The pamphlet,' 'reassured the "faithful" that, "as Allah the almighty had said", they could engage in sex with their female slaves, Christian or Jewish, "immediately" after their capture if they happened to be virgins. It didn't matter if the girls "hadn't reach puberty". The master could also have sex with a female who was no longer a virgin, provided her "uterus was purified".'

The pamphlet also stated that 'a female slave could be bought or sold because she was "merely property which can be disposed of" or "distributed just as all other parts of the estate are distributed". If she misbehaved, her "disciplinary beating" was permissible.' Allah had obviously said so, perhaps through an incandescent crack in the sky's black clouds.

Talking about her eight-month nightmare, Aniya was quite cool. She looked extremely uncomfortable only when the issue of pregnancy came up. 'The men I was "married" to had given me birth control pills,' she said, ending the conversation on the subject.

Ari had learnt to live with the monstrous, the inconceivable, the irrational, the ludicrous or the perilous. But here was another loathsome side of life that burst the framework of reality and filled him with disgust. The revulsion he felt, activated, as Hussein told him later, in the region of the brain called the anterior insular cortex, invaded his mouth and started rolling down to his stomach. Gripped by a moral vertigo, he excused himself and walked outside with Laura for some fresh air.

'What a nauseating, abominable situation...'

He did not need to say anything more. Laura, as disturbed as he was, grabbed his hand and held it for a while. When he felt better, he walked back to the hospital to say goodbye to Hussein. 'Perhaps we can meet again,' he told him.

'It will be a pleasure,' Hussein, looking at Laura, assured him.

Having taken a couple of days off to recover from the pain of his injury, Ari spent this time in his flat. He was visited by Laura when her work allowed her to visit, and read Eliza Kennedy's *I Take You* that had just been published. It was the story of a promiscuous lawyer in New York who prepares to marry her archaeologist fiancé but, to do so, she first has to overcome her antipathy to monogamy.

'Interesting,' Ari thought. 'Monogamy, they say, leaves a lot to be desired. But I love Laura, and this is it.'

That was the voice of his tender inner self. His body was loudly broadcasting a different message through the sharp pain coursing through his shoulder and his ribs.

When he was feeling better, he met Hussein for an early morning coffee in the plush surroundings of the XO bar of the Four Seasons hotel. Ari, who saw him first, recognised him from behind – his large bottom had made it easy. Laura joined them a few minutes later and was instantly complimented by Hussein for her good looks. The Syrian doctor then asked her what she would like to drink. He forgot to ask Ari the same question. They all settled on tea and were soon after fully engaged in a conversation that started when Laura asked the Syrian doctor why all the 'good' Muslims are bearded.

'Oh, Muhammad, Allah's Apostle,' Hussein said, 'instructed men to cut their moustaches short and leave the beard as it is. "Do the opposite of what the pagans do". That was necessary,' Hussein added, 'for political, religious and cultural reasons.'

'You mean 1,400 years ago?' asked Laura.

'Yes.'

'And it's applicable today whatever the circumstances?'

'Oh, well,' Hussein answered. 'That's a matter of interpretation.'

The chat very soon turned to the war and the role of the various rebel groups in it. When Hussein mentioned in this context the name of a Saudi prince, Laura, for reasons Ari could not understand, asked about that man's role in the war and, in particular, his connections with Jaysh al-Islam. The doctor's answer did not satisfy her. Having monopolized his attention, she did not, however, give up. She persisted, but the desired result kept drifting away unconcernedly.

Ari was not listening to their discussion. His attention had been hijacked by three people sitting close to him. One of them, a German, who he understood was an archaeologist, was telling the other two how she had become a celebrity in Palmyra because she had once washed a donkey.

'The poor animal,' she was saying, 'was very dirty and was being eaten by flies and other creatures. But nobody around seemed to care. So one day I decided to wash him. I used my share of water and an expensive German soap, but, as I discovered, all this had turned into a show. The whole village turned up to watch the event.

'"Mazmazelle", they said, meaning mademoiselle, "what are you doing? You're crazy". I ignored them, but I knew that the donkey was now a happy animal. All this happened twenty years ago,' she added. 'But last week, when I went to Palmyra again, people remembered me.'

'Mashallah,' the hotelier said. 'I remember you. You're the one who washed a donkey.'

They all laughed loudly. 'You must put the story on Facebook. People will love it,' one of her listeners managed to suggest before his telephone started emitting his personalised ring tone.

Ari refocused on the discussion at his table, which had now turned to more general questions. Carrying on with what she had been discussing with Ari a few days earlier, Laura had asked Hussein why the Arabs could not end the dysfunctional state of their affairs. A little puzzled, Hussein just smiled, while Ari, feeling uncomfortable, re-positioned himself on his chair. He hoped she would not go ahead with 'helpful' suggestions, which would disturb the sacred certainties of the regime.

'We don't want someone to come to Syria and tell us what to do in a political process,' Bashar al-Assad, Syria's ruler, addressing a cheering crowd, had already warned everybody after all. 'A country that is thousands of years old knows how to manage its affairs.'

'Please,' Ari said, mentally passing a message to Laura, 'remember the old saying: "Do not burst the bubbles that the Arab has put himself in".' Doing so would be like walking into a minefield of past errors and present cultural sensibilities. But in front of Hussein, he could not verbally pass onto her such a message.

Rather than stepping into the discussion, Ari instead chose to scan the pedestrians on the pavement outside. Hussein for his part, with a bitter smile of the kind usually used to greet an impropriety, looked at his nicotine-yellow nails and then proceeded to assure Laura that, if not for the jihadis, Syria would, as before, be on the regeneration path.

Their discussion was thankfully interrupted by an elderly woman at that point. She approached them very confidently asking if she could borrow their ashtray. They were happy to oblige, but the woman, from Torquay, 'the gateway to the English Riviera' as she told them, embarked on a little chat instead of moving on.

'I come to this hotel every year,' she said, 'and this despite the very troublesome earlier war years. And I'm always offered the same room overlooking the mountains. In the good old days, the lights of the houses that climb their slopes were like stars dancing at all-night parties.'

'That's nice,' Laura responded.

'But,' she added, 'a ghost peeps into my window every night.'

'Muslims do not believe in ghosts,' Hussein informed her. 'And if they don't believe in them, they don't exist. Do they?'

'The belief in ghosts,' he explained, 'comes from the pre-Islam times, "the times of ignorance". Believing in them is believing in a superstition. But we believe in jinns, spirits, good or bad. They were created before mankind from a smokeless flame of fire and dwell in the unseen universe. A jinn, assigned to every human born and replicating everything a person does, outlives the human but remains in the grave until the end of times.'

He stopped there as if his explanations were too abstruse for the woman's comprehension. Or because he got bored.

Before the woman started talking about her gluten-free diet as well, Ari and Laura remembered that they had an appointment to honour. They thanked Hussein for his time and left.

The excuse had elements of truth. Laura was meeting a Syrian arms dealer, though not for another two hours.

Chapter 7
At home with madness

To regain their peace of mind, Laura and Ari went for a short walk in the city's old bazaar, which was once again bustling with life. Cafés were crowded with people, including entire families, sellers pushed their goods and buyers moved between the rows. A women's volunteer orchestra was performing to the delight of the passers-by next to a big sign calling for young people to join the army.

Interestingly enough, Ari noticed, the city's roads were regularly swept and maintained in a decent condition despite the war.

The picture close to the Azem Palace, a beautiful sample of Damascene traditional houses built in 1750 and now housing the Museum of Arts and Popular Traditions, was not any different. Women with hijabs over their heads were sweeping the floors, and men, some with headscarves, were chatting with each other. One of them, a man with white hair holding a young boy in his arms, gave them a friendly smile. More friendly smiles welcomed them in what was the Temple of Jupiter as Ari was taking a photo of Laura, another one on top of the many he had already taken.

Minutes later, a sandstorm hit Damascus and they were forced to seek refuge inside the nearest café. The storm shrouded the city in a yellowish haze that masked a pale sun and the top of Mount Qasioun. It was bad, but nothing like the 'unprecedented' sandstorm that had hit Syria and Lebanon in September, killing twelve people and sending hundreds to hospitals with breathing difficulties. It was soon over and people moved into the open space to celebrate the return of bright sunshine.

The celebration was, however, short-lived as the news on the Syrian TV hit the people like a bombshell. Three suicide bombers had struck near the Stade de France in Saint-Denis while others had at the same time resorted to more suicide bombings and mass shootings at cafés, restaurants and a music venue in central Paris. The attackers had killed a hundred and thirty people, including eighty-nine at the Bataclan theatre, where they had taken hostages before engaging in a stand-off with police.

Isis claimed responsibility for it as it had in previous attacks, including the attack that had hit Tunisia in June.

Nearby people looked as pale as a lemon that had suddenly heard bad news. The only sound was the noise of jaws dropping.

'Why do they go to such extremes,' Ari wondered, as soon as he had picked up is jaw from the floor. The same question was on Laura's mind.

'Why? Do the jihadis want to punish the Western Powers for their involvement in the Middle East? Certainly. But how far would this take them? Nowhere actually. The Western Powers aren't going to be terrorised. Why then?'

'I'll tell you what I think,' Laura said. 'I think that their intention is to turn the Western states, and eventually Russia, too, against their own Muslim minorities. The Muslim minority, particularly in France, numbers millions. The minorities would then be forced to react and, as the jihadis hope, violently, in which case their Islamic war would be transformed into a civil war that would tear apart the various European nations. Should that be the case, we might as well postpone the arrival of the future.'

But then another looming question demanded their attention.

'Why,' Ari asked, 'has Isis convinced people in our part of the world to go to such extremes? Why does such brutality, almost unrivalled in modern history, attract thousands of Muslims from all over the world to Isis' ranks?'

'Good question,' Laura said after a minute's silence, which seemed to radiate the quandaries inherent in the answer. 'Good question, but what's the answer?'

Ari just looked at her.

'Something must certainly appeal to them,' she said eventually, after a minute fed only by silence. 'Something motivates them, inspires them, impregnates their imagination. What is it? The conviction that by indiscriminately killing those who oppose God and His Messenger, Muhammad, they give them just what they deserve? The Fire of Hell?'

'Yes and No,' Ari said, intrigued by the question. 'The issue has ended up being theological, but its roots are elsewhere. To begin with, you need to look at the injustice the Arabs have experienced for years and years.'

'You mean...' Laura started to say.

'I mean,' Ari continued, 'the Arabs gave their battle against foreign dominance when nationalism had captured their psyche, particularly in the 1950s and 1960s. But what did they end up with? Brutal and corrupt Republics. Their new rulers embezzled the national wealth and left their countries reeling under poverty.'

'Gaddafi,' Laura interrupted him, 'ruled Libya for more than four decades, yet he did not even build a decent hospital.'

'Exactly,' Ari answered. 'Nationalism had just failed to deliver the goods. And the interesting question here is why. Why was the wealth of their countries squandered? Why were people denied, just as they had been during the Ottoman rule, their rights?'

His voice, Laura noticed, was gradually rising. The frustration and bitterness that coloured it was also reflected in his eyes.

'Nationalism, as a result, appealed to them no longer,' he carried on. In doing so, he disregarded the people around him who had turned their heads to look at them. 'The Arabs, particularly the young ones, in effect rejected their world – it was at best irrelevant to them or at worst actively hostile. They wanted something else. But what was their choice? They massively endorsed what the "Arab Spring" had stood for, but ended up seeing their dreams crushed and their condition more benighted than ever. Dreams so readily degenerate into nightmares.'

Laura touched his hand, held it for a minute and, looking at him straight in the eyes, quietly told him to calm down. 'You don't want to attract their attention, do you?' Ari took a deep breath and carried on in quieter tone.

'The ending of the "Arab Spring" left the road open to the politicised religion of the jihadis. Targeted again were those who had treated the people as inferior human beings and deprived them of their dignity. Top of the list were those who had dominated their countries politically, culturally and economically. In other words, the Western Powers.

'The latter had carved up their land in line with their interests and backed up the local corrupt and tyrannical regimes in exchange for the benefits they accrued. The grotesque invasion of Iraq and those Powers' policy on Israel only inflamed their hatred further. It weatherproofed it.'

'The promise they made was that by asserting their values over the materialistic and avaricious West, they would get at least one scrap of superiority over it: spiritual superiority. "What we believe in, eternal life, is far superior to your trifling interests. What we stand for, oneness with God, stands miles apart from your petty aspirations. What we value, the word of God, is far above your frivolous concerns. And we're not afraid of death". Even if their death is their one and only history.' Ari's voice had been raised again.

'Let's move out,' Laura suggested.

They left the café where they had taken shelter from the sandstorm and moved out into the crowded street. A man who had not shaved for quite some time was humming a song with his eyes firmly fixed on the far end of the horizon. He bumped Ari out of his path and carried on without saying anything. The event was obviously beneath his notice. Preoccupied with his own thoughts, which were still swimming in his head, Ari did not say anything either. He carried on talking about the jihadi bombers instead.

'Despatching suicide bombers all over the planet,' he said, 'has the added advantage of giving wings to their wild fantasies of spreading the word of Islam all over the world. From Spain to India. Abu Bakr Naji, the Islamist strategist, had already given in his book, *The Management of Savagery,* a detailed blueprint for provoking the West into interventions. Such interventions, he held, would further rally the Muslims to jihad, leading to the ultimate defeat of the Dawlat al-Kufr, the State of Unbelief by the Dawlat al-Islam, the State of Islam.

'Quite explicit in his instructions,' he carried on, 'Abu Bakr Naji, a man unaware of his abnormality like all abnormal people, unwaveringly instructed the faithful to massacre the world. "We need to massacre", he said, "and to do that, we must adopt a ruthless policy in which hostages are brutally and graphically murdered unless our demands are met".

'As if what he was saying wasn't quite clear,' Ari continued, 'the Islamist strategist proceeded to illustrate his point by mentioning Banu Qurayza, a Jewish tribe in seventh-century northern Arabia. In punishment for a hostile act committed against Prophet Muhammad's native Meccan tribe, the tribe was annihilated in 627 AD. The men were beheaded and the women and children were enslaved.'

'This Abu Bakr Naji book you're talking about,' Laura said, 'must have turned into a bestseller among the jihadis.'

'In a sense yes,' Ari answered, 'though it was published on the internet. Mind you, Abu Bakr Naji was disenthralled from his worldly presence back in 2008 by a US drone strike.'

Ari's thinking moved onto a different track for a moment. He wondered how all these layers of rust over old beliefs, which the new religious fanatics persisted in seeing as the spiritual deposits of their past, did not seem to make them any less desirable. Like figures teleported from the distant past to the twenty-first century, they seemed instead enchanted by the primitivism of those beliefs, happy to seek refuge in them and dance to their tuneless music.

'One might well be tempted to think,' Ari carried on, practically talking to himself, 'religion seems to have come only to plunge the world into gloom. Moses, after all, had commanded the killing of idolaters and the burning of their cities and property as an offering to God, and St Augustine had endorsed "the just persecution the Church of Christ inflicts on the wicked". St Thomas Aquinas in his *Summa Theologica,* had likewise declared that heretics deserved "to be eliminated from the world by death" and Martin Luther had advocated the burning of synagogues and Jewish properties and in effect the murder of Jews, these "envenomed worms".'

Finding all this overwhelming, Ari tried to pause for a minute in order at least to take a deep breath. But he did not succeed. 'What is God's excuse for all this?' he asked himself, still as edgy as an overstretched guitar-string. 'He has no excuses. Or, if He has one, it's that He does not exist.' Taking his thinking a step forward, he decided that all this had, in the last analysis, nothing to do with God. 'It has, instead, to do with the law of self-destruction which has as much force in human affairs as the law of self-preservation.' For some reason, he did not, however, exteriorise his thinking. Instead, he asked Laura if she fancied an ice-cream.

'Why not,' she said, slightly worried about the overdrive of his tormented mind.

They silently enjoyed their ice creams, but Ari was soon after back on his story's horse. He wondered if the Islamists, prisoners of time, had just borrowed all their terrors from the past, or if they had also been improving their techniques. He was uncertain of the answer. But he was sure about one thing: they did not need any further training.

'What guides them is despair,' he concluded. 'And in their despair, encouraged by the propitious smile of their illusions, they're looking forward to joining the other world's eternal party.'

Dabiq, Isis's gruesome online magazine, had already said so when talking about our 'living through the end of times'. In its mythology, backed by its great advertising campaign, the forthcoming apocalypse, which all 'good' Muslims were eagerly anticipating, was only a matter of time. The scene for a cataclysmic showdown between the Muslims and the infidels, leading to the end of days, had been set. Mankind was to become history.

'It's written in the Quran,' Dabiq reassured everybody, outlining a concept darker than darkness itself. 'The Prophet Muhammad made it clear when he connected the war Isis has been fighting to Armageddon.' Their reading of celestial autocues together with some sort of inherent disinclination to think, had apparently convinced them that this was how it would all end.

'And who knows?' Ari said pessimistically. 'We may come close to it if they manage to get a hold of nuclear weapons. Yet their policy of despair and self-destruction, Freud's death-wish, is not a product of Islam. It's a product of the bruised Arab psyche, a waif moved by the tides of time they can't control.'

'Even if this policy of despair is taking them, together with innocent people from around the globe, to the very centre of hell?' Laura wondered.

'There are no innocent people, they would say. If you don't oppose the baddies or, even worse, support them, you're no longer innocent. Perhaps,' he added as an afterthought, 'this is something the politicians just cannot answer. It's the psychiatrists' job. Unless, of course, we accept that savagery is normal.'

'But miserably,' Laura interrupted him laughingly, 'the Arabs have not yet discovered the benefits of psychiatry.'

She missed Ari's response as, checking the time, she almost screamed. 'I should have left ten minutes ago. I've got an appointment with Houmam, the arms dealer. We're meeting at a police station in al-Midan of all places in twenty minutes.'

Al-Midan, a bustling neighbourhood with streets and alleys full of heritage and history, was not all that far away from the Old City. Rather than get a taxi, Laura decided to walk.

'Careful,' Ari said, repeating himself once again, the moment they were off their seats. 'The eggs of danger may be hatching much faster than you think.'

Back in his office and with the enervating burden of the mundane, Ari again started going through files, several of which had the word 'urgent' stamped on them. 'But they're all "urgent". Aren't they?'

When he had read a few and made some notes he needed to pass on, he got up to stretch his body. With a coffee cup in his hand, he went to say hello to the people working next door. They were all hard working individuals, both foreign and locals. One of them, Ali Barakat, instantly drew his attention because he had in front of him a black chalk drawing of Syrian men being taken by jihadis to the place they were going to be killed.

'Where did you find it?' Ari asked. 'It speaks volumes.'

'I drew it myself,' Ali answered.

'I don't believe it,' was Ari's instant reaction. 'This is a masterpiece.' Looking at the artwork, he remained silent for a while. 'It reminds me,' he added a minute later, 'of Francisco Goya's "Disasters of War" or even his "Saturn Devouring His Sons".' Reflecting a bit more, he corrected himself. 'Or it's more like his "A Lunatic Behind Bars".'

'Who is Goya?' Ali wondered.

'A great Spanish painter. One who penetratingly looked at the characters of the decaying monarchy and experienced the brutality with which Napoleon's army dealt with the Spanish people. His conclusion was that humanity is irrational and often bestial. Human madness was a major theme in his work.'

'Yes, madness is our daily diet,' Ali said sadly. 'From the day we're born.'

Very impressed, Ari advised Ali to carry on with his good work and was about to return to his own desk when the doorbell rang. Someone opened it to see a distressed man with shabby looks who asked to see a person responsible for the organization's work. The man identified himself as Jaafar Imad El Cheikh Ibrahim and had just managed, he said, to escape from the town where the factory he owned was now in ruins. His home was in Aleppo, the city many now called 'Syria's Stalingrad'.

Aleppo, the country's main trading and financial centre with a well-educated population and a history that went back to ancient times, was in fact being destroyed. Fast. The war was burning its way into all its neighbourhoods. The ancient bazaar and the once sleepy tree-lined boulevards where people lived and worked, time-worn markets where they went to trade and exquisite mosques, including the 11th century Great Mosque, were all now standing in ruins. Killing generations of Syrians, the war was also eradicating everything around them, including sites that had stood since the dawn of civilisation.

Ari gave the man, who had not shaved for weeks and was wearing a dirty white T-shirt, some time to say what he already knew.

Ruined and desperate, Jaafar could not stand either the endless destruction of his city or the rule of the jihadis. The latter included Jabhat al-Nusra, which both the United States and Russia considered a terrorist group, and Isis, which controlled the eastern and northern districts of the area. Here and there were other jihadi groups, including the Turkish-backed Ahrar al-Sham which worked with Jabhat al-Nusra.

'They've all brought us back to the Middle Ages,' Jaafar said.

The Kurdish-led Syrian Democratic Forces (SDF), supported by the Americans, were in the city's north-west part fighting not only against Isis, but also the Turkish-backed jihadi forces. 'Though the latter had denounced any kind of secular democratic government as un-Islamic, the British,' Jaafar observed, 'persisted in describing Ahrar al-Sham as a "moderate" force.'

'The jihadis,' he continued, 'have imposed their brutal rules on everybody. Al-Jolani, the Jabhat al-Nusra leader, dressed in army fatigues and a white turban just as the late al-Qaeda leader Osama bin Laden once had, has vowed to "protect jihad in Syria". In doing so, his group has repeatedly attacked all opposition to it, including the US-backed "moderate" groups. And Washington does nothing to help.

'There's no space for us,' Jaafar carried on, 'people whom Isis calls "the filthy and coward non-believers and the holders of the Christ emblem". The new generation in the Islamic State, the jihadis "promise", "will only grow steadfast on the path to Jihad" and will go as far as is necessary. For this new generation "loves death more than life".'

What he wanted was help to take his family out of Aleppo. As he was talking, his small figure had become slightly stooped. His hands clasped between his knees and his eyes stared at the varnished wooden floor. He was a broken man.

When he heard that Ari was Greek, the conversation changed focus. It also provided Jaafar the opportunity to give his loquacious nature a new outlet. He proudly recalled how the Syrians had helped the Greeks back in 1923, when thousands of them, uprooted from their homes in Asia Minor, had escaped to Aleppo.

'Twelve thousand Greeks and also Armenians and Assyrian Christians, all fleeing the onslaught of the Turks,' he said, 'arrived at Aleppo, starving and waiting to be helped. The situation, tragic and precarious, forced the town's authorities to ask the Greek government to prevent any more Greeks from reaching it. It was impossible, they had cabled, to admit more refugees.'

The story brought up feelings Ari could have done without. Misfortune seems to be the destination of every generation growing up in this part of the world. Some would say that this had been decreed by some sort of fate. If so, he did not know what name this fate responded to. But it was all rooted in a history which made no allowances to reason, humanity or values. Madness had taken over and reigned undisturbed for a very long time.

'History,' this "Fate" had apparently decreed, 'had to be written in blood and tears.'

He recalled Kavafi, the great Greek Alexandrian poet. 'Humanity,' he had said, "has no more honourable qualities. Those beyond are found among the gods." 'What a dispiriting thought,' he mumbled. 'But that's what it is. Isn't it?'

However, Ari had to respond to the request of his unexpected visitor. He believed his plea was genuine though he had not forgotten an old Syrian proverb that 'an Aleppine can even sell a dried donkey skin'. What the man wanted was, of course, far outside UMRWA's brief and totally beyond its abilities. But Ari could not bring himself to tell the poor man he could do nothing to help. All he ended up saying was how sorry he was upon hearing his story and how much he hoped it would end in the best possible way for him.

At the same time, he felt thoroughly ashamed on mankind's behalf. That was until the phone rang.

It was Laura. 'I was almost killed,' she said with a voice that reflected only horror in response to Ari's "hello".

'What?' Ari practically screamed.

'A bomb,' she continued, as if this explained everything.

'A bomb? What bomb?'

'The bomb that exploded inside the police station when I was there.'

'Have you been injured?'

'No.'

'OK. What happened.'

'I went to the police station where Houmam was waiting for me,' she flurriedly explained. 'We introduced ourselves to each other and got ready to move to a quiet place for a chat. Before doing so, I excused myself and went to the loo. That was the moment the bomb exploded. I ran out to see what had happened and there was destruction everywhere. The reception had been reduced to rubble. I asked the police officers what had happened.'

'And they said?'

'They said that a seven year old girl had entered the building, asking for help as she was lost. Then there was a blast. The child had a small home-made bomb attached to her body. The bomb was detonated by remote control. No one except the girl was killed. Houmam and a police officer suffered serious injuries.'

'Oh dear,' Ari managed to say as he was struggling to absorb Laura's news. 'You've been targeted.' He had no doubt she had.

'It looks like it,' she answered without hesitation. 'It's extremely unlikely that I just happened to be there when all this happened. The bombers must have known what I was up to. One of the arms traders I've contacted must have passed on the information to them.'

'And they used a child for the purpose.'

'The scums,' she said angrily. 'A child! But it's not the first time the jihadis have sent a child with a suicide belt. And surely it won't be the last. They do it in Syria, they do it in Iraq, Afghanistan and even in West Africa where Boko Haram has turned the children it has kidnapped into suicide bombers. It's Isis' policy, and a policy it's very proud of. It often takes children as young as five to the indoctrination rooms and convinces them they are "the generation that will conquer Baghdad, Jerusalem, Mecca and Rome".'

Though angry, Laura did not seem to have lost her composure. It was instead Ari who felt lost. He had difficulty absorbing the news and, more than that, he knew that the attempt on her life had also turned his own world upside down. Her being targeted meant she would have to leave Damascus. Were she to stay, she would only be earning her own death. The choice was clear and unambiguous.

At that point, he offered Jaafar his excuses and re-focused on the problem that had stormed into his life. He could not see how this would all end. Life, he thought, is not like fiction. Fictional events have templates and precedents – the events and experiences that inspired the story-teller. Reality, on the other hand, comes out of a clear blue sky. And it is always stranger than fiction. The thought again left him worried and baffled.

He wanted to meet her straightaway, but as her priorities had turned upside down, she had told him she would phone him later. She did so much later, when Ari had reached the four-star Dama Rose Hotel in Abu Rummaneh, the diplomatic quarter where Syrian president Bashar al-Assad has his private residence. He was to collect a present his father had sent him with one of his acquaintances.

Entering the hotel, he was struck by the spectacle. In its portico, a bride in full regalia escorted by her groom, having emerged from a white stretch limo, was walking into the hotel's gleaming marble lobby. Beautiful, heavily made up and imperious, she was chatting with the throng of guests and visitors. In a hall on the lower level, tables arrayed in flounced white damask were covered with dishes of cold and hot Syrian specialities.

Similar spectacles he had witnessed before. But this one, coming so soon after the attempt on Laura's life, highlighted life's contradictions in a most striking way. It burst the framework of his own reality. But, as his stammering thoughts reassured him, 'there's nothing unusual in this. Opposites live in the same neighbourhood.'

Laura had suggested he visits her flat. 'It's my turn to do the cooking,' she said over the phone in a tone of voice she would be expected to have if she had spent her day in Zeus' Gardens. The proposal was made in a way that did not leave space for refusal. It was as if everything that had happened in the last few hours was the product of his imagination. 'Unbelievable,' he thought. 'Is this what Englishness is about?'

Having nevertheless instantly tuned into her mindset, he asked her in response if she wanted him to buy anything.

'Yes, some tomatoes will do. And,' she added, 'some peace of mind please.'

He arrived at her flat and a loving teasing flame lit up their eyes as they hugged and kissed each other. Soon they were in the arms of the burning ecstasy to which they were delivered by the nocturnal nymphs.

Soon after, Laura started grilling some lamb cutlets. They were served in the company of a fine bottle of red wine, as fragrant and brusque as the blood of Dionysus. 'That's the best wine known to God or man,' she said as if they were in a Monet blissful picnic. Neither the flirtatious interaction nor the food could, of course, remove the anguish they were experiencing. The image of the ferocious attempt to end Laura's life was, like a ghost, haunting all the constituent parts of their existence. There was not much room for anything else, apart from anxiety and fear. The fear of the unknown. Its penetrating smell was steaming up around them.

The foreboding that had effortlessly settled in bed with this fear was not something they could pick up and throw out. 'You throw the sand against the wind, and the wind blows it back again'. The message it delivered weighed on their thoughts like a mountain.

Meanwhile, as Ari discovered, the BBC had already broadcast the report that Laura had sent about the bombing. The report gave no indication that she was or might have been the target. The story was also on the Syrian TV, which showed some blurred images of what looked like a blackened girl's head in a blanket and scenes of destruction inside the police station. Other reports suggested that the girl had been sent on her suicide mission with the blessing of her parents. Chilling footage in a video uploaded to YouTube by the jihadis actually showed her father telling her not to be afraid because she was on her way to heaven. Her mother, a woman wearing a burka, was seen hugging and kissing the girl before she left home never to return again.

The ghastliness both Ari and Laura were experiencing could not be put into words. They watched the pictures and said nothing. What relieved the tension up to a point was only the awareness of Laura's fortunate escape from the arms of death.

'Mere chance rules our lives,' Ari thought, once again recalling his own escape from death the day that the bomb had hit the place he had moved from only thirty seconds earlier. Thinking about that, however, was not important at the moment. Crucial, instead, was the question 'what's next?' How Laura would deal with the new situation she had on her hands. Would she, as one would expect, drop the Jordanian arms dealers' story and move to another part of the world? Or would she carry on until the bitter end? She still had not mentioned anything about it.

'She really has no choice,' Ari thought without saying anything. 'She has to go. If she stays, they'll get her.' He had no doubt about it. 'They'll get her.'

Her position was clarified soon after, as if she knew what he was thinking. 'I'll have to go,' she said with a voice coloured by the sadness that was invisibly dripping into their souls. 'Just another couple of days to get the confirmation of the facts I need. That's all. And then I'm off.'

'You mean you'll carry on with the story?'

'Yes. All I need is just a couple of days. What's a couple of days?'

Ari did not know what to say. If he were in her position, he would have made the same decision that she had. But it was not his life that was imperilled. It was hers and he did not want to encourage her to do what he himself would have done. All he said in response was 'it's not all that wise.' In her position, he would have said the same thing to himself.

Laura did not answer. 'Time for bed,' she said instead.

'Definitely.'

They walked to the bedroom, but all Ari could see were his hopes playing like a big fish in a shrinking seascape. He tried to recall something he had earlier told himself he must not forget. He could not. The thought had blown away and vanished without a trace. 'The stress must have affected me...' he mumbled, annoyed with himself. 'But perhaps,' his mind responded, 'this something will remember itself later.'

'Always the eternal optimist,' he mused.

Chapter 8
Cats, dogs and donkeys

When Ari returned to his office the next day he could not focus on anything in front of him. The outward and inward terrors that Laura's predicament had generated had stultified his mind and stifled his resolve. He wished for a minute that he could send his thinking to early retirement in Ekali, the leafy suburb of Athens. If only that was possible…

Conscientiously, he dispatched his concerns to the margins of his visual modality and instead tried to focus on work. Everything in front of him was urgent.

'What should be given priority?' he wondered. Yarmouk, a major camp hosting Palestinian refugees on the edge of the Syrian capital, was certainly on the top of the list. Samuels, his boss, had asked him to go there to see what the locals' humanitarian priorities were. 'I'll go there tomorrow,' he decided.

Despite the bloodcurdling uncertainties arising from Laura's difficulties, his decision made sense. Laura had told him earlier in the morning that she would be very busy for a while. The task ahead dominated her mind to such an extent that when Ari mentioned the Paris bombing in passing, she had not even bothered to respond.

'Nothing I've come across so far is as complicated as the situation in Syria,' she said, looking at him absently. 'It's not going to end well'.

'OK, enough of all this,' Ari muttered to himself.

'And the best I can do at the moment is focus on my own work,' she added. True to her word, she just disappeared from his antenna.

'Be careful,' Ari advised her again, while shivering at the thought of what might happen. The lights had been turned on, piercing the ominous clouds ahead.

UNRWA representatives had been in Yarmouk earlier, in April. The recent escalation in violence in the area had, however, once again made their involvement imperative. Like everyone else, he had no doubt that the locals desperately needed help – anything from hot meals and canned food to mattresses and blankets. All they needed was available, but in warehouses and tents in Damascus. Sacks of rice, and boxes of sugar, rice, beans, cooking oil and other essential foodstuff were piled high there, but nothing could be delivered.

Though a third of Syria's population were in dire need of food aid, the areas to deliver, particularly those controlled by Isis, had been made inaccessible by the government.

The Yarmouk camp had been established after the 1948 Arab-Israeli war that led to the displacement of hundreds of thousands of Palestinians. The number of the refugees increased following the 1956 new Arab-Israeli conflict – prior to the outbreak of Syria's civil war the town had become home to 160,000 residents. The number of Palestinian refugees in Syria, settled mostly in Yarmouk, Homs, Hama, Latakia and Aleppo, was altogether about 550,000.

Rebel forces had entered Yarmouk in December 2012, and from there they pushed on towards the capital. The Syrian government forces responded, as expected, with aerial bombardment. Thousands were, as a result, forced to flee to other parts of Syria and Lebanon in search of shelter. Soon after, forces loyal to Bashar al-Assad had succeeded in surrounding the camp and controlling access to it.

But the camp was now controlled by Jabhat al-Nusra, the al-Qaeda affiliate in Syria, and also Isis whose force was in nearby suburbs. The two groups had fought bloody battles against each other in other parts of Syria as Jabhat al-Nusra objected to the Isis global jihad. The enemy for Jabhat al-Nusra was the Bashar al-Assad regime. For Isis, on the other hand, 'the point of jihad', as its leaders had repeatedly said, 'is not to liberate land. Jihad, as defined by God, is fighting for and implementing the law of God'.

In Yarmouk, however, Isis and Jabhat al-Nusra worked together against the regime and the pro-Assad Palestinians whom they were reportedly beheading. Other groups of Palestinians were working together with them.

Ari visited the area together with James Garrahan and Brigitte Gravier, his colleagues, and also Mohammad Kamal Chehade, another colleague locally recruited. They were all fully aware that a visit to the camp was not without risks. To begin with, the Yarmouk Martyr's Brigade, a 'moderate' Islamist group, had previously detained UN peacekeepers visiting the area. Apart from this, the indiscriminate and disproportionate aerial bombings and ground attacks on residential areas by government forces and jihadis groups posed a risk nobody could ignore.

At the crossing, a man in a green camouflage uniform with a Kalashnikov rifle, stopped them to check what they were up to. After he had established their credentials, he relaxed and started chatting with them like a friendly neighbour. Almost oblivious to his immediate surroundings, he told them that he himself was a banker working until the war had forced him to stop his day job and man the barricades.

Ari wondered if he had received any training.

'Yes,' the man said when he was asked. 'I was given 40 days training and handed weapons by the army. I had to do it,' he added, 'because we have to stop these fundamentalists, fanatics and foreigners.'

They crossed the line when there was a gap in the gunfire.

Yarmouk, the city in which the dead outnumbered the living, was practically empty. The destruction caused by airstrikes, bombardments, fires and ferocious battles was overwhelming. With all sides using heavy weapons street by street, whole neighbourhoods, particularly those close to the main roads around the city, had been levelled. The city was a bombed-out wasteland. Buildings had often been blown up to prevent the advance of the regime's military forces and massive chunks of rubble, all that remained of destroyed buildings, even made movement for pedestrians exacting.

The UN had already warned that such tactics constituted massacres. But nobody would listen. 'Both sides,' Ari said, 'claim to have the good of the community at heart, while both in fact aim for political control in the pursuit of which they indulge in the worst excesses.'

'Well said,' said Brigitte.

'I didn't say that,' Ari answered. 'Thucydides did. He was talking about the thirty-year war between Athens and its empire, on the one hand, and the Peloponnesian League led by Sparta, on the other.'

It was, of course, not the only such instance one could recall.

Though a desert and a graveyard, Yarmouk nevertheless housed a population of about 18,000 people. Moving like famished ghosts, they were orbiting their sorrows without even a shack to haunt. Their situation embodied with startling vividness the tragedy of Syria's conflict like few other places. People lived amid intense shelling, deadly clashes and under the ineluctable menace of being shot by snipers. To stop the latter from targeting them, many had covered their alleys with huge white padded sheets strung from the upper floors of buildings.

The situation was so bad that hospitals in the areas surrounding the camp, including Yalda, Babila and Beit Saham, were flooded with wounded civilians from Yarmouk, and mosques were often blaring calls for blood donations.

Faced with what was practically a ghost town, Ari, standing close to a building riddled with bullets, stared at it for a minute, silent and almost breathless. Witnessing destruction of such phenomenal magnitude, the massive exodus of people from their homes and death on an unimagined scale was a gut-wrenching experience.

A proud and diverse society had been torn apart by passions that were no longer under control. And as a political solution to stop the fighting was still elusive, it was even more heart-breaking to think that the war would not be ending anytime soon.

'Yarmouk,' Ari told his colleagues, 'was showing the world what the costs of war had been: utter destruction and mass displacement of people. Victory, if and when it comes, will be celebrated on piles of rubble.'

As there was no food for anybody, people were dying of malnutrition. 'All I can give my kids to eat,' Abdullah, a resident told the UNRWA representatives, 'is wild plants. We pick and cook them.' His skin was like canvas, stretched tight against his bones. His capacity for suffering seemed to have deserted him. The man was lost in the agony of days that could not die. Others were living on grass. But even that was difficult as people had reportedly been shot by snipers while trying to gather grass to feed their starving children. For those kids and millions more, childhood had ended prematurely.

Earlier, in October 2013, the imam of Yarmouk's largest mosque had actually issued a fatwa that permitted people to eat cats, dogs and donkeys. Food from UNRWA that was allowed into Yarmouk had ended up in the hands of the rebels for their own use or for sale on the black market. Rebel leaders were often seen selling food at exorbitant prices to Yarmouk residents, just as they were doing in eastern Ghouta as well as in the capital's western suburb of Daraya. The same was the case in the nearby mountain towns of Zabadani, Madaya, and elsewhere.

When food had been delivered straight to the people in one instance, the hungry throng had filled the entire width of a street. One woman, gaunt with malnutrition, Ari was told, had fell down and was too weak to rise. She had died on the spot. Water was a huge problem, too.

'At 7am, I walk one kilometre to get water for my home,' a ten year old boy said. 'I usually spend five hours a day collecting water, but I only collect water every five days because it's only available every five days.'

Months and months after pipes were damaged by fighting, the water supply had still not returned and the water was dirty. An outbreak of typhoid in the camp during the summer of 2015 was not dealt with because even the most basic medical supplies were unavailable. Some help was eventually offered by UNRWA, which managed to operate a mobile health clinic set up in a cave and in a tent. They had both been converted into field hospitals. Still, women were reportedly dying in childbirth.

Heating was another huge problem too. 'There's no wood. We're burning furniture and clothes to keep warm,' another resident explained. 'People have burned their bedrooms, chairs, living rooms. We're also burning things which aren't purely wood, and this has caused many health problems. Even so, we can never insulate ourselves against the cold. Many of us wish to die but we just cannot end our lives,' Abdullah hopelessly concluded.

His words pointed to that invisible door through which all the chill of the world's failures and even the futility of their own efforts had entered, inaudibly and irrevocably. All they could do was watch the lyreless threnody performed in front of their eyes.

Ari phoned his boss with a feeling of dismalness. 'Never has the imperative for sustained humanitarian access been greater.' What he had found in the camp was nothing but bleakness – hopeless people with empty eyes, deprived of a vision of a decent life, begging for bread that would allow them to beg again. A feeling of respect for these people replaced the sorrow for their fate and simply overwhelmed him.

'Living without hope is heroic,' he whispered to Brigitte. 'It's actually more heroic than dying for your beliefs. It bestows on the soul a tragic greatness the jihadis will never understand.'

This was, of course, the situation not only in Yarmouk but all over Syria as the warring parties were refusing humanitarian agencies access to civilians in need. Up to 4.5 million people in Syria were actually living in hard-to-reach areas, including nearly 400,000 people in fifteen besieged locations.

But in Yarmouk, Ari also saw something else that filled his heart with hope. It was a man who, sitting on a pile of rubble, was playing his accordion. Even this small ray of life was enough to raise the temperature of his heart, twenty degrees below zero. 'Whatever happens,' he thought, 'the human spirit can still stand up and fight back.'

Depressed, Brigitte did not feel like sharing his optimism. Her heart seemed to have lost the hope that feeds the energy tanks. In the frozen featurelessness of that moment, her outlook had taken a quick, sanity-stealing trip south. 'The only reality is nothingness,' she despondently said, 'covered by a blanket of hypocrisy.' Searching for something, perhaps life's missing meaning, she remained unfocused for a while, just like the moonlight on the sea.

Ari had some water which had a sour taste, the same as wretchedness. Soon after, they all left the area. On their way back, they stopped at the rundown Rozana café, less than four hundred meters from the refugee camp, and had a *pollo* – a chilled mint and lemon drink – to recover from the nightmare they had found themselves trapped in. The drink was good, but not good enough. Their bones needed wine.

'I wonder,' Ari said after their first sip, 'how they feel about us – all employed by a powerful institution, paid a good salary, never deprived of the bare essentials, living the life we want to live. Do they feel jealous? Resentful? Envious?'

Nobody seemed eager to provide an answer. Nobody really wanted to think about it. Haunted by the horrible experience they had gone through, the capacity for thinking had deserted them, just like leaves deserting trees in autumn.

'I remember,' Ari carried on, as if he had not noticed their reluctance to engage in this sort of conversation, 'the day a Syrian tobacconist resentfully told me that I've got the job I have because I'm a European.'

'And you said...?' Brigitte asked.

'Silly man! I told him that he might be right. I wouldn't be where I am if I were in his position. But he wouldn't be where I am either if he were a European.'

Brigitte laughed. 'I see what you mean,' she said. 'Some people are never aware of their shortcomings without a label on them. But, on the other hand,' she acknowledged, 'if we were to wear the labels of our shortcomings, we would be covered with labels…'

The mood had just become a bit lighter to everybody's relief. An hour later, they were all back at the office, a place where they could temporarily hide themselves from all their eyes had witnessed. Quite disheartened by what he had seen, Ari was also totally convinced that the jihadis were unstoppable by arguments. He was ready for the worst. If religious himself, he would pray to God to save the world from all His faithful disciples, whatever their creed. People, he knew, are never as ebulliently evil as when they act out of religious beliefs.

He thought of Laura again, particularly as he had not heard anything from her. He wondered why she had not even sent him a short text to tell him not to worry. Though anxious, he crossed his fears and refocused on the situation at hand.

What crossed his mind was the lack of evidence of the Free Syrian Army's presence in Yarmouk. He wondered for a minute if they had any units in the area. To get an answer, he phoned Rami Abu Hadeed, a former army officer who had defected to the Free Syrian Army. He had helped him in the past when he had arranged for the delivery of medical supplies to residents of Eastern Ghouta, which was being mercilessly bombed by the Bashar al-Assad forces.

The Free Syrian Army and many other rebel groups, more than one hundred, represented what David Cameron, the British prime minister, had called the Syrian 'moderates'. Their groups did not belong, he told Parliament, to extremist groups and hence Britain could coordinate attacks with them on Isis, which posed a 'serious and undeniable' threat to the UK. For the jihadis, the FSA was nothing more than a puppet of the West and the United States in particular.

'How are you doing these days?' Ari asked Hadeed. 'You must be under huge pressure from several sides.'

'Yes, we are,' Hadeed said. 'Or, to be more precise, those who've been left behind are. I retired a couple of weeks ago.'

'Why?' a surprised Ari asked.

'You remember how we started back in 2011?'

Hadeed, whose face, Ari recalled, bore the deep marks of a habitual dissatisfaction, had answered Ari's question by posing another question himself.

The Free Syrian Army had been formed in 2011 by army deserters based in Turkey. Turkey, together with Saudi Arabia, Qatar and other states in the Middle East and with the support of Britain and the US, provided the rebels the political, military and logistic support they needed to become a force capable of overthrowing the regime. The US, in particular, had also promised them generous financial support and intelligence about the movements of troops loyal to Bashar al-Assad. Britain had, likewise, done the same. In 2013, the FSA had moved its headquarters to Idlib, in northern Syria.

'But soon after, we were overrun by the jihadis,' Hadeed said, his voice coloured by frustration. He was talking but also ruminating about the splendour of his army's failures. 'We just couldn't hold our ground. The problem was that rather than being a unified fighting force, we were nothing more than a loose network of brigades, with each one retaining its separate identity, agenda and command. Some of them,' he carried on, 'worked with hardline Islamist groups such as Jabhat al-Nusra and others against the Kurds in Syria. Even worse, some of them were just family gangs or simply criminals. As one might expect, ill-discipline and infighting inevitably led to a series of numbing setbacks and eventually to an operational paralysis.'

'Yes, I'm aware of it,' Ari responded, somehow surprised by the candour with which the man was delivering his verdict.

'Thousands of Free Syrian Army fighters and several major battalions,' Hadeed added, 'disenchanted with developments did, as a result, join the radical Islamic factions.'

'Yes, I remember the last time we spoke,' Ari interrupted him, 'you mentioned that Isis had just made you a springtime offer by issuing an ultimatum demanding that the FSA in al-Qadam, the neighbourhood next to Yarmouk, should accept their command. Refusal to do so, the FSA had been warned, would result in its destruction.'

'Correct,' Hadeed said. 'If you also remember, the Free Syrian Army as such had turned the offer down, but many of its fighters accepted it, thereby defecting to Isis. Isis had secured their loyalty with money and weapons.'

'Were you surprised this happened?' Ari asked.

'No,' Hadeed answered. 'Isis fighters got paid 80,000 Syrian lira ($250) a month, whereas the FSA men were only paid 5,000 lira (about

$20). In the past, we used to get much better money from Qatari and Turkish sources, but this funding was cut off when FSA units started to cooperate with pro-government forces against the jihadis.'

'So what you're in effect telling me is that the FSA basically exists on paper only,' Ari said.

'That's more or less correct,' Hadeed answered, in effect confirming that 'the Free Syrian Army hardly existed any more'. Cameron, Ari thought, having fallen asleep in the shade of his complacency, had obviously failed to realise that as much as he had failed to absorb that his intervention was only prolonging the country's agony.

'What's there is not an army,' Hadeed carried on. 'And jihadis like the Jabhat al-Nusra leader, Abu Mohhamad al-Jolani, who've actually claimed that there's no such thing as a Free Syrian Army, are not exaggerating. 'They would hardly have been doing so when the Free Syrian Army had handed them roughly half of the ammunition and weapons sent to them by the Americans.'

'Yes, I know. The FSA, they say, is just a "myth", a "fantasy",' Ari said. 'Or, as Isis itself put it, "there is no Free Syrian Army in the East of Syria any longer. All Free Syrian Army people there had joined the Islamic State". If not, 'moderate' rebel groups had signed a non-aggression agreement with Isis, as they had done south of Damascus, or been forced into dependence on the jihadis.'

But it was not only Hadeed or Ari who believed that the 'moderates' no longer existed. Many Americans were firmly of the opinion that there was no difference between what was left of them and extremist rebels in Syria. So were the 'Ruskies', who were bombing the brave 'moderates' fighting the army of Bashar al-Assad. Only the Western media, engaged in a hopeless effort to protect themselves against the truth they had consistently concealed, were still trying to convince their customers that the Russians were bombing the democratic opposition to Bashar al-Assad.

'Ridiculous,' Laura had once told him, referring to the promiscuity of the media's sympathies. 'All in tune with the dictates of their expediencies. Truth is just instrumentalised. But,' she had added dismissively, 'their arguments aren't tenable! Even if a majority of their readers or listeners have accepted them.'

'Yet,' Ari had teased her, 'you're part of the same media establishment.'

'Yes, I am,' she had answered. 'But I can't stomach the CIA's covert operations to train and arm extremists in Syria, with a budget approaching $1 billion a year. And it's not just me who says so. It's the US House Intelligence Committee whose classified debates were reported in *The Washington Post.*'

While talking to Hadeed, Ari's second telephone started ringing. It was the dry cleaning shop owner, who told him his clothes were ready for collection. Ari thanked him and returned immediately to Hadeed.

'Yes, sorry about that,' he said. 'We were talking about the FSA "moderate" groups still in existence. As far as I can tell, these groups are, in any case, anything but moderate. Their arrival in Aleppo for example, is remembered for their planting of 2,000-kilo bombs in the city centre and looting the city's schools. Isn't that so? And FSA groups have often been accused of summarily executing numerous prisoners. Even Iraq's deputy interior minister had accused them of atrocities.'

Hadeed suddenly seemed to be lost for words. He knew what Ari was talking about, but he could not bring himself to acknowledge it fully. 'Things aren't always what you wish or expect,' he murmured with a dysphoric voice, hesitant to expand on the subject.

Changing the subject slightly, Ari then asked Hadeed for confirmation that some FSA units were now reportedly joining Bashar al-Assad's army.

'The rise of Isis,' the ex-Syrian army officer said, 'has brought a dramatic reconciliation between moderate rebel and government factions. Outraged by the security state's brutal reaction at the start of the rebellion but now disillusioned with developments, many FSA fighters are now looking forward to discussing with Bashar al-Assad a "Syrian solution" to the war. Many of them realise that the only "accomplishment" of the war is the destruction of their own country.'

'Developments haven't been consistent with our illusions,' Hadeed said. He added that he would be glad to see Ari again, perhaps in the coffee shop outside Damascus where they had met before. No date was fixed.

Though tired after the long conversation, Ari returned to his desk to prepare for the meeting he was going to have with Richard Samuels, his boss, following his visit to Yarmouk. But, he wondered, what on earth could possibly be done in a situation such as the one he had come across. It looked totally hopeless. Yarmouk could only be helped by a major intervention by the Western Powers and Russia aiming at a ceasefire agreement, even a temporary one, which would allow the distribution of the badly needed first aid.

But it looked as if this would have to wait for a while. One could only hope it would at least arrive before the Second Coming.

Chapter 9
'God is Great'

Ari had a coffee while his stridently flowing thoughts turned back to Laura. He wondered again where she might be. She had become completely inaccessible for a while. As it turned out, it was not just him who had lost contact with her, but also her BBC colleague. He knew that when Mark Platt phoned him to ask if he knew where she was. He did not. He beeped her again after Mark's call a half dozen times without success and then he went to her flat. He repeatedly rang the doorbell only to receive no answer. All traces of her existence had vanished.

Back in his office, he had a quick chat with his boss, Samuels, who wanted some clarification of Ari's views on the situation in Yarmouk. Their discussion was, however, interrupted the moment the TV informed them that in response to the Paris terror attack, France had launched its biggest airstrike against Isis. Its target was the Isis headquarters in al-Raqqah. 'Christ had advised us,' Ari thought, 'to turn the other cheek. But he had never come across the jihadis.'

Struck by the news, everyone at the office remained stone silent for a while. The silence did not last long.

The phone rang and Mark Platt informed Ari that Laura's body had just been found in Douma, Eastern Ghouta. That was the city where the peaceful protests against the Syrian government had first broken out in March 2011 and which was now controlled by the rebels. It was close to the place where the body of Mohammed Yousef Awwad, an UNRWA relief worker, was earlier found after a mortar shell had hit his car.

A note pinned on Laura's body read: 'Allahu Akhbar' (God is Great). That was presumably the way Allah would 'fill out the earth with peace and justice'. That was also what the killers believed had secured them a place in Paradise. She was not the first journalist to be killed in Syria. More than seventy had already been killed since the war began, many of them before they could say goodbye to their lives.

Ari almost had an apoplectic seizure. He felt as if he had been hit by lightning. He was used to death since his arrival, but nothing he had experienced so far matched the anguish he was going through now. Flooded with emotions, he could not at first believe that Laura was no longer alive. A wild hope encouraged him to believe the news of her death was all part of a malicious rumour, a horrible dream or a mistake made by those who identified the body. It was just not possible that a 30-year old woman with such a sparkling personality and exuberant manners was no longer part of the wider scene and also his own world.

He wondered how such a thing could have happened. She had known that her job involved an element of risk, if for no other reason than she would often be in the wrong place at the wrong time. She had met colleagues in her line of reporting who would tell near-miss stories over a glass of beer, as if they were good jokes. Yet she was neither foolhardy nor as ambitious as to be prepared to risk her life for a story. She did not want to die.

Her death, he was certain, was anything but accidental. That could only mean that she was investigating a story which was bigger and much more dangerous than she had expected or imagined. But as he had lost contact with her for a while, he did not have a clue as to what the latest developments might have been.

His thoughts about it all for the time being had been overshadowed by his feelings. In Syria, he had, or he thought he had, established an intimate relation with death, a daily visitor to his world. But Laura's departure had just demonstrated that he was anything but at home with it. His heart was burning. His head was spinning. His body was numb. In the apoplectoid state he was in, words could not express the cataclysm his soul was swept up in.

He returned home and lay on his unmade bed, staring with open eyes into the darkness which had swallowed him. He found himself in the midst of an emotion in whose shadows he was melting, in a searing desert far beyond the land of his worst nightmares, in a void in which he could see his drowned hopes floating. She had died, gone to 'the other shore of the sea which has no other shore', and he felt something had died in him, too. When he finally fell asleep, all he could still see was the infinitude of pain.

The message he tweeted did not exactly reflect the depth of his despondency. It read: 'Laura Heineken, my lovely friend, killed by jihadis. I miss her terribly.' Some pictures of her taken by himself in

Damascus were placed on Instagram too. Many friends he had in various parts of the world, from Alexandria to Athens and from London to Brussels, tweeted back to him shocked at the news. They expressed their sorrow at Laura's going and their sympathy for his loss. Many wished him strength in dealing with his wretched universe.

One of them was his father, Kimon, who, as he said, was both very saddened about it and also very worried about him. He wanted to know if Ari had any additional information about her death and how he was feeling in a moment that his vision of a normal life had been broken. Kimon, a father like all others with gaps in his son's life, still did not know that Ari and Laura had formed a romantic partnership.

'Difficult to survive the era's madness,' Ari told him. 'But nothing is beyond the limits of our strength.' While switching off his Skype connection, he was anything but sure he believed what he had just said. But the truth was something he could not easily acknowledge even when talking to himself.

On the same day, he received another call from Athens. This time it was his old friend Pantelis, a lawyer and collector of unpaid bills. The devastating effect of the Greek crisis, now in its sixth year, and the huge financial difficulties Pantelis was experiencing, had shocked and dismayed Ari. To help, he had been sending him a small amount of money every month.

'Sorry, very sorry to hear of your loss,' Pantelis said, genuinely disturbed by Ari's trials. 'I can only hope there will not be many more deaths before this tragedy ends.'

Ari asked him how he was doing.

'The same as ever,' was the answer. 'We're still looking forward to the end of all these years of "humiliation and pain" and "the restoration of our dignity" which Tsipras had vowed to deliver before he was elected.'

'Words shaped with intent...' Ari said. He felt like saying something more, but he did not.

BBC staff had, in the meantime, paid full tribute to Laura. Interviews she had conducted in the past with Middle East leaders were repeatedly broadcast and various colleagues and public figures honoured her as a person and a professional. The messages on Twiter and Facebook likewise extolled her virtues.

'She was a wonderful woman, warm, caring, engaging and talented, fully committed to her job and respected by her colleagues,' most of them read. 'We are sickened to hear of her assassination, which is an assault on everybody who cares about and has faith in democracy.'

As if time had stopped and the earth had ceased to rotate on its axis, Ari wandered into his office the next day and, lost, busied himself with inconsequential tasks without thinking. He unpacked some office supplies, re-arranged what was in his drawers and shelves or filed all that he should have filed ages ago. He watered the unconcerned geranium by the window and even took the dust off the Neo Rauch painting on the wall behind his desk.

'What are you doing?' Brigitte asked him, full of sympathy for his frailty but also slightly alarmed by his state of mind.

'Nothing.'

'And what's this painting?'

'Just something my father bought in Leipzig back in 1993.'

He could have mentioned that his father had bought it for peanuts, but the same painting was worth a fortune now that Neo Rauch had become a celebrity. But he did not. Everything seemed incredibly far away, in effect dwindling to a nothingness he had never experienced before. He instead carried on with his cleaning of it. Whatever required no thinking and could detach him from his depressing thoughts was as good as a painkiller.

'I need her to be here,' he soliloquised in the sepulchral tone that defined his state of mind. 'I need her to assure me I exist at all.'

A photograph on his desk preserved the divine brightness of Laura's last smile. He looked at it and felt his sadness vehemently running in his blood. He withdrew to the past as if his memories could erase the ghastly images of the present.

He could see Laura walking with him to the Royal Festival Hall to listen to an Antonin Dvorák's Symphony or at the Royal Academy of Arts looking at Claude Monet's floral masterpieces. He could see her in Broadcasting House where he would occasionally go to collect her for a meal or in the Camden Town open-air market in which she was always looking for something unusual and interesting. More than anything else he could see her swimming like an eel through the crystal clear waters of Hydra, the island where they had spent a week together only a few months earlier, watching a film in Gardenia, the open air cinema, or enjoying their lobster spaghetti in Castello, a seaside restaurant with breathtaking views.

Her presence was so keenly felt that he fully expected to hear her ringing the doorbell of his home, enter with a loving smile and cross to the couch she liked with a mug full of coffee.

'Come and sit next to me, Ari,' he heard her saying. 'Come on. I miss you every moment I'm not with you.'

'I miss you, too, Laura. I miss your lovely presence, your indomitable spirit, the radiance of your immense fire that illuminates my life.'

But he knew the odylic force of her presence was only a memory lingering in his tormented mind. She was no longer around. The sun seemed to shine in vain. His gaze drifted to a point in the sky outside his window. 'If I could only turn back the clock...' His words floated in solemn silence through the universe. Unsurprisingly, the feedback was full of silence too.

By the time that both the Foreign Office and her brother had made all the necessary arrangements for the transfer of her body back home, Ari had managed to absorb a bit of the shock at her loss and partly recover possession of himself. The task in front of him now was to discover who her killers were and why they killed her. He owed it to her.

But who could they be? They could be members of Bashar al-Assad's security forces, alarmed by Laura's attempt to find out more about conditions in Sednaya, the military prison. The possibility seemed rather remote as Laura had not really started such an investigation. More than that, the regime was not interfering either directly or indirectly with reporting. In the experience of Damascus-based reporters, it accepted criticism as a part of the package. Besides, she was not involved in anything that could incur the wrath of the Assadists.

More likely, the guilty party was an arms dealer, the Jordanian intelligence, or one of the armed 1,000 opposition groups in Syria fighting against both the Damascus regime and also each other. Split by different political ideologies and territorial divides into many factions, the latter varied dramatically in terms of numbers and operational fighting strength. Each of them were trying to establish social and political control in one area of the country or another, occasionally co-ordinating its activities across a number of fronts but also fighting each other.

'Anything is possible,' his boss, the Jamaican Richard Samuels, told him the morning the two of them met to discuss the situation. 'But,' as Ari had no doubt, 'it won't be easy to work things out.'

Samuels, a high-profile spokesperson within the United Nations system since 2007, formerly a member of the BBC staff, had met Laura only once. Still, he was visibly very upset by her death. A very sensitive man, he had once, in 2014, when interviewed live in Jerusalem on al Jazeera about Palestinian children who had died from Israeli shelling in a UN school in Gaza, broken down in tears.

In trying to discover why and by whom she had been killed, Ari first had to make sure that he did not alienate himself from the various rebel groups which he could easily do by saying what they did not want to hear or something they might misinterpret. He also had to make sure he did not end up like Laura.

Giving himself no time for self-pity, as soon as he had recovered from the shock, he started looking for an answer. Certainties, something that would always be there like days and nights, he knew, were unavailable. In the world he inhabited, he could be sure of nothing.

The first thought that crossed his mind was to visit Laura's apartment where he might find some useful notes she might have left behind. Laura had, thankfully, given him a key. He was there in no time. Minimally furnished and uncluttered, the flat had a king-size bed, a desk, a couch with a flat TV set on the wall opposite it, and a pair of bedside cabinets. Its walk-in wardrobe seemed as if it was ready to take him in as a prisoner.

On the desk, he could see a couple of framed family photos, some out of date newspapers and take-away menus from shops nearby. On the kitchen's noticeboard, there was a photo of himself in a bathing suit taken in Hydra. He was on a windsurfing board.

Though it was still daylight, he switched on the light in an effort to dissolve the harrowing atmosphere, its eerie, unnatural stillness. His heart was beating fast, and his footsteps echoed like those of a verger in the Old St Peter's Basilica crypt. The flat had the vibes of a haunted ship. Yet he kept looking. What he was hoping he would find there was her laptop. But it was not there. It had not been found by her body either. What was also missing was her iPhone.

He searched her desk, as if the answer was on top of it, the bookcase and her bedside cabinets before going to the kitchen. He found nothing of interest. He made a coffee to steady himself and again looked inside every closet, even under her bed. Nothing. In the bathroom mirror, he only saw a blank face he barely recognised. He searched the mirror with his hands – it was definitely him. An imperceptible dolefulness pervaded him and would not go away.

'Looking for oil in Lausanne,' he thought, 'is more likely to produce results than looking for evidence here.' He decided he needed another coffee. 'I'll otherwise end up with an uninhabited brain-space.'

The thought hit him then that he had forgotten to search the pockets of her clothes hanging in the wardrobe. He re-opened it, and systematically went through everything, but had no luck. It looked as if all evidence had a pact with secrecy.

On his way out, just outside her front door, he met Laura's next door neighbour. She was a woman of similar age to Laura, with short brown hair covered by a scarf. She had just managed to slip into the lift through its sliding door after Ari had pressed the ground floor button. The little adventure had made her laugh in a way that sounded like the giggling of the stream on its way down the mountain of Parnassus. She was a Greek Orthodox Damascene employed by IBM, named Elia Bassem Fatime.

They chatted for a couple of minutes and she told Ari that she knew Laura. When Ari suggested that they meet to have a chat about her, she kindly agreed to meet him after work in the Old City. They met later in the day in the An-Naufara bar, just east of the Ummayad Mosque. He arrived after her, when she was saying goodbye to someone who was heading out. They talked a bit about life in Damascus.

'So much has changed,' she said. 'I used to walk down the street and know half the people I saw. The people today are not the ones I used to see. Most of my friends have emigrated. Outsiders have come in. It's like Damascus is my home, but also not my home.'

Ari asked her what she would like to drink.

'I don't like alcohol...' she replied. '...Just wine!'

They slowly shared a bottle of Marques de Casa Concha Chardonnay, which Elia was pouring ceremoniously into their glasses. The feeling she radiated every time she took a sip made Ari think that she would have no problem telling the difference between a Merlot and a Cabernet

Sauvignon. Appreciating her drink did not, however, stop her from often hiding her mouth with her hand to conceal a crooked front tooth she obviously could not come to terms with. She looked fixated, even obsessed, with the imperfection. It was called, Ari knew, body dysmorphic disorder, requiring the verbal approval of her looks as a means of calming her down.

'You're a lovely lady,' he said when the right opportunity appeared.

'Rubbish,' was her answer, offered with a self-deprecating smile, lacking the feminine helplessness expected in this part of the world. But she needed to hear Ari say so.

The discussion soon turned to Laura, whom Elia had seen in the morning, the day she was killed. Laura had been quite excited, Elia said, as she was after a big story which, she had jokingly said, was mentioned in the Domesday Book. She had not said what it was all about, but she was particularly furious with the Saudis who 'had gotten "too involved" with the Syrian civil war.'

Ari wondered what this could all be about. She had not mentioned anything to him about it, and this certainly meant that she had got hold of some information after he last saw her. Still, he asked Elia to recall everything Laura had talked about in the last few days before her death. She did so, but it was not of much help. They had chatted, she said, about life in Damascus now and before the war had started and, of course, about the way the savage conflict was developing. She was unhappy about the vanquishing of the 'Arab Spring' and the growth of the jihadi movement and objected to the support offered to the latter, principally by Saudi Arabia and Turkey, but also Jordan and Qatar.

Ari took a deep breath. He was not really getting anywhere. 'Work,' he mused, 'is 10% inspiration and 90% perspiration. The rest is luck. Luck is obviously out of luck. And so am I.'

At that point, a traditional story teller, a Hakawati, began his performance which made it impossible for them to continue their chat. Before they departed, Elia mentioned to Ari that she worked with a Greek girl, Maryam, whose father 'had been shot dead by the jihadis in front of his daughters. They'd pleaded for his life but they were ignored.' Words, obviously, had failed to reach their destination: the jihadis' heart.

'Horrible!' Ari said, at the same time brooding on the inadequacy of his response. 'Perhaps they weren't furnished with a heart,' he added a few seconds later. Out of curiosity, he then asked Elia if Maryam spoke Greek. 'The Syrian Greeks mostly speak Arabic,' she replied, 'though the older generations have a working knowledge of Greek.'

Apparently sure that he would be interested and without being asked, she carried on by offering Ari some more information. There was, she said, another group of a few thousand Greek-speaking people, all of them Muslims of Cretan origin, in Al-Hamidiyah, a town close to the Lebanese frontier, plus a significant Greco-Syrian population in Aleppo. Ari was vaguely familiar with this as several of them had reported that Greece had discriminated against them on account of their religion.

They finished their drinks and promised each other they would keep in touch. The meeting had provided no new information about Laura's death.

As Elia was about to go, a man and a woman sitting at the far end of the bar caught her eye. They exchanged greetings and the man, Ibrahim, introduced her to his sister and Elia introduced both of them to Ari. The man was from Baghdad. His sister, skinny as an excuse and married to a Syrian, was now living in Damascus. Their parents had both perished when a bomb, planted by Iraqi extremists, had exploded outside their garage in the Iraqi capital.

'How's life in Baghdad?' Ari asked him after they had all seated at his table.

'Horrible,' was Ibrahim's answer. 'And when I say horrible, I don't mean just the war and the bloodshed that continues unabated or the simmering sectarian tensions. I also mean our daily lives.'

'Meaning?'

'I finished university two years ago and I'm still looking for a job. I want to fall in love, get married, travel, do the things I want. But I can't. Life prohibits it. And then basic services are missing. We rely on generators as we have power cuts every three hours. We need a decent education system, but it's not there. Literacy rates are, as a result, plunging. Violence and also chaos have wrecked our lives.'

Ari and Elia listened without saying a word. Nothing they heard surprised them.

'Yes,' Elia said at the end, 'Isis is a big problem.'

'It's not just Isis,' Ibrahim retorted. 'Bagdad is battling to recapture territory from Isis, but everybody, the Sunnis, the Shi'ites, the Kurds and even the Yazidis are fighting each other at the same time. Split into different groups, they're also fighting among themselves. And this is one side of the problem.

'The other side,' Ibrahim continued, 'is the corruption that pervades everything. Much of the petrodollar wealth has vanished into the pockets of corrupt politicians. Thousands of non-existent soldiers are on the army's payroll. University degrees are purchased rather than earned. The élite is bleeding the country dry.'

'The removal of Saddam Hussein,' Ari said at the end, 'didn't take you all that far. Did it?'

'I wish my country had never been invaded,' Ibrahim replied. 'I wish Saddam was still in power. I didn't like him, but we would all be better off if he was still here. He was overthrown, but the peace and prosperity we were promised has still not arrived. Instead, our lives have been wrecked. By everyone involved in this war.'

Understanding his explosive burst of anger and frustration, Ari fell silent. Elia too. There really was not much they could say.

'Stupidity can never be defeated,' Elia eventually uttered.

Elia left as did Ari. He went to another café bar where he could have some peace for putting his thoughts into some semblance of order. He did not succeed as a group of noisy businessmen and the roar of the espresso machine interfered with them. He left the bar and sat on his motorbike for a while, recalling almost absent-mindedly the events of the last few days. Next to him, two youngsters were exchanging inarticulate monosyllables and laughing. Two smartly dressed women with their takeaway coffees in their hands were staring at them with dismissive looks on their faces.

A car trying to park close to him eventually forced him to move. As he did so, another car blared its horn in protest for not having been given priority. He set off for home, but on the way he decided to go first to the fruits and vegetables market to buy some fruits. Oranges, melons and bananas. He recalled that in Douma, a town 10 kilometres northeast of Damascus, sellers were dividing the bananas into smaller pieces as per request and selling them so that anyone could eat at least a little piece of banana.

'Eating a whole fruit seems to have become a fantasy,' he had told the fruit-seller.

'Never mind' he responded laughingly. 'Eating is an acquired habit anyway.' The man certainly had a good sense of humour.

But others, Ari knew, could not afford even that. They were surviving on what was growing in the wilderness of the fields. 'Dejeuner sur l'herbe,' Ari thought the fruit-seller might say.

The next day, he decided to visit Laura's flat again. Who knows, he might still find something interesting that he had missed before. The flat was cold, dark and unwelcoming as if death had temporarily rented it out and moved in. Ari opened the curtains, but then recalled that the curtains were open the last time he was there.

He stood for a while on one side of the window, peering down into the empty, bedimmed street. Who had shut them? The austere silence of the darkness with all its unsavoury odour was of no help. He started looking around but was now cautious of the unexpected, whatever that might be. He noticed that a few drawers, which he was sure he had shut last time he was there, were now half open. Somebody had obviously been in the flat after his last visit. But who? And what were they looking for? It proved, if further proof was needed, that Laura's death was anything but accidental, the work of some crazy jihadis.

'Crazy jihadis?' He laughed. 'As if there are normal, sensible, rational jihadis...'

He was hungry, but he did not care. Issues like this in the world he now inhabited were of no consequence. He nevertheless crossed the road to a coffee bar where he ordered a sandwich and a cardamom-infused coffee. It was then that another thought hit him. Considering that Laura's body had been found in Eastern Ghouta, where Jaysh al-Islam (the Army of Islam) had been recently engaged in heavy fighting with government forces, it might be worth making some enquiries there. The idea which was flashing through his mind, though still in its infancy, looked good. 'I should have thought of this much earlier,' he reproached himself.

He instantly got up and started slowly walking towards the door of the coffee shop. He reached it, stopped for a second as he realised he had still not paid for his coffee and was about to turn when he heard someone's squeaky voice just behind him. 'Going out?' He glanced over his shoulder. He had been blocking the doorway.

'No, sorry.' He was not sure he was heard by the owner of the voice which had addressed him as the man was already talking to someone else.

Laura, Ari kept thinking, could not have gone to Eastern Ghouta without a previous arrangement to meet someone, presumably a Jaysh al-

Islam official, in order to discuss something or to get help to proceed with something else she had in mind. To get some information, he needed to talk to Jaysh al-Islam people. He set the next day for that purpose.

But luck smiled on him or at least he thought it did, for the next morning Khaled Abdul-Majid, one of the Jaysh al-Islam leading members, called him at his office. The call came when the coffeemaker was gurgling and Ari had to ask him again for his name. The two of them had never met, but his name had been mentioned to him by Laura not all that long before her death.

Ari knew nothing about him or what he had discussed with Laura. But she had obviously mentioned Ari to Khaled, who was now suggesting that the two of them meet. The way he was talking about her made him think that he was the only person he knew in Syria who seemed to be personally affected by her death. Switching comfortably between Arabic and English, he explained on the phone that he had taken a liking to her.

Still, Ari felt, he was a Jaysh al-Islam fanatic.

Chapter 10
Bewildering problems

Jaysh al-Islam was quite a powerful force established by Saudi Arabia back in September 2013. A coalition of 60 Islamist and Salafist units, mostly operating around Damascus, it had been fighting both Bashar al-Assad and Jabhat al- Nusra, the Syrian section of al-Qaeda, whose expanding presence annoyed the Saudis.

Its aim, like that of Ahrar al-Sham, the member of the Islamic Front backed by both Turkey and Qatar, was the creation of an Islamic state under Sharia law. Its leader, Zahran Alloush had risen to prominence earlier, when his own group had bombed the National Security Bureau's headquarters in Damascus in 2012. The bomb had killed the defence minister and President Bashar al-Assad's brother-in-law. It was again him who called for the cleansing of all Alawites from Damascus, whom Sunnis regard as adherents of an obscure, even heretical cult, and of the Shi'ites, that 'filth'.

Earlier, Alloush had denounced democracy, a European import that is a means to hoodwink the people of Syria, and called for an Islamic state with Sharia law. Together with Ahrar al-Sham, his group also refused to join the Western-backed Free Syrian Army or to back the Kurdish fighters. The Kurdistan Workers Party, he had said once, 'embraced Hegel's philosophy and Hegel is a communist.'

But Jaysh al-Islam also bitterly opposed Isis, 'enemy number one of the Syrian revolution,' and condemned 'in the strongest terms' its assault in Paris. For Jaysh al-Islam, Isis had nothing to do with Islam. Hence, articulating its discontent with the Isis practices, it executed 18 Isis militants in the summer of 2015. It was in revenge for the beheadings of Jaysh al-Islam fighters by Isis. The execution, in which the executioners wore the orange clothes which Isis captives were forced to wear before their deaths and the victims black robes, was publicised on its website. The victims were shot at point-blank range with shotguns.

The brutality of Jaysh al-Islam or Ahrar al-Sham and other groupings under the banner of the Islamic Front was not far behind that of Isis. As Ari recalled, only recently had Jaysh al-Islam militants placed cages full of hundreds of captives as human shields against Syrian government air raids in the war-ravaged streets of Eastern Ghouta. The caged people were kidnapped Alawite military officers and their families. Videos of the trucks showing helpless, terrified men and women inside the thick metal fencing were shared on YouTube. 'If you want to bomb us and we die, they'll die like us,' a rebel in the video let everyone know.

It was one of the few times that when the government air force had attacked the rebels, several people in Damascus did not seem to mind it. 'The government was entitled to send a strong message', Mudhar, an Alawite loyalist in his twenties, had told Ari. 'They deserved it.' Sympathy for humanity sometimes seems to be in very short supply.

Ari and Khaled arranged to meet in a school in Douma, the administrative capital of Eastern Ghouta, a Jaysh al-Islam stronghold, in a couple of days. Meanwhile, another thought flashed through Ari's mind. Foreign intelligence networks must certainly know more about Laura's death than practically anybody else. He would have to look into it, except that he did not know whom they were represented by, where they were located or how they functioned. Many embassies including those of the US, UK, France, Italy or Greece had either closed or relocated to Beirut in 2012. Only a few countries, including Russia, Germany, the Czech Republic and also China, Cuba, India, Iran and Iraq maintained a full diplomatic presence in Damascus.

Whatever the difficulties, he had, however, to make a start. He asked Mark Platt, the BBC man who was thankfully in Damascus at the time for a meeting. It was he who had phoned to ask him if he knew why Laura had become inaccessible and then informed him of her death. The two of them had never met before, but this was no obstacle as Platt was as anxious as Ari to talk about his dead colleague.

The meeting took place in the celebrated Steed Café, in the eastern Qassa, a district of the capital. The manager welcomed them and led them to a table graced with red and white checked tablecloths and vases of flowers. Under three giant TV screens, perched next to portraits of President Bashar al-Assad, he took their order, which he passed onto a waiter. While they were waiting, he told them how popular his café was before the war. 'Still,' he added, 'we're optimistic. It was a lot worse last year.'

Platt, a friendly, casually dressed man in his mid-forties, had met Laura only a few times. Even so, she had quickly won his affection and respect. 'She was good at her job,' he said. 'Her sparkling presence was a source of inspiration to others.'

'Do you know what story she was after before she was killed?' Ari asked him, after the initial exchanges.

Platt shook his head. 'The only thing I know,' he said, 'is that she was in touch with somebody from Jaysh al-Islam, this powerful fundamentalist armed group active in the suburbs of Damascus.'

'Anything that has to do with the Saudis?' Ari persisted.

'Not that I know of.'

Ari had asked about the Saudis in the spur of the moment. But as soon as he had mentioned them, he recalled that the doctor he had met at Shami Hospital had practically been interrogated by Laura on the subject, when the three of them had met. The focus of her interest had seemed to be a Saudi prince, though Ari could not remember what it was all about as he had not been paying full attention. The only Saudi prince connected with Syria he could think of was Bandar bib Sultan, appointed in 2012 as the head of the Saudi intelligence and given the specific job of toppling the Syrian President. He had done his best to undermine him, albeit without success.

Ari thanked Platt for his time and they both got ready to go just as a woman walking into the restaurant caught their attention. She had strawberry-chestnut hair.

'We know her, don't we?' said Platt. 'She's a Hollywood actress, isn't she?'

'I think so,' said Ari. 'But what's her name?'

'Who remembers? But it's interesting to see what she looks like without makeup. What cosmetics, flattering studio lighting or airbrushing can do to a woman!'

Ari left. He had to meet Hussein, the doctor, once again. He phoned him and asked if he could steal a few minutes of his time to ask him a question. They met soon after. Ari arrived at his appointment quite late as at a checkpoint in Baghdad Street near Bab Tuma, one of the seven gates inside the historical walls of the city, an army officer had asked people to turn back due to the risk of incoming shelling. That was where, following the 16th century conquest of Antioch and Alexandretta by Ottoman Turks, the Greek Orthodox and the Greek Catholic churches for the Northern Levant had their seats.

Anything but surprised, Ari watched the spectacle for a minute. The officer's warning and the mortar shells fired now and then from the nearby Jubar or Duma made no difference whatsoever. People in the vicinity just did not seem to bother. Having acquired some sort of immunity against the miserable world they were living in, they just carried on with their activities.

'If I was meant to die,' a shopkeeper told Ari when the latter stepped into his shop to buy a packet of aspirin for a headache he had woken up with and which was still drumming behind his eyes, 'I'll just die. That's it.'

The attitude of two young boys, who in their dirty shirts weaved in and out of the gridlock trying to sell Ari a tissue box, was more or less the same. One of them was about nine and his brother looked no more than five. Displaced from their home in Idlib, which had been destroyed in the fighting, they were now trying to make a few Syrian pounds to help feed their family. Home for them was a building that was meant to be a school, but the local authorities had turned it into a shelter when displaced families started pouring in.

'We came to Damascus when our home was destroyed,' the older boy said as he wrapped his arm around his little brother's shoulder. Their smiles belied the sadness of their story, one that is all too familiar across this war-torn country.

Soon after, Ari was with Hussein. But the Syrian doctor was not as forthcoming as Ari had hoped. Perhaps the discussion that had preceded the topic that Ari wanted to discuss had not helped. It was when Hussein, a Shi'ite, lashed out at Isis, this 'insane, murderous cult', which had started all the trouble in the Middle East. Ari was, by temperament, never looking for arguments against views expressed by people he was discussing matters with.

Arguing a point rarely, if ever, made any difference, particularly when people were arguing without really understanding what they were talking about. Any talk under such circumstances was bound to carry as much weight as a soap bubble. But this time, he felt rather irritated by Hussein's comment. He felt history was being challenged by him just as it was in a report on Syria, published in a British tabloid he had just read on the internet. Uncertain as to whether he should be doing what he was doing, he got engaged in what, thankfully, turned out to be a very short debate on the topic.

'Yes, Isis is responsible for a lot of things,' Ari said. 'But if I'm to mention just one thing, Isis didn't exist in Iraq or anywhere else before the US-led invasion of Iraq. It was an Iraqi creation through which the Iraqi Sunnis channelled their inflexible anger at the Iraqi Shi'a regime and its Western backers. Whether insane or murderous, they expressed the main Iraqi Sunni political body, angry at the sectarian power grab by Nouri al-Maliki, the Shi'a Iraqi premier and US protégé. This fact, which had obviously eluded Barack Obama's attention, had thrown them into Isis' arms.'

While he was talking, he wondered again, as he had when he had raised this issue with Laura, when history begins. 'According to Homer,' he had said, 'the Greeks declared war on Troy to win Helen back. But if Zeus hadn't seduced Leda and if Leda hadn't given birth to Helen, Paris wouldn't have eloped with Helen and there would be no Trojan war.'

'So,' Laura had answered, 'the problem began with the tricky seduction of Leda by Zeus...'

'You may say so,' he had said, 'but the question about when history begins can't easily be answered even in the calm seclusion of history itself.'

Hussein's eyes had narrowed in apparent concentration. Being a Shi'ite himself, he could not identify with the hatred the Iraqi Sunnis felt for their Shi'a controlled government. He did not want to blame his Shi'ite brothers either.

'What a waste of time,' Ari thought after taking a deep breath in an effort to shut the sluices of discomfort the conversation had opened. Raising such an issue had not made any difference to the doctor's thinking. But if it had not made the discussion about Laura's death impossible, it had certainly made it difficult. This was the case despite Ari's subsequent attempt to pull himself away from the brink of the argument and solve the bridging problem by introducing a lighter subject for discussion: the numerous pigeons that were jumping on the nearby tables, impenetrably unconcerned about what was going on in Damascus, or even just around them.

Ari mentioned Laura's interest in the arms' black market and particularly in the arms' trade in which the Jordanian gang was involved. But Hussein did not seem to know anything about it.

'She didn't mention anything about it when talking to me,' he said. 'All she was interested in was information about a Saudi prince and his connections with the rebels. She didn't say why she was interested in him. In any case,' he added, 'there's nothing unusual about it. Connections don't mean a thing.'

Hussein's face wore a rather twisted smile, which did not look entirely free of calculation, and his mood became undecipherable, particularly at the moment he put his arm around Ari's shoulders, and wished him good luck with his enquiries. While his own phone was ringing, he watched him chatting with a few young people in tight tank tops before disappearing in a crowd of teenagers overwhelmed by the latest hipster fashion.

Ari was soon back in his office. He did not stay long. He left it together with Garrahan for lunch in one of the fast food stores nearby. While walking, they could again hear the sound of bombs exploding a few kilometres away. Bashar al-Assad's military jets were flying over them.

'Will this ever end?' an elderly man at the next table shouted. He was just talking to himself.

'It will. It will end,' Ari said to Garrahan, 'when the Arabs can manage to deal with their misfortunes effectively.'

'What on earth do you mean?' Garrahan asked.

'I'll tell you what I mean,' Ari said, 'but let's find a table first.'

They did so and ordered a pizza, which was really their excuse for a beer, necessary to refresh the soul.

'They need to see,' Ari said, while waiting for the pizza to arrive, 'their own contribution to their painful reality and re-assess their own culture before blaming others for their misfortunes. They need to look into their religion, which solely focuses on its ritualistic part rather than its spirit, into their politics, which rest on abuse of power, and into their culture, which relies on corruption, including nepotism, favouritism, bribery and cronyism. They need to break all links of habit and its seductive powers.'

'Well, of course. To have a chance, they need to reform their thinking,' Garrahan agreed. 'But this won't happen before the conversion of the Jews.'

'You're not serious, are you?' Ari asked, shocked.

'No, I'm not. But the portrayal of an Arab as one of the three Bs – billionaire, bomber or belly-dancer – won't easily go away.'

'Well, that's how some Americans, those who were born stupid, choose to see an Arab,' Ari retorted. 'But it doesn't mean a thing.'

The pizza they had ordered had still not arrived.

'Moliére,' Ari said, 'would have written another play between the time we ordered this pizza and the time it will be delivered. You know,' he added, 'his play, *The Would-be Gentleman*, was commissioned by the King, written, rehearsed and performed, all within five days.' Thankfully, they did not have to wait that long as the pizza arrived together with a second glass of beer. Their accelerated eating ended minutes later and Ari was able to continue.

'The Arabs do need to change,' he explained. 'To get ahead, they need to do what I mentioned already. They also need to review their cultural practices, which have marginalised women and also their family scripts, which, among other things, encourage a "wheel and deal" attitude even in personal relations. Alongside all this, they need to go for a governmental system that would mark the end of party edicts or dictatorial commands, which have been inflicted on them for centuries, and give people a voice. It's what they actually tried to do during the so-called "Arab Spring".'

Garrahan's attention was diverted for a moment when he heard his mobile ringing. It was his girlfriend, a local woman with a very high opinion of herself, who seemed determined to relay in full detail her adventures during her shopping expedition. When the call ended, Ari was only too ready to carry on. But before doing so, he could not resist asking Garrahan where he had met that woman.

'LoveHabibi,' he answered. 'A Damascus dating website.'

'Wow,' Ari said, as if in awe of Garrahan's sexual proclivities.

'I've got some more research to do in original sin,' the Irish explained with a faked seriousness that did not hide his beguilement.

'You've got many problems with women,' Ari teased him, 'but charming them isn't one of them.'

Garrahan' eyes twinkled with good humour, and Ari continued with his story. 'There is also a psychological aspect to it that takes you to roads unfrequented by the Arabs.'

Garrahan this time made a show of examining his coffee. 'Too much chicory in it,' he eventually said.

'Has he forgotten what we were talking about?' Ari wondered for a minute. He nevertheless ignored him and carried on.

'To get ahead, people need to win back their dignity and self-respect. This won't happen before they manage to overcome the feeling of inferiority towards the Western world resulting from centuries of foreign domination and under-achievement and the inescapable feeling of victimisation and humiliation.' Concluding his argument as if he was giving a lecture in front of a large audience, he added that blaming foreigners or their own brutal rulers 'may be useful in living without guilt. But disregarding reality only perpetuates the existing state of affairs. And this is what Isis has taken full advantage of.'

'I see your point,' Garrahan said, narrowing his eyes in apparent concentration. 'But perhaps, just perhaps, the problem is not the Arab history. It's Islam, which looks to me like an incurable disease.'

'Don't be too argute,' Ari taunted him. 'By demonising Islam, you only strengthen the Manichean vision of Isis. Islam is not represented by one school of thought. The many moderate trends which challenge the extremists will tell you a very different story.'

Garrahan pinched the bridge of his nose and swallowed back a yawn. His face wore the unguarded look of distaste. 'It's a funny old day,' he observed, groaning as he stretched.

It was about time to make a move.

As they were getting up, Ari teased Garrahan or perhaps himself, he was not sure. 'Well done, James. Once again, you survived my monologues. Till next time, of course ...'

'I'll be looking forward to it,' Garrahan answered as if he had meant it.

As they were about to go, they heard that a ceasefire agreement between the regime and Isis had been reached, providing for the evacuation of at least 2,000 Isis members plus a number of Jabhat al-Nusra fighters from Yarmouk. Its implementation was not expected to be easy, but the deal marked a success for President Bashar al-Assad. It increased his chances of reasserting control over a strategic area south of Damascus and it was, as people hoped, a step towards ending Syria's war.

Despite the optimism, the 2nd phase providing for the transfer of an estimated 4,000 jihadis from southern Damascus to Al-Raqqah did however hit the rocks. Instead of leaving, Isis only moved its fighters from certain districts in order to strengthen their positions inside the Yarmouk camp. The battle for southern Damascus was far from over.

Ari returned home and lay down on his bed for a while before meeting Elia as they had arranged over the phone. He could not, however, rest. His neighbour, a woman whom he had never met, would not stop singing. Passionate about her vocal talents, she would not end her practice before she was happy with her performance. But perfection somehow seemed to be beyond her reach.

'Choose your neighbour before you choose your house,' the Syrians say, he instantly recalled. 'How right they are!'

To escape his misery, he tried to read an old Maigret story by George Simenon, the prolific writer who, Ari could not forget, had once said that, though married, he continued to visit brothels accompanied by his wife. She advised him on the choice of girls. Funny, but in the state of mind he was in, he could not go beyond the first few pages.

He tried some poetry: Seamus Heaney. Poetry, Heaney had said, makes 'space-walk possible'. Still, he could not read. Disgruntled, he left his flat earlier than he had planned and went to meet Elia. But she was not there. 'Let's wait for a while,' he thought. 'Who knows what has happened.' She arrived ten minutes later.

'I'm so sorry,' she said. 'I had to deal with my mother. She went to a shop to buy a few things and on her way out, she put the receipt in her bag instead of the banknote she had been given as change and threw the note into the rubbish bin.'

'Worse things can happen,' Ari said in sympathy. 'Someone once told me his aunt had put her shoes in the refrigerator. Shall we go for a walk?' he then asked.

'I would love to,' Elia answered.

They sauntered around the shrine of Sayyida Zeinab, daughter of the Shi'a martyr Ali and granddaughter of Muhammad. The shrine was a beautiful Iranian-style mosque in southern Damascus that attracts Shi'a Muslim pilgrims from Iran and around the world. Syrian pilgrims in black chador stood in its courtyard while a young girl in their company was dressed as a Syrian military officer.

Elia was relieved that life in Damascus was becoming easier. 'Even a few months ago,' she said, 'we had to live with the constant sound of explosions. Once, in the Christian district of the city, four rockets shot from the rebel districts fell on one street in 48 hours and I happened to be there. One of them hit the church and a woman died in the explosion. Another injured woman was screaming. Still, like everybody else, I managed to get used to it. But not my nephews. They had come from Germany to spend their holidays in the Syrian capital and were struggling to adjust.'

An elderly man, who later told Ari that he was an Armenian, sitting in a fold-up chair in front of his shop, looked at them as if he knew what they were talking about. In sympathy with Bashar al-Assad, he had hung his picture on the wall with the words 'Yes, we are with you'. Ari and Elia stopped and took a look at his shop's crafts for sale. Ari asked him how life was these days. Despite his fossilized spine, the man stood up and asked them to repeat the question.

'It's fine now,' he eventually answered, quite lucidly, refusing to give way to fear. 'Not like the times when a rocket landed across the street. The wall up there fell,' he said, gesturing towards the opposite building. 'You can see what remains of it: stone pocked with shrapnel holes.' Some other buildings were pierced with gigantic holes, and so charred and damaged that they were close to collapse. 'I hope,' he added now from behind his antique desk, 'our government will defeat these evil men, these criminals, these terrorists who strike down the civilians.'

Ari wondered when he had put Bashar al-Assad's photo up on his wall. 'Before or after the Russians got involved in the war?' The man, like many in the winter of their lives, was hard of hearing and Ari had to repeat the question.

'Who remembers,' he eventually responded, while engagingly leaning on the window sill. 'Ask me what happened fifty years ago and I'll tell you.' His memory seemed loyal to his distant past, but not to his recent past.

Almost before he finished his sentence, a group with two strollers and a half-dozen other kids, all of them teasing each other and begging the elders for ice cream, noisily stepped into their path. Elia left at that point as she had an appointment with her hairdresser, and Ari wandered among the vicinity's rambling souks in an effort to clear his mind. He then returned home and had a glass of mineral water before he took his clothes to the laundrette. He wished he could take his mind to the laundrette, too.

While waiting for the washing machine to finish spinning, a student, who was waiting there for his wash to finish too, joked that the days when women were taking care of this sort of business were obviously over. Ari was not sure whether the young man regretted this development or not. While agreeing with him, he refrained from comment, which might open the way to a conversation he was in no mood to have.

The next day he was in Douma.

Chapter 11
A force with a bad breth

Douma was the city where hundreds of people had died, following president Bashar al-Assad's attack against it with chemical weapons in 2013. The regime's action, the deadliest chemical deadliest chemical deadliest chemical attack since the Iran-Iraq war, had sent shockwaves throughout the whole world. It was what had forced the West to consider military action against it. Action was eventually averted but only after the Syrian government had accepted a US–Russian negotiated deal to turn over 'every single bit' of its chemical weapons stockpile for destruction.

Government forces had since imposed a devastating siege on Eastern Ghouta. The Syrian army had been bombarding it regularly while the rebels were launching rockets and mortar shells into the capital. Despondent, in April 2015, Zahran Alloush, the Jaysh al-Islam commander, rushed to Istanbul to discuss with the Turkish government ways to lift the siege in al-Ghouta.

Meanwhile, the 'moderate' rebels had launched an attack on those they suspected might not be on their side. In one instance, Ari was told by Ahmed, a Sunni like most of the inhabitants of Eastern Ghouta whom he had recently met, they had assembled a large group and started to ask who was Christian or Alawite. The Sunnis refused to betray their neighbours, but the rebels were merciless in return. 'They killed people in front of our eyes,' Ahmed said.

Hit among others was Ahmed's wife and his 12-year-old daughter. The latter received a bullet in the thigh. His wife was hit in the neck. 'She died in front of me,' he added. In the ensuing chaos, he had left his son grieving over his dead mother and he had taken his badly injured daughter to search for urgent medical help.

All one could see in the city of 175,000 people, where Ari was to meet Khaled, were destroyed houses, burnt cars, and hills of bricks, pipes, timber and rusted water tanks. Glimpses of streets engulfed by uneven piles of brick, rooftops tilted askew and steel reinforcement bars pulled apart like spaghetti were seen by the outside world through videos posted by rebels and rescue workers. Residents, cut off from the main electricity grid for two years, were, as elsewhere, relying on generators and other sources of light at night. Jaysh al-Islam fighters and their families were known to have abundant food on their table, but the rest of the population was starving.

Starvation for the government was a weapon of war as ghastly as the cruel action of the rebels.

Still, children playing on an old bus next to the ruins of a destroyed apartment block waved to Ari as he approached them. So did a man adjusting his satellite dish on the outside of a partially destroyed block of flats. Ari, who had for a moment felt disoriented, had stopped his motorbike in front of him to ask where exactly the school was. The man, Mahmood, came down, shook hands with him, pointed in the direction of the school, and asked what was bringing Ari to this part of town. Ari then asked him how he and his family were coping. The answer did not surprise him.

The family group lived in one funky and damp bedroom and one smaller room doubled as a kitchen and bathroom. The house often had no electricity or water and the bedroom was incredibly hot, humid and dark. Nine people lived in it, including three children, who did not go to school because the family did not have the means to buy them uniforms, books and satchels.

Ari did not expect anything different, but the scale of the calamity as it unfolded in front of his eyes defied ordinary comprehension.

Armed with directions, he was soon at the school. Khaled, however, was not there. Kindly, the school's head teacher offered him a coffee and guided him to a quiet corner where they could enjoy it in peace. The once white walls of the room now had a dingy yellow colour under a layer of damp. While they were sipping their coffee, the man started talking about the horrifying and intense experiences they were going through.

'Teachers, just like doctors and government officials,' he said, 'are regarded as authority figures and are frequently targeted by the rebels. Sometimes they are also kidnapped from their place of work.'

'Why?' asked Ari.

'Jaysh al-Islam objects,' the head teacher said, 'to the liberal and secular school syllabus of Syria. It objects, in particular, to the study of religion, which, embracing both Christianity and Islam, propounded a message of religious tolerance.

'They want us to embrace salafism and also eliminate anything which promotes Syrian nationalism.'

Salafism, as Ari already knew from the young years of his life spent in Egypt, produced and spread by Saudi Arabia, is a form of Islamic fundamentalism attached to the way the first three generations of Muhammad's followers practised their religion. Salafism is rooted in the word salaf or 'forefathers' and is erroneously known in the west as Wahhabism.

But as Islam spread across a vast region over time, it had to adjust to numerous other faiths and cultures and also to the demands of power and politics. It became, as a result, more pragmatic. For traditionalists this nevertheless amounted to obliquitous deviationism that made a holy jihad necessary for the return to the 'purity' of the early days. Their movement inspired a later figure, Muhammad ibn Abd al-Wahhab, an eighteenth century theologian, whose most puritanical understanding of his religion had a huge and continuing impact on the Salafist movement. Wahhabism, one form of puritanical Salafism, was actually named after him. The alliance, which Abd al-Wahhab formed in 1744 with the local ruler, Muhammad ibn Saud was strengthened by the marriage of the cleric's daughter to the emir's son.

The entire House of Saudis was, as a result, viewed as directly descending from Wahhab. This turned Wahhabism into the spiritual and ideological weapon for the expansion of the Saudi royal family's political and military power and influence. It also provided one of the wellsprings for the jihadi crusade which overwhelmed the moderate versions of Islam in many countries, planted the seeds of terrorism and led to head-chopping expeditions and thousands of deaths.

But the man who brought salafism into the 20th Century was the Egyptian thinker Sayyid Qutb. Born in a small village in Upper Egypt when the 20th century was still a toddler, he had spent two years in the US in the late 1940s only to be left disgusted by what he viewed as the unbridled godless materialism and debauchery of the capitalist world. His fundamentalist Islamic outlook was, as a result, honed harder. Back in Egypt, he developed the view that the West was imposing its control directly or indirectly over the region with the collaboration of local rulers who might claim to be Muslims, but who had in fact deviated so far from the right path that they should no longer be considered such. For Qutb, 'the philosopher of the Islamic revolution', offensive jihad against both the West and its local agents was the only way for the Muslim world to redeem itself. Killing a Takfir, an 'impure' apostate, was an obligatory and meritorious act.

Qutb was hanged in 1966 on charges of involvement in a Muslim Brotherhood plot to assassinate the nationalist President Gamal Abdel Nasser. His ideas have, however, lived on in the 24 books he wrote, which have been read by tens of millions, and in his connections with people like Ayman al-Zawahiri, another Egyptian who was the current al-Qaeda leader. Qutb's views, which inspired his followers to rationalise even unprovoked mass murder as righteous defence of an embattled faith, were shared by Bin Laden.

But given the kingdom's central role in the making of the West's Middle East policy, the gradual Wahhabisation of the Muslim world was tolerated, tacitly condoned or even supported by the Western Powers rather than confronted. It was what, with the blessing of US President Reagan, had created the first jihadi army in Afghanistan.

'Supporting the Jihadis suited the West,' Ali Mahnoor, a Pakistani hotelier who was in Damascus at the time, had told Ari. The two of them had met the day that Besher Yaziji, the Syrian Minister of Tourism, had welcomed a delegation of International Peace Supporters. 'Hence,' Mahnoor carried on in an angry voice gliding through his clenched teeth, 'the rapid expansion of Saudi influence in all Muslim countries, including Pakistan. It began to grow in the 1970s, when Riyadh's ultra-religious establishment teamed up with Pakistan's military ruler, General Zia ul-Hag, and also when the US offered its support to Afghanistan's mujahideen.'

The tone of the hotelier's voice reflected an anger, un-tempered by time, which was also evident when he was talking about indoctrinated young Pakistani Islamists.

'They've been washing their feet as part of their daily ablutions in my hotel's hand basins,' he exploded.

'The religious schools established by Saudi Arabia in rural communities during those years, the madrassas, to plant extreme religious views in the minds of Pakistani children and teach them that they have a sacred duty to fight infidels,' he carried on, 'have grown dramatically since. In 1956, there were only 244 such schools. Today, in some areas of Pakistan, they outnumber the underfunded public schools.'

A young female employee, whose job was to monitor media coverage of the war for the ministry of information and who had joined their conversation, added: 'A network of more than 30,000 such schools today provide the human resource for militant causes and up to 2,000 of them are involved in violent activities. The toxic role Saudi Arabia plays in promoting the most intolerant strains of Islam across the Muslim world provides the building block for the very groups which the West is fighting.'

It was not, of course, only in Pakistan that the Saudis were heavily investing in building mosques, madrasas, schools, and Sunni cultural centres. The tsunami of money they unleashed in India alone ensured – and this just from 2011 to 2013 – the arrival of some 25,000 Saudi clerics sent to preach religious intolerance, i.e., the extreme Wahhabist fundamentalist strain. Their presence was also felt throughout the entire Muslim world, from Afghanistan, Malaysia and Indonesia to Libya and Nigeria.

In Afghanistan, they supported the mujahedeen against the Soviets with money and fighters in a way that gave rise to the Taliban and eventually to al-Qaeda. In Bosnia, they provided aid to the Bosnian Muslims in the wars that broke up Yugoslavia and brought the Wahhabi strain of Islam to Europe. In Chechnya, they helped to radicalize further the local Muslims. In Europe, too, they devoted billions of dollars to fund the establishment of fundamentalist Islamic groups in a number of European countries, which produced the European Islamist terrorists. The growth of madrasas was explosive but only where Iran did not hold sway.

The Saudis, as Hilary Clinton admitted in her private emails, funded 'the Sunni terrorist groups worldwide'.

'Mind you,' the Pakistani hotelier added, 'funds are funnelled to the terrorists not only through such networks but also through Islamic NGOs, which fail to comply with the basic laws governing charitable organisations. Some of them have actually been actively involved even in the jihadis' efforts to develop weapons of mass destruction.'

In 2013, the European Union eventually declared Wahhabism to be the main source of global terrorism. Saudi Arabia, 'a godfather to terrorists everywhere', was supposed to have been cornered. This was the case particularly after the 9/11 atrocity which was mainly carried out by Saudi terrorists backed by powerful members of the Saudi élite.

Yet Riyadh is still considered by the US and British governments a critical partner in counter-terrorism operations and in the fight against Isis. Apparently, maintaining their partnership with Saudi Arabia and the Gulf monarchies has for both the American and the British governments taken priority over the elimination of terrorist organisations such as al-Qaeda, al-Nusra, Isis and the Taliban.

And this despite the views of senior officials in the White House and the State Department and even the concerns of President Barack Obama himself. The latter, Jeffrey Goldberg reported in *The Atlantic* following numerous interviews with him, 'often harshly questioned the role that America's Sunni Arab allies play in fomenting anti-American terrorism'. Obama, Goldberg said, 'is clearly irritated that foreign policy orthodoxy compels him to treat Saudi Arabia as an ally'. He could also have mentioned Turkey, Qatar or Pakistan.

Hence the complete failure of the Americans' vastly expensive 'War on Terror', the fiasco that accompanied their Middle East policy.

But in the meantime, despite their supporting it, the Americans fell out with the Saudi monarchy. The Saudis to begin with, had never reconciled themselves to the US-led invasion of Iraq, not because it toppled Saddam Hussein, but because it led to Shi'a majority rule in that country. They objected further to the nuclear deal struck between the USA and Iran, which enabled Iran to join again the international community, and they baulked at what they perceived as US complacency in the face of Iran's advances in Iraq, Syria, Lebanon and Yemen. For the Saudis, those advances far outweighed western perceptions of Isis jihadism as the main threat inside and outside the Middle East.

They also bitterly objected to the support the Americans offered to the Egyptian 'Arab Spring' that toppled the Egyptian dictator Hosni Mubarak and brought Mohamed Morsi, head of the Muslim Brotherhood, to power. The US-backed military coup led by General Abdel-Fattah al-Sisi against Morsi in 2013 did, however, delight them. Morsi, as many held, might be preparing an Islamic coup d'etat, but he himself had proclaimed that his Islamism was not in conflict with democracy. It was this concoction of Islamism and democracy that drove the Saudis up the wall. Connecting

Islamism with democracy was for them bound to lead to the emergence of a rival band of pan-Islamism that was as intolerable to them as the emergence of someone else claiming to represent Islam. Rather than Egypt, Qatar or Turkey, the kingdom was supposed to be its protector. Anything else was viewed as an existential threat to the Saudi monarchy and undermined the Saudi interventionist policies in Syria, Yemen and Libya.

To protect its imperialist interests, Saudi Arabia declared the Muslim Brotherhood a terrorist organisation, and this despite the Brotherhood's full backing by both Qatar and Turkey. Soon after, in March 2014, in response to Qatar's support for Ahrar al-Sham and other groups in Syria with connections to the Brotherhood, it also withdrew its ambassador from Doha. Qatar, the Gulf nation with the potential to outshine the Saudi kingdom, and also indirectly Turkey, which was increasingly leaning towards the Brotherhood's ideology, had been given a warning. So had the US President Barack Obama, who was accused of betraying a US ally.

The creation of what eventually became Isis was the response of leading Saudis to what they perceived as disastrous American failures in the Middle East. The Americans were aware of it, but they ironically ended up actively grooming it. The Saudis had, as a result, not only created a powerful and venomous force in the Muslim world, one 'with very bad breath', as Laura had once said, but they had also stifled, or they had tried to, the emergence of a 'moderate' Muslim opposition to it. They were, thus, primarily responsible for the terror that, in the name of Wahhabism, plagued the entire region and the Muslim world.

Though a product of Saudi ideals, money and weapons, Saudi Arabia lost, however, control of Isis when the jihadists adopted a more extreme version of the Saudi extreme religious doctrine. The Saudi version, Isis claimed, did not reflect the original ideas abandoned during the reign of the fourth caliph in the 7th century AD. Declaring war on Saudi Arabia, which had joined the 'crusaders', Isis vowed 'to liberate the "Land of the Two Holy Mosques" once their mission in Syria had been accomplished.

Mecca and Medina, the epicentre of Islam, had to be the capital of Baghdadi's caliphate. As it happened, Saudi Arabia was also the largest producer and exporter of oil.

Bolstered by supportive parents, teachers in Eastern Ghouta tried to resist the Islamist pressure, but standing up to armed men required unlimited reserves of courage. The case of the head mistress of one school in Eastern Ghouta, 'one of the bravest and admirable women', was brought to Ari's attention.

'The rebels,' the head teacher said, 'had separated boys from girls, ended sports for girls, and cancelled art lessons and also the teaching of physics. They also wanted the school to stop teaching girls science and mathematics and emphasise the importance of jihad. The head-mistress refused to cooperate and was imprisoned before being offered cash to bring in the Wahhabi school syllabus. Still the woman stood her ground. Having no other option, she finally escaped with her two children to government-held territory. Unfortunately, her story had a tragic sequel. A few weeks later, a mortar landed in the garden outside where her two sons were playing, killing one of them and injuring the other.'

Khaled, a man in his early-thirties with a face hidden behind a long black beard and an earnest and steady gaze, made his appearance at that point. He apologised for his late arrival, due to unforeseen circumstances – 'a traffic jam', as he said facetiously. Such 'traffic jams' were a frequent occurrence – hence, as he said, 'yesterday I missed the Man United game.'

'Lucky you,' Ari answered. 'They lost once again.'

They carried on chatting for a bit about the English Premier League and then Khaled asked Ari what a Greek was doing in the midst of it all.

What he meant was a Greek Christian from Greece as opposed to the Greek Orthodox Christians who were to be found mostly in the western part of the country or in Damascus. Those he knew, he added, did not support Bashar al-Assad, but they would never join the rebels. Ari avoided getting into a discussion with him about the Syrian Greeks and the Greek Orthodox Church of Antioch, the largest and oldest of Syria's Christian churches with about 500,000 members. In any case, they were not exactly Greeks. The term only referred to their use of Greek in liturgy. The majority of them considered themselves Arabs and were speaking Arabic in its Levantine variant.

He did, however, agree with Khaled that they would never join Isis or Jabhat al-Nusra. He kept to himself the knowledge that many had already joined Bashar al-Assad, not out of love, but to stop the advance of the Islamists. This, as Ari already knew, was one reason the Syrian government officials were always much friendlier to him as opposed to his British colleagues. In any case, whether in government or opposition circles, Syrians, just as all Arabs, trusted the Greeks more than the Western Europeans.

'History certainly had something to do with it,' Khaled acknowledged.

Curious about him, and particularly about his English, which was pretty good, Ari asked how he had managed it.

'Oh,' he said, 'I spent six years in Glasgow. Studying at the University.' Then he joked. 'Besides I always carry my "Dixionary" with me.'

This, Ari decided, explained not only his good command of the English language, but also his mild way of dealing with the world in which he had now found himself. He then asked him about Laura. How he had met this 'lovely and intelligent girl', as he had described her.

His answer cut as quick as a wink. 'Following an attack by the Bashar al-Assad air forces, which had caused a large number of casualties among the civilian population,' he said, 'she'd come to Douma, in Eastern Ghouta, to get a clearer picture of what had taken place. While there, she'd tripped over some metal rubbish, the remains of a car, and I ran to help her. All I did was offer her some hydrogen peroxide a bit later to treat a few minor cuts and scrapes.'

The treatment had taken place while the two of them shared some tea – something that offered them the opportunity to discuss the situation in Eastern Ghouta and developments in other parts of Syria. But during this chat, Laura had also mentioned that she was working on something that had to do with the Syrian jihadis' foreign connections and this something had been traced to Eastern Ghouta.

'Didn't she mention the Jordanian intelligence's involvement in the weapons black market, guns and ammunition sent by the Americans and the Saudis to the Jordanians for the Syrian rebels that were appropriated by its officers?' Ari asked.

'No,' was Khaled's reply.

Though friendly, his attitude left something to be desired. When pushed by Ari for something that would at least look substantial, he stared at the open doorway and the brilliant rectangle of light beyond and then muttered something, which trembled on the verge of incoherence. It probably meant 'sorry, I don't have any details'.

Ari swallowed a couple of times to relieve the dryness of his throat. Rather irritated, he felt like telling Khaled that he could forget about the 'details' and instead focus on the essentials. But he said nothing. Followed by Khaled, he then moved towards the exit. When they shook hands, he sensed that Khaled was about to tell him something. The words seemed to be on the tip of his tongue, but he chose to leave them where they were. Ari again felt he was robbed of the answer.

'Perhaps,' he thought, 'Khaled had something important to say, but he wouldn't say it before I've earned his confidence. But what do I need to do to win him over?'

Despite the exasperation with his attitude, he nevertheless felt that there was something engaging about him. He was definitely a driven person, but he was also refined, polite and surprisingly soft-spoken – certainly not the kind of person who would behead the infidels. His six years in Scotland had familiarized him with European culture and had given him insights that many of his compatriots lacked.

His heart, Ari felt with nascent sympathy, was in the right place but his mind was still vacillating between the requirements of his convictions as a human being and those as an Islamic activist. Perhaps he would one day know better as to which side he should throw his weight.

'Except,' Ari scornfully told himself, 'one can always find a number of good reasons to end up doing the wrong thing.'

As he was about to leave, Mohammad Nofal Yassin, a Palestinian from the Yarmouk refugee camp who was in receipt of some help from the UNRWA Development Programme Ari was working for, approached him to thank him again for all the help he and his family had received. He placed his right hand on his heart as a signal of affection. After he had given his thanks, he castigated Isis for its vicious attacks on Palestinians.

'Isis,' he said, 'has even been silent about the recent Palestinian uprising against Israeli forces occupying the West Bank and did not care about their struggle to win a homeland.'

The Palestinian cause was for the jihadis a nationalist cause and as such irreverent and sacrilegious.

'What's Israel's position on this?' Ari asked as if he did not know.

'Israel plays chicken with Isis,' Yassin said. On the one hand, it's never been overtly supportive of the jihadis. On the other, it would rather see Isis running Syria than Bashar al-Assad. If Isis wins, Hezbollah will lose its backing from Syria, Syria itself will no longer be Israel's concern, and Iranian influence in the region will be neutralised. Besides, Israel and Isis both share the same hostility towards Hamas and the Palestinian Authority.'

'So, you say,' Ari interrupted him, 'the enemy of my enemy is my friend.'

'Yes,' Yassin said. 'The Israelis themselves have actually said so. "We don't want Isis defeated in this war". Given that, Israel was pretty reluctant to support US military actions against Isis.'

'This is also what has turned Israel into a de-facto partner of Saudi Arabia. Strategically speaking, Israel's main enemy in the Middle East is Iran – not because it's developing nuclear weapons but because it challenges Israel's hegemony. But Iran is also Saudi Arabia's enemy.'

'And what do you say is Isis' position vis-à-vis Israel?' Ari asked.

'Isis hasn't launched a single attack against the Jewish State,' Yassin said. 'And that's a fact. Its top priority is building up a firm base to be used as a springboard in its "holy war" against the Shi'a power centres – the Hezbollah group plus Syria, Iran and Iraq. Its successful conclusion will be followed by the targeting of the Sunni monarchies of the Persian Gulf – Saudi Arabia and its neighbours. Once those Powers have been "dealt with", Isis would then be ready to launch a "holy war" against Israel. At least that's what they say.'

'This, I'm sure, suits Israel very well,' Ari said.

'It does,' was Yassin's response. 'And if the Isis plans ever materialise, Israel, together with other anti-Isis forces from Saudi Arabia to the United States, will take care of it.'

Ari did not delve into the Arab-Israeli saga further. So Yassin, after lighting a cigarette, asked Ari what had brought him to the area. He was told that it was all about Laura's death.

'I've seen her here,' the Palestinian said rather apprehensively. 'She was having a tense meeting with Ahmed Zaman, the head of Jaysh al-Islam's intelligence, and Omar Tawfeek, the head of the Saudi overseas operations. The meeting,' he added, 'had taken place in the badly damaged Haresta neighbourhood of Damascus.'

'What were they talking about?' Ari asked.

'I wish I knew.'

Yassin's statement was definitely important, but in what sense? There was no way Ari could tell. He asked Khaled, who was still around, if he knew anything about it. Khaled confirmed that he had seen them talking, but he did not know what they were talking about. He had nevertheless at last confirmed something, which Ari read as a veiled reference to something more substantial. To make any progress, he had to see either Zaman or Tawfeek or both. The latter, Khaled told him, was virtually unreachable as nobody knew where his business would take him the next day. Zaman, on the other hand, was a bit easier to trace.

'Easier, but not easy,' Ari thought, 'as his whereabouts had to remain secret if the Syrian air force were not to target him.'

Getting out of the building, he encountered about twenty children, all with round drooping eyes, silently staring as their street was filled with the rumble of a tanker delivering water provided by his own organisation through a local contractor. Their drawn faces were as grey as the concrete buildings all around them. They were certainly maturing twice as fast as Europe's children. One of them was wearing a T-shirt with a sarcastic message addressed to the West: 'You can't feed the poor but you can fund a war'.

'How true,' Ari thought.

Further down the road, a pushcart vendor was selling cucumbers, zucchini and eggplants. Ari asked him how he secured his food supplies. In the meantime, Zaman emerged from behind the tanker and was walking towards the building. Ari instantly recognised him from photos he had seen on the internet. Tall, scrawny, haughty, he was walking on the rugged terrain as if he was above the world that surrounded him. Ari wondered for a minute what would make such a man laugh. He stopped him and, after introducing himself, asked him if he could give him a few minutes.

'What do you want?' Zaman asked abruptly, striding ahead to the front door of the building. His attitude of self-conscious aggressiveness and his stride pattern remained unchanged.

'What you, Tawfeek and Laura were talking about when she came to see you.'

Zaman gave him a cold yellow stare, said nothing and continued walking.

'OK. Let's cut corners.' Though preserving his gravity, Ari was fast losing his patience. 'Was it about the black market arms deals the Jordanian officials are engaged in?'

'I don't know what you're talking about,' Zaman still sitting in the same attitude retorted. This and the uncompromising tone of his words did not leave Ari much hope.

'I'm not asking you to confirm the Jordanians' deals,' Ari clarified. 'I'm asking you if this was the topic you and Laura were discussing.'

'I don't remember.'

'You must.'

'No, I don't.'

'Listen,' Ari carried on. 'This woman was murdered and I want to know who murdered her. Is it the Jordanians? And don't tell me you don't know. You must have at least some idea. Something that could put me on their trail.'

Zaman did not seem sure how to react. On one hand, he did not want to alienate Ari. UMRWA's work, if and when it could be done in Eastern Ghouta, an area besieged by the army, was of the kind that offered his rebels some very valuable relief. On the other, he was not willing to pass on anything. Therefore he stuck to his guns.

'I said I don't remember, and I don't remember because nothing substantial was raised in the meeting you're talking about.'

'You're not covering for the Jordanian thieves, are you?' Ari persisted. His question could be seen as rhetorical, but both he and Zaman knew that it was not.

'Get out of my way,' was Zaman's answer. He was already in the building, surrounded by a small army.

Nothing he had said was quotable. But his inimical attitude had left miles of space for interpretation. There was certainly something he did not want to talk about.

'What was it exactly?' Ari wondered.

Chapter 12
A few centuries back

As fatigue had sapped his strength, Ari returned to the Old City determined to have a break. It was all too much. 'Perhaps,' he thought, 'I need to take a course in laziness as I've never been good at it.' But he was fully aware that what he really needed was to retire for a while from human wretchedness in order to alleviate the tension that forced him to pay overtime the tension-readers working inside him. He needed to escape his empty, silent nights with their echo of yesterday's talk, disperse the fog of inadequacy that had settled upon him and distance himself for at least a day or two from his constant introspection.

'Even a Bedouin is better company than my own thoughts,' his inner self told him in a voice soaked in misery. Still, the thought put a gut-wrenching smile on his face.

'What I really need,' he reflected once again, 'is a friend with whom I could be myself. I need a gentle smile, a kind word, an understanding presence. Loneliness and grief are very bad partners.'

He could have phoned James Garrahan, his Irish colleague, but chose not to. Meeting with him would inevitably lead to more work-dominated talk. He could have gone to the Four Seasons hotel where journalists and NGOs representatives would be enjoying a few drinks at the bar. But again he was in no mood for engaging in meaningless chatter or to listen to the latest 'funny' Arab-centred soporific jokes.

To beat his haunting loneliness, he needed a different connection. Maryam, the Syrian-Greek girl, who Elia had mentioned might be the answer. While thinking about it, he was skyped by Kimon, his father.

'How are you doing?'

'Well, OK.'

'So sorry that life is so hard for you.'

'It's OK, don't worry. I manage.'

He could see his father's concern on his wrinkled face on the screen.

'And you?' Ari asked him.

'Old age, you know. It never comes on its own. The silent working of immutable laws make sure of it.'

He was getting close to his eightieth birthday.

His father, he knew, was not threatened by any condition that could suddenly end his life. He could still hold his body in a perpendicular position and walk almost as vigorously as in his earlier years. 'I'm indestructible,' he had once said to Ari. He looked as if he believed it. After all, he had never been sick a day in his life. But he was still not the same man Ari remembered from the old days. Something had changed in him. He had lost his interest in what was going on around him. He was out of tune with his time.

As the editor of an Alexandria Greek daily, he was once interested in politics. But what he would now say was 'Never mind. Nothing changes. They're all the same.' Perhaps, Ari had thought in his earlier days, the man lacked the quota of ambition and aggression people need in the world of politics to leave their mark behind. Or, perhaps, he felt he was really too honest to be a politician. He was not so sure now. He was interested in business, too, but money-making was now 'not important'.

'What is important?' Ari asked.

'I can't think of anything.'

'Films perhaps?'

'Boring.'

'Holidays?'

'I'm happy where I am.'

'Going to a good restaurant?'

'Not interested.'

'Friends?'

'The best are dead.'

'But something must appeal to you!'

Kimon thought for a minute. 'Your mother's cooking.'

His mother was no longer alive. She had been killed in 2000, when an Air France Concorde had crashed during take-off from Paris, after striking debris on the runway. A hundred and thirteen had died in the crash. Ariadne's thread seemed to be linking Kimon only to the past. His wife's death must have left a deeper mark on his life than Ari had imagined. Or, he wondered, perhaps this is what happens when people get old and no longer have any ambitions. 'I'll know when I get close to his age,' he decided. 'If I survive Syria, of course.'

Anyway, he once again reassured his father that he was coping with all the current difficulties pretty well and urged him to find something interesting to do with his time.

'Why don't you write your memoirs?' he asked. 'You've got interesting things to say and you're now legally old enough to say them.' They liked to tease each other. 'Or you can learn to play the piano. You always wanted to.'

'I love you,' Kimon said in response.

'I love you, too,' Ari said. And he meant it. He had very fond memories of his father.

He then phoned Maryam and started explaining to her who he was. She stopped him short because Elia had already talked to her about him. Her welcoming voice indicated that Elia had apparently not just mentioned him to her, but had also said something very nice about him. To justify his call, he asked her a few general questions to which he already knew the answers and to which she was only too happy to respond. When she asked him how he was managing in her war-torn country and in the turbulent world his state of mind had taken up residence, he told her how 'bloody difficult' his life in Damascus had become.

The plain acknowledgment of his feelings was something he regretted only a moment later. 'I should have kept my mouth shut,' he told himself with some anger. 'I don't know her and even if I did, I should be able to control my emotions better. I'm losing it.'

'So sorry,' she responded, full of sympathy.

'Well! She didn't think I'm a cretin,' he thought, quite relieved.

But, as he needed the presence in his life of a warm human being at the moment, he took his initiative a step further. Though his thoughts were blushing in embarrassment, he asked her if she was free the next day, which was a Friday, to meet for a drink. Her answer was what he had hoped for.

'Yes, that would be nice.'

'Yes, it would be,' he answered by repeating what she had just said, relieved that he had performed as well as he might expect. He looked for something more to say, but words, just like those elusive coins needed to activate a public telephone, were not available.

They met the next day in a café close to her flat. Ari did not know what she looked like, but when they met, he was taken aback by her warmth and her charm. She was doe-eyed and had long dark hair and a dancer's stomach. She was holding in her arms a glowing smile and looked to be in her mid-twenties. More importantly, she looked quite contemporary even if her heavy caramel-coloured case inscribed with her initials seemed to be telling a different story. She had bought it, she said, in the pre-Christmas sale.

They had a coffee under a thoroughly be-smoked oil-painting of old Damascus and chatted for a while. The topic was her family and then inevitably the situation in Aleppo where her roots were traced.

'Aleppo,' she said with sadness, 'is now controlled by Jaysh al-Fatah, the new coalition of jihadi groups formed last March under the supervision and coordination of a Saudi cleric, Dr Abdullah al-Muhaysini, and the backing of Saudi Arabia, Turkey and Qatar. It includes, as you know, Jabhat al-Nusra, the Salafist terrorists of Ahrar al-Sham and another five small jihadi groups. Their resources are different, but they act together.'

'Yes, I know all about it,' Ari said, unwilling to go into the story. He was not exactly in the right mood to talk politics. Laura's death continued to leave heavy footprints on his daily life and dominated his mind. He needed, he knew, something different that would, at least, enable him to leave himself behind for a while. This might again give him a positive frame of mind, re-energise him, enable him to build up his strength.

'And they are being supplied daily cash, weapons, artillery...' Maryam carried on as if she had not noticed his unwillingness to talk about it, '...not just bullets and guns. All trucked across Turkey's borders with Syria. Turkey had turned a blind eye to Isis and al-Qaeda activities on its side of the border. This is what enabled them to establish networks in a string of southern Turkish towns and forge links with traders and smugglers. They were all operating relatively overtly for quite some time.'

Hoping against hope that he was not crossing any boundaries, though he knew he was, Ari interrupted her to suggest they meet again the next day. 'It's my day off,' he said, 'and we can possibly take a ride on my motorbike to Maaloula.'

Maaloula, the 14th century Christian town, was just about 50 kilometres to the Northeast of Damascus. The town, a symbol of Christian endurance, was rising from the ruins after its eight month occupation by a Jabhat al-Nusra force committed to the pertinacious pursuit of its goal: the obliteration of its Christian past.

'I would be very happy to,' she answered with ineffable delight, evidence of her unconsumed love for life. 'I've been there, but ages ago.'

The next day, they were on their way. Although it was quite chilly, the journey through the scenic route was both safe and pleasant. On arrival, they had a lentil soup and a sfiha, the Middle eastern pizza, and sauntered through the Old City's narrow alleyways for a while. The streets had been thoroughly cleared of rubble and rubbish from the collapsed buildings.

'It's so homely here,' Maryam said. 'So old and yet so fresh.'

She waved hello to two kids with sparkling eyes on the side of the road. They waved back.

Proceeding on, they visited the early fourth-century monastery of Mar Sarkis (St Sergius) and Bacchus, dedicated to two Roman soldiers executed for their Christian faith. Entering it, Ari crossed himself instinctively – three fingers, right to left as the Greek Orthodox Christian ritual dictated.

It was what he had always done since childhood. His family was not religious, but they would always go to church on Good Friday and on Saturday, when during the midnight service the Greeks would celebrate with hymns and fireworks Christ's resurrection. The event had little to do with religion. What required its observance was instead tradition and the need to honour it as a means of protecting one's own identity. This was particularly the case when globalisation threatened to turn the entire world into a US cultural colony.

Maryam did the same. They both lit a candle and watched its flexuous, dancing flame. The subtle fragrance of the spiritual deposits of the past had sirenized their spirit. The church had been cleaned and repaired. Little, however, could be done in the adjacent convent from which many of its centuries old icons and books had been stolen or destroyed. As clean and refreshed as it could be was the Orthodox monastery of Mar Takla.

Money for repairing churches, Ari and Maryam heard, had come from Greek and Russian Orthodox and Catholic churches in Syria, Lebanon and further afield. The Aramaic Institute was being reconstructed with French aid.

Talking to the locals, for whom Aramaic, the language spoken by Christ was still used as a living language, was a most interesting experience. They explained how the town's Muslims and Christians were living together peacefully, respecting each other's communal and religious traditions and practices. This lasted until the 1980s, when the Muslim Brotherhood arrived and began to convert the local Muslims to the Saudi Arabian intolerant Wahhabism. The converts subsequently joined the 'moderate' Free Syrian Army whose forces, backed up by Jabhat al-Nusra, attacked Maaloula, and started destroying the Christian sanctuaries.

There was, of course, nothing unusual about it. One of the most obvious and shocking aspects of this war was the systematic destruction of ancient cultural and archaeological heritage sites and artefacts. The damage to magnificent sites like the temples of Bel and Baalshamin at Palmyra had already made headlines. But Christian churches and ancient monasteries, Shi'a mosques and shrines and anything depicting figures had also been targeted and destroyed. Museums had been looted and embellishments had been removed even from Sunni mosques. All this was in line with Isis' puritanical vision of Islam, which was leaving no space for anything that was not dedicated to Allah.

'I pray this will never, never happen again,' the old woman they were chatting with told Ari and Maryam. 'I pray to all saints for this, a different one every day.' The fire in her eyes seemed to have died long ago. Another woman standing next to them whispered to Maryam that the old woman's son had been killed in the war.

'He and his companions were burned to death in barrels. We don't know if they had hidden there or if the jihadis had placed them in the barrels and set them on fire as a grisly form of execution.'

'When you are dead,' the woman added, quoting a Syrian proverb, 'your sister's tears will dry as time goes on, your widow's tears will cease in another person's arms, but your mother will mourn you until she dies. A mother's grief is never tempered by time.' Broken, the old woman was now ready to die. 'In my coffin,' she had asked, 'be sure to put my needle and plenty of thread. I need something to pass my time in the other world.'

Maryam looked at Ari with a feeling coloured by despondency.

Hearing what had happened in town, they were both very saddened, but looking at the locals' effort to re-establish some sort of normality was heart-warming. Even if everything else is destroyed, the spirit, invisible and unconquerable, is always there to affirm life eternally. While reflecting on this, a young boy approached them to ask if they wanted a letter written by a Christian something like sixteen centuries ago. He wanted 'only one hundred US dollars for it'.

The spirit, 'invisible and unconquerable,' said Ari speaking loudly to himself rather than to Maryam, 'would never fail to honour the old traditions either.'

'You've got a point,' she answered with a smile as she pushed her hair breeze-ruffled hair back into place.

Just as they were about to get on his motorbike, he was hit by another thought. The force behind Maaloula's destruction was again, as in so many other cases, not the local community's old rivalries, but the Saudis' determination to turn back the wheel of history. They provided through their Wahha virulent variant of Islam the jihadis' ideology and the breeding ground for extremism. 'Madness,' he thought, 'is not a medical condition. It's a lubricant.'

As soon as Maryam put her jacket on and wrapped her scarf around her neck, she climbed on Ari's motorbike, and soon after, they left behind Maaloula and the thorny mountain valleys of Qalamoun, close to the Lebanese border, where the Syrian army was fighting the al-Qaeda forces. Christianity in that mountain had been eradicated hundreds of years earlier, during the Ottoman rule.

The ride back to Damascus took a bit longer than they expected. The sky had not fallen in line with the prediction of the weather forecaster and they encountered some rain. Delighted nevertheless with the enjoyable experience in such a unique place, they promised each other they would meet again.

'I hope your boyfriend won't mind it,' Ari said, though he knew the answer.

'I don't have one,' she replied, embarrassed because her blushing had been seen by Ari. 'I was in love once, but it ended.'

Refreshed from the short distance he had taken from his convoluted world, Ari tried the next day to re-focus on his daily routines, the epic of the everyday. Whatever his inner self was calling for, the demands of his work had to be given priority. But he did not have time to work out the day's schedule. His thoughts were interrupted when Brigitte Gravier, his Belgian colleague with a luminous virtue that lit her un-powdered face, stormed into his office in a state of mind he had never seen her in before.

'Did you hear the news?' She was practically shouting.

'What news?'

'The Turks.'

'What about the Turks?'

'They shot down a Russian aircraft.'

'Oh dear,' Ari managed to say.

His TV was instantly on. On the screen was the weather report. A couple of minutes later came the news. A Russian SU-24, the news reader was saying, had just been shot down by Turkish F-16s in the Turkey-Syria border area and crashed in the mountainous Jabal Turkmen area of the Syrian province of Latakia. The aircraft had just completed another bombing run against Islamists, 5.5 km south of Turkey. The pilot was killed by Turkmen as he parachuted into government-held territory.

'What's the date today?' Ari asked.

'November the 24th,' she answered.

'Mark this date,' Ari continued. 'We may trace the origins of the Third World War to this date.'

'How come?'

'Wait to see how the Russians will react and what NATO will do in response.'

Turkey claimed, the news reader continued, that the aircraft was flying over Turkish airspace. Russia insisted that it was hit over Syrian territory, penetrated by Turkish F-16s. US military officials said that the downed plane had entered Turkish airspace for a few seconds only. They did not have to wait for too long to hear how Russia reacted. The Russian President attacked the Turks as 'the accomplices of terrorists' and demanded an apology which the Turkish Prime Minister instantly ruled out. In response, Russia deployed a good number of its sophisticated S-400 anti-aircraft missiles at the Hmeimim airbase in Syria. Their deployment was bound to affect developments on the battlefield.

Russia also suspended the reciprocal visa-free regime with Turkey and banned charter flights to and from Turkey. Other measures included the limitation or even the banning of imports from Turkey and restrictions in the work of Turkish companies in Russia. A top destination for Russian tourists and also an important exporter of Turkish agricultural products to Russia, Turkey was bound to be hit hard.

'Anything more than that,' Ari told Brigitte, 'would be nothing less than a declaration of war with missiles flowing in all directions.'

NATO, in the meantime, was at a loss. The last time a NATO state had shot down a Russian or Soviet plane was in the 1950s. The Alliance's Secretary-General immediately declared that its members 'stand in solidarity with Turkey'. What this meant was, however, extremely unclear. Would the NATO alliance go to war with Russia as an act of solidarity with one of its members which was nevertheless out of tune with its own policy? The fingerprints of uncertainty were everywhere.

Ari recalled a chat he had with Laura on this issue. That was when Turkey had increased its military involvement in Syria and the danger of a conflict with Russia looked increasingly imminent. Laura was as uncertain of the future as he was. 'Anything is possible,' she had said. 'Things can easily get out of hand. Erdogan and his Islamist-rooted Justice and Development party are only looking for trouble. They are determined to provide the "leadership" they believe Turkey's neighbours in the Balkans, the Middle East, the Caucasus and Central Asia 'expect' from his own country. He believes Turkey deserves to be the leader of the Islamic world on account of its Ottoman heritage and geographical potential. His foreign policy is ideologically-driven and therefore very dangerous.'

'He and his colleagues live in a world of fantasies, their neo-Ottoman fantasies,' Ari had said. 'Their world is coloured by their imagination. And the blood of the Kurds, too, by the way.'

Laura was of course familiar with all this from earlier times, when she was in Egypt, where, following the end of the Muslim Brotherhood's short-lived reign, Turkey had persisted in supporting the Islamists against the new regime of Abdel el-Sisi.

Brigitte's views were not all that different. 'The country's neo-Ottoman ambitions,' she told Ari, 'haven't come out of the blue. They've been articulated by Ahmed Davutoglu, the architect of Turkey's foreign policy for over a decade. He had openly described Turkey as the core country for setting a new order in all the areas which a century earlier were part of the Ottoman Empire.'

'We have to think big,' Davutoglu had said. 'Last century was only a parenthesis for us. We will close that parenthesis. We will do so without going to war, or calling anyone an enemy. We will again tie Sarajevo to Damascus, Benghazi, Erzurum and Batumi.' As alarm bells were ringing all around, he added: 'We have never and will never have our eye on anyone's land, based on a historic background.'

Yet, at the same time, Turkey was preparing to invade Syria and had already invaded Iraq.

'The pro-government Turkish media,' Ari added, 'have hailed him as a powerful leader following in the footsteps of Ottoman sultans. He was for them the spiritual heir of Abdulhamid II, the sultan who adopted the policy of pan-Islamism.' Davutoglu had argued that the nation states established after the breakup of the Ottoman Empire were artificial state entities. Given this, Turkey was entitled 'to carve out its own *Lebensraum*'.

'The use of such an unpardonable word,' Ari said, 'wasn't a slip of the tongue. He knew what he was saying. And what he was saying reflected the true state of his thinking.'

His *Lebensraum* provided for the cultural and economic integration of the Islamic world in an area without borders under the leadership of Turkey. It also meant Turkey's economic hegemony over the Caucasus, the Balkans and the Middle East. Davutoglu, Ari recalled, had first introduced his pan-Islamist ideas when he was an International Relations professor at Marmara University in 2001. He had subsequently expanded his vision on several occasions as in 2009, before he assumed public office, when he declared:

'We are the new Ottomans. Whatever we lost between 1911 and 1923, whatever lands we withdrew from, we shall once again be there between 2011 and 2023.'

The opportunity to act on his grandiose neo-Ottoman scheme and turn Turkey into the leader of the Islamic world, Turkey believed, had arrived when the 'Arab Spring' revolutions broke out in various Arab countries. Erdogan, the 'sultan', predicted the old order would give way to a regional 'Muslim Brotherhood belt' under his leadership. His 'prediction' was of course as good as a racing certainty.

'How on earth could he believe this sort of thing,' Ari told Brigitte, 'is totally beyond my comprehension. The man must have been living in the clouds.'

'Or possess extra-mundane powers,' she laughingly suggested.

Pursuing the fantasies he was heavily addicted to, Erdogan sided with the Arab countries' Islamic opposition movements, including the jihadis, and actively supported them with funds, arms and ammunition. Embroiled in the internal affairs of Bahrain, Egypt, Iraq, Libya, Syria and Yemen, he also ended up at loggerheads with Turkey's traditional Western allies as well as Russia, Iran and Greece. In the case of Greece, he challenged the 1923 borders between the two countries.

'At Lausanne,' he said, 'we gave away the (Greek) islands that you could shout across to. The Lausanne treaty did not do us justice.'

Apart from Syria, where the situation got out of hand, so did the situation in Iraq. Turkish troops were being sent into Iraqi land since the 1990s, and despite the Iraqi government's denouncing their arrival as 'a violation of Iraq's sovereignty and security', they gradually expanded their presence. They did the same soon after the shooting down of the Russian Su-24 too, when the Turkish government despatched another large and heavily armed contingent with tanks and armoured personnel carriers into Iraq. The intention behind the move, Erdogan said, was to help train local Kurdish and Sunni Arab forces in the impending battle to retake the city of Mosul from Isis.

The move, the Turkish President hoped, would prevent the establishment of an embryonic new Kurdish state, assert Turkey's influence in the region and, more importantly, place it in a position to act militarily when the Iraqis would start the battle to re-take Mosul from Isis. Turkey, when that happened, would be part of the operation whether the Iraqis liked it or not.

'It seems that the Turks,' Brigitte said, 'consider Mosul a Turkish province that was cut off from the Ottoman Empire after World War One, and are dreaming of its re-occupation.'

'Or,' Ari added, 'they're aiming for the creation of a Sunni power centre in northern Iraq – a sort of "Sunnistan" under their control, bound, if it ever happened, to hasten the partition of Iraq. Whatever,' he added, 'what Isis started by challenging the Sykes-Picot frontiers, those arbitrary lines drawn in the sand, Turkey seems determined to finish for its own benefit.

'Erdogan's purpose,' he carried on, 'is the re-drawing of his country's frontiers in the first place with Syria and Iraq. Hence his pompous imperial approach embodied in his assumption of responsibilities. He claims history has bestowed upon Turkey the task to protect "the hundreds of millions of its brothers in the geographical regions to which it had been historically and culturally bound". Taking his thinking a step further, Erdogan added that "certain historians believe that the Turkish national borders extend to Cyprus, Aleppo, Batumi, Mosul, Erbil, Kirtzali, Varna, and the Aegean islands". They just forgot to mention a passing cloud of asteroids.'

'That's why he's been urging Turkish women,' Brigitte said, 'to produce at least three babies each.'

Angry, Iraq threatened Turkey with military action if it failed to remove the troops it had sent to Iraq's northern region. 'We don't want war with Ankara,' the Iraqi prime minister said, 'but we're ready for it.' Stepping in, U.S. President Barack Obama advised the Turkish government to withdraw its military forces from Iraq. 'The battle of Mosul,' the Americans added later, 'is Iraq's battle.' Of the same opinion was the Arab League whose statement on the issue, expressing a rare coming together of states amid divisions over the wars in Yemen and Syria, was evidence of wider Arab concerns over Turkey's role in the Middle East.

Still Turkey, laughing at Baghdad's threat of military action, refused to give way. Mosul, 'a city of Sunni Arabs and Turkmen', it declared, 'could not be controlled by the Shi'ite government of Baghdad'. President Erdogan accordingly informed the Iraqi Prime Minister 'we will do what we want to do.' 'We don't need permission for this, and we don't plan on getting it,' he added later. The US once again cautioned Turkey to stop playing its new and dangerous war games in Iraq's glasshouse, but again to no avail.

'The Iraqis, backed by the Americans,' Brigitte said, 'are determined to protect Mosul from Turkey and the Americans are not likely to let the Turks attack the Kurdish forces. Rather than teaming up to fight Isis, they're all jockeying for future influence. I wonder,' she concluded, in a sentence that embraced all of the ongoing uncertainties, 'what, if cornered, will the Americans choose to do at the end.'

It was a very good question. The Turks had gravely complicated the US-led coalition efforts to push Isis out of Mosul and al-Raqqah. Even worse, assuming that Isis was ousted one day, they seemed ready to turn these areas into a battleground again. Peace, without a home at the moment, seemed bound to remain homeless in the future, too.

Chapter 13
Plots with room for improvements

Ari phoned Khaled the next day and asked if he could arrange for him a meeting with Zahroun Alloush, leader of Jaysh al-Islam. With an unpromising voice, Khaled said he would look into it. Such a meeting was bound to be difficult under any circumstances. It was even more difficult on the day that presidential vehicles with Bashar al-Assad in one of them, going through the wealthy, upmarket Malki area of Damascus, were hit with grad rockets.

The attack was claimed by two Islamist groups, Liwa al-Islam and Liwa Tahrir al-Sham, both parties of Jaysh al-Islam, and was denied by the government in a short statement sandwiched between endless news stories about the war. But stories about plots to assassinate the Syrian President had never ceased to reach the ears of the various foreign missions in the country. Their outlines remained fuzzy, but they did sometimes make the news.

In one of them, in 2013, Israel had been reported as helping the Islamists to carry out an attack on the Syrian President. It did so, Israeli media explained, because the Israelis, shocked at his ability to resist the rebellion, were mulling other ways to topple him. An attack on his life was apparently also carried out later on, when two armed groups claimed they had fired several artillery shells and hit his motorcade as he travelled through the Malki area of Damascus. He was in that instance on his way to attend prayers at the start of the Muslim holiday of Eid al-Fitr. The Syrian government denied it had happened. It had also denied another rumoured, unsuccessful attempt in the early part of 2015, when two French nationals, smuggled into the country by Jabhat al-Nusra militants, were arrested.

Plots against the Syrian President's life often involved coaxing people who had access to the presidential palace into betraying him. A plot by the Turkish intelligence to do so in conjunction with the French intelligence, but defused by the Syrian security apparatus, had also already received a mention in this respect. Bashar al-Assad himself was convinced that Turkey or Saudi Arabia would assassinate him rather than launch a military attack on Syria. The legitimacy of his being treated as a military target was not really disputed either in Europe or the US. Assassinations like the killing of dozens of pro-government businessmen, TV personalities, officials and their families who had been found shot dead in their homes or killed in hit-and-run attacks on the street did not seem to be illegitimate either.

The news about the latest attempt on Bashar al-Assad's life spread like a fire in a warehouse. But what was still unknown was that only a week before this attempt, members of Jayish al-Islam who had infiltrated the household staff of President Bashar al-Assad, were discovered, arrested and killed by the president's security. Their plan, as Ari discovered later, was to kill the dictator by planting explosives inside detergent containers in the library of the presidential palace in the west of Damascus, located at a hilltop fortress that sprawls across the plateau of Mount Mezzeh. Designed by the celebrated Japanese architect Kenzö Tange, best known for designing the Hiroshima Peace Memorial Museum, the palace, which overlooks the city, is composed of vast white planes of Carrara marble, punctuated by thin arrow-slit windows.

For security reasons, Bashar al-Assad was living elsewhere. On that day, however, he was expected to be at the palace's library in the guesthouse, a discreet half-mile or so from the main building. The armed rebels were no more than five kilometres away. The discovery of the conspirators was made possible when a bawab, the porter of the bloc of flats in central Damascus, observed the comings and goings of some visitors, and, alarmed by the conspiratorial expressions on their faces, made it a point to overhear bits of their discussions. He then informed the authorities.

It was something that had not happened by chance. Doormen kept tabs on the personal lives of the residents and constituted a self-appointed but vaguely state-sponsored information network. As in other instances, men on the ground were often more important than the electronic means of surveillance.

Focused on the effort to find Laura's murderers, Ari did not pay much attention to all this. Attacks, bombings and killings were after all a daily phenomenon like the prosaic severity of the daily tasks that give bread. What preoccupied him, instead, was who might have the information he needed to unravel the mystery of Laura's murder. She had often, he recalled, talked about arms dealers, and one of them who could guide him was Abu Ahmad, the arms dealer from Hama with the chubby and freckled face. The man had in the past requested UNRWA's help for his family stuck in that town and Ari had helped by making a couple of phone calls to his colleagues in the area.

Pleased to see him again, Ahmad let a hint of a smile appear on his thick, sensual lips before shaking hands with Ari. In the process, he squeezed the signet ring he was wearing into Ari's little finger. 'To be honest,' he said when Ari asked him the question, 'I've heard a rumour, but I don't know anything about the Jordanian intelligence's involvement in the arms smuggling operation.' Ari did not like his 'to be honest', but he could not say anything. Ahmad was nevertheless happy to expand on the way that the arms black market operates.

'Dealers,' he said, 'use a network of drivers and smugglers to hide munitions in trucks delivering civilian goods such as vegetables and materials for construction. Fuel trucks are used a lot, because they come back to Isis territory empty. They're moving in and out of Isis territory like crazy.'

But it was not only weapons destined for delivery to the rebels that were being traded. 'Munitions from Moscow and Tehran that are meant for Mr Assad,' he said, 'are another top source of weaponry bought on the black market. The customers like Russian products – they buy Iranian stuff too, but cheaply.' While talking, his callused hands kept wandering in the empty space in front of him. It looked as if he would not be able to communicate his thoughts otherwise.

'Stopping the trade in an area with few economic opportunities left is next to impossible,' he added with all the wisdom his experiences had endowed him. 'Every time an arms trader flees, many more, desperate for a chance to make money, are there to replace him. Today, it's all about money,' he concluded. 'Nobody gives a toss who you are... They just care about the dollar.'

Ari thanked him for his help and, when on his own, he Googled the words *Jordanian arms dealers*. 'I should have done it days ago,' he told himself. He got nothing as he was getting no signal.

His next target was the British and the American intelligence men in Damascus, who should, he believed, have some information about Laura's death. Finding out who they were was, however, quite a difficult task as people in their position do not advertise their services to the public – if it is indeed the 'public' whom they serve. He was totally out of his depth with all this. He had never been trained in intelligence work, he was not connected with the right sources, and in any case, his job did not provide him with enough time to pursue his investigation. Perhaps all he was doing was wasting his time.

Dismissing the difficulties ahead, he decided that priority had to be given to meeting the Western intelligence representatives in Damascus. He talked to his boss and then he contacted Rami Abu Hadeed, the FSA colonel. They arranged to meet the next morning.

Early the next day, he jumped on his motorbike and headed towards their meeting place. At some point, the road was blocked. The neighbourhood's bread maker told him that a car bomb had just exploded and killed a brigadier from the air force intelligence. That was the most feared of several overlapping Mukhabarat, the regime's security branches. The explosion, Ari was sure, must have left the brigadier as surprised as nothing else in his entire life. In a chilling novelty, his killing was filmed by Ahrar al-Sham, the Islamist group, and was networked socially on YouTube for everyone to enjoy.

Still, the bread maker did not seem to care. He casually looked up at what was going on in the street and then went back to pounding the dough. People were as used to such atrocities as people in other parts of the world are used to traffic jams.

'To hell with it all,' Ari told himself. 'That's not what life is about.'

Then he became aware of the scrumptious smell coming from the bakery. It was that of fresh-baked bread. A sudden flash of memory rushed him back to the years before the tail of the quirky 20th century had left the scene, and the world he was in vanished at a stroke. Holding time in his hands, he was back at his home in Ekali, the northern suburb of Athens, to the peaceful times of his youth, when days were full of energy and nights full of dreams.

He used to go to his local bakery to buy bread for his family. But when back home, a good portion of it had already been eaten. 'You can't do this sort of thing,' his mother had always reminded him to no avail. Fresh bread, hot from the oven, was a delicacy. Irresistible! He wished he could re-live his early life for just a while. But, whatever one offered it in exchange, time would not be persuaded to run backwards.

Cushioned by his memories and also delayed, he arrived late to his appointment. The colonel, a man who, helped by his hennaed hair was wearing his years with distinction, was still there waiting for him. Thankfully, he did not seem to think that Ari's late arrival was due to some vague relic of colonial oppression. They shook hands and ordered some zouhourat, that delicious tea with a light yellow colour and a delicate, flowery flavour, made from hibiscus flowers.

Initially, the discussion revolved around developments in the war zones and within the Free Syrian Army.

The FSA, the colonel said, which prior to September 2012 had operated from Hatay, known as the Sanjak of Alexandretta, had deployed units in various parts of Syria, but it was now facing almost insurmountable difficulties. Mentioning Sanjak, where his career as a rebel had started, coloured his voice with an undisguised sadness.

Sanjak had been governed by an autonomous regime within the French-mandated State of Syria as provided by the secret and notorious 1916 Sykes-Picot Agreement. Included in its territory, which was considered an integral part of Syria and which was inhabited by Arabic-speaking Alawites (50%), Turkish Sunni Muslims (30%) and Christians (20%), were the cities of Alexandretta (Iskenderum) and Antioch (Antakya), the pre-Islamic capital of Syria.

The ethnic composition of the province was, however, of no interest to Turkey. Hatay, Mustafa Kemal, the founder of the Republic of Turkey maintained, had been a Turkish homeland for 4,000 years. To back up his point, he had cited the 'findings' of the Turkish 'scientific' Sun Language Theory, which held that ancient peoples of Anatolia and the Middle East such as the Sumerians and Hittites, were related to the Turks. Coming from Central Asia, the Turks had, however, appeared in Anatolia mostly during the 11th century.

The same 'scientific' theory had suggested that all human languages can essentially be traced back to Turkic roots. 'Going, perhaps, as far back as Adam and Eve,' Ari had told himself when he had first heard of it. 'Or even before time was born! Wow!'

In 1938, the region, the centre of the Hellenistic Seleucid Empire and later on an important regional centre of the Roman Empire, was offered to Turkey by France as an inducement to join the war against Hitler. Turkey, of course, never did. In the same year, the Turkish army entered Hatay and expelled most of its Alawite and Armenian inhabitants. The next year, following a referendum that has been viewed as both phoney and rigged, particularly as thousands of Turks had been transferred into the area, Hatay was annexed by Turkey.

The colonel stood up. 'We still call this land *Liwaaa aliskenderuna* and consider it an integral part of our territory. The smell of history is all over our differences and disputes.'

Ari and the colonel walked to a green area nearby. They sat on a bench, but not before the colonel spread his handkerchief on it like David Suchet in the TV series Agatha Christie's Poirot.

They briefly talked about Laura's death this time. Rami Abu Hadeed had never met her – a recent photo of her Ari himself had taken in Via Recta, the Roman street that runs from east to west in the Old City of Damascus, did not help matters. The colonel had no information to offer. In his deep voice, sandpapery from years of smoking, he did confirm, however, that it was rather unlikely in his view that Laura's death had been accidental.

Ari asked him to arrange for him a meeting with Abdul-Ilah al-Bashir, the Free Syrian Army's chief of staff since 2014. Given his position, the latter might be able to tell him something the others were not familiar with. And then the critical question, which Ari tried to make sound as casual as asking him if he could pass onto him the salt, perfunctorily entered the stage.

'In Damascus, who's in charge of MI6 and also the CIA?'

Hadeed, who did not ooze away at the question, crossed his legs, revealing his veined ankles, before he answered. 'Mark Hollinger, known in Damascus as a Business Development manager, and Rod Kreegan, known as the representative of a US private bank.'

'Do you know them?' Ari proceeded to ask.

'Of course I do,' was the answer. 'It was initially their predecessors and then they themselves who facilitated the establishment and growth of the Free Syrian Army. They offered advice, contacts, money and eventually the delivery of lots of weapons to our units.'

Out of curiosity this time, Ari asked him one more question. 'Doesn't the Mukhabarat know what they're doing?'

'Of course it does,' Hadeed answered. 'But taking for granted that the foreign intelligence groups will be represented here anyway, it prefers to deal with individuals it knows as opposed to people it hasn't yet identified. In any case, they are under surveillance.'

Ari thanked him for his help and got up, ready to leave. But the FSA officer stopped him. 'I want to ask you for a favour now,' he said. 'Can you help me and my family escape to Greece and from there to Germany?'

Ari was dumbfounded.

'Everyone is leaving the country,' Hadeed said. 'My wife dreams of Germany's free medical care. Our older son, you know, has eye problems and our younger one suffers from asthma. She's terrified that before they could be smuggled to Europe, they would be swallowed up by the Syrian military. With their health problems, she's convinced they wouldn't survive for long.'

He knew he was not the only one who was thinking of escaping to Europe. 'Every day,' he said, 'you hear someone else is leaving.'

The discomfort he was experiencing while talking to Ari about it was only too evident.

'You have to think about the safety of your family,' he added as if to justify his request. 'I want to remain in Syria,' he murmured, giving voice to his residual melancholy. 'But by staying, I'm gambling with my life, my wife's life and the life of my children. This is beyond my endurance.'

He then lapsed for a few moments into a somnambulistic bewailing. The cigarette in his hand wobbled and its inch-long ash dropped to the floor. The fire in his eyes seemed to have gone out. His life seemed to be ebbing away.

Caught in the middle of a vicious war that had already caused mass destruction, hundreds of thousands of deaths, homelessness, widespread hunger and in the Isis occupied areas the kind of brutality civilisation had thought it had left behind, the colonel was not, of course, the only one who wanted to run away from it all. The feeling was shared by the millions who had been forced to sleep in camps, spent any money they had on paying smugglers for travel, and risked their lives crossing borders and seas. Rather than improving, the situation was meanwhile getting worse as the Syrian and Russian air forces kept hammering the rebel-controlled areas while innocent and desperate people were trying to escape the front lines.

As everyone knew, more than 4.5 million people had already fled Syria since the war began in 2011 and some 7.6 million were internally displaced and in urgent need of help.

The colonel's request put Ari on the spot. On the one hand, he wondered whether he himself would choose to stay on if he lived in a half-derelict house without food, water or electricity. But on the other, it was not his job to facilitate the escape of Syrians to Europe. Besides, other people held entirely different views on the same issue. Another Syrian, for example, who Ari had met in a packed event that took place in Damascus' Christian quarter, was determined to stay on because, as he had said, 'our country needs us!'

'OK! I'll see if and what I can possibly do...' He did not finish the sentence as he did not know how best to end it exactly.

His vague promise did not remove the colonel's anxiety from his face, now a sitting tenant. Still, Hadeed smiled at the end. The smile related to something else: the woman close to them who was admonishing her child for something he had done.

'In the old days,' he said, 'Syrian mothers used the name of Richard Coeur de Lion to silence their children.

'Yes, of course,' Ari answered. 'He was the leader of the Third Crusade and responsible for the massacre of Ayyadieh – the slaughter in cold blood of 3,000 Muslim soldiers alongside women and children. Saladin's forces were of course enraged. The events had herringboned their psyche like army tanks. Difficult to erase them from the book of memory.'

They left it at that and promised to keep in touch.

Chapter 14
Deliberate ignorance

Back home at the end of the day, Ari had some ready-made food, as tasty as the soles of his shoes would have been. 'Next time, I'll eat the packet and throw away the contents,' he decided. A moment later, on reading the back of the food container, he realised that he was supposed to have cooked it. Too late.

Soon after, he was in his bed. Sleep was not, however, easy. In the stillness of the night, he could hear the echo of Laura's voice, while his unmoored mind, exposed to the waves that the mystery of her death had given rise to, remained ungovernable. He emerged from the ruins of his night very early in the morning, before the light erupted in his room. The morning looked unruffled, but his disposition was unchanged.

His next job was to find the telephone number of the 'Business Development manager'. When he did, he phoned him and told him he wanted some advice on a project that could help the Palestinian refugees. Hollinger agreed to see him in his office in the Old City the next day.

He arrived at Hollinger's office early in the morning. An elder Syrian on the ground floor opened the building's door for him with hands which, knotted with arthritis, shook as he switched its handle.

On the building's humble third floor office, Hollinger opened the door for him and motioned him inside. He was not a man easily describable. All one could definitely say about him was that he did not have any facial disfigurements, did not limp or did not stutter. Though in charge of a fully-fledged network of informants, safe communication channels and a number of safe houses, he was on his own at the moment. Anything but welcoming, he just gazed at Ari with the crisp formality endemic to some root and fibre English people. He was X-raying him.

'Oh, you're Greek,' were his first words, slowly enunciated in his posh accent. His bottom lip almost did not move.

'Indeed,' Ari said.

'You don't see a lot of cricket in Greece,' he said as seriously as he would have if talking about the weather.

'Was it a joke?' Ari wondered. 'None at all, thank God,' he responded with a hint of mockery creeping into his voice.

Hollinger did not seem to think that Ari's response was a joke. Jokes require the appropriate context and have to obey some rules, anything but evident on this occasion.

Ari had heard that agents are trained to be good actors, i.e., convincingly become the person their job demands them to be. Looking distant and formal, as Hollinger did, did not seem to meet this requirement. But perhaps he was wrong. He hoped that, at least, the man would have the critical thinking necessary for his job.

Going straight into the subject he wanted to discuss, he talked about Laura, mentioning, in particular, her investigation.

'So sorry to hear of her death,' Hollinger said as soon as Ari mentioned her name. 'I didn't know her, but I'm very sorry.' His voice was flat and dry, and it came through barely moving lips without expression or intonation. The man looked as if he needed to borrow some feeling to ensure his words made an impact. But sorrow cannot be rented.

'I know,' Ari said, 'that she had come across information relating to the black market arms trade the Jordanian intelligence operatives were benefiting from. What have you heard about it? Is there anything useful you could tell me?'

Hollinger listened to Ari, occasionally raising an enquiring eye before blankly staring at the ceiling. In tune with his disquieting remoteness, he asked no questions.

'This man has elevated his blank receptiveness,' Ari decided, 'into a form of art.'

'Sorry, no,' Hollinger said eventually. 'But if I hear of something interesting I'll pass it onto you.' With a rather economical smile, intended to convey an almost creditable impression of concern, he glanced at his watch. 'I'm afraid…' he started saying.

Ari did not let him finish. 'Well, I'm off now. Many thanks for your time.' They shook hands, but when opening the door to walk out of his office, Ari nearly collided with a tall, bearded Arab man. He stood there, perhaps impersonating a door, practically blocking the way.

'Excuse me,' Ari said. The Arab made way without uttering a single word. 'How strange,' Ari thought.

The American, Rob Kreegan, the US Defence Intelligence Agency man known in Damascus as the representative of a US private bank, was next. They had arranged to meet at the 17th century al-Mamlouka hotel, in the Christian quarter of the ancient city. When Ari arrived there, he was approached by another man, an American with a face reddened with age and probably whiskey, who introduced himself as Simon Weaver.

'Kreegan could not make it,' Weaver said, 'because he had to go to another meeting at the Damascus Securities Exchange.'

A waiter welcomed them soon after with a smiling 'good morning' to which Weaver replied with a cough. Still smiling, he led them to a table in the hotel's courtyard under a citrus tree. Weaver rather stiffly asked Ari what he would like to drink. They settled for orange juice, ordered it and exchanged glances at each other for a minute. It looked as though they were taking stock of each other.

For some reason, Ari could not make the man out. He looked like someone who could reduce any colour to grey, a broken man. His gaze was skittering and unfocused. Worse, he appeared to be on the edge, sort of emotionally numb and disconnected, stuck. The singleness of purpose one would expect to see in him was not there. Perhaps he had some big family problems at home or perhaps the constant stress under which he had to perform his duties had taken its toll.

The world they lived in, Ari thought, could certainly drive someone insane. It had done so to many intelligence agents who had, as a result, retired early or to Vietnam and later Afghanistan and Iraq war veterans. The Americans called it Post Traumatic Stress Disorder, a term that described the psychological injury many of them had to deal with. 'This is what sometimes happens to people when leaders are committed to the merciless pursuit of self-interest regardless of the means employed for the purpose,' Ari thought. 'The ends justify the means. Don't they?'

He recalled here Madeleine Albright, the former US Secretary of State. Asked if the price to disarm Iraq of weapons of mass destruction and to free the Iraqi people was worth the death of half a million Iraqi children, she had replied, 'We think the price is worth it.' No matter how many were killed, there were always more left behind after all.

The astounding callousness of her approach was indeed staggering. Ari had often wondered if her conscience had ever caused her a sleepless night. But perhaps her conscience had been muted.

'How is it going?' Ari asked in an effort to start the conversation. He did not have anything in particular in mind. After completing the examination of the wisteria, the 'banker' answered, 'Bloody difficult.' His voice was as colourless as the wind and the amphibology of his words a bit perplexing. He clarified what he meant when he added, 'He won't give up.' He meant Bashar al-Assad.

'No, he won't,' Ari agreed with him. 'And this may tell us that it may well be better to let things go the way they're going as anything else is likely to be more complicated and dangerous.'

The banker's assistant, wearing an expression of voluptuous languor, did not respond immediately. His glass, which was not quite centred on its mat, had captured his attention. Carefully, he repositioned it. 'No,' he said afterwards in a resigned tone that lacked conviction. 'We'll carry on until all this ends as it must.'

'Carry on with what?' Ari wondered for a minute. 'Supplying the "moderates" with weapons worth billions of dollars, which end up in the hands of the jihadis? Placing their faith in the hands of the non-Isis Islamists who've been as responsible for so many horrible crimes as everybody else? Carrying on with a war that has killed hundreds of thousands and turned millions into refugees?

'Perhaps human despair was none of the Americans' concerns. Or of anybody else's. Whatever,' his thinking rolled on, 'one thing is now certain. The West's policy in Syria is in ruins. It's just not possible to back the Islamist offensive against the secular regime of Bashar al-Assad. Whether members of Isis, Jabhat al-Nusra or the other terrorist groups Saudi Arabia, Qatar and Turkey have set up, what the Islamists aim for is the world's return to the darkest ages humanity has experienced.

'Backing a movement that demands the establishment of a democratic regime is one thing. But as this movement has collapsed, the only force left against Bashar al-Assad is the anti-regime Islamists! Should the West back them up? If yes and if, as a result, they won power, both a medieval theocratic system would have re-surfaced and a powerful force to oppose the West's strategic designs in the area would have emerged. The West would be the loser.

'Looking at the problem in these terms,' Ari wondered, 'who then is really the West's main enemy in Syria? The Syrian regime or the jihadists?'

He had no doubts about it. 'The enemy at this stage,' he said, carrying on with his internal dialogue, 'is only the jihadists. And if this is accepted, all the armed groups now need to be defined not in terms of their position vis-à-vis Bashar al-Assad, but in terms of their position vis-à-vis the Isis jihadists. Except that apart from the Kurds, no other group is committed to the war against Isis.

'And this means that these groups, whether backed up by the US itself, Turkey, Saudi Arabia, Qatar, Jordan, the Emirates or whoever else, are not the West's friends and allies. As long as the main enemy is Isis, friends are only the Kurds and the Syrian regime.'

Restrained, he pulled himself away from the brink of the argument with Weaver, by raising the issue of Laura's death. He did not expect a considered answer. And indeed the banker's response delivered in a weary voice was as unhelpful as one could expect. 'No, sorry, I haven't heard anything.'

Following his 'I'm sorry', they both quickly glanced at each other and then looked away into the distance of the garden. The birds, free from existential problems and political misjudgements, kept singing the same songs they had sang in the time of the Seleucid Empire.

The Syrian government representatives working with UNRWA subsequently brought Ari in touch with Mukhabarat, the Syrian Military Intelligence Directorate that functioned under the direct control of Bashar al-Assad. This was a force whose agents in their unofficial uniform of black leather jackets and dress pants were everywhere. Their power rested, indeed, on their visibility.

Though all too powerful, Mukhabarat was, however, trying at the time to recover from a highly painful double-cross that occurred when one of its officers, General Mahmoud Abu Araj, gave Western-backed rebels vital intelligence that led to the loss of Tal Al Harra. The latter was an electronic warfare station 50 kilometres south of Damascus, set up by Mukhabarat to intercept Israeli communications and also to hunt for the source of the leaks that resulted in the killing of dozens of military personnel wrongly accused of treason.

The Mukhabarat officer Ari met, Ahmed, a self-assured middle-aged man, welcomed him warmly enough, but he claimed at the same time that he had no idea what Laura was involved with and much less who had sent her to her grave. As opposed to Hollinger, to whom Ari had mentioned

Laura's interest in the Jordanian intelligence's arms trade, he said nothing about it to the Syrian intelligence officer. Were he to do so, he would be moving into areas he did not want to enter. Passing on intelligence from one side to another was not his business.

Disappointed, he only asked Ahmed if some other officer might have information only to hear that if such information existed, he would certainly know about it.

'But how about CCTV?' Ari persisted.

'Good question. But sorry, no! The particular spot where Laura's body was found is not covered by any security camera.'

Equally unhelpful was Derrick Fischer, the irritatingly eve-tempered German foreign intelligence agency's representative. BND was lately working with the regime's intelligence against Isis. Its agents were travelling to the war-torn country to work out, together with the Syrians, the best ways to deal with the jihadis and, in doing so, they were also collecting information about Syrian extremists who had emigrated to Germany.

Although Ari tended to accept that the various intelligence networks had no information about Laura's killers as yet, he could not stomach the British Intelligence's detachment from the murder of a BBC journalist. Frustrated once again, he returned to his office.

Jaafar, the man from Aleppo who had visited him a few weeks earlier asking for help to bring his family out of the wrecked city, was waiting there to see him. His clothes had not seen any service for months. On his hands, there were liver-spots, which seemed to have appeared as suddenly as mushrooms.

He had heard, he said, of Laura's death. He was very sorry about it and would be happy to be of help, if Ari needed any. In return, he would appreciate some assistance to get his family out of Aleppo. Ari wondered how Jaafar had heard about Laura's death.

'It was on the news,' the man said.

But the news bulletins had of course not mentioned that Ari was her friend.

'OK,' Ari said. 'I'll think about it.'

But sensing Ari's reluctance to commit himself, the Aleppo man, who kept repeating Ari's name as if its repetition was proof of his sincerity, proceeded to make a suggestion he obviously thought Ari could not turn down.

'I've got lots of contacts in the arms black market, and these contacts might well provide a lead.'

Ari thanked him and again told him that he would think about it. A second later, another thought crossed his mind. 'Did you know Laura?' he asked. 'Have the two of you ever met?'

The short answer was, 'No.'

Jaafar left soon after, but not before he asked Ari his final question.

'You haven't got a cigarette, have you?'

'No, sorry, I don't smoke.'

Ari stared at the ceiling for a while, wondering how come a man, who only a short while ago seemed to be standing at the edge of a breakdown, had suddenly turned into an activist. 'And why this sort of suggestion? Did he know something, which he had not mentioned? Did he know what Laura was involved with before she was killed? And if yes, in what capacity?'

He could not work any of it out. It all looked as purposefully ambiguous as a Kandinsky painting. Once again, the universe seemed to be full of mysteries. 'What happens to the hole after you eat the bagel?' He hoped the question in front of him did not have the same intricately combined absurdities and amplitudes.

Partly because he needed to and partly in order to escape the nightmare in which he was trapped, he tried to focus on the requests for help which had reached him the day before from Latakia, Syria's seaside resort. But his head was splitting into many parts and the pain of Laura's loss, fierce and unrestrainable, kept coursing through his arteries. The footprints of his tormented mind were visible in everything he did.

The Syrian army forces were at the time making quick advances in Latakia, recapturing many villages and hills, many of them along the Turkish border, from the rebels. In this, they were supported by the Russian air force and the S-400 surface-to-air missile weapon systems deployed by the Russians in the area since the very end of September. Latakia, a city that had seen massive protests against the Bashar al-Assad regime in 2011, all of which were suppressed with elaborate brutality, had never fallen into the hands of the jihadis. Throughout the war, it continued to look like a Mediterranean holiday resort to which Damascenes would come to for a break and, in the summer, a swim.

Yet the war was too close for comfort. If nothing else, people were reminded of it by thousands of photos of young men, all casualties of the war, which adorned the walls of houses and shops in practically every block in the government-controlled villages. They were soldiers, 'martyrs' for their families and friends, killed in the fight against the rebels.

'Part of the martyrdom culture encouraged by the regime,' Ari was told by his boss.

On the province's frontlines, far away, at the edge of Idlib, the picture was, however, different. The beauty of the resort had given way to destroyed villages, abandoned homes, burnt cars and rusting military equipment. In the fields and hills separating the government from the jihadi forces, fires were often raging next to clouds of flies feasting on decaying, unburied bodies.

The question for Ari was how the Latakia Palestinians could be helped through the provision of cash, accommodation, food and non-food items. The latter included blankets, mattresses, tarpaulins, clothing sets and kitchen sets plus schooling facilities, vocational training and whatever was essential for the health care of the population. Health care included whatever was necessary to mitigate the risk of disease: regular garbage collection, rehabilitation of sewage system infrastructure, supply of chemicals for treatment, equipment, spare parts, and fuel for camps and host communities.

It was a tall order, but UNRWA had a history of care for the Palestinians as good as that of its dedicated staff.

As soon as he finished reading the various notes, Ari started making his own notes which he printed out an hour later and passed to other staff members. He was sure they would take good care of his instructions. He passed on a copy of them to his boss, Samuels, too. The latter took a look at them with his glasses perched on the bridge of his nose, and fired his question without looking up. 'Is this a report or Encyclopedia Britannica?'

'Oh, boss…' Ari said as if in despair.

As he was leaving, his telephone rang. It was Maryam.

'How are you?' she asked, rather embarrassed at taking the initiative to re-establish contact between the two of them. Ari was pleased to hear from her, but he too felt a bit embarrassed for having placed her in this position by not taking the initiative himself.

'Oh, pretty well,' he answered, before asking her how she was doing.

She told him she was doing fine and then, trying hard to find the right words, she wondered if he was free 'the day after tomorrow'. 'I mean in the evening,' she carried on, 'to escort me to a party. It's a party that a friend I know from my school days is giving in Abu Rummaneh.' That was the posh neighbourhood that housed some of the capital's best houses and several embassies.

'The friend,' she said, 'is one of the three daughters of Ibrahim al-Shaar, a Syrian military leader who is now the Minister of the Interior. He faces sanctions that the European Union placed against him back in 2011 because of his involvement in the violent treatment of demonstrators. In 2012, following an explosion at a national security building in Damascus, he was injured.'

Ari told her he would only be too happy to escort her to the party. He would be at her place in good time so that they could go together in her car.

Having his morning coffee at a nearby café the next day, Ari checked as usual the BBC website to see what was going on in the world, tweeted something about Maaloula and then started to plan his day. A burst of laughter from a group seated next to him jarred him out of his thoughts soon after. At the same time, his mobile rang. Michael Kay, a member of the BBC staff in Beirut, was on the line. He was in Damascus for a couple of days, he said, and, if Ari could manage it, he would like to see him.

They met for lunch in the Naranj restaurant, on the iconic Straight Street in Damascus' Old City. The restaurant had a stunning reputation as it had hosted 37 heads of state over the years. Michael was obviously familiar with it. Ari had heard of it, but he had never been there. If he had, he would not have been carrying his motorbike helmet under his arm.

The journalist, a bearded, casually-dressed, easy going man in his mid-thirties, arrived and the two of them instantly spotted each other. Ari, in any case, would have had no difficulty recognising him. He had seen him reporting for the BBC and admired the way his mind worked. As they arrived early, only a few tables were taken by young people eating hummus, eggplant puree and salads. They settled in one of them, ordered a beer and chatted for a while in an effort to get to know each other.

'An Arabic-speaking Greek! Wow!' Michael exclaimed while his soft, watery blue eyes took stock of his interlocutor.

'Childhood in Egypt,' Ari explained. 'And then some work in Athens.'

In the paper that Michael had brought with him, he could see that Arsenal had beaten Dinamo Zagreb three – nil and was moving onto the next stage of the Champions League competition.

'It won't go very far, I'm afraid,' Michael said in passing seeing that Ari's attention had been drawn to the newspaper's headline. 'Arsenal is not what it used to be. Wenger has grown lethargic in the last few years.'

Ari was not sure he agreed with him.

'Well, things are difficult right now,' he answered, 'but, as with everything, there are ups and downs.' Expressing his hope rather than belief, he added that he might well get through at the end.

They then turned their attention to Laura. Not having any precise information, Michael talked in general about her approach to the crisis and, in particular, about her distaste for the Islamic Front, which was still for the West part of the anti-regime's 'moderate' forces. She did not agree with it.

The Islamic Front had been formed with the backing and the active involvement of Saudi Arabia, Qatar and Turkey in November 2013. It replaced the preceding Syrian Islamic Front alliance. The latter was a grouping that had co-operated with al-Qaeda, and included in its ranks the hard-line Islamist groups Jayish al-Islam and also Ahrar al-Sham. The latter, whose public profile the Qatari-based al-Jazeera news network had done its best to raise, had been heavily funded by Qatar in an effort to check the increase in Saudi influence. The new Front claimed it commanded a force of 45,000 fighters, many of them 'foreign brothers who supported us in jihad'. Its aim was to 'topple the Bashar al-Assad regime completely and build an Islamic state'.

The Saudis had bankrolled the training programme of its members and supplied them with several thousand guided anti-tank missiles, which had done serious damage to the ageing Syrian troop carriers and tanks throughout 2015. They themselves and the other Gulf Cooperation Council states – Bahrain, Kuwait, Oman, Qatar and the United Arab Emirates – were, meanwhile, being supplied by the US with everything, from attack helicopters and ballistic missile defence systems to precision guided munitions.

But when the Islamic Front attacked the Free Syrian Army, the US and Britain decided to suspend assistance to it. They did not nevertheless classify it as an enemy they had to deal with.

'This,' Ari said, 'was a grave mistake. Focusing only on Isis was the West's strategic failure.'

'It's a shame,' Michael said, 'to support the Front's jihadis in what's supposed to be an effort to restore democracy in Syria. Actually, more than that, it's suicidal. The jihadis are only out there to kill democracy.'

'Rightly so,' Ari interrupted him. 'There're no longer any "moderates" in this war. The Free Syrian Army has practically disintegrated. Low morale, distrust of its leaders, failures to create any "liberated zones" and, don't forget, lack of payment have led to massive desertions to Jabhat al-Nusra or to the government. Talking about "moderates" is a joke.'

'Yes, of course,' Michael agreed. 'Only recently, I don't exactly remember when, the head of the US Central Command admitted that out of the 54 fighters they had sent to Syria, only four or five of them still remained in the field. Just like another group of 75 men, rather than fight the jihadis, they declared that they wouldn't cooperate with the US. They handed over their weapons to Jabhat al-Nusra.'

'Beautiful, isn't it?' he concluded. 'Putin wasn't wrong,' he added wryly. 'He said that sending arms to the area that could end up in the wrong hands only proved that the leaders of the American-led intervention in Syria had mush for brains.'

The setbacks the Americans had suffered had been so overwhelming that they had actually abandoned their paraplegic plan to build an army from the ground up to fight Isis. The help their illusions had offered for the purpose had ended.

'Yet,' he carried on as if what he had just said needed some further explanation, 'our government and also our media are happy to back the opposition to Bashar al-Assad, whether this opposition is the terrorists of Jabhat al-Nusra or the jihadis of Ahrar al-Sham. And what gets me is their cynical tendency to describe any grabbing of government-controlled zones by the Islamic Front as a "liberation".'

'It's so disgraceful,' he added with barely hidden disgust. The focus of the conversation had now shifted. The Western media had come into the picture. 'Influence,' Michael carried on, 'can so easily be bought in our countries by Arab and pro-Israel funders. Once I myself even heard one US administration official refer to his own country as "Arab-occupied territory". We're fed, as a result, rubbish. The State Department, to mention just one example, believes, as its leaked memo of August 2014 made clear, that Isis is funded by Qatar and Saudi Arabia, yet our compliant journalists are eager to tell us that it supports itself through the sale of oil, taxes and antiquities'.

'Their reports,' Ari said, 'are often as accurate as the Arab media reports on the "murder" of Princess Diana. She was killed because "she was carrying Dodi's child and the Queen of England couldn't bear the thought of a Muslim becoming the heir to the throne".'

They both had a good laugh. They needed it. 'Yes, stories are often fabricated,' Ari added. 'Truth can easily be manufactured. You do, by the way, remember the Nariyah story, don't you?'

'No, what is it?'

'Nariyah, the nurse, was the only witness to an atrocity committed by Iraqi troops back in 1991. They took babies out of their incubators in a Kuwait hospital and let them die. The case drew the media's attention for months before the 1991 Gulf War and helped its selling to the public. It was only a year later that we heard that Nayirah's last name was al-Sabah, that she was the daughter of the Kuwaiti ambassador to the US, she had never been a nurse and she was never in Kuwait in 1991.

'Awful,' Michael said, unwilling to hide his animation. 'What we feed the public...' He could have mentioned in this respect some 'monumental errors' the BBC had admitted it had made. But he chose not to. They both knew that truth is often a bemused bystander in the battle between two parties.

Inevitably, they briefly talked about the future, both agreeing that the choice now was between the jihadis and Bashar al-Assad. There was no way the US could turn back the clock. 'The West,' Michael said, 'has to accept that five years of wishful thinking has ruined Syria. It has to stop propping up the so-called moderate opposition, which is not moderate at all, and help the Syrian army to deal with Isis. It's time we got real, we owe it to the Syrian people,' he concluded.

Returning to Laura's death, Michael did, however, mention almost incidentally that she had at some point, placed the emphasis on the

Saudis' critical involvement in the Syrian crisis. Once again, Ari was not sure how to assess Laura's thinking.

'Was what she had said about the Saudis a general comment about their policy or did she have something particular in mind? And what about the Jordanian black-marketers whose unveiling would cause a major scandal?'

But she was not there to tell him. All he could hear was the echo of a voice long silenced.

Having finished their lunch, the two of them wandered out into the streets for a while where people were enjoying the fragrant scent of the jasmine and the slightly cooler temperatures. Youngsters, who could not afford to eat at Naranj, were gathered here and there, consuming snacks and ice cream. In the distance, the minarets of mosques were bathing in a green light. The city was quiet, relaxed, open again to tea and gossip.

Yet a minute later, the neighbourhood entered a state of alert with every vehicle being searched by soldiers or scruffy militiamen in camouflage trousers and T-shirts. Something like an imminent car bombing or suicide attack had obviously reached their ears. It was a false alarm. Life certainly kept going on, but death was never far away. Customers in the city's busy cafés were constantly reminded of it by the thuds of outgoing government guns and the rolling explosions of the barrel bombs dropped on the rebel-held suburb of Daraya.

Daraya, in Western Ghouta, only a mile or so from President Bashar al-Assad's home, was a crucial battleground for both government forces and rebels. It held a strategically vital position near a military airport and it was a gateway to the city centre. Under tight siege since 2012, it had no access to essential services, such as running water and electricity. Out of its pre-war 80,000 population, only 8,000 were still living there.

Chapter 15
A few glasses of champagne

The very next day, he was in front of Maryam's door, ringing her doorbell. She welcomed him with a big, ingratiating smile and led him straight to her car, a modest Fiat with an old registration number. The destination was Abu Rummaneh, the exclusive Damascus neighbourhood. Traffic was sometimes busy but also sometimes relaxed, allowing them to take a look at what was going on.

Passing a car showroom, they could see a big sign in front of it: 'We are a Female Friendly Facility'. A little further down the road, there was a picture of a Barbie on a shop window. Ari made a casual reference to it only to see Maryam disconcertedly take her eyes off the road towards the pavement. The irate driver behind gunned his engine and pulled past her. Ari could see a disgusted look on his face.

Taking a deep breath before giving herself permission to explode, she furiously explained that barbies are banned in Saudi Arabia. 'They are, as they say, a threat to morality. They are offensive to Islam.'

'Really?' was all Ari could say.

If he intended to say something more, he was not given a chance, for she instantly embarked upon a tirade against the Saudis whose abysmal record on everything that concerned women she found exasperating. 'A woman can't go anywhere, even to do a bit of shopping or see the doctor, unless accompanied by a male guardian. A female teenager, by the way, who went out without a man and was gang-raped was given a punishment of more lashes than one of her rapists by the court.'

Ari was, of course, familiar with all this, but he let her carry on because she needed to express her ire. Having turned her back on feminine frippery, she did just that.

'Women can't drive,' she said, 'because the Saudi clerics hold that such a thing "undermines social values". They can't open a bank account without their husbands' permission. And in the majority of public buildings, including offices, banks and universities, they have to use separate entrances designed for women only. Public transportation, parks, beaches and amusement parks are, likewise, segregated in most parts of the country. And, of course, they must adhere to the dress code dictated by the Islamic law – cover their bodies with the burqa, this everyday clothing designed as a walking prison.'

'On the other hand,' Ari added with a smile, 'they are absolutely free to enjoy all the pleasures of domestic life.'

But Maryam had not finished. 'They've even proposed,' she added, 'hosting an Olympic Games without women. The women who had joined them have been denounced by hard-line clerics as "prostitutes". Women in shorts are obviously too much for men to handle. And intelligence is of course a drawback in a woman.'

'Thankfully,' Ari said, 'they're at least not expected to commit suicide upon the death of their husbands.'

'And thankfully again,' Maryam responded in the same lighter tone, 'sometimes men treat their many wives as if they were members of the family.' She paused, but only briefly. 'And even talk to them, albeit in monosyllables.'

'What they'll tell you with unimpeachable sincerity,' Ari said in a way that changed the focus of the conversation, 'is that "universality" simply stands for our own standards. "Universal values" reflect nothing more than our own profane values. Theirs, of course, are universal because they have been decreed by Allah, God preserve his soul.'

'Wow,' she said.

By then, they were passing in front of the National Museum of Damascus. Ari had been there before and the memories the saunter in front of history's gate had evoked were still with him. There was of course nothing to see there. Following the looting of the museum in Mosul and other Iraqi sites, the Syrians, determined to avoid a similar fate, had shipped about 300,000 items from all their museums to secret protected locations.

At the entrance of the museum featured the central doorway to the Qasr al-Hayr al-Gharbi castle, originally located in Palmyra and built by the Umayyad Caliph in the Byzantine architectural style in 727 AD. Its star exhibit was the fully-reassembled 2nd-century synagogue from Dura-Europos. The latter's walls were covered with Talmudic injunctions and bright figurative paintings of biblical scenes. The museum exhibited exquisite pre-classical, Arab Islamic, classical and Byzantine collections.

But its halls were now empty as were the glass cases on which an occasional placard was the only reminder of the treasures that once sat on these shelves. Its walls were, likewise, stripped bare, brown squares and rectangles standing in for the priceless paintings that once hung there. In the tree-lined garden outside, he recalled that ancient sarcophaguses resting on their plinths were shielded by concrete shells to protect them from mortar attacks. Little pigeons, naked, were washing themselves in the fountain.

'Syria,' Maryam said, 'has seen chunks of its rich cultural heritage broken, bulldozed or looted by militias and terror groups. Isis has destroyed ancient sites in Nimrud and Hatra, and Aleppo's old town and its ancient souks are burnt. Shrines and artefacts have been stolen by gangs to be sold abroad. Palmyra was damaged, too, but thankfully the archaeologists removed almost all of the ancient busts and statues from its Roman ruins before the place was overrun.'

The land had behind it a history of thousands of years which its laundered memory could recall with pride.

Soon after, they were in Amena's spacious house. Its beautiful outdoor water feature, its fine French doors, which were concealed inside behind white slatted blinds, and its wooden ceilings immediately hit their eyes. Many people were already there when they arrived, including some ladies with jewellery on their up-lifted breasts. They were all chatting as if determined to prove the meretricious vanities of their class. Vanity and her sisters, avarice and envy, were permanent features of their world. 'As they are in our world,' Ari's sense of fairness whispered.

Thankfully for Ari, Maryam knew quite a few of them, both Syrians and Europeans, to whom she introduced him. They were all quite pleasant, eager to ask him questions about his work or solicit his views on current developments. Occasionally they would attempt a joke.

'Why can't he dial 911?'

'He can't find the eleven on the phone!'

At some point, Maryam introduced Ari to Amena, the host, who engaged him for a while in a discussion about London. She had spent a few years there studying at University College. 'I love London,' she said with genuine affection, 'and if and when I have a chance, I would love to go back there again.' Her Jean-Claude Ellena perfume delicately enhanced her almost inconsumable presence.

Her father, the Interior Minister, who had just joined them, greeted everybody. Amena introduced Ari to him. The Minister, a smartly-dressed man with leather shoes in which he could see his face and an authentic-seeming smile shook hands with Ari. He and his government, he said, were 'very grateful for all the help UMWRA was giving to the Syrian people.'

'What's going on is tragic,' he added. 'I hope it will all end quite soon.'

A middle-aged man, with a protruding belly and with looks that reassured everyone that he was exempt from intellectual influences, was standing next to him. Unwilling to break his taciturnity, he made no contribution to the conversation. Neither Amena nor Maryam had introduced him to Ari.

Talking, however, was not all that easy as the band, which loudly played Sufjan Stevens, Joanna Newsom and other British or American songwriters' songs, would not give it the hearing space required. Many people were enjoying their champagne and others were dancing. A few girls were twerking.

It was a picture of Damascus that Ari was familiar with. Whatever happened in other parts of the country, the affluent Damascene middle class just carried on as before. Business had, of course, been affected, but the lifestyle that the country had adopted, when in the last ten years before the war it had opened up to Western culture, had not. Many of these people could move to Europe. But they had not. Neither rebel sympathizers nor government boosters, they had just stayed on in government-controlled areas partly because they were pretty safe and partly because they did not want to share the fate of those Syrian refugees who had escaped the Syrian war. They knew that most of them lived in miserable conditions.

'The situation abroad is humiliating,' they would often say.

The new confidence projected by the government following the Russian intervention had also encouraged them to believe that the end of the war was not far away. Hope brings confidence, however temporary, and one could sniff it everywhere.

Like everyone else in the country, people were tired of this war.

'Five years ago, when it all started,' a bank manager told Ari in the party, 'Syrian society was spilt into two camps – those who supported the president and those who opposed him. Now people from the two opposing sides are trying to find a common language. They still don't share the same views. They accept, however, that there are different points of view, which means that a different model of co-existence and tolerance is gradually emerging.'

Another middle-aged man who had joined the conversation hit a different note. 'We've been fighting for our existence for five years, and we will not lose,' he said. 'We fought the Ottoman Turks for 400 years. There is no way we'll fall.'

The conversation ended there as they had exhausted their conversational resources. With a glass in his hand, Ari then moved around a bit and exchanged a few words with people here and there until his eye caught Simon Cole. He was sitting at the end of a big armchair, talking with a group of about six men, both Syrians and Europeans. Ari had not seen him since he had left the LSE, in which both did their doctoral dissertations. He waved at him, and Cole instantly got up to shake hands with him.

'You've changed a lot...' Ari started the conversation. 'You've improved with age like a good malt.'

They both laughed. 'Oh, I've just aged,' was Cole's response.

'What are you up to here in Damascus?' Ari asked.

'Passing on the wisdom of the West to Syrian students,' Cole said with sarcastic playfulness. 'I've got a job as a visiting lecturer at the Economy and Public Administration Faculty of the University of Damascus.'

'It sounds good,' Ari said.

They both recalled some stories from their student days, exchanged a few opinions on the state of the country that hosted them both and then Cole proceeded to tell Ari a pretty weird story. He had been approached, he said, by a Syrian security man who wanted him to turn into an informer and provide information about any anti-regime activities within the University. Cole had turned the suggestion down only to be blackmailed by the same man a few days later. 'Either you give me ten thousand US dollars,' he had bluntly said when he had "accidentally" met him in a bar, 'or I'll make sure you're thrown out of the country.'

Cole had asked for a couple of days to think about it before they met again. The security man agreed, but he had never showed up at the agreed appointment. It was only the day after that Cole discovered that the man had been killed when a rocket had hit his neighbourhood.

Maryam joined Ari at that point and he introduced her to Cole, who complimented her on her dress. She looked, Ari thought, elegant without ostentatiousness. They all took another glass of champagne, clinked glasses and exchanged some practical information relating to their respective jobs. A woman in a white deep V neck open blouse and a flirtatious presence then joined their group. Cole introduced her.

'She's Adeela. She is at the University with me.'

'You teach there? Ari asked.

'No, I do secretarial work.' Fully aware of the impact she was making, and with an elaborate weariness, she then inserted a cigarette between her cadaverous lips. It was this awareness that had empowered her to cut short Cole, who was speaking the moment she had joined them. Soon after, Maryam gave Ari a lift back to his flat. But the day was not yet over.

'That damned man, the one standing next to the Minister,' she said with a bitterness dressed in casual clothes when they were back in her car, 'is the one who'd interrogated me at the police headquarters back in 2011. He had left me in a damp and chilly police cell, without any food, water or sleep for 48 hours, and then he attacked me with questions about my network of friends involved in what he called a "plot" against the regime.'

'Oh, you were active against it,' Ari said as if he had not guessed.

'Of course I was. Who wasn't?' A smile broke across her face as she was apparently recollecting something from those days.

'We'd started our pro-democracy peaceful demonstrations demanding an end to Assad's authoritarian rule in March 2011. That was after the arrest and torture of some teenagers who had painted revolutionary slogans on a school wall. But our peaceful rallies were infiltrated by armed Islamists, who opened fire, often from rooftops, against both the police and civilians.

'Unfortunately,' Maryam carried on, 'our struggle for democracy was ruthlessly exploited right from the beginning by forces hostile to democracy, like Saudi Arabia, Turkey and the United Arab Emirates. They instantly poured hundreds of millions of dollars and thousands of tons of weapons into the arms of anyone who would fight against Assad. These Powers were so determined to take down the regime that they didn't even hesitate to start a proxy Sunni-Shia war, as the US Vice-

President Joe Biden had admitted when talking to students at Harvard in October 2014.

'The firing drew in the armed forces who, in turn, opened fire on us, killing several. More people, as a result, took to the streets in daily nationwide protests. The contagious fervour of the "Arab Spring" that had spread across all the Middle East had imbibed every pore of our body. But only one section of our opposition to the regime was linked to violence. Yet our movement was hijacked by the Islamists and soon their insurrection, taking cover under the street demonstrations, was underway.'

'And you were part of it,' Ari said, stating the obvious.

'Yes, I was. I had no illusions about the risks of activism. There were plenty of stories about arrests and torture in the Mukhabarat detention centres – the regime's security agents were known for their inane brutality. Young men were disappearing and their families were being told months later to go and collect their bodies in body bags. So at some point, I had to leave my home. I was no longer secure in it.'

'And...?' Ari asked.

'Well, they found me and they arrested me. They wanted information about my friends in the resistance movement and, more than that, they wanted to trim my wings and teach me a lesson: "You need to fear us". The fear ceremony,' she added, 'was conducted by that man who was standing next to the Minister. I'd refused to say anything, and was taken back to the cell where I was beaten with a cable and sticks. I was released after a few days.'

'How revolting,' Ari said. 'Give people the opportunity and they'll turn into monsters.' He was fully aware of the regime of terror Bashar al-Assad had installed after the first demonstrations against him broke out.

'And yet,' he added, 'you've turned into his supporter.'

'His fate,' Maryam said, 'is nothing to me compared to the fate of Syria – the country, the people, the children. A Syrian is being killed somewhere in the country every moment. We need to stop the killing. That comes first and stands above anything else. It's what Syria demands.'

Ari could not agree more with her. However, as she had hinted, that was only the first step towards the new Syria she was dreaming of. 'You'll all have to do an awful lot if and when peace arrives,' he said. 'The Arabic culture needs to be shaken up. And this is not easy.'

'I know,' Maryam said. 'We first need to establish a democratic state in which the rule of law is observed as much as we need to shake off the corruption that has become a deadly and almost incurable disease. We need to end the historic meddling of foreign Powers into our affairs, re-set our priorities socially and culturally and give women the place in society they are denied. We need to strive for excellence in all fields and put an end to our deficiencies, which are plainly evident to the rich Arab kids who attend foreign universities. We need to feel proud of ourselves again.'

Ari was listening totally fascinated. She carried on. He could not stop her even if he wanted to.

'What is required is honest self-reflection that will allow us to address the problems inherent in the dysfunctional Arab culture and the family scripts, which provide fertile ground for all the wrong things, and also in the Muslim religion. The Muslims seem to have forgotten Prophet Muhammad's call to them to be loving and caring human beings, both toward each other as well as toward the world around them. They indulge in religion, but they've never absorbed the true teachings of God.'

'They would,' Ari facetiously retorted, 'within a secular society.'

'Of course,' she said, at this point ending her rather long verbal journey, which had necessitated numerous stops, with a few more words. 'We need to stop blaming others for our misfortunes. We have to take the responsibility for them. Otherwise, it's the old story of the bad workman blaming his tools.'

Ari was no longer wondering what exactly he liked about her. She was certainly beautiful and good-natured and at least a generation away from the old country's concepts of family. But she was actually more than all that. She had a spirited presence that enlivened everything around her. He wondered for a minute whether Laura would like her as much as he did. He was not inclined to work out the answer.

When it came to goodbye, he received a peck on both cheeks before stepping out of her car.

Chapter 16
'Is your art equal to it?'

Back home, he started thinking of Laura once again. Travelling into the past, he recalled the time when, talking with Israeli journalists, she was arguing as vigorously as Maryam in favour of a Palestinian homeland. This was after Israeli Justice Minister Tzipi Livni, formerly chief negotiator with the Palestinians in the nine-month peace process that had been suspended by Israel the month before, had a meeting in London with the Palestinian Authority President Mahmoud Abbas. The meeting had been denounced by Israeli Prime Minister Benjamin Netanyahu.

'Israel would not negotiate with a Palestinian government that is united with Hamas, a terrorist organisation,' Netanyahu had told Livni before the meeting. Joining it, 'you will represent only yourself and not the government of Israel.' Economy Minister Naftali Branson described Livni as 'a satellite lost in orbit, with no connection to the planet Earth'. According to a tweeted message, Laura had told Ari later on, Branson was paid by his wife, a professional pastry chef, £25 per hour to listen to her dreams at breakfast. On the other hand, someone added, he was paying a psychiatrist a much larger amount of money to cure her of her distaste of him.

But Livni was backed by the Israeli Labour. And also by Laura herself, who fiercely argued with some of her Israeli fellow journalists for the right of the Palestinians to a homeland, denied to them by the Israeli government. The argument, which had started in a good spirit, had ended in acrimony.

'This woman certainly had ideals and convictions,' Ari told himself once again. 'And the courage to stand up for them.'

Recalling the times they had spent together made everything else look trivial and unimportant. The memories forced the world he was living in to shrink. He was missing her as much as reality its lost dreams. 'I love you,' he said as if she was standing next to him.

'I love you too,' she chimed in from the other side of beyond.

To escape his excruciating thoughts, he turned on his TV. It might help, he thought. He did not, of course, expect that anything of interest would be on as, apart from anything else, it was late at night. Most of what was usually on his TV was just, as someone had scathingly described it, crap the channels put out to fill the gaps between commercials.

As it happened, an old episode from Bab al-Hara, one of the most popular television series in the Arab world, was on. The series chronicled the daily happenings and family dramas in a neighbourhood in Damascus during the French rule in the inter-war period. Episodes usually contained some minacious actions by malicious characters, which slowly marinated into a flippant melodrama. He watched it for a while and then switched it off. His last image before doing so was the hapless expression of a spokesman promoting some polyunsaturated yogurt. It reminded him of the yogurt in his fridge which had gone mouldy.

At his office early the next day, he came across Jaafar, the refugee from Aleppo, who was waiting for him at the building's reception area.

'Good morning,' he said quite cheerfully. 'I've been wondering if I can help you with your investigation. It seems to me that Laura's death has something to do with the Jordanian security's commercial activities.'

Ari was taken aback.

'What makes you think that this is the case?'

'A friend in the same business,' Jaafar said, 'has told me of her interest in this business because she had asked him for details.'

'Who's this "friend" of yours?' Ari asked.

'He isn't here now,' Jaafar replied. 'He's left for Beirut.'

'No, I mean who is he, not where is he.'

'Well, he's a man in the same business as the Jordanians.'

'OK,' Ari said. 'What did this "friend" of yours tell you? What exactly was Laura looking for? Who are the Jordanians involved in the black market sale of weapons given to them by the Americans and the Saudis to pass onto the rebels?'

'I know very little about it,' Jaafar replied with exaggerated earnestness. 'Give me some details and I'll come back to you with more. The information I have is that something went wrong in Jordan with the delivery of a large quantity of weapons from Saudi Arabia.'

'Well,' Ari thought, 'that explains why Laura was interested in the activities of some Saudi prince.' But he said nothing. Something, he felt, was wrong as this man, Jaafar, who, appearing out of the blue, had offered him his services in exchange for something which seemed pretty remote, i.e. the escape of his family from the Aleppo hell. He certainly was not naturally stupid. But what was he after? Rather than bother to find the answer to this question, Ari closed his notebook, screwed the top back on his black pen and decided to end the miserable insipidity of the moment. He told the man to come back if he had something specific to pass on.

Jaafar did not like the suggestion. But Ari did not try to dispel his misgivings.

Instead, he again visited Mark Hollinger to talk to him about the possible Jordanian involvement in Laura's murder. But Hollinger did not want to hear a word about it. Having repeated that he knew nothing about Laura's movements, he did, however, venture to suggest that her murder was probably the work of jihadis.

'They enjoy killing westerners, their "oppressors",' he said, 'and when they have the opportunity, they take it.' Following a prolonged silence at the end of which Ari felt he had grown a beard, he added that 'it's very likely that this is what has unfortunately happened.' The smile that accompanied his last few words was Napoleon's smile – a smile in which the teeth are shown, but the eyes do not smile.

'Hollinger,' Ari thought again, 'seems to have elevated dissembling a story to an art.'

'Yet,' Ari insisted, 'she was trying to unravel the Jordanian story. This is not a story with the smell of ordinariness. It's a major scandal involving powerful people determined to go to the bitter end to frustrate its exposure. It's a story that must have certainly earned her many enemies.'

Hollinger's vinegary expression, which, Ari was sure he frequently wore, underpinned by his silence, remained totally unchanged.

'Yes, speech is silver,' Ari, quite irritated, almost said. 'But silence is golden. Isn't it?' The words in his mouth chose the very last minute to remain where they were.

Out of Hollinger's office and upset by the penuriousness of his discussion with him, he wandered the Old City without any sense of direction for a while. Without realising it, the walk took him to Souq al-Saroujah, the area with a cluster of backpacker hotels he had never explored. Those in its Merjeh Square, the red light district of Damascus, often doubled as brothels, were places women alone were advised to avoid. None of them featured on the list recommended by the government. And this despite the fact that the government's accreditation agency would often give highly suspect inflated ratings to hotels owned by Syrian chains or those that had paid a baksheesh to the authorities.

Dispirited, he watched two men for a couple of minutes involved in a bad argument, exchanging insults with impassionate profanity, before walking back to the Old City. While there, he came across a woman who was wearily pushing a shopping trolley full of rags. He helped her push the trolley onto the pavement. On the wall facing it, graffiti read 'Assad for eternity'. Another read: 'I love you Lulu'.

In the meantime, he again decided to try his luck with Rob Kreegan, Mark Hollinger's US counterpart, and subsequently went to his office unannounced. But Kreegan, on his way out, superciliously asked Ari to telephone for an appointment, and then drifted away. Ari was once again left feeling despondent and wondering why the sun had disappeared half an hour ahead of schedule.

'I don't know where I'm going,' he told himself with a heavy dose of sarcasm. 'But I must be making progress... I must. Very slowly of course. Except that any slower and I would be moving backwards in time.'

The elbows of his days were leaning on the water of futility. He felt frustrated, impotent, weak, even a muddle-headed fool. People, he thought, were just laughing behind his back after having gone to see them in order to ask questions to which nobody would give him an answer. At the end, he pushed to the background, albeit with some effort, this merciless dissecting of his inadequacies and re-focused on what he needed to do.

Very strangely, he came across Kreegan in a bar only an hour later. Ari was seated there at the time, enjoying a beer and listening to the noisy conversation of a group of Syrians about the European Union and its policy on the refugees.

'Many EU countries,' one of them was saying, 'can't take the pressure. They feel they can't absorb the millions of refugees who arrive in their land and at some point, pushed by fear, resentment or racial prejudice, they'll completely block all new arrivals. That will be bad news for us, but it will also be bad news for the EU. It could lead to its splitting and eventual disintegration.'

The discussion made Ari think about how Greece was supposed to deal with something like a million of refugees who had crossed its borders on the way to safety if Europe refused to share the responsibility. He stopped thinking about it when his eye caught Kreegan.

The American, whose impregnable body fortification indicated that he might be wearing a bullet proof vest, was accompanied by another American, a young fellow with the face of an extra in a riot scene. In the heavily word-polluted atmosphere, he greeted Ari in a slightly mocking way and then attentively listened to his words for just a few minutes. At the end, he drew his eyebrows together as if he had come across a preposterous question. 'No, sorry,' he said emphatically while his hawkish eyes were piercing Ari. 'I don't know anything about it.'

'You don't know anything about the Jordanian intelligence agents who've turned into arms dealers, either?' Ari persisted.

'Never heard of them.'

Despite his heavy-handed approach, which indicated something different, perhaps, Ari thought, he might indeed not know anything about Laura's death. He did not nevertheless believe that he did not. Still, this changed nothing on the ground.

'So, all this is news to you,' he said at the end as if he wanted to put Kreegan in his place.

'Don't be silly,' the American answered with elaborated dismay. 'This isn't news. It's just stories invented by people in love with their fantasies.'

He then pretended to check his phone for messages and Ari was moved out of his awareness field. He was back into it a minute later when Kreegan re-addressed him. 'But, anyway, I have to say mazel tov to you. You're doing very well in your search for an answer.'

Ari was as surprised as the Virgin Mary in Leonardo's Annunciation. He never expected such a statement from Kreegan. 'He didn't really mean it, did he?' he thought. 'No, he didn't! If nothing else, the deliberate way he had punctuated his words did not make them sound like a compliment. In fact, Ari thought later, the multi-interpretability of his words highlighted only what they concealed.

Hoping to get the lead he needed, he next tried to meet General Salim Idris, the leader of the secular Free Syria Army whom the jihadis viewed as a man lacking the right religious convictions. But he had no luck. The General, as he was told on the phone, was out of town.

In what turned out to be a long dreary afternoon, he then walked out of the bar only to bump into a man who oddly squinted at him once and then again. He smelled of dampness and stale tobacco. Ignoring him, he phoned Sergei, the Russian 'cultural' attaché, who was happy to see him in the Russian embassy, a multi-store building in Omar Ben Al Khattab Street. He went straight there, passed the armed security's checks, left his motorbike in the embassy's parking space and then walked to its reception area where Sergei arrived soon after.

The 'cultural' attaché, a man in the last days of his departing youth, asked him if he cared for a drink. They settled for a cup of tea and, opening the conversation, Ari asked him if he had been in Damascus long. 'It will be a year next week,' the latter answered before asking Ari how long he had been in the Syrian capital himself.

'Just over three months,' Ari answered, at the same time thinking that what he had gone through in these three months was what others experienced in a lifetime.

Ari did not really expect Sergei to provide any information about Laura's death. But he did still ask him, explaining at the same time that his interest in her was due to a personal connection.

'She was a very good friend. A great friend.'

'Very sad,' Sergei answered. 'But in the world we choose to live in, just like frogs around a pond, one can only expect the worst. This is one of the reasons we're trying to bring back some order.'

This was not, of course, the reason Russia was in Syria. But Ari kept his mouth buttoned up. If he had said something, he would have mentioned Russia's strategic interests in the country, its key naval facility at the port of Tartus and its forces at the Hmeimim airbase in Latakia.

'Russia has been trying to stabilise the situation,' Sergei said, 'to create conditions for a political compromise that would end the five-year conflict. It did so in July 2011, when President Medvedev tried, together with Chancellor Angela Merkel, to find a consensus for a strategy that would persuade the Syrian government to begin a constructive dialogue with protesters. And it did the same in December 2011, when it condemned the violence to which all parties had resorted, including the disproportionate use of force by the Syrian authorities.'

'Bashar al-Assad had gone too far,' Ari added. 'The repression on which his power rested was bound to lead to an explosion.'

'Russia's attempt, in January 2012,' Sergei continued, 'to get the West to agree terms for the replacement of Bashar al-Assad was dictated by the same desire to stop the war. But the West, convinced at the time that the Syrian regime was about to collapse, only ignored it. And then, in 2014, the talks known as Geneva II broke down after only two rounds because the Syrian government refused to discuss the demands of the opposition. Negotiation is an exotic fruit in this part of the world. Yes,' Sergei acknowledged as if he wanted to shift responsibility for the Syrian tragedy from Russia's shoulders, 'the Syrian government has made mistakes, very many mistakes.

'And these mistakes,' he carried on, 'contributed to dragging the country into the civil war. In June 2013, President Putin actually said that Assad's refusal to undertake any reform had led to the current situation in Syria. Had he done so, Putin had added, what we're seeing in Syria today would have never happened.'

'Bashar al-Assad,' Ari interrupted him, 'must have lost, as a result, his no claims bonuses.'

Sergei just smiled as if this was an inconsequential joke.

Russia had, of course, objected to the US threats of strikes against Syria in response to its use of chemical weapons, instead proposing the placing of these weapons under international control before their subsequent destruction. No matter how much it wanted to turn the Bashar al-Assad regime into an agreeable proposition, it had no intention of replacing it with a new, Western-backed regime. Vital interests were at stake. The emphasis therefore remained on reform.

This was the case in September 2015, too, when President Putin called once again for a united, international effort to fight the threat of Isis. His call was accompanied by the suggestion that Bashar al-Assad was ready to integrate a part of the opposition into the state's administration. As the situation had changed, the West was this time more willing to listen. President Assad, the British Prime Minister David Cameron said, can possibly be part of a deal during a transition period, though not part of Syria's future in the long term.

'Well, that was a step forward,' Ari agreed. 'It's about time we stop dredging up old rivalries as if we were still going through the Cold War.

Russia's interests should be acknowledged. In any case, despite its comparatively light military footprint, Russia had achieved its central goal of securing the Assad regime. Unless the West wants to start the Third World War, it can do nothing in Syria now.'

Rather diplomatically, Sergei refrained from putting his thoughts this way. 'Russia,' he said instead, 'wants to see an end to this war.'

'That's absolutely vital,' was Ari's response. 'But Russia must also do its best to ensure the rights of the Syrian citizens are fully recognised and respected.'

'Sure,' said Sergei, albeit with much less conviction while still searching his vocabulary for the right words. He could not find them. His wordbook seemed to be as poor as a moth's all of a sudden.

'And by the way,' Ari carried on, 'would Russia be as determined to see Syria's pre-war borders re-established? If the Turks, for example, recognised the Bashar al-Assad regime, would Russia be willing to let Turkey occupy the Kurdish part of the country? I'm speaking theoretically, of course.'

'You're wasting your breath,' Sergei said. 'No such thing is ever going to happen.'

'I wouldn't be so sure,' Ari almost said. 'The temporary and opportunistic support Russia now offers to the Kurds can easily, if it suited its interests, turn into clinical indifference to their fate. But, of course, you can never know what twists the plot has in stock.' He did not, however, say anything.

Soon after, the topic changed as neither of them wanted to continue this discussion. It was Sergei who took the initiative. 'When politics are out of the way,' he said, 'I might one day write a book about my experiences in Syria.'

'That sounds great,' Ari responded. 'By the way,' he carried on, 'do you know the story about the experiences Anna Akhmatova, the Russian poet, has chronicled?'

'What story?'

'A woman in a prison queue in Leningrad,' Ari said, 'enduring the terror of Stalin's regime and blue with cold, asked Akhmatova if she could fully describe it all. "Is your art equal to it?" she had said, thinking that what they were going through was beyond any description.'

'Oh those times…' Sergei could only say, obviously dismayed by the reference to the Soviet past.

Still, as the two of them had for some reason formed a sort of a personal connection which only the future could define, Sergei invited Ari to his Moscow house, if and when he decided to visit Russia.

'I'll keep it in mind,' Ari assured him.

Chapter 17
Certainties and uncertainties

A s Ari was going back to his office, the subterranean feeling at work in him that he was being shadowed started growing again. It was the kind of feeling created when you see something from the corner of your eye, but there is nothing there to sustain your inferences when you look. He had nothing to substantiate this feeling. All that was there was just thoughts swamped by instinct, the increasing consciousness of all the perplexing circumstances he had found himself in, a vague awareness that something was wrong.

And then the next question popped up. 'What was likely to happen if his fear was not the product of his hyperactive imagination? Who might be interested in his movements? The US intelligence? The jihadis? The regime's secret police?' Whoever it might be, he knew that the moment to face the most extreme form of censorship was now on the express train.

The idea had first struck him, three or four days earlier, when he had gone to a meeting that the Syrian Minister of Tourism had held in honour of a group of International Peace Supporters. Among others, present in the event was Jeremy Gardner, the BBC Middle East correspondent, who had arranged to interview the Minister privately at the end of the meeting. Ari was introduced to him, but there was no time for anything more as the Minister had signalled for Gardner to join him in a private space.

As the meeting had ended, Ari exchanged a few short glances devoid of any meaning with a few people and moved towards the exit. It was then when a Syrian had approached him. He introduced himself as a reporter for the *San Jose Mercury News*, a Californian daily, and then started asking him questions about his work. Ari could not imagine that the *San Jose Mercury News* would have a correspondent in Damascus and later, when he checked with the Syrian Ministry of Information, his assumption was confirmed.

After a few general questions, the Syrian 'reporter' started asking him questions relating to Laura' death. Ari, who liked neither him nor the nature of his questions, offered a very brief answer and then walked out.

There was no way a reporter of a parochial US newspaper would know anything about Laura's personal life.

The incident could have easily been forgotten if, a couple of days later, Ari had not seen the 'reporter' in the company of Rob Kreegan, the US Defence Intelligence Agency man, in a smoke-filled café in the Old Damascus. The two of them, Kreegan and the 'reporter', had made a very brief contact, the kind one makes when apologising to someone for accidentally elbowing him in a crowded London train. But in a split second, the 'reporter' had passed something onto Kreegan.

Perhaps a memory stick, the contemporary Vitelian tablet, with documents or photographs?

Ari had heard that an agent's training included, among other things, role playing in real locations, such as parks or cafés where the trainee had to demonstrate that the meeting took place securely. Kreegan looked as if he had played the part well. He was a master of dissimulation.

And if the 'reporter' had passed on information to him, Ari wondered, how accurate would that information be? Misinformation had been the foundation on which the West's mistaken decisions had been made.

His uneasy feeling was reinforced ten minutes later, when he stopped to exchange a few words with Kreegan. Repulsed by the previous trivialities and determined to force an explanation, he told him that he knew that Laura was in touch with Jaysh al-Islam, which had something to do with her death. Kreegan laughed while his face, darkened by the subdued light, remained as inscrutable as before.

'No, it wasn't Jaysh al-Islam she was in contact with,' he said eventually, with all the pleasure of a man in love with his lies. 'It was Jabhat al-Nusra.' He did not go into any detail as the rest was presumably implied from context. Then, as if wishing to dispel any doubts still in the air, he said that he had a photo of her with Jabhat al-Nusra fighters taken just before her death. His body language appeared to be very neutral.

Ari did not believe him. What he said, a diversion from the truth, just did not fit in with anything that had crossed the threshold of his ears so far about her movements. 'He's lying,' he decided. 'But then why this demonstration of sheer cussedness? Why this parsimoniousness with the truth? Who and what was he trying to conceal?' But he knew now that it would be easier to persuade a tree to move to another location than force Kreegan to part with the truth.

The issue at the moment was not, however, Kreegan's statement, but his connection with the Syrian 'correspondent' of the American newspaper.

Seeing the Syrian 'reporter' together with Kreegan made sense according to his mental reconnaissance, but only in the context of a professional relationship between them. Agents, briefed and debriefed, were used all the time, often for cash in exchange for intelligence, often fabricated. But, on the other hand, he could not wrap himself in certainties. It was possible that the 'reporter' was not an informer. Or, aware that he had now started fantasising, he could be an informer working as a double agent like that Jordanian doctor who had been recruited by the CIA after he had said that he had penetrated al-Qaeda's leadership. Exposed as a double agent soon after, he had blown himself up at a remote base in Afghanistan, killing seven CIA employees.

The absurd connection he had just made disturbed him. 'At the mercy of events,' he thought, 'I'm just losing it.'

The word 'absurd' hit a nerve. 'In the nonsensical, irrational, incongruous world we live,' another part of him argued, 'nothing is absurd. In fact, absurdity reigns supreme. Giacometti's figures, Kafka's novels or the work of Edvard Munch have amply demonstrated it. So have the writings of Heidegger, Sartre, Camus and other existentialist philosophers, the plays of Beckett, Ionesco and other post-war absurdist playwrights or the paintings of Francis Bacon and Damien Hirst. Absurdity in their gravity-free visual space is their response to the absurd world we live in – the rise of fascism, the War, the Holocaust, the nuclear attacks on Hiroshima and Nagasaki or our daily mess. We've been swallowed by the absurd.'

'In any case, even if the assumption I'm making now is absurd,' he thought again, 'there are certainly other absurdities of greater consequence. Like the "liberation" of Iraq by George W. Bush and Tony Blair.'

In the meantime, Kreegan, whom he wanted to ask one or two more questions, gave Ari a cold smile as if they had straightened out all the details, turned his back in an ungallant way and marched away. Ari remained where he was, watching him disappear into the crowd. 'Perhaps,' he reflected, 'I shouldn't have gone that far with him. I knew I wouldn't get anything out of him. By pushing him, I may have entrapped myself in something I may well regret later.'

Whatever, the footprints of truth were still untraceable. Unsettled by the episode, he walked back to his office. At its front door, he looked for the building's concierge to ask if he had observed anything unusual, strange or suspicious. He could not find him anywhere. 'Where is he?' he asked the ground floor office man who had just emerged from nowhere.

'He's just been arrested,' the man said.

'Oh God! What's he done?'

'His wife had reported him to the police and they arrested him.'

'His wife reported him to the police for his political activities?'

'No. She reported him because he had uploaded her contact details to a porn site.'

'Why?'

'He wanted to exact revenge on her for her infidelity. She was sleeping with another man.'

The woman was angry at her husband, the neighbour added, but she was angry at herself, too, because she had failed before all that had happened 'to enlarge his mind'. Ari was not sure the man was serious.

Back at his office, he discovered a message on his answering machine. It was Cole who wondered if they could meet for a drink. But, as he was about to return the call, Jaafar stepped in to ask Ari if he had any news.

'I can tell you,' he said, 'that Saudi Arabian arms shipments, Kalashnikov assault rifles, mortars and rocket-propelled grenades bought in bulk in the Balkans and elsewhere around Eastern Europe, were being stolen by Jordanian officials.'

'Which officials?'

'I don't know.' His professed ignorance and impenetrable demeanour had started to get on Ari's nerves.

'But I know,' Jaafar carried on, 'that these weapons, worth millions of dollars, were sold in Jordan at bazaars in Ma'an, Sahab, and in the Jordan Valley.'

'I take it that the Jordanian government is fully aware of what's happened,' Ari said.

'I'm sure they are,' Jaafar replied, 'particularly as they are themselves implicated in the siphoning of truckloads full of stolen weapons. So,' the Aleppo man continued, 'what did Laura know about it?' Rather than offering information, Jaafar was instead trying to get information about it all from Ari. The sterile conversation was leading nowhere and continuing it made no sense.

'I don't have anything which could answer your question,' Ari said in a manner which indicated that the time for Jaafar to go had arrived. Jaafar got the point.

'Tell me if you get hold of anything that may help and I'll cross-check it and tell you the result,' he said before walking out.

A minute later, Garrahan rescued Ari from his nightmares by suggesting another visit to the gym. 'It's gym day tomorrow,' he announced. 'When do we meet?'

In a selfie of his mood, all Ari could see was a willow tree heaped in unremitting despair. He almost told Garrahan that his day had been pre-empted by his need to square his thinking. Yet, in the end, he decided to give the idea a go. 'Eight o'clock,' he replied.

They met early the next morning in the gym itself and after changing into their gym clothes they went straight for a coffee.

'It tastes like cough medicine,' Garrahan moaned after the first sip. But then, in a different tone, he added, 'I must tell you a joke I've just heard.' The good mood he was in had opened the gate to an almost manic loquaciousness. 'A local drives up to a checkpoint in the Northern Irish countryside only to find a masked man pointing a gun at his head. "Catholic or Protestant?" roars the balaclava, in a minacious mid-Ulster brogue. "Jew", says the driver, thinking fast. But the balaclava goes ballistic, hollering at a colleague further up the road. "Jackpot, Mohammed. We've found one!"

The unavoidable could not, however, be indefinitely postponed and soon after, they found themselves lifting weights and running on the treadmill. The Swedish woman Garrahan's eyes were searching for was not there.

'Next time, let's try the swimming pool,' Ari helpfully suggested. Feeling like grass left out for the night, Garrahan just looked at him silently.

When they had finished, they perambulated for a while until their legs took them to the famous Hamidiyah Souq, a shoppers' paradise with the smell of cumin and other delightful essences. Located inside the old walled city of Damascus, the Souq runs the entire length of the wall to the front entrance of the Umayyad Mosque. Countless shops on both sides of the walkway are happily living together with many street vendors hawking their wares. Available for sale is everything one may want, from clothing, rugs and kitchen items to souvenirs, paintings, leather and copper goods, mosaics, spices and teas, artefacts, antiques or sweet desserts. Many shops specialise in various areas – there is a silver market, a wool market or a brides market.

Ari and Garrahan aimlessly walked around, stopping where their curiosity invited them to do so and chatting with the vendors. As opposed to those in other Arab countries, the latter did not hassle them or try to force them to spend their money on their goods. They left them alone to browse the items on display until they were ready to buy.

'It's such a relief to see just friendly faces,' Ari said. 'Their attitude actually tempts me to buy something.' He did just that.

Acting impulsively, he bought an antique 19th century Syrian Ottoman Shamshir Broad with a very large blade and an original, fully matching scabbard. The blade, in fine condition on both sides, was fully covered in Arabic script of very interesting Kufic design. The scabbard was mounted with silver overlaid fittings designed in the same style as the gold script on the blade.

'What are you going to do with it?' asked Garrahan, whose amazement had almost turned him into stone.

'Time will decide,' was the cryptic answer. Ari could not think of a better one. 'Well, it was a bargain,' he rather unconvincingly said later. He was aware that this was a lie. He had bought the sword to bring some succour to his battered soul.

As time for a drink had arrived, they sat down at a bar and ordered a beer. Ari was feeling rather relaxed for a change. The gym, the shopping and the pleasant lassitude of the afternoon idleness to which he had delivered himself had calmed him down. A beer, he hoped, would only contribute further to the refreshment of his mind and might also help to make the afternoon as pleasant as Schubert's Ave Maria. But it was not to be.

Pierro, the Italian journalist, appeared with a big smile on his face. The smile died the moment he made eye contact with Ari because Ari instantly reminded him of Laura.

'How terrible,' he said. 'How brutal, inhumane, vicious their action was. How horrible to lose such a gentle, kind and intelligent woman who was going to be a big star in the media world. I still can't recover from her loss. I'd had tears in my eyes when I heard about it.'

Though the dandified expression of his feelings was only too evident, Pierro looked genuine in his reactions. Ari asked him if he happened to know anything about the circumstances that led to her death. 'No, sorry,' was the answer. 'I wish I did.'

Ari, after introducing him to Garrahan, asked him why he was still in Damascus. 'You said you would only be here for two weeks or so.'

'Yes, I did, but things changed.'

Pierro, in his turn, recalled that Ari had told him that he had been born in Alexandria. 'I thought,' he said, 'that the Greeks had been expelled from Egypt by Nasser ages ago.'

'Oh dear!' was Ari's immediate reaction. 'Now we'll have to talk about Nasser.'

Following the Anglo-French Suez invasion in 1956, many British, French and Jewish people had, indeed, been expelled from the country. Then, in 1957, Nasser introduced the Egyptianisation laws which nationalised British, French and also Greek and Jewish assets, including banks, insurance companies and other commercial property. All foreign companies had to turn into Egyptian-registered ones with majority Egyptian shareholding and Egyptian management.

'That's not exactly true,' he said, responding to Pierro's comment. 'Nasser didn't expel the Greeks. The Greek-Egyptian community was gradually being reduced in size since the 1930s and declined further in the 1950s, but something like fifteen thousand Greeks were still in Egypt after Nasser.' His answer did not, as he had hoped, end the conversation.

Rather than address the waiter, who was unprofitably waiting for his attention, Pierro instead chose to argue with Ari. 'My understanding is that the Greeks were purged from Nasserite Egypt. Their expulsion was a clear-cut case of ethnic cleansing.'

'Sorry, that's not the case,' Ari answered. The tone of his voice, he realized, had unintentionally risen. 'Yes, Greeks were driven away in their thousands. But this was primarily due to their own poor adaptability to Egypt's postcolonial conditions. They just couldn't adjust to the structural changes Nasser had introduced. They had, as a result, lost confidence in their future. Adjustment wasn't possible for another reason, too,' he carried on while placing his glass back onto the table as calmly as he could.

He did not really want to talk about the situation in Egypt more than half a century ago and Pierro's insistence irritated him. But what also irritated him was the topic itself, which had brought back disturbing memories.

'The Greeks never learnt Arabic,' he explained. 'Moreover, they avoided close relations with people outside the narrow circle of their own churches, clubs and societies. Their linguistic and cultural distance from the natives grew even more because of their Hellenic-centric education.'

Pierro listened but the seat he was sitting on did not seem to be as comfortable as before. Garraham, for his part, excused himself as he had to go to the loo. 'Our mother, nature's imperious voice,' he explained. Yet Ari could not stop this time.

'There's one more thing I need to say,' he added. 'Despite their strong sympathies and genuine sense of solidarity towards the Egyptians, their Eurocentric perspective alienated them from the locals. The Egyptians were, unfortunately, perceived in stereotypical terms as a less civilised, potentially fanatical and usually unreliable crowd.'

'Well...' Pierro conceded while trying to be as calm as a summer day. 'This tells us something about the current situation too.'

They both knew that the cultural gap between the westerners and the Arabs, and all it implied, was still one of the most important factors in the ongoing confrontation between the two.

At that point, a woman close to them giggled rather loudly at something her companion had said. Having attracted attention and become rather embarrassed, she fluttered her eyelashes and then clamped a hand over her mouth. Garrahan, who had not missed the occasion, gave her a look full of amiability. She returned the look with a graceful smile of innocence that instantly uplifted Garrahan's spirit.

'And how did you end up speaking Arabic?' Pierro gave his last shot.

'Thanks to my father, Kimon. He was not of the same school of thought.'

Ari and Pierro decided with Garrahan's full-hearted agreement that, as the issue had been thoroughly debated, to settle for a stronger drink. It was served by a woman whose youthful cheerfulness compensated for her obvious lack of experience. They all enjoyed their beer and the playful crowd in front of them. Soon after, they prepared to leave.

It was then that Ari's eye caught a bearded Arab he had seen at the office of the Syrian Minister of Tourism. The man, in his forties, wearing a dark Didashah, the loose, one piece robe, and a three-piece red and white head cover, pretended he was checking the menu, but his eye was chaining him down. This time, Ari felt, there was no mistake. He was definitely being followed. But as anger began to burn inside his chest through the film of apprehension, his phone rang. Mohammad Nofal Yassin, the Palestinian from Yarmouk, was on the line.

'I've promised you,' he said, 'that I would call you if I remember something else from the meeting between the Saudi intelligence man and the Jaysh al-Islam man, on the one hand, and Laura on the other.'

'I'm listening,' Ari responded eagerly.

'I didn't hear, as I said, what they were talking about. Their words were drifting through the door, but they were undeterminable. I did, however, hear the word "killing". It was in connection with someone who had been killed or was to be killed. It looked as if Laura was reacting strongly to what this word related to.'

'Who's been killed?' Ari wondered. 'There was no way of telling as hundreds were being killed daily. Or who might be killed, or, if he were to use a more accurate word, murdered? Again, there was no way of telling. And how did the Jordanians fit into this web of conspiracies that seemed to be enmeshing so many players in what was a very deadly play? Who knows? And what was bringing the Saudis into the picture?'

The mystery seemed unfathomable and his patience had been thinned. He desperately needed to get through this torrent of uncertainties, find a lead, flesh out the story and end his restlessness, ever present like pins and needles in his back and in his head. Even if he wanted to, he could not disenthrall his mind from all this. In the meantime, and as the bearded Arab seemed to be out of sight, another question had started taking root in his thinking.

'Why were the Saudis discussing this Jordanian business with Jaysh al-Islam? The issue was very serious, but it certainly did not primarily concern the Syrian Islamists. It was something to be resolved only between the Jordanian government and the Americans. Or between the Saudis and the Jordanians. Something in all this did not make sense.'

One could, of course, argue that everything made sense except that sometimes, as when looking at Phyllida Barlow's sculptures, it just takes a while to figure out what sense is. Formless shapes dredged up from the unconscious and simultaneously both monstrous and benign can certainly, at least at first glance, look deprived of any sense.

Chapter 18
Conflicting priorities

Before deciding what was the next step in his investigation, Ari was instructed to investigate the situation in Hama, a city 213 km north of Damascus. Jund al-Aqsa, a subunit within Jabhat al-Nusra, was trying to take it over from government forces.

Hama, a stronghold of the Muslim Brotherhood, had a miserable history.

The Brotherhood, a Sunni group with an Islamist ideology, had engaged in a full-scale confrontation with the secular, 'un-Islamic' Ba'athist regime. The war between the two sides had started back in 1964, when the rebels attacked everything the party represented, and continued particularly between 1976 and 1982, when the Brotherhood, together with other Islamist groups, engaged in a long campaign of hit-and-run attacks against government officials and military installations. They also attacked Soviet military and civilian advisers.

One of the most serious attacks occurred in June 1979 when Muslim Brotherhood gunmen killed 50 Alawi cadets at the military academy in Aleppo. Another one, again carried out by the Brotherhood in the densely populated al-Azbakiyah neighbourhood of central Damascus in 1981, had killed more than 200 civilians and military men. Terrorist attacks centred around urban centres such as Damascus, Aleppo, Hama, Homs and the coastal cities of Lattakia and Tartus. In 1980, an attack was also made on the life of president Hafez al-Assad, father of Bashar al-Assad.

The government's response to this campaign of terror was absolutely ruthless. Following the 1982 insurrection in Hama, which housed the headquarters of the Brotherhood, and determined to crash for good the armed Islamist opposition, government forces had laid siege to the city for three-weeks. The town was mercilessly bombarded before the government forces combed the ground and killed all surviving rebels they could find. Casualties were calculated between 3,000 and 30,000.

It was, some claimed after the event, the single bloodiest assault by an Arab ruler against his own people in modern times. Following the crushing of the Hama uprising, the Islamist insurrection was broken and the regime was again in control. The massacre has since been referenced in Syria as the 'events'.

As if this was not bad enough, Hama was again the frontline between government forces and the Islamists every single year since the start of the civil war. The city, where a huge demonstration of people had demanded the departure of Bashar al-Assad in 2011, was attacked by the government's army. Hundreds had reportedly died. The area had since been the target of large scale jihadi attacks which the government had always repelled.

UMRWA was interested in the area because it was home to thousands of Palestinians.

Ari took the trip to the tortured city together with Brigitte, his Belgian colleague. They chatted on the way about the war, their work, the latest films and, while talking about food, they stopped to have some. Brigitte opted for the famous vegetarian falafel sandwich, and Ari went for a fatteh, the typical Damascene dish. It was made up of soaked bread, chickpeas and lamb with the typical garnish of a little pickle and nuts.

While they were eating, Brigitte mentioned her experiences in the hills above the city of Tartus, on the Mediterranean coast. The provincial governor, she said, had unveiled in a village an art fair entitled 'Tartus: Mother of Martyrs' to which 30 commissioned sculptors had contributed pieces of their work, dedicated to Syria's fallen. Most of them included literal representations of mothers, along with local motifs, like Phoenician boats and a phoenix rising from the ashes.

'The unveiling of the statues was attended by hundreds of war-wounded and relatives of soldiers who had died in the conflict. "These people have died so that the others should have life", the governor said.'

'They were the lucky ones,' Ari said. 'They can't die again.'

His tone of voice reflected the feeling of resignation he was experiencing more often as time passed. Those same words were on the lips of millions of people, all those in the midst of the worst disaster in their living memory. They were the words of their despair.

'Interesting,' Ari added. 'The government is determined to burnish the cultural cachet of the families whose children, brothers and fathers have been killed while defending Bashar al-Assad's regime. A similar culture has grown in Iran and in the areas controlled by Hezbollah. But that's how it goes. Endless wars need heroes.'

As he was talking, a golden retriever started barking and Brigitte got up to calm him down. 'My brother,' she said, 'had a similar dog. But he died.'

'I didn't know your brother has died...'

'Not my brother. The dog!'

They were in Hama soon after but Brigitte, in the meantime, had lost her usual energy as the vegetables she had eaten earlier had caused her a stomach upset. They were probably not properly washed. Still, they both collected the information they needed thanks to, among others, a 50-year-old grey-haired general, who dressed in a black sports hat, a brand new Russian camouflage smock – 'a gift from our friends', he called it – and black boots, missed no opportunity to thank 'Abu Ali Putin'. That was the name the Syrian army generals had affectionately given to the Russian President.

An elderly man with thick, callused fingers, ingrained with soil so deeply that it could not be washed away, happened to overhear him. He sucked his cigarette, narrowing his eyes as the smoke stung them, said nothing and then walked away to a small green area to piss.

To remind himself what he should include in his report later on, when he was back at his office, Ari made a handwritten note, which he hoped he would be able to decipher later on. His handwriting was so unreadable that even he himself could not read what he had put down sometimes. 'Just like Marx,' he told himself. While in London, Marx had applied for a job as a railway clerk but was rejected because of his unreadable handwriting.

The note recorded, or at least it intended to, that the Hama people, apart from medicines and food, also needed prosthetics and other assistive devices, including wheelchairs, hearing aids and walking sticks or crutches. The war had created a situation which could never emerge from the womb of even Hollywood's fertile imagination.

Back from Hama, Ari had a free day and rested. The rest helped him to relax, but not to any great extent as images from Hama and other parts of Syria were devilishly lurking in his head. They had all taken permanent residence in it. Tantalisingly, he could not help but think about Laura too, whose agonised death he had involuntarily reconstructed in his head and which would not let him sleep at times.

There was no way he could ever switch off. He acknowledged it and then proceeded to offer himself a piece of advice. 'Be true to yourself, and all will go well.' But would it?

He closed his eyes and again he saw Laura for a moment. She was smiling at him like the spring.

Spending the first half of the day at home, he cooked something as it had been some time since his last meal, had a cup of Ovaltine and then phoned Nibal Bassem Fatime, a senior member of the UNHCR, the UN Refugee Agency, for a chat. They arranged to meet at the latter's office in Kafr Sousa, a neighbourhood in the south-western part of the capital, home to the Syrian Council of Ministers and the Syrian Ministry of Foreign Affairs.

Ari left his flat and, while walking to his motorbike, he came across a young fellow wearing a T-shirt in which he was asking the world 'I'm crazy. What's your excuse?' He wondered for a minute what his was. But maybe he was not crazy. Maybe he was just mad, living in harmony with the madness around him. Survival in his world was after all conditional on the individual's adaptability to madness.

He met Nibal, a Syrian doctor close to retirement, whom he had met before in meetings between representatives of organisations involved in charity work. In the balmy winter the city was enjoying, they went out for a short walk and then sat in one of the nearby bars for a refreshment. A man he had seen before in the street was now inside, barricaded behind a newspaper. Perhaps the man had nothing better to do. 'I shouldn't be getting paranoid,' Ari advised himself.

Nibal was a traditional man wearing the time-honoured keffiyeh. A gold watch fob, his father's, stretched across the front of his waistcoat. It was occasionally being pulled out 'like a bucket from a well'. He ordered an aniseed tea that was served in an elegant glass. Ari ordered an Arabic coffee served in a tiny espresso cup. The doctor told him how tired he was as he had just come back from Lebanon. But the journey, he added, was much easier than before. 'A year and a half ago, one had to go through plumes of smoke, caused by shelling or airstrikes, streamed upwards from rebel-controlled areas to the horizon.'

It was the time that the Syrians expected the war would last forever or that Isis would sooner or later advance to Damascus. But this time there was none of that. The four-lane highway from Damascus to the border,

Ari was told, was well-maintained with army checkpoints, albeit fewer than before, dotted along it. Still, security was not totally guaranteed. Militants and ordinary thugs did periodically come down from the mountains and ambushed isolated cars with trucks or SUVs. Anyone stopped was lucky to get away with their lives and the loss of just their valuables.

When the army was not around, drivers were left with no option but to race from or to the border at high speed. 'No tickets for speeding on this highway,' Nibal joked. But they would stop at the checkpoints as the Lebanese soldiers, just like their Syrian colleagues, were instructed to shoot to kill if a driver failed to stop.

Crossing the border into Lebanon was not always that easy. The Lebanese, already burdened with 1.2 million refugees, were not eager to allow Syrians to enter their country.

'The sure way to get a visa,' Nibal said, 'is to go armed with an air ticket in your pocket to fly out of Beirut.'

'Or perhaps,' Ari thought, 'with enough money for a large bribe.'

Despite all the difficulties, homeless, unemployed, distraught, humiliated or frightened, thousands of Syrians were, however, still taking the risk in what was often a hopeless attempt to escape the undiluted horror of the war. Workplaces across the country had emptied and even the Syrian military was suffering a major manpower shortage.

'So sad,' Ari said. 'And equally sad is the fact that nobody can do anything about it either here or in Europe. Europe has turned its back on the Syrian tragedy. The plight of the refugees, as it has been nonchalantly made clear, is none of its concerns. At least,' Ari finished, adding an optimistic note, 'though life here is most disagreeable, not every Syrian is eager to leave.'

'I wouldn't,' Nibal said emphatically. 'It's a question that comes up time and again when I'm in Beirut. People keep asking me "wouldn't you be happier, safer, more relaxed in Lebanon?" And my answer is always the same. "No, I am going back. Damascus is my city!"'

'It is, indeed,' Ari thought. 'But it wouldn't be the same if Damascus had suffered the fate of its suburbs and your home was in ruins.' But he chose not to say anything.

'But my brother, the architect,' Nibal added, 'has gone. He left the country last year.'

'Where's he gone?'

'Santiago.'

'Why?'

'He couldn't think of anything further away.'

The two of them finished their drinks, wished each other good luck and cordially shook hands. Soon after, Ari phoned Maryam.

'Interested in going to the movies?' he asked.

'I would love to,' she answered with barely hidden enthusiasm.

'Stars Wars: The Force Awakens?'

'Great! It has received a great review by Plato in his Theory of Forms.'

He laughed.

'Your complexion looks a little weathered from your work,' Maryam said, after exchanging hellos. 'It must be very hard.'

He had noticed the same thing himself in the morning while he was shaving. 'It's not easy,' he responded without going into further detail. In doing so, he would have no choice but to express his frustration at the way things were going. And this would certainly spoil the evening. They watched the film in the Cinemacity, which, like all the others, attracted mainly male cinema-goers, and then, watched and graded by many anonymous eyes, they went to its Japanese restaurant for some food.

'For a long and healthy life,' Maryam joked, 'eat olives. We in Syria still say olives for breakfast give you energy all day.'

'I would rather go for the yolk of an egg with a spoonful of rum,' Ari joked.

Maryam laughed and carried on recalling the old times. 'Houses,' she said, 'would wake up to the sweet baking smells of bakeries and patisseries seen in every corner. Food played an important part in life, particularly the delicious desserts – the more syrupy, the better.' She laughed. 'We still enjoy them. People love to gather around a table full of delicious desserts and tell love stories from the past. Desserts are nearly always offered as a present when people visit family or friends.'

'Funny! It's the same in Greece,' Ari said. 'In England, people bring wine.'

He then asked her if being a Christian had given her any problems in a Muslim country.

'I've never had any problems,' Maryam answered. 'Muslims have always been very helpful in every respect. It was a Muslim who helped me to get my current job. Syria is a melting pot of religion and ethnicities. And mixed marriages are palpably and unmistakably commonplace. Things have, of course, changed since the start of the war. Human kindness, a key to a tolerable life, is in rather short supply these days.'

As they walked out of the restaurant, a man Ari did not recognise approached them with a big smile on his face.

'Oh, Mustafa,' Maryam shouted, 'how nice to see you! Mustafa,' she explained to Ari, 'is a Muslim preacher who, together with his wife, fled their home in Aleppo after rebels had burnt down their pharmaceutical factory. They did so, they told him, because his son was in the army.'

'My son was killed last March,' Mustafa added, with great sadness in his eyes. 'But that's something you can only expect. In peace, sons bury their fathers. In war, fathers bury sons.'

'Do you have other children?' Ari asked Mustafa.

'Yes, another son who's with me now. He sells sandwiches outside the university.'

'And you live where?' Ari carried on.

'In a room the local authority has provided. Nice, though its only furniture is a mattress on the floor.'

'Well, at least you're still alive,' Ari said encouragingly. But he was, of course, feeling sorry for the man, another member of an upper middle-class family whose fortune had been destroyed in the war and whose life had been delivered into the hands of such 'God-sponsored' brutality. This made him think of the waiter, a refugee from Idlib, for whom he had left an insufficient tip. As it happened, he did not have enough change.

'How thoughtless of me,' he told himself reprehensively. 'When I'm there again, I'll make amends for my omission.' The commitment positively affected the unpleasant feeling that sat on his face.

Back at the office the next day, he again had to deal with Jaafar, who wanted to know if there was any progress with Ari's enquiries about Laura's murder. He himself appeared convinced that Saudi Arabia, importing weapons and ammunition to fight both the Syrian President and also Shi'ite rebel groups in Yemen, was not averse to giving Isis a bit of help in terms of arms supplies.

'Well, we know that,' Ari responded, a bit irritated as the discussion was once again turning out to be a waste of time. 'Don't we?'

'The same is the case with Turkey,' Jaafar continued, 'as its primary objective is to defeat and contain the Kurds.'

It was the last time Ari saw Jaafar. He was murdered a couple of days later. A note attached to his body read 'That's what happens to police informers'.

Ari was once again shocked at the turn of the events. Life, as he was experiencing it, seemed determined to vindicate the claims of the unexpected. Anything, no matter how many light years away it was from the limits of sober probability, was only just around the corner. Rather depressed, he could only see a future taking them to the ultimate frontiers of darkness. 'Perhaps,' he thought, 'there is no such a thing as the future. The future is nothing but an illusion.' But he would not give up his enquiries into Laura's death.

Except, as he discovered, he could not once again carry on with it, at least for a while. His life was a jumble of conflicting priorities.

Chapter 19
A past without a future

T
hree of the UNRWA staff, all Syrians, taken by militants in Aleppo, had all ended up in al-Raqqah, the capital of the Isis caliphate. Calls that Richard Samuels, Ari's boss, had made to the Isis headquarters demanding their release had produced no results. They were captured, he was told, because they were engaged in spying for the regime.

What Samuels had nevertheless been given to understand during these calls was that their release was negotiable in exchange for a number of Isis prisoners held by the Bashar al-Assad forces in the outskirts of Aleppo. Samuels, a man clothed in a humility which concealed his brilliance from those who did not know him, asked Ari if he would be willing to mediate between the two sides by going to al-Raqqah.

'But how do you know they're being held in Al-Raqqah? Ari asked him.

'I just do,' was the answer. 'Surveillance systems tapping into global communications networks and hoovering up data have told us so. By "us", I of course mean London which has passed on the information to us.'

'And by "London", you mean GCHQ, the Cheltenham-based spy agency, and its peers, MI6 and MI5?'

'Yes.'

'Whose eavesdropping practises and interception of personal data sets has been denounced as too intrusive?'

'Yes,' Samuels said again, but this time with a smile which could be interpreted in many different ways.

'I'm very impressed,' Ari said. 'What they can do these days…'

Still on the same subject, he asked Samuels whether he was in Damascus when an Isis man from New Zealand had inadvertently revealed his precise location by posting geotagged tweets.

'What?' asked Samuels.

'I read about it in *Time* magazine,' Ari said. 'The man, I don't remember his name, had tweeted, posting a picture of his burned passport, that his mission to Syria was a "one-way trip". An intelligence group used the tweet geo-location information to place the man in a specific house in a Syrian town. When he realised that he was geotagged with his precise coordinates, he deleted all the 45 tweets.'

'They'll soon know what we do in our bedrooms, too,' said Samuels.

'They do already,' Ari answered. 'Their eyes and ears are everywhere, from our smartphones, TV sets and air conditioners to our cameras, refrigerators and Wifi-enabled toys.'

They dropped the subject and again focused on the nature of the mission Samuels was talking about.

Ari was of two minds. On the one hand, his boss' confidence in his skills and ability to do such a demanding job thrilled every fibre of his body. In his short career at UNRWA, he had been given some very demanding tasks, but nothing of this magnitude had crossed his path before. The idea of crossing the doorway to al-Raqqah's hostile infinity was nevertheless a nightmare. Al-Raqqah, everybody would tell him, had to be avoided at all costs.

This city, on the north bank of the Euphrates River, had initially been controlled by the Free Syrian Army. Overwhelmed by Isis in 2013, it was given a choice: to join Isis or face death. When that occurred, Ari was told by Salem al-Meslet, an arms dealer who had survived the onslaught, a ghastly and hair-raising development had followed.

'First,' al-Meslet said, 'Isis killed the soldiers. Then it killed civilians. The jihadis chopped off heads and put them beside the roads and the main square. They executed women as well as men. Videos of deaths and beheadings were broadcast in every square in which even imams, mostly Saudis or Egyptians, were carrying Kalashnikovs and wearing a loaded suicide belt.'

'I'm sure the videos have left a very favourable impression on them,' Ari said.

'These spiritual nonentities…They loved them.'

Most of the Isis fighters in al-Raqqah, al-Meslet added, were foreigners: Tunisians, Saudis, Jordanians, Egyptians, Moroccans, Turkish, Afghans but also Russians, French and British. Other foreign fighters from Uzbekistan, Tajikistan, Chechnya or Daghestan had burrowed themselves in northern Syria, mainly around Aleppo and Idlib. They were all fighting against the government, but they were also often doggedly engaged in infighting between themselves.

This made Ari wonder whether defeating Isis militarily in Syria would solve the problem the world had to deal with.

To begin with, the end of Isis through aerial bombardment could not be taken for granted. Some were actually arguing that it was helping it, instead, by recruiting for it more and more young people from all over the world. But even if Isis was defeated, at least another fifteen rebel forces in Syria were ready to succeed it. And even if it was expelled from the areas it occupied, the problems behind its emergence, not only in Iraq and Syria, but also in Egypt, Libya, Yemen, Saudi Arabia or even the Ivory Coast or the Caucasus region would remain.

The fact was that, following the western interventions in Iraq, Libya and Syria, the corrupt and brutal regimes of the area had either ended up in chaos and sectarian and tribal upheaval as in Iraq, Syria, Libya and Yemen or descended into their old degenerate selves as in Egypt or Tunisia.

'Belief systems,' Ari thought, 'cannot be bombed. They were, as was the case here, deeply rooted in the psyche of the jihadis, who, whatever the outcome of a battle, saw themselves as the winners. If they killed you, they had won the battle. If they got killed, they would go to heaven.' The story of a frustrated would-be suicide bomber Ari had heard illustrated the point. Bewitched by his naivety, he screamed at his captors:

'I was just ten minutes away from being united with the Prophet Muhammad!'

'Some people,' Ari thought, 'think they are born posthumously. But, I wonder, would the suicide bomber be screaming again, at his own funeral this time, for all the wrong assumptions he had made when still alive? Who knows? Perhaps yes, if death makes you wiser.'

He remembered he had told the story to Garrahan as soon as he had heard it. Dismayed at the mind-numbing flood of developments, Garrahan could only ask, sarcastically, if the would-be suicide bomber had taken out travel insurance for his astral trip. 'What else can you possibly say,' he added with a voice coloured by frustration.

His train of thought, he realised, had been derailed again. He realised it when he was told that somebody who called himself Gottfried Schwegler was waiting to speak to him on the phone.

'I'm a Swiss lawyer,' the man said, 'and work for a big Swiss legal firm. I'm authorised to make a contribution towards the welfare of the

Palestinian refugees in Syria. The funds available have been bequeathed to these people by an individual, a woman who died in Lausanne three weeks ago. I need your advice.'

'Fantastic,' Ari said, although unsure as to what exactly was going on. But the Agency was underfunded and the offer seemed promising.

'Do you have anything in particular in mind?' he asked with a voice intentionally nonchalant.

'I'm looking forward to your suggestions,' the man replied.

'OK. Come over. I'm happy to discuss matters with you.'

Schwegler, a middle-aged Swiss lawyer who looked exactly like a Swiss lawyer, appeared soon after in UNRWA's office. He accepted a coffee and, while enjoying it unhurriedly, started asking questions relating to the needs of the Palestinian population and the organisation's work in the field.

'We provide basic services and humanitarian assistance to the 450,000 Palestine refugees who are still in Syria,' Ari said. 'They live through one of the worst humanitarian crises in decades. When we can, we help them with food parcels, blankets, medical support, hygiene kits, sanitary items, schooling, cash assistance. But we can't reach many areas at all. The severe escalation of violence in Yarmouk last April, for example, compounded the extreme hardships of civilians trapped there with the suspension of the Agency's access to the area.'

'How exactly do you operate?'

'The Agency,' Ari responded, 'operates and provides services via 12 community-based organizations. But let me check to give you the exact details.'

He got up and picked up a big yellow file from the shelves with lots of documents in it.

'Oh yes, here we are. We have 12 food distribution centres, 15 health centres, 11 health points, 44 UNRWA schools, 55 non-UNRWA schools, 11 UNRWA shelters, 2 UNRWA-supported shelters, 21 recreational spaces, and 8 safe-learning spaces supervised by teaching staff and psychosocial support counsellors to provide protected spaces where refugee children can learn and play. The safe-learning spaces provide educational support to 3,114 female and 2,411 male students.'

'Quite impressive,' the Swiss lawyer said.

'Do you want more details? You want me to carry on?' Ari asked.

'Yes, please do.'

'In cooperation with WHO,' Ari continued, 'UNRWA vaccinated 2,237 children with the first dose of oral polio vaccine in 2015. More than 12,000 refugees were also reached in polio awareness campaigns. UNRWA further developed and implemented frequent nationwide hygiene awareness campaigns to reduce the risks of communicable disease outbreaks, particularly those related to poor access to water and sanitation.'

'OK. I get the picture,' Schwegler said.

It was then Ari's turn to ask the question that would determine the weight of his conversation with the Swiss lawyer. 'What kind of contribution do you have in mind?'

'About ten million dollars,' was the answer.

'Wow,' was Ari's reaction.

At that point, he excused himself and went to see Samuels, his boss, who invited both Schwegler and Ari to his office for some more discussion. At the end, Ari asked Schwegler if he would be interested in going for dinner somewhere in the Old City. Schwegler agreed.

The Swiss lawyer was collected from his hotel at 8.00 o'clock in the evening, and they both started walking to Leila's Restaurant. Once there, they were taken straight to its rooftop seating area, known for its great views of the Umayyad Mosque. They could still see it. The night had not yet rendered it invisible.

'This is a great place,' Schwegler said. 'Well chosen.'

He then lapsed into silence while adjusting and re-adjusting his glasses on his nose. In front of him, there was an English version of the menu, but he could not work out what the various dishes were. 'Bloody difficult,' he said at the end in an almost frosty tone. 'I can't make sense of it at all.'

With Ari's help, he eventually ordered a traditional Arabic meal together with some wine. As soon as this was done, Ari excused himself to visit the WC and, in doing so, he bumped into a white-haired man. They apologised to each other. The man had the accent of someone who had grown up in the sunset zone.

'American?' Ari asked him.

'Yes. From Buffalo, New York.'

'Long time here?'

'Forty years or so.'

'You must love the city,' Ari said.

'Very much so,' said the American, who identified himself as Thomas. 'Just look around you,' he added, gesturing around. 'There's no other place like this in the world.'

'And you're not afraid.'

'My government has repeatedly warned me that I may be kidnapped. But I feel extremely safe. Proof of it is that I still haven't been kidnapped! By the way,' he added, 'the Syrian people are not terrorists. They are the most honest, down-to-earth, loving people in the world.'

'Nice to hear that,' Ari said on his way back to the Swiss lawyer. 'And nice meeting you.'

'Funny,' Schwegler remarked. 'Wine is not on the menu, but you can get it if you just ask the waiter.'

'They don't want to be bombed by the jihadis,' Ari joked in reply.

As the Swiss lawyer was not exactly a deipnosophist, he confined his response to a few words. 'I hope,' he said, 'we'll see the end of their reign quite soon.'

'We might,' Ari responded, rather unconvincingly. 'It's amazing,' he then added as if he were speaking to himself, 'how much the Islamists' power has advanced over just a few years. But the men in black didn't appear out of the blue.'

'No?' Schwegler said, not sure what Ari was talking about.

'I mean they've been coming for years, and they've been coming with our help.'

'What do you mean?' the Swiss lawyer, still not understanding what Ari was saying, asked again.

'Well, where shall I begin? Perhaps with the beginning,' Ari replied. 'It all started back in 1979, after the Soviet invasion and the subsequent ten years occupation of Afghanistan. And nobody seemed to have a clue what it was all leading to. Funded by Saudi Arabians, Osama Bin Laden's mainly Islamist Afghan mujahedeen guerrillas networked with jihadi groups in Pakistan and elsewhere. They did also attract some 35,000 volunteers who, thinking there's not much else to do between birth and death, flocked to their training camps from around the world. They joined what al-Qaeda itself called "the first real jihad". In no time, Al-Qaeda turned into the dominant force.'

'Yes, of course, Osama Bin Laden,' was Schwegler's response.

'In this, and as long as the enemy was the Soviets,' Ari continued, 'the jihadis had the active support of president Ronald Reagan. He passed onto them hundreds of millions of dollars and helped to turn Afghanistan into the Soviet Union's Vietnam. Reagan was very proud of it. But in the process, he'd miserably failed to notice that he had also helped al-Qaeda to emerge as a vehicle for a wider global jihad with the United States as its prime target. It all underlined the CIA's dismal performance ever since, which is not going to disappear into the mists of history.'

'Yes,' Schwegler said. 'The US' top priority at the time was to defeat the Soviets.'

'Correct,' Ari answered, 'but with Islamist, not American troops on the front line. The consequence was the 9/11 attack. The thousands of fighters trained in Afghanistan,' Ari continued, 'became the torch-bearers of jihad in the rest of the world. But the formative Afghan experience had also provided the Islamic terrorists the combat-hardened jihadi leaders and the strategists who were to play an instrumental role in the emergence of the Isis of today. One of the latter,' Ari carried on, 'was the Jordanian jihadi Abu Musab al-Zarqawi, who ended up being the direct parent of Isis in almost every way.'

'I'm not familiar with their names,' Schwegler penitently explained. 'They are next to impossible to pronounce.'

Ari had another sip of wine. He needed it as the story was too harrowing. That was obvious even to the woman at the next table who, as he realised at that point, was staring at both of them with eyes full of curiosity. She was probably wondering how people could be engaged in what was obviously a serious discussion in a place like this, a place you come to have a care-free time?

When she realised that Ari was looking at her, she pretended to look for the waiter just as she probably had done in the past, when men were glancing at her, even briefly.

'So, is this how Isis was formed?' Schwegler asked.

'I'll tell you, but it involves a lot of detail,' Ari said. 'I once tried to tell the story to someone who asked me the same question only to hear at the end that I was clogging his brain with useless information.'

'OK. Go ahead,' was Schwegler's response. He did not seem disoriented by the verbal bombardment he was being subjected to. He genuinely seemed interested in the story.

'Al-Zarqawi, the one I mentioned earlier,' Ari carried on, 'like many others, had spent the 1990s in Afghanistan. There he connected, among others, with Abu Abdullah al-Muhajir, the ideologue whose writings provided religious cover for the most brutal excesses, including the killing of both Shi'a "infidels" and Sunni "apostates". "The brutality of beheading is intended. It pleases God and His Prophet", al-Muhajir wrote. He had obviously forgotten he was human and he should, as such, have no connection with such a God. Al-Zarqawi was also influenced by the Islamist strategist Abu Bakr Naji, whose book, *The Management of Savagery,* instructed al-Qaeda to resort to massacres in order to create a new Islamic caliphate.'

'Religion for the insane,' Schwegler exclaimed.

'Madness gone mad,' Ari replied. 'They love to collect groups of dead bodies as much as a stamp collector loves to collect new sets of stamps.'

'Following the 9/11 attacks, the US and its allies changed their policy towards the jihadis and bombed and invaded Afghanistan. It also launched a wider "War on Terror" against al-Qaeda. The latter's power in Afghanistan started to diminish rapidly. But at the same time, the ongoing US drone campaigns radicalised segments of the local population in Pakistan and turned the lawless border between the two countries into a breeding ground for terrorist activity.

'Osama Bid Laden urgently needed another battlefield, and the US provided it in 2003 with the invasion of Iraq. The invasion had been made necessary, president George W Bush and prime minister Tony Blair claimed, on account of both Iraq's production of weapons of mass destruction and its support for international terrorists.

'Of course, it was all a fabrication.'

'Indeed,' Schwegler agreed. 'A mountain of lies.'

'But it was also a huge mistake, the greatest strategic screw-up since Hitler's invasion of Russia, as someone has said. It released the country's sectarian demons. Together with all the other mistakes made in the pursuit of the West's interfering policy in the Middle East, it dramatically destabilised the region, produced millions of deaths and refugees and led to the development of international terrorism. The jihadis had virtually no presence in Iraq prior to the invasion.'

Meanwhile, he was watching to see if there were any signs of impatience on Schwegler's part such as shifting his legs, examining the faces of people moving around or raising trivial issues such as the size of their napkins. So far there was none. Schwegler, Ari thought, did not need any lessons in patience.

'So, what led to the emergence of the jihadis in Iraq?' the Swiss lawyer asked.

'The invaders toppled Sadam Hussein,' Ari said, 'but they also thoughtlessly destroyed Iraq's security structure and dissolved its army. Critically, they also disempowered the Sunnis, who under Saddam's tightly-controlled Ba'ath Party regime, enjoyed pride of place over the majority Shi'a. The Sunnis were enraged under the circumstances and, following the Americans' withdrawal from Iraq in 2011, they revolted. The state of "savagery" that Abu Bakr Naji had envisaged had been created.

'Abu Musab Zarqawi moved in. Soon after, he was organising deadly, brutal and provocative attacks primarily aimed at the Shi'ite majority, plunging Iraq into all-out civil war. Bin Laden urged him to stop the bloodshed against the Shi'ites and focus on the far enemy, the Americans. He was ignored.'

At that point, a smiling man brought them the main course: a kebab karaz made with lamb meatballs, cherries, pine nuts and pomegranate molasses for Ari and a kebab khashkhash made with rolled lamb with chilli pepper, parsley, garlic and pine nuts for Schwegler.

'Delicious,' he almost screamed.

Ari agreed with a smiling nod.

Excluding minor remarks about the lighting in the restaurant, the endearingly unpolished face of a young woman who took a seat close to them, and the city's traffic jams, they both enjoyed the food and the wine amid long spaces of silence. Not focusing on their dinner would practically be a sin that neither of them were prepared to commit.

But as soon as they had finished and were ready to carry on with the story, Ari seemed to have momentarily lost his train of thought. 'Where were we?' he asked. 'Oh yes, we were talking about Zarqawi. Zarqawi at first refused to pledge allegiance to Osama Bin Laden but changed his mind later on. His group became the official al-Qaeda branch in Iraq. The two men, however, were never on the same page. Bin Laden wanted al-Qaeda to focus on U.S. targets while Zarqawi emphasized sectarian war and attacks on both Shi'ite and Sunni apostates against whom his troops acted with incredible brutality. Bin Laden was dead against it and, from his point of view, rightly so because Zarqawi's tactics alienated the Muslims.'

'So,' hazarding a guess, Schwegler said, 'they split.'

'Not exactly,' Ari said. 'There was no split. In the meantime, the Al Qaeda indiscriminate violence in Iraq had led to a backlash from the Sunni tribes, which badly hit Zarqawi's group. The crisis it faced accelerated after his death in 2006 from a U.S. air strike. New leader of Al-Qaeda in Iraq became the man known by his nom de guerre, Abu Bakr al-Baghdadi.

'Baghdadi, together with 20,000 Iraqi inmates, had been detained by the Americans in Iraq's Bucca concentration Camp for years until his release. Though a jihadi by trade, the Americans had let him go because he was judged to be a low-risk fighter. Perhaps, they thought so,' Ari added, 'because he was not only a keen football fan, but he had also created a soccer team for mosque regulars in his youth. "I'm Iraq's Maradona" he had joked.'

'In different circumstances, we would only laugh at it,' Schwegler suggested.

'But then the Syrian crisis began. And Al-Baghdadi,' Ari continued, 'moved his operations from Iraq to Syria where he joined the rebellion against Bashar al-Assad. Soon after, in April 2013, he announced the merger of his forces in Iraq and Syria and, out-bin Landening Osama bin Laden, he proclaimed the creation of the "Islamic State in Iraq and the Levant" (Isis). Ayman al-Zawahiri, leader of both al-Qaeda and Jabhat al-Nusra, its Syrian spinoff, and a man who lacked Osama bin Laden's charisma, rejected the move.

'As a result, Isis and Jabhat al-Nusra ended up at each other's throats. Hundreds were killed in vicious internecine clashes, which ended with Isis being driven out of most of north-west Syria by Jabhat al-Nusra and allied Syrian rebel factions. But Isis took over al-Raqqah, a provincial city in the north-east, and made it its capital. Many of the foreign jihadi groups who had joined Jabhat al-Nusra then joined Isis. It looked to them a tougher and more radical proposition.'

By that time, Ari and Schwegler had eaten their dessert, a chocolate muhallabia each, and set out for the road. Though summer was some way behind them, the evening was quite pleasant. Trees and grasses, still unambiguously green, had, however, an exhausted air. They had run out of summer days.

'What a beautiful evening,' Ari said before continuing with the story. Its conclusion seemed to be only a few blocks away.

'Taking advantage of the Sunni anger against the government the Americans had put into place in Iraq, Isis, aided by former Saddam Hussein loyalists, swept through Iraq's cities and villages with bewildering speed. Of particular importance here was the capture of Mosul. It gave the jihadis the opportunity to ridicule the American rose-tinted multibillion-backed claim that they had rebuilt the Iraqi army. It also enabled them to grab the Iraqi forces' sophisticated American weapons, a part of which was diverted to their Syrian headquarters in al-Raqqah. But it also empowered them to steal the show from al-Qaeda central and take over the leadership of the global jihadi movement.

'Following the capture of Mosul, the jihadis then moved swiftly down the Tigris river valley and seized other towns as well, including Tikrit, Saddam Hussein's old hometown. Thousands of Iraqi military recruits in the big military base on Tikrit's outskirts surrendered to Isis. 1,700 of them, all Shi'ites, were shot dead. Videos and pictures showing their execution by black-clad Islamists were posted by Isis itself on the internet.'

'Good Lord,' was all Schwegler could say in the face of such shocking and bloodthirsty jihadi exhibitionism.

'Al-Qaeda, meanwhile, had shifted the emphasis to targeting military and security targets instead of public markets or mosques. Befriending local communities instead of attacking them, it also got involved in trucking and delivering gas, bread, water and other staple food supplies to the civilian population.'

"Well, a snake is a snake, wherever it lays its eggs,' was the Swiss lawyer's unexpected response.

'Soon after, on the 29th of June 2014,' Ari carried on, 'the Islamists proclaimed the establishment of a "caliphate" – a state governed in accordance with Islamic law, or Sharia, by God's deputy on Earth, or caliph. Abu Bakr al-Baghdadi, the fountain of all wisdom, was declared the caliph and "leader for Muslims everywhere". His staggering move, of huge significance and resonance within Islam and an act of extraordinary ambition, took many by surprise. A caliph is supposed to be the successor of the Prophet Muhammad and the one destined to lead the caliphate to the land of glory.'

'Quite a lot of history must be behind it all,' Schwegler assumed.

'Yes, of course,' Ari answered. 'Striving for the leadership of global jihadism,' he then carried on, 'Abu Bakr al-Baghdadi was claiming nothing less than the mantle of the Prophet and of his successors who carried Islam into vast new realms of conquest and expansion. Inspired, thousands more foreign fighters flocked to Syria and Iraq to join the fight. Al-Qaeda was marginalized.'

'So, in the space of just a few months,' Schwegler interrupted him, 'Isis had blasted its way from obscurity to the centre of the world stage.'

'In doing so,' Ari carried on, 'it had also torn to pieces the Sykes-Picot agreement which Abu Bakr al-Baghdadi had vowed to terminate – "we'll not stop", he said, "until we hit the last nail in the coffin of the Sykes–Picot conspiracy". His "we" incidentally only meant "I". And, indeed, the geopolitical structure of the Middle East, particularly in Syria and Iraq, is not what it used to be. Frontiers in this part of the world are essentially defenceless today. Or they don't seem to matter.

'But the mass killings of Yazidis in 2014 and the Isis attack on the Kurdish capital eventually triggered the US air strikes that were joined by fourteen other nations. In September last year, after Isis had besieged the Kurdish-held town of Kobane on the Turkish border, the US-led air campaign was extended to Syria. Meanwhile, the jihadis had been advancing southwards towards Baghdad, massacring their adversaries and threatening to eradicate the country's many ethnic and religious minorities. Mankind's slaughter was always made in the name of God.

'At the same time, the grotesque outgrowth of Sunni rage was metastasising to other parts of the Arab world. The jihadis in Libya pledged allegiance to Baghdadi – we've heard of their arrival last February, when they carved out an enclave along the 200km of Libyan central coastline. It was on one of its beaches, if you remember, that armed with the moral sense of a wolf, they beheaded a group of 21 bewildered Egyptian Christian workers in orange jumpsuits. In the promotional video Isis produced, the blood of the victims was mingling with the waters of the Mediterranean.'

'Prime-time entertainment,' Schwegler interposed sarcastically. 'Moments of suculent beauty…'

'Allegiance to Baghdadi,' Ari carried on, 'was also pledged by the Ansar Beit al-Maqdis jihadi faction in Egypt's Sinai. Meanwhile, Isis's tentacles spread deeper into Africa in March 2015 when Boko Haram in Nigeria took the oath of loyalty to him. Similar developments occurred in other dysfunctional states – Yemen, Pakistan, Somalia, Mali or Afghanistan.

'In the latter country, which the Americans had "liberated" not all that long ago, Isis had already created a force that numbered several thousand fighters linked to the jihadis in Iraq and Syria. They incidentally stood in opposition to the thousands of Taliban rebels.'

'Unbelievable,' Schwegler murmured, as if talking to himself. He was so shocked that the few words he offered in addition seemed to tremble on the verge of incoherence. In any case, they could hardly be heard as a woman's dog very close to them had suddenly started barking for no apparent reason. It must have done so, Ari decided, as a matter of principle.

'Horrified, the US and its allies, particularly Britain and France, who Barak Obama, the US President had hinted, had in the case of Libya been asleep on the wheel, were completely powerless to halt Isis' advances. Sirte, the Mediterranean town where Muammar Gaddafi, the dictator, was born and died, turned into an urban stronghold to rival Mosul in Iraq and the Syrian city al-Raqqah. This, in turn, contributed to the rise of well-armed criminal and militant groups and fuelled conflicts in Tunisia, Algeria, Niger, Chad, Sudan and Egypt.'

Both tired, Ari and Schwegler decided at that point to make a move to their beds. It was already quite late. Schwegler thanked Ari for all the information he had so generously shared with him and then walked to the Beit Al-Mamlouka hotel, a luxurious 17th century building in the city's Christian quarter.

Ari was on his motorbike. His mouth was exhausted from the two hours of talking, but he was deeply impressed by Schwegler's interest in the details of such a complicated story.

'I'm sure,' he thought, 'he won't remember half of it tomorrow. But he'll at least be clearer about one or two things.'

Chapter 20
Beyond the known boundaries

The next day, after a good night's sleep, Ari called the building contractor that the Public Works Ministry had recommended to find out what ten million dollars could build. He needed to give Schwegler some sort of an estimate.

'Quite a lot,' the man – Sayid was his name – responded. 'But I'll tell you what. Give me the job and you can have ten percent of it, one million dollars, in your bank within 24 hours.'

Ari was flabbergasted. For a minute, his ears, uncertain as to what had been said, refused to accept it. 'You'll pay me to give you the job?' he asked, with incredulity only too evident in his voice. Perhaps he had just misheard him.

'One million. And nobody will know.'

'You disgust me...' Ari angrily belaboured him. 'You're a disgrace. People in your country starve to death, and all you're interested in is profiting from their tragedy. Aren't you ashamed of yourself? Don't you have any kind of humanity in you? Don't you...?'

He did not manage to say anything more as Sayid, immune to shame, cut him short, but only to repeat his offer. 'One million dollars. Think about it and when you're ready, we can discuss matters again.' He then hung up.

Ari needed time to recover from the shock caused by the moral numbness of the man and his refusal to acknowledge any responsibility towards his fellow countrymen. People for him were nothing more than a commodity. The man had the moral sense of a cat. He served himself a generous dose of the brown liquid produced by his coffee maker and, with the mug in his hand, he addressed the others close to him.

'Would you believe it? I asked the building contractor recommended to me by the Ministry of Public Works what he could build with ten million dollars and he instantly tried to bribe me to give him the job. I can't believe it. The bastard.'

Mohammad Chehade, his colleague, looked at him and burst into laughter. 'Oh,' he said sarcastically, 'the poor man must have accidentally mislaid his moral compass.' Amazed at Ari's moral outburst, he carried on and asked him why he could not believe it. 'I thought you were familiar with our culture. This is the way things are done in our part of the world. Don't tell me you didn't know...'

Ari collapsed into a chair. It really was all too much. Chehade was right, and Ari knew it. What he had come up against was not something unexpected. It was an everyday occurrence, backed up by the thriving Arab culture of corruption to which the contractor's greasy hands were now so generously contributing. Why was he so surprised? Certainly by the crudity of the 'offer' made without any artful subterfuges and the emotional ruthlessness of the contractor. And upset? Because of all it symbolised. Moral anaesthesia.

The building contractor was not an individual lost in his own schemes. Having internalised old attitudes through growing up with them, he was the representative of a world from which he refused to move away. He was deeply attached to his Ottoman roots. The requirements of decency were beyond his reach.

'You're right,' he told Chehade a minute later. 'This is something one can only take for granted.'

He moved his arms up and down like a pelican folding its wings and, without another word, he moved back to his office. But the issue was still burning inside him. He recalled Aristotle. 'The moral virtues,' the ancient philosopher said, 'are engendered in us neither by nor contrary to nature. We are constituted by nature to receive them, but their development in us is due to habit.'

'Yes,' he decided, 'it's as he said. Except that what we've habitually learnt to cultivate is our deficiencies and failings. We've got principles, yes, and values and ideals. But principles are unprofitable and as such unsuitable. We're, therefore, not grounded in them. Our roots are, instead, in habits, the bad habits dictated by expediency. Expediency is in fact the only principle we adhere to.'

Tartuffe, Moliere's hypocrite, also came to mind. 'I'm obedient to God,' he said, 'whenever it's expedient'. He was obviously blind to what missuited him.

'But such an attitude is based on habit, and habits are unfortunately deeply engrained, and also loyal to us. As loyal as the habit of getting up in the morning.'

Regardless of his other priorities, the labyrinth of thoughts he seemed to have settled in was not easy to escape from. 'This can't be that true,' he told himself having again re-adjusted his thinking. 'The world is not only inhabited by wicked people. Many people, people I know, would always act decently whatever the circumstances. Their poverty is proof of it,' his cynical self added. 'But we don't hear from them. Why? Because the agenda is set by the slimy, the vile and the vicious.'

'Not a very uplifting thought!' he muttered. 'But all you have to do is get used to it! Incurable optimism doesn't take you anywhere!' He almost felt like giving up. You just cannot cope with people emancipated from every value. 'Perhaps,' he told himself, 'things would be a lot easier if I didn't care as much as I do.' He had heard himself talking like this time and again. There was no point wasting his energy. He could do nothing to change the world.

'Nobody gives a toss.' But that was not really him and he knew it.

'You carry on,' he told himself, 'even if you know you can never win. You don't do it for the world. You only do it for your own sake. Don't give up. Just don't give up! Anyway,' he reminded himself, "the world turns and the world changes, but one thing does not change: the perpetual struggle of Good and Evil".' They were not his, but T. S. Eliot's words.

'No, I won't give up,' he said almost loudly, having emerged from his somnambulatory abstraction. The speaker was now his sense of self-respect, dignity and pride, all in tune with his system's cadence.

'Yes, absolutely,' another voice told him. 'But stop manning the barricades of civilisation for a while and instead see what he wants.' 'He' was Cole, whose call he had not yet returned.

Putting his philosophical woefulness aside, he picked up the receiver and called his number. He could not get through. Cole, as he told him later, had turned up the music in his iPod's headphones so much that only a suicide bomber in his flat could penetrate the bubble he was in. Ari eventually managed to get through. All Cole happily wanted was to meet in town for a drink.

They did meet later, when the day had crossed the horizon line, in a bar. Among other things, they discussed the offer of help made by the Swiss lawyer, which was still in the air. He needed, Schwegler had told Ari, to discuss matters with his board of directors. Ari also mentioned the building contractor's attempt to bribe him, focusing now on his own very negative emotional reaction to it.

'It made me feel like giving up for just a moment. Reality, bent on its own business, makes no room for hope. Or, even worse, it has outlawed it.'

'Oh well, don't worry,' Cole responded. 'If there's conscience, there's hope. And you better not forget this. Anyway,' he said, adding what he probably thought was a helpful lie, 'nothing is beyond the limits of our strength.'

'Bullshit!' Ari thought. But he did not say it. He assured him instead that he was right. But he was not feeling any better, something that his wan expression could only confirm. If it were to become agreeable, reality would have to be reinvented.

The discussion then turned to the current situation. 'I wonder,' Cole said, 'if the end of the war is any nearer.'

'Perhaps it is,' Ari said sceptically. 'The strikes by the Russian and coalition air forces may end up forcing the jihadis out of Syria. The price they're paying is heavy: they've reportedly lost around 2,500 fighters just in the last few weeks and 15,000 since the air strikes began in August 2014 in both Syria and Iraq. But with a population of perhaps 10 million acquiescent Sunnis to draw on in Iraq and Syria, recruiting is not much of a problem.'

'It's quite alarming,' Cole reflected. 'More so,' he carried on, 'because Isis doesn't not exist just in Syria and Iraq. It has major constituency supporters in almost all Arab countries, including Saudi Arabia, Kuwait, Lebanon and Jordan, and in several Western countries. Even if the caliphate is gone, the war is bound to continue with attacks on targets all over the world. Battles against the jihadis might well be won here or there, but defeating Isis militarily would not end the global jihad.'

'You're right,' Ari agreed with him. 'The war is primarily ideological which means that what has to be defeated is the jihadis' pernicious ideology. If not, new generations of young militants are bound to make their presence felt for a long time to come.'

By this time, they had emptied their glasses and wondered whether they should go for another round.

'And who's going to fight this ideological battle on humanity's behalf?' Cole asked ironically, before the decision to go for another drink or not had been made. He did not expect an answer.

'Well, not the West, unless you think capitalism can do the job. After all, consumerism is another religion, capable of dissolving in its melting pot all other religions. But the West itself can't see any other picture apart from that which its own strategic and commercial interests dictate. And certainly not the Russians, who are only concerned with their strategic interests in the Mediterranean. The battle has to be won by their moderate co-religionists in the first place.'

'So you think that the moderate Muslims will protect mankind against itself?' Cole asked. The optimist in Ari oozed away at his friend's question, asked with such a generous dose of incredulity. The air was instantly filled with feelings of despondency.

'Let's talk about something else,' Ari suggested, as his mind flew apace to the words of Antonio Gramsci, the Italian Marxist theorist: 'I'm a pessimist because of intelligence, but an optimist because of will.'

'What?' asked Cole.

'Another drink?'

'Sure.'

They ordered the drinks and Ari then asked Cole if their current life affected his sleep. All he wanted was to change the focus of the conversation to something more digestible by asking this question. The jovial triviality of the moment did, however, disappear the moment Cole opened his mouth.

'I have a recurrent dream which seizes me during the wee hours of the morning.'

'What's that?' Ari asked.

'A recurrent dream,' Cole answered, 'is a dream that comes frequently and repetitively.'

'No, for God's sake,' Ari said. 'I know what a recurrent dream is. What's your recurrent dream?'

'I've been constantly dreaming of going through my bedroom mirror to find myself back home on a specific day, the 10th of June, 1996. I was just ten years old then. Being back in time, I knew what had happened between then and now. I knew, in other words, what life had in store for the people I knew and loved.

'In my dream, I'm trying to persuade one of my mum's friends, a married woman, who, I remember, had an inappropriate dalliance with one of her colleagues, not to go to work on that day. She was, by the way, an actress participating in the making of a film. Knowing that she was going to be in a very bad, deadly accident, I urged her as strongly as I could not go to work. But she wouldn't listen.

'In the film, she was on her way to a business meeting in the sports car she was provided with on that day. At some point, she went to light a cigarette while rolling down the window. In doing so, she was unaware of the leaking bottle of hair bleach containing hydrogen peroxide that was in the door of her car. This stuff is a highly inflammable material used for creating peroxide-based explosives like the ones used in the 2005 London bombings. The combination of it and her lighter's flame instantaneously turned her car into a fireball.

'Screaming, she was burnt alive while nobody close to her could do anything to help. The car burnt to a shell and she was identified from her dental records.

'I keep dreaming the same dream time and again, always urging her not to go work on that day and always failing to persuade her. It's a nightmare I often wake up from at night, very distressed.'

'What a dream!' Ari said. 'Very, very weird. Did you, by the way, fancy that woman?'

'For God's sake,' Cole answered. 'I was only ten.'

'Well, what can I tell you? Your recurrent dream relates either to that woman or, more likely, to hell, the world we live in.'

'Whatever the interpretation,' Cole answered, 'what I want to find out is how I stop having this dream.'

'Sorry, I can't help you. I don't have a clue,' Ari responded. 'When you're back in England, do ask a psychotherapist.'

Wanting to move the chat to greener fields, Ari then asked Cole to talk about something else.

'Tell me, how's your new girlfriend?'

'You mean the one who's uninhibited by the paper-thin walls?' Cole asked, laughing loudly.

'Yes, that one.'

'Oh I've known her for quite some time, but we made it only recently. She's a nurse.'

'Really?'

'Yes, she specialises in circumcisions. She circumcised a boy recently, and she told me the boy's father asked her before the operation to be careful because the boy hadn't had this experience before.'

They had a good laugh and kept talking like old midwives for a little longer. Even so, the feeling of despondency remained with Ari. Later on, back at home, he prepared for his trip to al-Raqqah. This primarily involved his psychological preparation for what might well be a one-way journey. It involved a big decision, the biggest ever in his life, which, if wrong, he would not even be alive to regret.

'On the other hand,' he told himself, 'if I get through this, I'll have plenty of material for a new chapter in my future autobiography.' A minute later, he decided, 'you aren't funny.'

As he knew, given the enormous risks involved, going on behalf of his organisation to al-Raqqah was not obligatory. Considering that sixteen UNRWA staff members had already lost their lives since the conflict had begun and thirty-one others were missing or presumed detained, extreme situations were, as a rule, avoided. Ari, like all his colleagues, had a choice.

Despite the advice of a couple of people he knew and also his own better judgment, he decided to cross the bridge of hesitation. He would visit the jihadis' headquarters to negotiate the release of his fellow-workers. What shifted the balance in favour of such a perilous decision was his hope, extremely thin though it was, that he would get some information regarding Laura's murder. He knew, of course, that such an expectation was nothing but a fantasy.

In going for it, he was also somehow helped by Khaled, who assured him that his cousin, an Isis member, would be there to help, if help was needed.

Though the battle between his mind and his spirit fiercely carried on, he eventually decided to make the move. But on the blade of his decision, he was anything but comfortable. His heart was still flooded with endless waves of anxiety, which sometimes brought every muscle of his ligaments to a standstill, and his head was pounding. He had no doubt that this trip would test his courage, his endurance, his commitments, even his faith in himself. He was also fully aware that his life would be at risk – even the simplest incident could turn him into another dead body in a dirty street.

'But at least I'll be done with the dentist then,' he ruefully humoured himself. The smile disappeared from his face only a second later, when he wondered whether Laura had wrestled with the same question when she was thinking of extending her stay in Damascus 'just for a couple of days'. 'Of course she had,' was his instant reaction. 'Of course she had. She knew very well she was risking her life. But she couldn't adjust to a lesser sky.'

Before leaving Damascus, he visited Ibrahim al-Shaar, the Minister of Interior, whom he had met at his daughter's house. His intention was to ask him if there were any concessions that could be made to Isis in return for the release of the three prisoners.

While waiting outside his office, he could not fail to notice a very sad woman sitting opposite him. She wanted, as she said, to ask if the Minister had any information about her son, whether he was still alive or not. He had left his home, she said, and had not come back. She had phoned 131, the landline number where enquiries about missing persons could be addressed, but they did not know anything.

'I tried a broker,' she added, 'whom I paid a large sum of money to get the information I wanted. But all I got were requests for additional payments.'

The Minister opened his door at that moment and asked Ari to come in.

'Since I'm going to al-Raqqah to discuss with Isis the release of the three hostages,' Ari said after the initial niceties, 'I need to know what you could possibly offer them in return.'

The deadpan expression on the Minister's face gave the answer. 'Nothing whatsoever.'

'I understand the problem,' Ari carried on. 'But something has to be done. We can't let these three people die.'

'I understand the problem,' the Minister, with a smile on one side of his mouth, replied using the exact same words. 'But we can't negotiate with terrorists.'

After a wearisome debate, at the end of which he moved to the land of 'perhaps', the Minister asked Ari which prisoners Isis wanted to see released in return. Ari did not, of course, have the answer to that. He had to talk to Isis first. What he finally got from the Minister was a vague promise that he would look into it once he knew exactly what Isis demanded.

Rafiq Shahadah, the head of Syria's Military Intelligence Directorate, was as difficult.

'We can't negotiate with Isis,' he said. 'Once we start, there'll be no end to it.'

As far as Shahadah was concerned, the three Syrian nationals Isis had captured did not apparently count for all that much. On the other hand, Ari knew, the man had a point. But at least in the end, he, just like the Minister, promised to look into it once he knew Isis' demands. As the talk on the subject had practically ended, Ari thought for a moment of asking him if he had any information about Laura's murder. For some reason, he did not. It was perhaps because he assumed he would get nothing from the man. But as he was about to leave his office, the Syrian official asked him a question that totally took him by surprise.

'How are you doing with your investigation into Miss Heineken's death?' Shahadah asked.

'Good lord,' Ari wondered. 'Do they now have the means of mental bugging to keep tabs on what everyone is thinking?' He abruptly stopped as he realised he was nearly thinking aloud.

'I didn't know you were interested,' he said instead.

'Oh yes, we are,' he was assured. 'Her killing was anything but accidental. It was ordered by a foreign Power.'

'The Jordanian secret service's involvement in the stealing of weapons destined for delivery to the rebels?'

'No,' said the head of Syria's Military Intelligence Directorate. 'It was something far more serious.'

'What?'

'The Saudis' heavy involvement in Syria's affairs.'

'Meaning?'

'I'm not sure.'

Ari did not know whether to believe him or not. Anyone could make up stories for sale to the public just like Scheherazade, the wife of King Shahryar, who entertained her husband with new stories for One Thousand and One Nights in order to escape execution. In the same way anyone would be happy to mislead you if it suited his interests. But a blind instinct was telling him that the man was not leading him to something he had made up. His story afforded glimpses of other possibilities with which he did not feel he should quarrel.

'And how did Miss Heineken fit into it?' he asked.

'Ask Jaysh al-Islam,' was the answer.

Again Ari was taken aback. The intelligence network of the Syrian government apparently extended beyond what he had imagined were its limits. Obviously, there was no such a thing as secrecy. Midas, he remembered from his school days, punished by Apollo with a pair of ass' ears, had managed to conceal his deformity. But as he could not keep the secret, he had dug a hole in the river-bank and whispered to it 'King Midas has ass's ears'. He thought he was safe. But the reed which sprouted from the bank whispered the secret to everybody who passed by.

'Secrets simply cannot be kept,' he decided. 'Particularly if they are embedded with helpful lies.'

'Were your forces first on the scene of the crime?' he asked, as if this was going to make any difference. He knew the question did not make sense.

'You can't always be the first on the scene,' the man answered. 'Even Nemesis isn't omnipotent.'

Ari nodded as though he had known it all along. But the fact was that he could not cope at the moment with the issue Rafiq Shahadah had so casually raised. Al-Raqqa, sitting on the precipice of the big Unknown, had taken priority.

Wishing to make some progress, the next day he proceeded to contact the Isis headquarters in al-Raqqah and ended up speaking to Abu Mohammed al-Adnani, the Islamic State's' chief spokesman. His name rang a bell. The US State Department had offered a reward of up to five million dollars for information leading to his capture.

He explained to him that he was being sent by his organisation to negotiate the release of the three hostages and was promised a safe stay. But even if al-Adnani kept his promise, the journey itself was very dangerous as even buses had been shot at, particularly when gangs were manning the frontlines.

Crossing the lines into Isis territory had its own problems. But it was not impossible. Front lines were not as hermetically sealed as one might expect. Every other morning, for example, a bus used to arrive from Damascus to al-Raqqah, carrying mostly women, who wanted to join their families for a while. The same was true the other way round, except that people were not easily allowed to leave al-Raqqah to another city. Those like the eight Moroccans holding Dutch citizenship who did so without the explicit permission of the caliphate were charged with 'treason' and executed.

Ari had prepared himself for the hazardous journey, both emotionally and physically. He had made sure, among other things, his clothes, modest and black in colour, did not inhibit his movements and, more importantly, did not offend the jihadis' notion of fashion. Even his bag was black. The idea of getting a three-piece head cover was turned down the very first moment it crossed his mind. Seeing himself in a head cover actually made him laugh.

He also got a new mobile phone as he did not want to delete anything which Isis would find objectionable from his own – music, racy pictures, videos – or names of people, emails etc. Isis might well thoroughly check what was on it and copy it, destroy it or use it for its own purposes.

He left Damascus very early in the morning, when beaded dew-drops were still on the tree leaves. Driving at night, when total darkness enveloped the roads, was even more dangerous than in the daytime. He was to reach al-Raqqah through Homs and Hama from where he would have to start a new journey to the Isis 'capital'. It was a journey through government and also rebel-held territories. The idea of going there by coach did not appeal to him. Though a poster advertising the bus route read 'Feel safe with us', the journey was expected to last anything from 20 hours to three days.

He instead jumped on his motorbike.

Chapter 21
With the 'soldiers of God'

Driving through the haunted landscape, Ari was once again wondering whether he would manage to get through this alive. One problem was the sporadic shelling along the road. Apart from this, rebels or ordinary thugs did periodically ambush isolated cars with trucks or SUVs. People who got away with their lives and the loss of just their valuables would have to thank their good luck forever.

It would be worse if the captors viewed you as a commodity. A foreign head commanded a high price.

He did not know what reception the Isis fighters manning the checkpoints would give him either. In fact, you could never know if you would cross the line safely or be shot at. Much depended on the mood of the fighters at the checkpoint.

The countryside looked as still as a photograph at various points. Now and then, old men were leading goats, and children were playing amid the stone facades of their ruined villages. Elsewhere along the way, there were soldiers manning the numerous blocs. They were armed with all sort of weapons: AK variant rifles, US military-issued M16, CQ, German Heckler & Koch G3 and Belgian FN Herstal FAL type rifles. Supported by the Syrian army's new Russian T-90 tanks, they were also helped by Russians, who were there to train the Syrian tank crews. The Russians also maintained an eastern base of forward air controllers to guide the Sukhoi bombers to their night-time targets.

At some point, he was stopped by soldiers cowed behind scarves to protect themselves from the desert wind that cut like a knife. They were holding Kalashnikovs in their hands.

'There's lots of shelling ahead,' he was informed. Confirmation of it, if it was needed, was offered by the sight of a burnt-out bus less than 50 metres away. 'It was hit with rocket-propelled grenades or it drove over a hidden mine left for the army,' another driver told him. 'Thirty-eight passengers were killed in that bus.' Further down, there were two rusting oil tankers and next to them a sewage truck hit by a rocket. Its stink was still there and cars were trying to dodge the deluge of excrement.

'Not like a Constable painting,' Ari thought.

A helicopter, flying low, passed above them and disappeared in the distance. So did the buzzards. They vanished into a crack of stone where they were camping.

His arrival in the Isis capital, he carried on thinking after the shelling had ceased, was also extremely dangerous. The unequivocal threat the Islamic state represented to any foreign party was a fact of life. Outsiders had been beheaded and, as a result, even the most enterprising and daring westerners would hesitate being anywhere near them. In fact, very few had.

Up until Homs, the dual-carriageway was clear enough. The Syrian air strikes had kept the Isis men away from it. In central Homs, which he at last reached, all he could see were ruins – acres of blitzed homes and apartment blocks and shops still dripping with broken water mains and sewage. He passed it and, following the signposts to al-Raqqah, turned right.

 Close to the line dividing the two camps, he came across the Syrian army gun lines, firing their 130mm artillery every minute. Shells were exploding across the valley and a great curtain of blue smoke was ascending into the sky. The impact of the explosions was now and then visible through it. After nearly ten hours, he eventually reached the Isis-controlled areas. He could see from the distance the heavy damage done to it by the Syrian artillery and the Russians. Roads had been torn up by their missiles and trees ripped apart with their huge trunks lying down the hillsides like giant skittles.

He left his motorbike with the Syrian forces and then crossed the line dividing the two camps. In doing so, an officer, who posed as a man who liked to light his cigarettes from the shells whizzing beneath his nose, sarcastically wished Ari a safe return. He wore no identification or badge. Militiamen seated beside old Russian self-propelled guns and smoking cheap Russian cigarettes laughed. They all apparently thought that the good wishes he had conveyed to Ari were nothing but a joke.

When the two sides had ceased fire for a while, Ari seized the opportunity and trudged from the government-held territory into what was a no-man's land. Walking through craters in the ground, he was soon in what was viewed as Isis territory. The jihadis, who at the moment had laid down on their backs warming their lice, arrested him instantly. Having been interrogated for half an hour, he was then taken for the long trip to al-Raqqah.

Interestingly, all the way to the province's capital, his custodians, all of them 'soldiers of God', kept talking about the forthcoming Armageddon and the martyrdom on the path of Allah. They were certain this would assure them a place in paradise, whereas the Book says, 'theirs shall be the dark-eyed houris, chaste as hidden pearls: a guerdon for their deeds'.

'Who knows,' Ari thought, 'they may also be provided with free mobile phones for communication with the other dead fellows.'

It was this belief that had ensured the endless supply of recruits willing to blow themselves to pieces in suicide attacks, euphemistically called 'martyrdom-seeking operations'. It was also what had turned Isis into a formidable fighting force, hard to beat in strictly military terms. As if he wanted to produce evidence of the strength of his beliefs, a masked Jabhat al-Nusra fighter shouted with the profound conviction of a jihadi killer the moment he made eye contact with Ari. 'Glory to the great and all-powerful Allah, Lord of the worlds!'

The man, like the other jihadis, looked possessed. 'His hotline to God,' Ari thought, 'the product of his early-acquired senility, must have been recently re-activated.' His dark eyes, blazing with a fierce anger, seemed fixed on the eternity the non-believers, all those who had consigned themselves to perdition, could obviously not access.

In a cloud, which no beneficial influence could penetrate, he then continued for the benefit of the unblessed, in this instance Ari. 'God has sent us the faithful pupil, Abu Bakr al-Baghdadi, bearing the fire of Islam to clean the world from parasites and fake Islamic savages of the Middle East. Inshallah.'

His total and unequivocal certainty that the future belongs to them, delivered by his impassionate gibberish, was pierced by volleys of gunfire. A loud explosion nearby sent acrid smoke billowing into the air.

'Well,' Ari thought while trying to overcome what was something more than a twinge of uneasiness, 'greed is obviously not the only thing left in our world these days.'

In al-Raqqah, he was taken to a building devastated by the air strikes, which on that day housed the Isis security headquarters, and was briefly interrogated by a hard-looking man, one of its officers. Lots of anonymous eyes were watching and appraising him but nobody said a word. Many of them were kids who had never soiled their hands with work – only with blood. Work, perhaps, was not appropriate for those Allah had selected to spread his message.

He explained what he wanted and asked to see Abu Mohammed al-Adnani, Isis' chief spokesman, and possibly Abu Bakr al-Baghdadi, the 'caliph' himself. Escorted by two armed guards, as if he were their prisoner, he was then allowed to walk out onto the city's streets. He was told to be back soon. Walking around, he exchanged a few words with a child who was sitting in a pushchair filled with cartons collected to use for heating. He was so thin you could put your hand on his belly and feel his backbone. Another child was sweeping debris off a road at a site damaged by bombs.

'Where are you from?' he asked them.

'A village,' they said.

'What village?'

'Oh, it's so small and poor that it doesn't have a name.'

'When do you attend school?' was his next question.

He already knew the answer: never. Schools had closed in January after Isis had decided to rewrite the curriculum and cut out the 'un-Islamic' teachings contained in the schoolbooks. This included the removal of all images, even those the children's brain could not decode. Reading was obviously a dangerous amusement and thoughts a useless burden. Books that did not advance Islam were viewed, in any case, as meaningless and worthless. They were often burnt.

Ari recalled that in 642 AD, when Alexandria was captured by caliph Umar, the Islamists destroyed its famous library that contained hundreds of thousands of scrolls including ancient works of incalculable value. Umar's instructions to his military commander had clarified: 'If those books are in agreement with the Quran, we have no need of them. And if they are opposed to the Quran, destroy them.' The Islamists, it was said later, had found the library books sufficient to 'heat the baths of the city for six months'.

The children did not answer his question. Wondering why on earth he had asked them, he said nothing more on the subject. To hide his verbal stillness, he instead walked to a little shop nearby and bought a packet of biscuits and some salted peanuts. He tore open the packet, offered a couple to each of them and while chewing one himself, he watched a group of youngsters kicking a ball. He wondered whether a man, surely an official, standing on a rooftop in the effort to find a signal for his cell phone managed to get what he was after. He probably had not as he was spitting angrily on the street beneath. Perhaps, Ari thought, he imagined he was somewhere else, in a library.

In the market where he found himself soon after, he could see a number of women always accompanied by a male guardian, a husband, brother or father. All of them had to wear niqabs, the headdress that completely covers the face and the head, as well as black gloves and loose dark clothing. They could not use perfume and they were not allowed to talk loudly in the markets. Billboards along the road reminded them what they should or should not do, and so did the presence of the gun-toting police women, members of the al-Khansa Brigades. Men were likewise required to wear loose fitting pants with hems falling above the ankles.

Other billboards reassured everybody that Isis 'will win despite the global coalition'. The names of jihadi groups were spray-painted on what was left of the buildings' walls. Black flags appeared in many places. He walked further down the road towards a hospital that was flooded with injured people, several of them civilians. Like others, this hospital was also experiencing severe shortages of medical personnel and medicines. Its infrastructure had been destroyed. Electricity and clean water was largely unavailable.

A further hundred metres away, a small crowd assembled for reasons Ari could not work out, kept shouting very loudly. He wished he had never gone to see what they were up to. A woman was being stoned to death for adultery. Her screams in the shadows pierced the air like a bird's that had come back to an empty nest. They did not last long. A man next to him stared into space like a zombie. The place had burnt its bridges to civilisation.

Al-Hisba, the special police, ever-present, was always ready to ensure adherence to its moral laws. People had to attend the daily prayers, witness the beheadings of 'traitors,' refrain from smoking and only listen to religious songs. In the same spirit, satellite dishes were destroyed so that people would not be consuming 'un-Islamic' programmes, and police had been stopping people on the streets to check their mobile phones for inappropriate pictures. Such an offence could earn the offenders a flogging.

To police the town the security forces were helped by the culture of spying which particularly encouraged the youngsters to become informants. In many instances, the latter were acting out of fear or the need to survive in desperate circumstances, i.e., to earn the day's bread.

Tired at that point, Ari stopped for a glass of water in a kiosk selling sandwiches while wondering how people could possibly cope in the face of such difficulties. Each of them had lost at least one or more members of his or her family and most had lost their homes. They were starving and denied all the facilities the modern world provides, from running water and electricity to heating and medical care. On top of all this, they were deprived, not just of their most elementary rights, but also of their dignity and self-respect.

Even if all the suffering ended the day after, they would have to live with its long-lasting legacy and the psychological traumas the war had caused for years. 'What they had been hit by,' he thought unable to hold back his sadness, 'was nothing less than a psychological tsunami.' Words to describe this cataclysm could not really be found in any language.

His reflections were interrupted by the arrival of groups of young jihadis, members of the 'Turkish Brigade', known for its sniper strength, and German Muslims, reputed for their unblemished eagerness to carry out suicide attacks. The number of foreign fighters joining the jihadis in Syria and Iraq, someone had said or written, Ari could not remember, was close to 27,000 from 86 countries, more than half of them from the Middle East and North Africa.

Apart from the Turks, they all hung around talking loudly. The Turks instead focused on listening to, via intercepted walkie-talkie frequencies, exchanges between Kurdish peshmerga fighters in which the words 'kebab', 'chicken tikka' and 'salad' were frequently repeated. Ari did not have a clue what all of this was about. It was only later, when he returned to Damascus, that the arms dealer he knew told him that 'kebab' stood for a heavy machine gun and 'salad' for Kalashnikov ammunition.

'You've got explosive bullets, penetrating bullets — a mix, just like salad,' he laughed.

Ari, hoping to see the people in charge of the city's business, returned to the dilapidated building where he had initially been taken. The tension he had experienced when first there had somehow subsided as his credentials had been fully established. 'Perhaps,' he thought, 'they intend to negotiate seriously. Khaled's cousin's talk with the leaders and the officials present might have also helped to this end.' Still, people would not engage him in any discussion. He was only told he had to wait, which he did before being taken to a space tunnelled under the surface of the earth. It was not the only such space. Isis had dug a city underneath the town to protect its people from air strikes. A minute later, several Isis officials arrived.

He realised soon after why he had been taken there. Russian air forces had started bombarding al-Raqqah once again. The rebel fighters' monitor control screens had detected the incoming air attack, but they could of course do nothing to prevent the blow. Useless, likewise, was Isis' sophisticated equipment, such as guided anti-tank missiles – Russian Kornet and Metis systems, Chinese HJ-8, and European MILAN and HOT missiles.

Russia was two months into its bombing campaign on Syria and its strikes had hit numerous military targets, including various 'moderate' Islamist factions backed by Saudi Arabia, Turkey and Qatar, particularly in Idlib, Latakia and Hama. But the bombing had inevitably also caused many non-combatant deaths as, expecting the air raids, the jihadis were operating among civilians whom they often used as a human shield.

People were shouting orders, running in and out of the tunnel or talking furiously over their iPhones. An injured official, who had been brought in from the street outside, was receiving some attention, which did not, however, seem to be doing him any good. A little further away, there was a small group of men, whom the rest were treating quite respectfully, talking over a phone device.

One of them, whom Ari recognised instantly, was the 'caliph'. He eyed him with a consuming curiosity.

In his mid-forties, bearded, slightly bald and bespectacled, he was in full command of what was going on. He was definitely a crane among chickens, and looked as if he was ascending into eternity. The serious injuries he had received in Iraq earlier, in March, following a coalition air strike, from which he had still not fully recovered, did not seem to make a difference.

At the moment, he was talking on a walkie-talkie whose controlling impulse had been pre-set to make its interception difficult. The talk, Ari was stunned to hear, was about a plan to increase dramatically the tension in the relations between the Russians and the Americans in order to force the latter to act in the way Turkey and Saudi Arabia desired. It involved the use of jihadi surface to air missiles against each other's warplanes.

'The "evidence" will be in place,' Abu Bakr al-Baghdadi was saying to the person at the other end of the line, 'to prove to the Russians that Americans had shot down their planes and to the Americans that Russians had shot down their own.'

His ferocious energy was spreading all around him. In his company, Ari decided, one could easily lose the habit of thinking.

He recalled that the year before, top Turkish officials had been caught talking about staging something similar: an attack on the Tomb of Suleiman Shah, a sovereign piece of Turkish territory in Syria, that was to be used as a pretext to intervene militarily against the Syrian regime. The audio recording of their talk had been anonymously leaked on YouTube and was subsequently banned in Turkey by the Turkish Prime Minister.

Was Recep Tayyip Erdogan now ready to engineer a new excuse, which would inadvertently lead to a major clash over Syria? And how would he benefit from it? Trying to avert an incident like the one Ari had just accidentally heard about, only about a month earlier, in October 2015, military officials of Russia and the US had signed a 'memorandum of understanding', which included specific instructions for air crews to follow in order to 'deconflict' their respective air operations over Syria. It also provided for the creation of a ground communications link between the two sides in the event air communications failed.

A similar understanding had been reached earlier, in September, between President Putin and Israeli Prime Minister Benjamin Netanyahu. The 'hotline' established between the two leaders ensured that there would be no misunderstandings or accidental shoot downs. To avoid any mistakes, they even agreed to engage in joint air exercises. Everyone knew, as the Syrians themselves would say, that 'a little spark could kindle a great fire'.

The execution of the plan, the 'caliph' believed, would force them, the Americans and the Russians, to confront each other in which case the

Turks, on the side of the Americans, would be free to act in the former Ottoman lands as they wished.

The possibility that such action might lead to an armed clash between the Russians and the Americans in Syria had not escaped Baghdadi. But he did not seem to care about it. All that he and the Turkish and Saudi Arabian sponsors of the plan cared about was the defeat of Bashar al-Assad followed by the defeat of the Syrian Kurds, which was Turkey's prime objective, and of the Iranians, which was the main goal of the Saudis. For Isis itself, hostilities between the two super-Powers would, God willing, open the gates to Armageddon and to a life in which the centuries are but a moment.

'It would be fun,' the 'caliph' reassured everyone around him condescendingly, but with a boisterous laugh. He was now standing on a stool to be nearer to heaven.

'Looking forward to it,' they all roared with pleasure. They were certain that nothing could deprive them of its delectation.

'Well, well,' Ari told himself. 'That's why the Americans had given him one hundred death sentences to run more or less concurrently.'

They had done so not only because of his ruthlessness, but also because they believed that the future of Isis depended on him. If they killed him, one part of the jihadis would follow the road he had opened and announce a new caliphate. Another would split off and return to al-Qaeda. Others would turn into gangs, following whoever was strongest.

The al-Baghdadi project was supported by the head of MIT, Turkey's National Intelligence Organization, and had the full backing of Recep Tayyip Erdogan, the authoritarian Turkish President with Sultanism on his brain. This became clear to Ari, not during the radio conversation between Abu Bakr al-Baghdadi and his interlocutor but soon after, when the Isis leader reported the head of MIT's words for the benefit of his colleagues.

'We won't let Vladimir Putin,' the Turkish intelligence boss had stressed, 'smother Syria's Islamist revolution. If the West doesn't put aside its cynical mentalité and thwart his plans, we have to take action ourselves.'

That was after Putin had asked the Turkish Ambassador in Moscow to tell his 'dictator president to go to hell along with all his Isis terrorists'.

The Russian intervention in Syria had caused a devastating setback to Erdogan's efforts to overthrow Syria's secular President Bashar al-Assad and also to secure a role for himself as a major player in the Mediterranean and the Middle East. Rather than expanding the country's influence, he ended up alone and at odds with just about everyone. His neo-Ottoman policy was in shambles.

Alienated from his Western allies, who had also become openly critical of his penchant for an oriental style of authoritarianism, and the countries in Turkey's immediate neighbourhood, he also had to deal with problems with Russia and Iran, even with Israel, Armenia, Cyprus and Greece.

'I'll tell you the real reason Erdogan is determined to overthrow Bashar al-Assad,' Pierro, the Italian journalist, had laughingly told Ari a couple of weeks earlier, when the two of them met again, albeit accidentally, in Damascus. 'It's for personal reasons.'

'He's angry at the Syrian President and his wife, Asma, both close to Erdogan and his wife in the earlier days. Asma, in an email to her husband, described the Turkish president as a thug who had read only one book and his wife as a frump interested only in shopping. Her email had been intercepted by the Turkish intelligence and passed on to Erdogan. The rest, as they say, is history.'

Asma Assad, who had grown up in the middle class English world, had graduated from London's King's College and pursued a career in international investment banking before moving to Damascus at the age of 25 and marrying the Syrian President.

'Well,' Ari said. 'Germans have said far worse things about Erdogan.'

'Whatever,' he added, 'developments had curtailed his dreams in a world in which, as he had clarified, he wasn't to be addressed as "Your Excellency". This obviously wasn't good enough. He had to be called, Turkish satirists said, "The Mightiest and Humblest Ruler of All History".'

But there was nothing funny about it particularly as all opponents of the Turkish President were not too long after branded 'traitors' and 'terrorists' and were savaged by both his regime and its uncultured oafs. 'The fact that an individual could be a deputy, an academic, an author, a journalist or the director of an NGO,' Erdogan himself said in an effort to explain his naked power grab, 'does not change the fact that that person is a terrorist.'

'They call me a dictator,' he added, 'but I don't care. It goes in one ear and comes out the other.'

Chapter 22
When the cat cried 'Allah'

Turkey, a NATO member country, was challenging NATO's worldview and, in doing so, it was raising major security issues. This was gradually more and more apparent since its involvement in Syria's affairs, back in June 2011.

It was then when Erdogan, in the spirit of his neo-Ottoman authoritarianism, assembled in Istanbul a number of Syrian rebel leaders to work out a plan for a regime change in Syria. Subsequently, he offered the Islamists arms and through MIT, the Turkish intelligence, training in clandestine work. Prime beneficiaries were the Islamic Front and in particular Ahrar al-Sham, the Turkish-sponsored Islamist group, and also the Syrian Turkmen brigades. The latter, with Chechen fighters in their ranks, worked closely with Jabhat al-Nusra in north Latakia, and in the northern areas of the Idlib and Aleppo.

Evidence of the Turkish scheme to arm the rebels was published in May 2015 in Cumhuriyet, the Turkish daily, but two of its journalists were jailed as a result. 'So what if the MIT trucks were filled with weapons?' Erdogan was quoted later in an attempt to dismiss the disclosure as unimportant.

At the same time, Turkey turned a blind eye towards the jihadis and let the country become their most important strategic base by far. The 'jihadi highway' allowed Isis and other rebel groups, particularly in 2013 and 2014, to come and go freely, import heavy ammunition into Syria and develop a cross-border black market oil trade.

Exasperated, the German government, which viewed the Erdogan government as 'the central action platform for Islamic groups', decided to supply Turkey only with limited intelligence information about the Isis movements. The conviction was that rather than use any such information against the jihadis, Turkey might use it to assist them. With barely controlled fury, Vladimir Putin, the Russian President, had meanwhile called the Turks 'the accomplices of terrorists'. This was after the Turks had shot down a Russian Su-24 plane over the Turkish-Syrian border. Russian officials had also claimed that Turkey's President Recep Erdogan and his family were personally involved in a multi-million dollar oil smuggling operation that funded Isis terrorists and the smuggling of arms.

'This is tough on Erdogan,' Ari thought, 'but at least the man has an income rich in zeroes to ease the pain.'

His declared combined earnings were estimated to be around 58 million dollars a year – he was No. 1 on the list of the world's 10 highest-paid political figures. Just his palace, which he had transformed at the cost of 600 million dollars, had 1,150 rooms, enough to turn him into the target of the Turkish satirists. But whatever the claims about Erdogan's illegal income, pocketed with as many hands as Durga, Hinduism's Mother Goddess, it was undisputable that Turkey was the main consumer of the oil stolen from Syria and Iraq.

This was something the Americans could not stop. The jihadis, as a result, could freely use the crossing points to and from Syria to export crude oil originating from Isis controlled oilfields, and import weapons. Likewise, though Turkey had joined the coalition against the terror organisation, the number of air attacks Turkey was launching against Isis was nothing compared to those against the Kurds. The Americans were furious.

Not surprisingly, their requests for permission to use Turkish air bases against Isis were ignored for a long period. They were finally approved only as of late July 2015, and the US was able to use the Incirlic Air Base in southern Turkey to launch air attacks against Isis. But the Americans had been forced to offer a quid pro quo: they turned a blind eye to Turkish strikes against the Kurds, the only successful ground force in the war against Isis. Largely mute in the face of the blatant Turkish military's onslaught against the Kurds remained the reaction in Western Europe too. Very little attention continued likewise to attract Turkey's involvement on the side of the Islamists in Syria.

Still Erdogan, furious like a deserted bride, fiercely objected to the support the Americans were giving to both the Syrian and the Iraqi Kurds in their fight against Isis. To counter it, he had proposed the establishment of what he called a 'safe' zone all along the northern Syrian border that covered the 900 km frontline area where the Kurds are largely the majority ethnic population. The 'safe zone' talk was, of course, arrant rubbish.

It would involve the invasion of Syria's northern regions by the ground troops of 'friendly' nations, i.e. Turkey, which would keep the Kurdish militants at bay. The reference to 'friendly' nations related only to those which were supporting the extremist groups. Such a zone would also re-introduce Erdogan, the Turkish leader, as a leading figure in a war in which he had been marginalised. More importantly, it would bolster Turkey's claims to be a vital interlocutor in an eventual resolution of the conflict.

What the latter entailed was disclosed by Turkish pro-government media, which proclaimed Aleppo as the 82nd province of Turkey. One of them, Takvim, a daily newspaper, even featured a map of the buffer zone that included Aleppo, Idlib and the north of Latakia as part of the future Turkish state.

Fearing the worst, Washington and its European allies rejected the 'buffer zone' proposal. Accepting it, accepting Turkey's war against the Syrian Kurds in other words, would have made it impossible for the coalition to carry on the war against Isis. Apart from this, Turkish boots on the Syrian ground, serving only the expansionist Turkish designs, would complicate the Americans' efforts to defeat Isis and could also drag the US into a conflict with Russia. Members of the American military even argued that Turkey did not deserve the protection of the alliance if the situation got out of control. Besides, they could not see which countries, apart from Turkey, would supply the ground forces necessary for the purpose.

'Hilary Clinton,' Ari thought, 'if she was still the head of the State Department, would have accepted the Turkish "safe zone proposal".'

In any case, for the US and its NATO allies, the Kurds were an asset rather than a hindrance. The US-led coalition actually relied almost exclusively on Iraqi Kurdish peshmerga fighters and Syrian Kurdish militia to fight Isis on the ground. The enemy was Isis whose rise had created a grave threat to the socio-religious makeup of the Middle East and to global security.

Living these thoughts aside, Ari re-focused on his own situation. He knew that overhearing the story had sealed his own fate. The jihadis would never let him get away with the information he had so accidentally acquired because the 'caliph' whose eye had caught him, did not expect him to understand Arabic. Sweat poured down his arms and rolled down his spine as he was digesting the incredible news he had heard. He blankly stared at the wall, struggling to get a grip on his runaway nerves, and then focused for a while on his breathing. He was gasping for breath, he realized, like a fish out of water and needed to fill his lungs with air properly.

'Get him,' the 'caliph' barked at his guards.

'Wait a minute,' somebody said. Ari recognised the voice was his own.

Several armed Islamists practically lifted him off the ground immediately, emptied out his pockets – his iPhone, UN card, bank cards and his cash, threw him deep underground, into the bowels of the compound, and locked the door behind them. He remained there for a few hours in the full knowledge that his life was over. He had partly prepared himself for it when he had accepted Samuels' suggestion, but the callousness of reality had very different colours to what he had imagined.

'Nothing unusual in all this,' he reminded himself as he leaned against the wet, almost glistening wall. 'Things always have one appearance when far away, and quite another when looked at closely.'

Yet the vertiginous feeling this created was something he had never experienced before. He was in unknown territory, in the arms of a darkness of hostile infinity he could almost touch with his fingers. The situation challenged his final endurance, tested his courage, and took him to the limits of his indefatigability. The only thing he could now rely upon was his spirit, which had to conquer his fears.

The enemy, he decided while sitting on the damp, grimy floor with his back against the wall, was not the jihadis. It was his fear, the fear that was trickling all the way down his spine before moving to his head. The danger was in his thinking if the latter was left at the mercy of this fear.

'If there is any chance of survival,' he told himself, 'your impertinent thinking has to chill out, become as unemotional as a number.'

Just an hour older since he overheard Baghdadi talking over the phone, his outlook had changed beyond belief. In the dark and empty room with wet, almost glistening walls, his thoughts first travelled to his parents, Laura and his friends before moving to his student days, a time of hope that he could make a bit of a difference to the world. He recalled his dreams and disappointments, his successes and his failures, the options he had declined. But he regretted nothing. He was a fighter, fighting for a good cause, and a fighter never gives up. Anger had already burnt the icy shield of desperation and fear away and was turning into a fury barely controlled.

All of this was suddenly interrupted when Russian jets launched another attack on al-Raqqah and the whole area was shaken. The thought crossed his mind that it would be a relief if he died from a Russian bomb rather than at the hands of the jihadis. He would not enjoy, he was sure, being beheaded.

Thankfully, the next moment a bomb hit the building he was in and a wall noisily collapsed in a cloud of smoke. Despite the confusion and the panic he was experiencing, he breezed through the damaged door. No guards outside it. The building was engulfed in an eerie, unnatural stillness only occasionally disturbed by something that sounded like the utterances of an immured spirit wailing for its life.

It came from a door next to him. He paused for a moment and then opened it. 'Anybody there?' he hallooed. It was only a hungry cat clawing and whining at the door in an effort to escape. He gave it a biscuit he still had in his pocket and, as a Muslim would say, the cat cried 'Allah'. So Ari decided.

Out in the street, fighters were shouting and a teenage girl, who had been injured, was screaming for help. An older woman had put her arm around her and a man was calling 110 for an ambulance, if he could ever get one. Another woman next to them had sank her head into her hands. A few steps ahead, an Isis official of a senior rank, if he were to be judged by his looks, seemed to have already passed to a place where no letters could be forwarded.

Seeing both civilians and rebels hit by the airstrikes brought back to Ari all he had heard about the tactics of the Islamists. 'They used us as human shields,' a refugee from Aleppo had once told him in Damascus. 'They would deploy their militants among the houses and in the streets. They would say it is to maintain order, but they were in fact hiding among us.' It was exactly what he was witnessing here.

Moving slowly, he approached the dead rebel officer only to discover that he was not yet dead. His head was bleeding and splotches of saliva were all around his mouth. Yet an almost imperceptible smile on his face had brought a flicker of life back to his haggard features.

'He must be happy,' Ari thought. 'He's about to make his acquaintance with Allah. And perhaps, who knows, with some born-again virgins too.' He did so a minute later.

His face, Ari was sure, looked more dignified now than when he was alive. Some sort of respect for the man who was suffering his fate with such discretion grew in him without his being fully aware of it. No matter how obtuse his beliefs were, the jihadi was still ready to forego life for them, to hand out the most important gift we're given – life itself. 'Isn't this,' Ari thought, 'what the early Christians were doing when persecuted by the Romans?'

He did not have time to think about it as the man's eyes were now shut for good and a cloud of insects was already buzzing around his body. It was only then that Ari noticed the mobile phone in his hand. He was apparently talking to someone when he was hit. He quickly picked it up and moved into another half-demolished building where he was on his own. He called his boss, Richard Samuels, who did not answer the call. While the cold was biting at his skin, he then called Robert Forester, the veteran Middle East British correspondent. He had met him a couple of times the month before in Damascus, when Forester needed information about the relief work UMWRA was doing.

Thankfully, the call was answered immediately, and Ari, almost breathless, told him about the plan to bring Russia and the US into a military conflict in Syria. Sucking some air back into his lungs, Forester asked for details and Ari expanded by recalling every bit of what he had heard. At the end, he promised him he would keep him in the picture if anything new came to his attention.

As soon as he had finished, he was filled with an immense relief, which soon turned into a breathless inarticulate excitement. 'Even if I'm to die in the next minute,' he told himself, 'I've frustrated the realisation of this almost unbelievable and catastrophic plan.' Forester, he was sure, would immediately give it publicity and the conspirators hands would be tied.

To be on the safe side, he also thought of speaking with Michael Kay, the BBC journalist, but no matter how frantically he ransacked his memory, he just could not remember his telephone number. From now on, the issue was his own survival. But he desperately needed sleep. His shoulders slumped in exhaustion and his eyelids seemed determined to close the doors to the day. But sleep would have to wait.

Hoping he would be able to help, he phoned the Jaysh al-Islam man in Damascus, Laura's friend, and explained to him what he wanted in a low and measured tone. For a long moment, Khaled remained as quiet as the Sphinx.

When he finally spoke, he assured Ari he would contact his own Isis acquaintances in al-Raqqah and offer them a small bribe to help him escape to the capital. Checkpoints were often lucrative business through the smuggling of people and food. Isis tolerated much less graft than others, but it was still as vulnerable to the region's deep-seated corruption as were the 'moderate' rebels or the secular Syrian regime. Ghost armies enabled corrupt commanders to pocket the pay of non-existent soldiers, funds raised for food subsidies were embezzled, fake medicine orders enriched officials and so did the smuggling of refugees. Patronage, which bought loyalty, was as flourishing as in Damascus.

Fortunes raised this way were often spirited over the border into Turkey, sometimes by the fraudsters themselves. One of the latter who had ran off with lots of money had tweeted a former comrade: 'What caliphate? You idiots'. Whether members of Isis or of the 'moderate' groups, rebels often prized financial gains over their political commitments or radical ideology.

Two hours later, when the bombing had stopped, an Isis member, Abdul, came to see him in the same dilapidated house from which he had made the phone call to Robert Forester. He offered to help but asked for a fifty thousand dollars payment. Ari had turned into a hostage of an Isis gang. The train back to civilisation seemed to have been cancelled. But he did not give up. In the time-honoured Middle-Eastern tradition, he immediately engaged his 'helper' in negotiations regarding the price for his 'help' and managed to cut it down to a tenth. Payment would be made in Damascus as Ari could not oblige on the spot.

The deal had been struck, but Ari could take nothing for granted at the same time. The year before, he knew, Anthony Loyd, the foreign correspondent for *The Times*, had been kidnapped, shot and badly wounded by a man he had thought of as a trusted fixer. Abdul sensed his unease and did his best to reassure him that he could be fully trusted.

'I'm a good man,' he said. 'I stick to my word.'

'His words,' Ari thought, 'could be trusted but no more than an inscription on a tombstone commemorating the virtues of the dead.' But he had no choice.

The journey back to Damascus, initially by a car Abdul had managed to find, and then by Ari's motorbike was quite a terrifying experience involving 23 checkpoints before his arrival in the capital. At one of them, Isis members would not let him and his 'helper' through before contacting al-Raqqah, which, if they did, would turn him into a prisoner again. Abdul pretended he was fully behind their decision, but when he got the chance, he jumped on the car with Ari and ran away in a burst of speed. Shots hit the car but neither of them.

Relieved to see that the main danger was now behind them, Ari tried to phone his boss on their way to Homs. But, as he discovered, his mobile's battery had died. He asked a shopkeeper if he could use his mobile phone. For some reason, the man refused. 'He's the kind of person,' Ari told his 'helper', 'who wouldn't do anything for anyone, if he could help it.' Abdul seemed to agree. His own mobile was broken.

In the ochreous haze of expiring sunlight, they stopped in Homs for the night. One of the few hotels was, thankfully, still operating in the city. As soon as they entered it, a big ludicrous sign in the reception area welcomed them with the words:

'Notice to residents: Will guests requiring of partners for sleeping or purposes male and female both please most kindly request the desk of reception. M Hassan, General Manager.'

'Such utter nonsense. It almost rivals,' Ari thought, 'the reports on Syria by Fox Broadcasting Company.'

The General Manager, a man who had the personality of a hard-boiled egg, welcomed them himself and offered them a hot drink. Intrigued by Ari's presence in his part of the world, he then asked him what he was up to in Syria. Ari told him he was working for UNRWA. When they finished their drinks, the hotelier gave him the key to a room and, with a bland smile on his face, he told Ari that he could also have a girl, if he wanted.

'It's on the house,' he added, just to make sure that the offer was correctly perceived as a gesture of good will.

'No, thanks,' Ari told him. 'I'm rather tired this evening. But I would like, if it is possible, to borrow your phone?'

'Of course you can,' was the answer.

This time, he managed to speak to Samuels, to whom he explained briefly that he had a 'very difficult' journey and that he would be back soon.

Fully aware of all the problems inherent in the situation, Ari immediately contacted Hollinger and Kreegan when back in Damascus and gave them a first-hand account of what had happened. For some reason, they did not seem impressed despite the fact that a military clash between the Americans and the Russians in Syria was by no means unthinkable. It could easily occur even accidentally.

He also had a meeting with Alexander Kinshak, the Russian ambassador in his embassy, which had been struck by shells in October, fired by rebels while hundreds of Damascenes were outside it in support of the Russian air strikes. Unable to do anything more about the Isis plans, Ari then talked to Richard Samuels about the bribe promised to the Isis man who had taken him out of al-Raqqah and he was promised the issue would be taken care of.

Later in the same day, he also met Robert Forester, who was reluctant to send the story to his newspaper before talking to Ari. He had met him before, but the story this time was of huge importance and the only evidence Forester had to back it up was Ari's testimony. He had to see him at least, Ari knew, to hear him face to face and, among other things, to assess his credibility in person.

Forester arrived at Ari's office and, without wasting any words, he asked him to explain the circumstances under which he had found himself in al-Raqqah. He also wanted him to repeat word by word what he had heard. Ari did so, but Forester was still not happy. He asked for details relating to Abu Bakr al-Baghdadi himself – what he looked like, what he was wearing, how he interacted with his colleagues, what the exact words were that he had used – and also relating to al-Raqqah itself. At the end, convinced that Ari had not made up the story, he thanked him and left.

The story appeared in the *Independent*, the British daily, a couple of days later and became the top story all over the world. Turkey's reaction was, as one could only expect, quite violent. A very bad-tempered Erdogan denounced it as a fabrication and attacked the Western media for the bias with which they were allegedly dealing with his country.

'It's all a lie,' he said in a press conference which turned into prime time entertainment as he was trying to hold back his wrath for the unexpected disclosure of his plans. 'It's the work of irresponsible journalists who'll go for anything sensational without regard for the truth.'

Truth for him was a word that had had its day. The lie was his home. Take it away and he would be left homeless.

Yet, while they reproduced the essence of the story, the Western media tended to soft-pedal their reaction to the Turkish plot. 'It's what a family does when it tries to minimise the importance of something wrong another family member had done,' Forester told Ari over the phone.

What the various governments were secretly doing in response to the news was not what Ari could know. But he knew that this diabolical plan was now dead.

Chapter 23
A Christmas street party

Relieved, Ari took a walk in the capital's 19th century Marjeh Square where it was only too easy to forget that war was raging even in its outskirts. 'Forgetting apparently,' he told himself, 'is the road to happiness.' The thought had not crossed his mind before and he thought about it again: 'Happiness does occasionally visit us for sure,' he told himself. 'Yet life is nothing but pain. The more we therefore forget, the better off we are.' He decided such a conclusion had to be the subject of more circumspection. He did not exactly feel at home with it.

'At any rate,' an afterthought hit him, 'life is full of things destined to be forgotten. We don't have to try to forget.'

He had been away from the capital for only a few days, but his experience in al-Raqqah had cut so deep that he almost felt like a tourist back in Damascus. Re-entering daily life, he noticed everything routine had blocked. The mix of rural refugees and urbanites in front of him were calmly enjoying the breezy café culture. Women in black abayas and others in cropped jeans were taking their strolls in the afternoon's crepuscular light. Supermarket shelves were well stocked, restaurants were well booked and at the city's top hotels, evening receptions and wedding celebrations carried on as in the good old times.

The city exhumed an air of serenity that made possible what is viewed as normal interaction. Only the power cuts, regular but promptly filled by humming generators in the city's chic venues, managed to halt the party temporarily.

Syria might be crumbling and the war was taking its toll. Nearly everyone had lost loved family members or friends, many had been crippled by the bomb explosions, many had lost their businesses, millions now living in Damascus had lost their home. Many of them had nowhere to go for months, if not years, to come. And everyone seemed resigned to the possibility of sudden death. But life carried on. It had to.

This, Ari thought, might just reflect the adaptability of human nature. People, after all, were tired of war and all they wanted was a normal life, a life in which their unfenced existence would not be threatened.

'Enough is enough,' a 21-year-old with bleached-blonde hair who worked as a bartender at night while studying for her fine art degree, told him later that evening. 'People are tired of war and just want to live a normal life.' She was listening at the time to the Levantine-Western fusion of Shamstep. Leaving behind the traumatic experiences they were still going through, the youngsters in particular were now looking forward to simple pleasures – enjoying a beer, watching football or smoking their nargiles at popular bars.

They were all, obviously, members of 'the evil generation, who neglected prayers and followed sensual desires', bound, as Allah said, 'to be thrown into Hell' to wash its floors endlessly. 'Just like the elderly Jews,' Ari suddenly recalled what he had read somewhere, 'who were cleaning the Nazi streets with toothbrushes amidst laughing crowds'. But the tranquillity also underscored the success of Bashar al-Assad in insulating his seat of power from the devastation that had swept much of the country.

Though he needed time to recover from the al-Raqqah horror, Ari decided to re-focus on Laura's murder. Perhaps, he thought, he would be able to get some information about it from the anti-Bashar al-Assad forces in the Ain Tarma neighbourhood of the Syrian capital. Someone had mentioned, albeit vaguely, the possibility. Despite the raging fierce clashes in the area between Syrian soldiers and rebel fighters, he did have a go. But his efforts again produced no results.

He returned to the Old City and, as he stopped in a pub, the pub Sharqi, next door to the noisier bar '80s' where youngsters liked to watch football, his eye caught Mark Hollinger, the MI6 man. A stone's throw away, he was getting into a car. He waved at him, but Hollinger disappeared into the car without returning the greeting. It was actually at that moment that the events of the last few days really caught up with him.

Tired, drained and slightly disoriented as life had already given him too much to evaluate, Ari was left staring in his essence's outer space. Swallowed into the imponderable future, his thinking was derailed. Fatigue had worn him down.

'All I want,' he decided, listlessly leaning his head against the table, 'is a rest from existence. A holiday from human frailty in a faraway place, unfamiliar with man's enemies – his self-interest, his pride, his prejudices, his stupidity.' Brooding on his thoughts, he went back in time for a minute. 'Where are the days,' he wondered, 'when I was looking forward to all the exciting things which were impatiently waiting in my future's reception room?'

None of this was there any more. The old days seemed to be part of his past life, the life he had lived before he was born. Or the product of his colourful imagination. His perturbing thoughts that hovered across his face were thankfully swept away the moment a woman close to him started screaming at someone who was taking a photograph of her.

'I've told you so many times I don't want to be photographed,' he heard her saying.

Ari had met a woman like this before, when on holiday in Sardinia. Angry, and probably emboldened by the wine she had already had, she had thrown what was left in her glass at the photographer's face. Equally angrily, the photographer loudly urged her not to take her bad temper with her everywhere she went.

Looking at the photographer, Ari gave him a sympathetic smile, which was not returned. It was caught, however, by a woman, a young and attractive ash-blonde European, who smiled at Ari in sympathy with his embarrassment.

'Well, what can you say,' he said to her. 'There are people and then there are people. If we were all the same, life would be boring.'

'True,' she answered with a strongly accented voice.

'You are…?' Ari asked her.

'Swedish,' she answered.

'And you're going to a gym in Chafeek Jabri Street,' Ari carried on.

'Yes. But how on earth do you know that?' she asked, totally amazed.

'The filigrees of air,' he answered, 'whispered it to me.'

As she continued looking at him, quite puzzled, he explained that Garrahan, his Irish colleague had talked to him about 'a beautiful Swede he had met at the gym'.

'You mean James?' she asked.

'Yes.'

'We've met there a couple of times,' she said, 'and we casually talked about the gym's facilities. I never knew his surname or what he's doing in Damascus.'

'He works for UNRWA,' Ari informed her. 'And you?'

'I work for a NGO, which has partnered with WHO in the effort to alleviate the suffering we see all around,' she said.

They chatted about their work and, at the end, Ari asked her if she wanted to give him her number to pass it on to Garrahan. 'James, you mean,' she corrected him. She gave it to him and the next day Ari was talking to Garrahan.

'Would you be prepared to buy me dinner in exchange for some vital information?' he asked.

'Piss off,' the Irishman said without looking up from the papers in front of him.

'It relates to Sanni,' Ari insisted.

'Who's Sanni?'

'A blond Swede.'

'Where would you like your dinner?' Garrahan had surrendered.

They met the same evening and for some reason they gobbled up all the food that was heaped on their plates to a prodigal fullness. Only divine aid could help them digest it. Garrahan did not only pay for it, but he also paid for an extra bottle of wine in a moment of reckless extravagance. Later on, he asked Ari if he had any Rennies.

Over the next few days, Ari, though tired, contacted various foreign and Syrian information officers and members of the Free Syrian Army. Still, nothing useful emerged concerning Laura's murder. Other information kept, however, coming in almost effortlessly.

That was the case when Ari shared a coffee with Adnan, an arms dealer, in the rebel-held area of Eastern Ghouta. His interlocutor, a man with aquiline features, a taste for fast deals and a mouth radiating a sort of perpetual sneer, had no difficulty admitting that 'Isis buy like mad. Every day. Demand is so high,' he boasted like an auctioneer who wanted to encourage more bids, 'that my phone rings almost non-stop. I can barely keep up with the demand for the goods.'

The dealer had no difficulty admitting that supplying weapons to both the rebels fighting Isis and Isis itself netted him a commission from 10 to 20 per cent in every multimillion dollar deal.

'Most of the weapons I take to the rebels,' he added, 'are stolen from government forces. I transport the entire load past the security officers and, needless to say, with their blessing. If I'm ever caught, I can negotiate with them on a cash basis. The arms dealers located in Egypt,

Syria, Libya, Gaza or Iraq,' he added, 'are now using Facebook to sell a wide range of weapons, including missiles and tanks. Jordanian intelligence operatives are involved in this trade, too. They systematically steal weapons shipped into Jordan by the Central Intelligence Agency and Saudi Arabia, weapons which are intended for Syrian rebels, and sell them to arms merchants on the black market.

'Yet the biggest black market in the country is currently the border provinces of Idlib and Aleppo. It's there that the Gulf backers of the rebels send truckloads of munitions through the Turkish border which corrupt fighters divert to local dealers.' Ideology, obviously, hardly matters. On Facebook, the arms sales are listed under a variety of categories such as 'Sports' or 'Shopping'. 'Delivery,' he added with a smile, 'is free if you pick it up in the given locations. But it can also be delivered within 24 hours.'

'I hate Isis,' Adnan said at the end, 'but this doesn't matter as long as I'm making a good profit.' He finished the sentence by rubbing his fingers together to indicate the financial windfalls involved.

To an outsider, all this made little sense, considering that Isis had seized hundreds of millions of dollars' worth of weapons when it captured Iraq's second city, Mosul, in the summer of 2014. Having looted, captured or illicitly traded from poorly secured Iraqi military stocks, it had since acquired much more. Its arsenal included US-made Abrams tanks, M–16 rifles and MK–19 40mm grenade launchers, seized from the Iraqi army, to Russian M–46 130mm field guns taken from the Syrian forces.

Isis, however, still needed ammunition: rounds for Kalashnikovs, medium-calibre machine guns and 14.5mm and 12.5mm anti-aircraft guns. It also needed rocket-propelled grenades and sniper bullets and also truck bombs, suicide vests and improvised explosive devices. As it turned out, the best sources of ammunition were its enemies, including both the rebels and the Syrian army, both of which would sell supplies to black market traders who then sold them to Isis dealers. A significant portion of its weapons had also come from key military bases captured in Syria.

Everybody was of course very familiar with this as, apart from anything else, exchanges between emirs and the weapons 'centres' were often heard on walkie-talkies.

Meanwhile, early in December, following a ceasefire deal with the government, the city of Homs, once dubbed 'the capital of the revolution' against Bashar al-Assad, was evacuated by the remnants of the rebels and returned to government control. The regime's victory in Homs, helped by the relentless Russian bombing of the city, which caused many civilian casualties, indicated to Isis that it had to escalate its response.

All hell seemed to break loose at that point. 'American' surface-to-air missiles launched by rebel brigades in the Turkmen region of Bayirbucak, in north-west Syria, came close to downing a Russian warplane within days. If the Russians reciprocated by hitting American targets, the door to the apocalypse would have opened.

'It's coming,' Mohammed Qurabi al-Ghazal, an imam whom Ari had accidentally met in Douma the day after, had happily informed him. 'Isaiah has prophesised it when he announced that Damascus would someday become a "heap of ruins". 'This prophecy,' he added with the certainty of someone in the know, 'is being fulfilled at this very moment. The destruction of Damascus would be followed by the Third World War, which, followed by the apocalypse, would give birth to God's new world.

'The end of time scenario,' the imam had explained to Ari, 'involves the emergence of a redeemer called al-Mahdi, the "guided one", who would rule for a number of years before the Day of Judgment comes. The final battle between al-Mahdi's forces – tall soldiers with long black hair and beards, dressed in black and carrying the prophet's black banner – and the Christian Romans would take place in Dabiq in northern Syria. After this, run from Damascus, the world "will be filled with justice" as the only faith on that day will be the religion of Allah'.

'If Allah,' Ari thought of saying, 'hadn't instead created another race blessed with the ability to think.'

He nevertheless kept his mouth shut. 'Self-deception,' he thought, 'seems to be as essential for some as the blade of a knife is for others. They need it to survive or, if Islamists, to blow themselves to pieces. Still, their beliefs presupposed and demanded the abdication of reason. But the world is full of people belonging to different centuries.'

'Al-Mahdi,' Ari told the imam, 'is not mentioned in the Quran.'

'Well,' al-Ghazal answered, 'Mohammed had prophesised about him.'

Meanwhile, Christmas was around the corner and Ari was thinking about what on earth he would be doing on a day that people at home would be getting together with their families around a turkey, which, everyone assumed, would be only too happy to join the celebration.

He went home, had a shower, listened to CNN with a cold drink in his hand and then called Elia, Laura's neighbour. They met the same evening in the Old City and walked by the many souks. The modern new shopping centres and supermarkets had not as yet replaced the folkish Arab tradition which ensured souks carried on, not just as commercial centres, but as gathering places where people could socialise.

'Who needs cable TV,' Elia joked, 'when you have places like this?'

Before going to a restaurant, Ari bought a Christmas card for his father, Kimon, wrote a few words on it wishing him a merry Christmas, and put it in a postal box.

'What's on the menu tonight,' Elia asked when they sat down, as if dining out together was part of their daily routine.

Ari liked the Syrian cuisine, quite similar to other Levantine cuisines, mainly Lebanese, Palestinian, Jordanian and Iraqi. They ordered a selection of appetizers, followed by that torpedo-shaped fried croquette stuffed with cooked minced lamb, onion and sautéed pine nuts he had tried a few times before. Plus a Bargylus bottle of wine.

The evening rolled on pleasantly. They talked about Elia's job with the IBM – she was, she told Ari, a Configuration Management Administrator – and the work pressures she had to deal with as they were short-staffed. She also talked about the way she looked for relief from these work pressures outside of work hours.

'Yesterday evening,' she said, giving Ari an example, 'I went to Galerie Albal, a loud, Western-style coffee house with an art gallery above.'

It was the place where the city's bohemian types congregated. This reminded Ari of the day in Hydra when, together with Laura, he had gone to the Hydra Workshop, a former warehouse on the harbour waterfront. In its modest but beautifully proportioned space many famous artists had exhibited their work. The exhibiting artist the day they visited the place was Anne Collier, a Los Angeles born, New York based artist, whose striking works depicted cropped photographic images of the female body.

Elia asked Ari if he had managed to get any information regarding Laura's murder, but as he had nothing to say in response, the conversation on the subject ended in no time. But this did not prevent Ari from talking about Laura – his time with her in London, her stories from other Arab countries in which she had worked or their days in Damascus. He only stopped when, embarrassed, he realised that, despite Elia's understanding of his emotions, he had gone over the top. Feeling rather worn out, he wondered for a minute what the point of all this was. Whatever he thought or said about her, she was and remained dead.

By the time they had finished their second Bargylus bottle and drained their glasses, it was quite late. Time to leave. He offered her a drive back on his motorbike, which she gladly accepted, and at her front door she gave him a goodbye hug.

The next morning, Maryam was on the phone.

'What are you doing for Christmas?' she asked.

'Not much,' he said. 'Perhaps I'll try to finish a report my boss requested ages ago.'

'Don't be silly,' she joked. 'Do come over to share our turkey. My mother and my two sisters would only be too happy to welcome you here.'

Her father, he remembered Elia had told him, had been shot in front of his daughters by the jihadis.

He arrived at Maryam's small flat on Christmas day, carrying a Christmas pudding and a bottle of red wine. He felt most welcome from the very first moment. Each member of the family gave him a hug and Elisa, Maryam's mother, kissed him on both cheeks. They talked about Christmas, which since the time the civil war had started had turned out to be a very low key affair. The situation, he was told, was quite different a few years back.

'But this year,' Maryam said, 'things are different. Together with a feeling of security, what has now come back is also the old Christmas spirit of kindness, generosity and compassion. Damascus has re-discovered its multi-culturalism, which the jihadis seem so determined to eradicate.'

Around a table that did not leave much elbow space, they had the turkey, which they enjoyed, and some wine to help the food go down. Following a steaming mug of coffee, they then watched on TV *The Producers*, the Hollywood comedy written and directed by Mel Brooks. Soon after, they all went out to join the celebrations in Bab Touma, Damascus' historic Christian Quarter.

Ari could not believe his eyes. A 27-meter tall Christmas tree in George Khoury Square was twinkling with Christmas lights.

The district was decorated with crazy Christmas light displays beneath which thousands of people, Christians and Muslims, were moving around in Christmas hats. Several were dressed as angels, some of them biblically incorrect, or white-bearded Father Christmases. Groups were singing Jingle Bells, bands in corners or on vans were playing contemporary tunes, individuals were blowing their shiny trumpets or banging their brightly-coloured drums. Waves of intoxicating uproar, formed from a thousand disparate voices, were hitting the streets one after another. Many people were dancing.

Others could be found in the numerous small stores the city was peppered with, piling up their bags with embroidered silk cloths, hand-carved wooden boxes, and freshly-mixed perfume along with the latest Barbie dolls and toy cars. Several of them were probably just back from the capital's front against the jihadis.

Ari was stunned. Yes, the clouds of war were not shadowing Damascus as they did even a few months before, but this festivity explosion was beyond his expectations. The number of Christians had, of course, dramatically increased as Christian refugees had settled in the capital to escape the religious persecution and the horror of the war in other parts of the country. But it was not the numbers that made the difference. It was the people's determination to put the country's troubles to the back of their minds. Not for good, but for at least one day.

The celebration had the blessing of Syrian President Bashar al-Assad. Though not a Christian, a few days earlier he had visited the Notre Dame de Damas Church, an ancient cathedral located just two kilometres from the rebel-held neighbourhood of Jobar in Eastern Ghouta, where he attended the Christmas choral presentation. The mood in the streets of Damascus, Ari decided, had definitely changed. But so it had in all other cities from which the jihadis had been thrown out.

People who had fled their cities had started going back to their homes, though their homes often had no roof, and the words 'Syria, Bashar al-Assad' were spray-painted over their walls in red. The Jabhat al-Nusra slogans had been obliterated apart from the word 'Allah', which had remained untouched. There were fewer checkpoints in all those places and people could drive to Aleppo up the highway again or to the Lebanese border.

There were even instances, Ari had heard, of Free Syrian army soldiers sharing a coffee or a meal with government soldiers. Some of them, after forswearing their opposition to the government, had been allowed to keep their light weapons and to access food and medicine. Others had been allowed to return to the ranks of the army they had deserted.

Ari once again wondered how there were still people in Washington eager to gamble in the effort to overthrow Bashar al-Assad, and together with him, in all likelihood, his secular regime in order to take the country to a darkness no eye could penetrate. He communicated his thoughts to Maryam, whose short, crisply-articulated response was 'they're drooling idiots'.

At play, there was, of course, as Ari knew, something more than the sheer force of those people's idiocy, enough by itself to overwhelm a public uninterested in remote enquiries. It was the interests of the idiots' backers, all those who were able to dictate developments through the hidden parallelogram of forces they had built up.

But this was not the time for any serious discussion. Maryam and her sisters were dancing in the streets, singing and laughing and moving from one place to another to enjoy, if possible, every bit of what was a massive Christmas party. The event was something, Ari knew, that would stay in his memory for good. The future would not be able to forget it.

Chapter 24
'Unfounded speculation'

Having rested for a while, both physically and mentally, Ari returned to work after a couple of days with enough energy to light up a street. But before he had settled into his office, his telephone rang. It was a man with a Texan accent who identified himself as Arthur Parker. He got straight to the point.

'I'm interested in getting involved in a big business project here in Syria,' he said with a thick coat of self-confidence over his voice.

'What do you have in mind?' Ari asked, curious rather than interested.

'Construction. More than five million houses and stores have been destroyed in this country and need to be rebuilt.'

Ari could hardly believe his ears. 'And why are you phoning me?' he asked.

'Because UNRWA,' the American said, 'must be interested in financing a project that will provide housing to a few thousand Palestinians.'

'What's going on in his mind? Doesn't he know that the country is on fire?' Ari wondered for a minute. 'But the country is still at war,' he retorted.

'The war will end soon,' the American said confidently with all the authority of his ostentatiously virile tone of voice. 'The Russian air campaign will make sure of it. And when this happens, which will be soon, somebody must be around to start the reconstruction.'

'Yes,' Ari thought, 'somebody like the Swiss-French LafargeHolcim cement company which financed the terror activities of jihadi groups, including those blacklisted by the West, in order to maintain its operations in northern Syria.' The company had been sued by the European Centre for Constitutional and Human Rights and had admitted that its practices were 'unacceptable'. But, of course, Ari said nothing about it all. Doing so would serve no purpose whatsoever.

The conversation, which had begun desultorily, had already gathered a swift energy. What Parker wanted, as he made clear, was a meeting with Ari whose professed enthusiasm for it was nevertheless disproportionate to its anticipated returns. Ari passed on the request to Samuels, his boss, and Samuels suggested that they would lose nothing by meeting this 'gentleman'. Ari called him back and arranged to meet him at his office later that day.

Parker appeared on time, shook hands with Ari and stared intently into his eyes for a minute, like an optometrist seeking a flaw. Without the usual niceties of etiquette he then got straight to the point. 'The general population will need houses and stores, the provision of which will require huge efforts for years to come. The opportunities here are endless and the Palestinians can benefit from what we offer.'

'Who's "we"?' Ari asked, as he had perhaps missed something.

'It's a big construction corporation based in Denver, Colorado.'

'And you're ready to bring cranes and scaffolding?'

'We will be pretty soon.'

'So will the Iranian developers with ties to the government,' Ari teased him.

'Really?' Palmer seemed surprised. Like all free enterprise propagandists, he hated competition in any form.

'Yes, they're interested in doing business in well-off Shi'ite majority neighbourhoods in Syria's capital.'

'We'll beat them,' the American said confidently.

'Yes, if the Russians let you. Anyway,' Ari added, 'you're welcome to give us your exact requirements and we'll see if and how we can work together.'

That was all that Palmer wanted: the reassurance. For him, that was the beginning of a grand adventure no other American had attempted in the Middle East. While talking, his eyes mirrored his calculating intelligence.

'Mind you,' Ari said at what seemed to be the end of their conversation, 'the needs of the Syrians go far beyond their housing requirements. 70% of the population is without access to adequate drinking water, four out of five people live in poverty, and more than 2 million children are out of school. Helping 13.5 million people, including 6 million children, will require more than 3 billion dollars in just 2016 alone.'

'That's not my problem,' the developer answered. He then looked out of the window to see if his car and his chauffer were still where he had left them. In doing so, he bumped into Brigitte. He apologised to her with a smile absent from his face until that moment and then walked away full of energy and purpose.

Moving away from such fanciful ideas, Ari returned to his desk on which nothing fanciful could be detected. In the evening, he saw Parker on the Syrian TV giving an interview about his grand reconstruction plans. 'My sense of reality will never stop being taken by surprise,' he decided once again. The thought had already crossed his mind many times.

A day later, a phone call from Rami Abu Hadeed, the FSA colonel who had asked Ari for help to escape to Greece, informed him that somebody called Ibrahim Suleiman was in town. He wondered if that man, who, Hadeed had incidentally said, loved to entertain people by telling them jokes about Jews, could manage his and his family's departure to Europe. Ari contacted him for his own reasons and arranged a meeting for the next morning.

Ibrahim Suleiman, a man who looked like Jimmy Hoffa, the US Labour leader who was sent to prison for fraud and conspiracy, was a member of the anti-Assad Turkmen brigades smuggling refugees to the Turkish town of Çeşme. From there, payment of $3,000 per person would secure the desperate Syrians a place on a dinghy to cross into one of the nearby Greek islands. The vessels were often rotten and overcrowded and therefore likely to sink. Many actually did. But having no home to return to, the refugees had no option but to try their luck.

'I was afraid,' Mohammad Nofal Yassin, a 40-year-old baker who had fled with his wife and four children from Yarmouk, had emailed Ari's office from Chios island in November, 'that I had made a terrible mistake. I was told there would only be 35 people on the dinghy, but there was more than 60. We refused to board. But we realised that staying was not an option. There was no home to return to.'

He and his family had fearfully clambered into the dinghy only to run into trouble fifty minutes later and in the middle of the night. The boat had run out of fuel. Thankfully, the Greek coastguard had picked them up and the rescued family was taken to Chios.

The meeting with Ibrahim Suleiman took place in Deir al-Asafir, a town in Eastern Ghouta. Ibrahim welcomed Ari as if he were an old friend, grumbled about life, which denied him the comforts he felt he was entitled to, and, without invitation, briefly talked about the end of time scenario and the emergence of al-Mahdi. His pronouncement seemed infected by a bug similar to those that cause the most profitable diseases to the benefit of the pharmaceutical companies.

But he also very proudly told Ari that the 'American' missiles used against the Russian planes had been launched from the Aleppo area by Turkmen, his people. The latter's militias were at the time being attacked by the Syrian army which was again backed by Russian air power.

The Turkmen, mainly concentrated in the north part of Syria and numbering something close to 200,000, had never been recognised by the Syrian regime as an ethnic minority. As soon as the uprising against Bashar al-Assad had started in 2011, they formed the Syrian Turkmen Brigades, which, trained by Turkey, took up arms against the regime. In the following years, they worked together with other armed groups, including the Jabhat al-Nusra Front and the Islamist Ahrar al-Sham.

Ibrahim offered to take Ari to the areas controlled by the 'moderate' brigades. 'They need,' he added, in an effort to dissolve the cloud of suspicion he detected on Ari's face, 'all the help they could get. The civilian casualties are horrendous. The Russians bomb us indiscriminately.'

He almost failed to finish his sentence as he sneezed a few times. He had, he said as he was wiping his hands on his trousers, a cold. 'He has not washed,' Ari thought, 'since the death of JFK.'

What the man did not mention was that the Russian strikes aimed at the 'moderates' were directed at the number of Turkmen villages in the far north-west of Syria which had been occupied by hundreds of Chechen fighters for many months.

Russian air strikes, which began in September 2015, had killed about 1,000 civilians up to that point in Syria. It was a story that once again offered the opportunity for a sad reflection on the consequences of war, any war. To a Greek, like Ari, the loss of innocent civilians brought back an inherited painful memory – the allied bombing of Piraeus on Tuesday, the 11th of January 1944.

Flying from Italy on that day, 84 American B-17 bombers had appeared over Piraeus, which, like the rest of Greece, was under German occupation. The Greeks flooded the streets and, watched by German army units, began to celebrate. The celebrations did not last long as the pitiless and relentless bombing of the city that destroyed entire neighbourhoods began. The bombardment continued by the RAF on the same day. It was reported that the allied air attack had killed a minimum of 700 Greek civilians and 12 German soldiers. The attack had infuriated the Greeks to such an extent that the Germans, taking advantage of it, 'celebrated' the allied bombardment with a series of propaganda postal stamps.

'Concern for humanity,' Ari thought, 'is there, well-embalmed in a bank vault. But this is history. Let's focus on the moment.'

In doing so, he could only see his concerns growing. Either the man was just trying to impress him or, alternatively, he was seeking his approval for reasons he could not work out. Suspecting that the offer to visit the place represented a threat, he eventually just negated it. Its breath stunk. Even if it was not a trap, he was convinced it was nothing less than an invitation to commit suicide.

He instead asked Ibrahim for proof of what he was saying. The latter, eager to show the world what his race could do but also ready to accept £10K for the information, gave Ari what he needed. It related to the supply of the ground-to-air missiles, their transfer to Aleppo, the name of the rebel unit that had fired them and also its location. Ari passed on the information to the Russian 'cultural' attaché, who was happy to receive it. He passed it to the Americans, too, deservedly so as they paid for Ibrahim's bribe.

Ibrahim was happy. 'It's always a pleasure to make a profit off the Jews,' he told Ari when he was handed the money.

With ground-to-air Russian missiles it had bought from the 'moderate' rebels who had bought them from Bashar al-Assad's forces, Isis subsequently downed one of the US jets. But by this time, its game was up. The Americans did not fall into the trap and the only result was the intensification of the bombing of Isis resources.

But as his investigation into Laura's murder was not progressing, Ari decided to re-focus on it. He tried to recall what Laura had told him about Khaled and what exactly the latter had said or hinted at when the two of them had met. He was even trying to re-read his body language. It indicated, he felt, some discomfort, which he was rather unsuccessfully trying to hide. He needed to meet him again. He was sure he knew something about Laura's death, which he did not want to pass on.

As he thought a bit more about it all, he also felt sure that Mark Hollinger, the MI6 man in Damascus, also had information which he did not want to pass onto him. Wondering who the man really was, and what his verbal mist concealed, he decided to collect some information about him. But this had to wait for a while until the arrival of the New Year the next day.

The first day of January was quite cold. Still, this did not prevent the Syrians, used as they were to the inclemency of their winters, from enjoying their day in the Damascus parks. Apart from calling Khaled to arrange a meeting, that was all Ari did too. But Khaled's phone seemed to be out of order.

He next called Mark Hollinger to arrange another meeting, but he was told that this was not possible. Hollinger had to go for 'a meeting with officials of the Central Bank of Syria'. Ari told him the meeting would not last for more than five minutes and Hollinger reluctantly gave way. First thing the next morning, Ari was at his office. Hollinger opened the door and, with arms crossed over his chest, bluntly asked Ari what he wanted to talk about.

'Give me a minute and I'll tell you,' Ari said. 'There's a train of thought that the Saudis were involved in the murder of Laura. That was at least what Elia Bassem Fatime and Michael Kay seemed to think and what Khaled had hinted at. The Saudis' involvement was somehow evident in what Mohammad Nofal Yassin, the Palestinian from Yarmouk, has told me. In addition, Rafiq Shahadah, the head of the Syrian military intelligence Directorate, has also clearly implied the same thing. Saudi Arabians were involved in the killing of Laura. Why? What was their reason? Did it have to do,' he asked, 'with the Jordanian business, or, as it seems to me, with something else. Whatever,' he asked at the end rather bluntly, 'why had the Saudis ordered her execution?'

Quite undemonstrative of his thoughts and biding his time, Hollinger said nothing. Ari wished he could intercept what he was thinking, but he did not possess the right equipment. The technological revolution had not gone all that far as yet. Thoughts were still invisible. 'But if Hollinger's silence could speak, what would it say? Perhaps it didn't need to say anything. Just its odour was saying more than one thousand words.' The interval of silence sat for a while between them like a third person.

Hollinger eventually dismissed Ari's suspicions with a smile that conveyed both amusement and malevolence, the same Ebenezer Scrooge would have offered to someone who attempted to assist him in counting his gold. Ari's assertion, he added with sinister conciseness, was 'unfounded speculation'. Laura 'had been killed by the jihadis.

'The problem,' he concluded while putting his jacket on, ready to leave his office, 'is not any non-existent Saudi involvement in Laura's murder. It's instead her meddling in things that her imagination had produced.'

In spite of his imperturbable disposition, his voice sounded lame and shoddy. Even worse, its tone had something vaguely threatening. It made Ari instantly recall another similar situation, which he had come across in Alexandria, from the time he was a kid. He had witnessed a car accident which had led to a woman being killed. The driver, apparently obeying the traffic laws whenever it suited him, had not stopped at the red light and had driven straight into her. Yet he had refused to take any responsibility for it. 'It wasn't my fault,' he had blatantly told Ari, 'and don't you dare to tell anyone stories your imagination has produced.'

He walked out of Hollinger's office still wondering why on earth the intelligence man had totally refused to consider at least the possibility that Laura had indeed been involved in unravelling a nasty story. Anything like it was, for him, 'unlicensed speculation'.

As soon as he was out on the street, he heard the sound of a car door slamming. The young man who emerged from the car, a Peugeot-207, seemed to take an intense interest in him. Only three meters away, he was eyeballing Ari, squinting against the curl of smoke rising from the cigarette dangling from his lips. In front of him, there were empty crisp-packets he had just thrown away. His looks gave him shivers.

Ari stopped dead in his tracks for a second as if he had been unplugged. He stared back and quickly studied him. His face had a vicious scar that diagonally ran across it, from his forehead to his chin. It appeared that whatever had cut him had mutilated his left eye in the process. Something looked very wrong here. He had, Ari decided, been targeted.

He started wondering for a minute why he had gone to Hollinger's office to ask the questions he did, why he did not carry on with his UMWRA work without trying to identify the killers of Laura, why he had after all come to Damascus rather than stay in London and enjoy all the good things the UK capital offers. If he had had the sense, he would have at least removed himself from the story, dropped clean out of the race. He would be in his Hampstead flat improvising, like Paganini, his music-related performance, or in the Emirates Stadium watching an Arsenal game. Not in a city where death happily kept setting traps for everybody everywhere.

He dismissed all the thoughts he was wrapped up in a moment later. He was where he was because the road in front of him had always been the road of the soul. Anything else would just not be him. It would falsely represent a part of himself that just was not there. All he needed now was another cup of coffee, on top of those he already had knocked back.

He did not go for it. He instead tried Khaled's number. Khaled, who answered the call this time, told him that he could come to see him the next day, if he wished.

This arrangement suited Ari as the 'moderates' discontent the media had been reporting about had attracted his attention. He wanted to find out more about their plans in the Eastern Ghouta meeting of community leaders, held in order to find new ways to ensure their survival.

Chapter 25
Tomorrow is totally unscripted

Ari's planned journey to Douma was not going to be easy, and he knew it. On Christmas day, Zahran Alloush, the leader of the all-powerful Jaysh al-Islam, and five other senior leaders had been killed in an airstrike in Eastern Ghouta. Their death was a major blow to the opposition and a coup for Syria's intelligence, which, having successfully infiltrated the Jaysh al-Islam's high command, knew the precise location of their meeting.

In addition, the Riyadh conference, to which the Saudis had invited 'moderate' groups fighting the Bashar al-Assad regime inside Syria, had broken down. Though Isis and Jabhat al-Nusra were not invited to take part, Jaysh al-Islam and Ahrar al-Sham, the 'moderate and legitimate' opposition groups according to Saudi Arabia, were there. The latter did, however, pull out of the talks because, as it let everyone know, the conference had abandoned the prospect of an Islamist Syria.

The situation, meanwhile, was getting even more tense when regime and Kurdish forces began to push Isis back into an area between Aleppo and Azaz in north-western Syria. It was through this area that Turkey provided the Islamists with the aid they needed. In this, the Kurds had the active support of Russia whose jets began blitzing the positions of the Islamists.

Erdogan was once again beside himself. He could order the sun to rise every day, but here he had a situation he could not handle. The Kurds, who had partnered with Bashar al-Assad, were now partnered with the Americans in Eastern Syria and with the Russians in Western Syria. This was shifting the dynamics of the war in a way Turkey found utterly objectionable. His presumption of leading a neo-Ottoman Sunni revival had just boiled down to a revived war with the Kurds. It was far from what he had been scheming.

In response, Turkey started bombing the Syrian Kurds advancing against the Islamists in Asaz. It also started talks with Saudi Arabia to work out the joint deployment of ground troops in Syria. Such a move seemed even more vital now as remains of the Free Syrian Army units, after their original desertion, had reportedly been reincorporating into the Syrian army. Mohammed bib Salman, the Saudi Defence minister, was all in favour of the Turkish suggestion. Dismayed at Russia's military intervention, he had already warned Russia that its involvement in Syria was bound to have 'dangerous consequences'.

Saudi Arabian clerics had, meanwhile, declared a jihad against Russian and Syrian government forces and urged all Sunni Muslims to join the battle against Bashar al-Assad.

Neither Turkey nor Saudi Arabia could, however, advance the idea of a military intervention. The necessary US support was lacking. The Obama administration was not interested in getting dragged further into the Syrian conflict and it would not endorse the multilateral military intervention Turkey and Saudi Arabia had in mind. Such an intervention was likely to create more problems than it would solve. It was filled with danger.

Apart from anything else, if Saudi and Turkish forces were deployed at Syria's north-western border, they would be inside Russia's operational theatre. That meant that even the slightest of incidents between the Turkish and Russian forces could have very dramatic consequences. It could lead to a war between the two countries in which case NATO might well have to invoke article 5 of the Washington treaty which states that an attack on one member of the alliance is an attack on all of them.

This would be a total nightmare for the US.

And if the Saudis attacked Iranians fighting on the side of the Syrian President, this could easily lead to a war between those two countries. Even if none of this happened, the occupation of Kurdish areas in Syria by Turkey looked quite disagreeable.

Given all these problems, the Americans had no intention whatsoever of letting regional actors call the shots. But in the arms of their ineptitude, they had inevitably lost control of developments on the ground. They knew that air strikes alone, constant and deadly as they were, had their limitations. Isis could be beaten but only in co-ordination with a cohesive, motivated ground force which the West had no intention whatsoever of providing. Hence they relied on the Kurdish Peshmerga.

But sticking to their guns required a shift in their policy towards Turkey and Saudi Arabia, their major allies in the area, which they were resolutely reluctant to contemplate almost since the very beginning of the

Syrian war. Perceptions in Washington were nevertheless now gradually shifting. The Turkey and Saudi Arabia-backed 'moderates', who had until then enjoyed the backing of the US, were now quickly going out of favour, too.

Totally disenchanted with them, the Obama administration had even warned them later on that they would face 'dire consequences' if they did not dissociate from the Jabhat al-Nusra terrorists, the most effective force fighting the Bashar al-Assad regime. In doing so, President Obama made crystal clear to everybody that the war on the regime had ended. The only enemy in Syria was now the Isis jihadists.

'It was what the Americans should have done ages ago,' Ari thought as he was watching the news on CNN. 'But they didn't have the guts.'

The shift in the American approach was deeply controversial within the Obama administration and infuriated the 'moderate' factions affiliated with al-Qaeda. The American demand to isolate the extremists, one of their representatives argued, was 'irrational and immoral'. Dissociation with Jabhat al-Nusra was neither desirable for them, nor even possible as they were all part of the same interlocking hideous machine. Hence the shift in the American approach was met with outright opposition by both the 'moderates' and their backers, Turkey and Saudi Arabia.

The US, the latter two Powers claimed, had abandoned 'the mainstream Sunni rebels'. Isolating Jabhat al-Nusra, they further argued, would only benefit Bashar al-Assad.

In response, the Americans increased their reliance on the Kurds. But this only aggravated the problems between the US on one side and Turkey and Saudi Arabia on the other. A daunted Ahmet Davutoglu, the Turkish Prime Minister, even threatened the 'harshest reaction' if the Kurds continued their fight against Isis in the border areas. The threat implied a full scale Turkish invasion.

Alarmed, the UN Security Council urged Turkey to 'comply with international law'. The US and the EU likewise called on its government to hold fire. Meanwhile, as information had reached his ears that Turkey had a contingency plan to seize the NATO nuclear arsenal at Incirlik, President Obama ordered the removal of all nuclear attack planes from Turkey.

Enraged, the Turks warned the US government that relations between the two countries would be 'seriously damaged' if Washington insisted on supporting the Kurdish militia in the battle to drive Isis out of Syria. The US, they argued, should rely instead on Turkish forces and the Syrian 'moderates' they backed in the battle to re-take al-Raqqah in particular. They had even presented to the US their own battle plan for the purpose. Yet the US did not want to hear a word about it.

The Saudis, for their part, again called for the overthrowing of President Bashar al-Assad. The call was made despite the reservations of Western leaders who had indicated that the Syrian President should stay on during a transition stage for an unspecified time. But this only angered the Saudis and the Turks further. 'The Americans are running away from their responsibilities,' a senior Saudi official in Riyadh said. 'They have done nothing but enable Putin...' The exact words he used in his denunciation of the Americans' 'incompetent' policy were carefully omitted from the news agencies' reports.

To show their own competence, the Saudis announced in Riyadh the formation of a global 'Islamic Alliance' of 34 countries, including Egypt, Qatar, Turkey, Pakistan, Malaysia and Nigeria. Though its purpose was to combat terrorism, Isis was not specifically mentioned. Its formation nevertheless had nothing to do with 'terrorism'. It was all a show for the benefit of the United States, Russia and most importantly Iran. Saudi Arabia was the 'leader' of the Muslim world.

On January 2, 2016, to demonstrate their own competence, the Saudis did also proceed, just like Isis, to behead 47 people, including the revered Shi'a cleric Sheikh Nimr Baqr al-Nimr. His 'crime' was the rejection of the Saudi wahhabism and his call for free elections. All that was missing from this heinous demonstration of their religious beliefs was footage of the decapitations.

The executions caused a storm of protests in many Arab countries, but once again the West, though uneasy at the grotesque butchery, chose not to notice it. The country whose decisions controlled the ebb and flow of trillions of oil-generated dollars along with its strategic location and control of the Sunni Muslim fortunes, ensured the West had to go on paying obeisance to all the regional head-choppers.

In the meantime, the Americans had started to pursue more actively their goals in the area. The threat of a new international war has spurred on both them and the Russians, but also several of their regional and local allies, including the Kurds, to throw their weight behind a truce for the first time. This might, hopefully, be followed by a negotiated settlement between the Syrian regime and the 'moderate' rebels. All of them could then turn their weapons against both Isis and the Jabhat al-Nusra Front.

Adopted earlier, such a policy would have seemed a long shot, but what would have proved intractable for nearly five years was now a real possibility. That would, of course, be the case provided the local rivalries in Syria had been ironed out. Should that be the case, the Isis caliphate could not look forward to a long life.

But the plan was not easy to implement as there were no agreed upon lists of terrorist organisations to exempt from the cease-fire arrangements. Jabhat al-Nusra was an internationally sanctioned terrorist group, Ahrar al-Sham, the Turkish-backed group, had been designated as a terrorist group even by the United Arab Emirates, and Jaysh al-Islam, the Saudi-backed group, had been involved in numerous terrorist activities. U.S. Secretary of State John Kerry had once referred to the latter two groups as terrorist groups, though a State Department spokesman later repudiated his comments.

All of them, committed to creating an Islamic State under Sharia law, had denounced any kind of secular democratic government as un-Islamic, and had vowed to expel Shi'ite Muslims, including Syria's Alawite minority, from Syria. The Quran was to be their only source of law and they were nothing less than valiant helmsman of the antediluvian catastrophe.

But, on the other hand, the Americans were not prepared to confront them. Attacking them would effectively kill the Syrian opposition and further cement Bashar al-Assad's grip on power. Their policy, as deformed as the body of Toulouse-Lautrec, had put the Americans in a bind. They either had to side with the jihadists and support the establishment of a theocratic Islamic state or, without saying so in so many words, side with the Assad regime. At that late stage, they seemed inclined to take the latter course.

This exasperated the Turks, the Saudis and also the 'moderates' they were sponsoring in Syria. The latter, if the Americans were to pursue such a course, were ready to confront them militarily. Their discontent had already manifested itself not only in Syria but also in Turkey itself where Islamists had protested in front of the NATO military base in Incirlik, which was used by the Americans to bomb Isis.

'Muslim blood,' they held, 'can't be spilled through military action from Incirlik.'

The void seemed unbridgeable. The Americans were, in fact, outraged over Turkey, who, despite repeated warnings, continued 'shamelessly and openly to back the jihadis'. Its involvement in the war was ostensibly directed against Isis, but its real target was the Kurds whose submission to its rule was for the Turks a must. The Kurds had to be kept 'in their place'. Keeping them 'in their place' also offered Turkey the excuse to proceed with its planned territorial expansion into northern Syrian and also northern Iraq territories in tune with Erdogan's Ottoman dream of recapturing part of the land lost to Turkey at the end of the First World War.

Ari, in his office, was thinking about all the incredible ramifications of the incrassating Syrian 'plot'. Turkey's militancy in particular, he was sure, constituted a major threat to the US designs in the region, which the US was anything but likely to tolerate.

'But what could the US do to change the course of events? How could President Obama put an end to the subversion of his administration's plans by both the conservative American establishment and also by Turkey and Saudi Arabia? Whichever way he chose to go there was a price to be paid. There were no black and white solutions, nothing was as simple as a Madeira cake.'

Ari was thinking hard about it, but he still could not work out the way that the Americans would go.

'Erdogan has the upper hand and would continue to do so unless the US rhetoric turned into action against him. But what action? Bomb Turkey? Out of the question. Drive him out of power? Yes, but how? A coup d'état?'

His instant reaction to that thought was 'Don't be silly. The Americans wouldn't dare do such a thing against a major NATO ally. But what if Erdogan was determined to force the pace of developments in Syria, the Middle East and, given the Russian involvement, possibly in the world, too? If yes, who would then be in charge of the US foreign policy? Obama or Erdogan?'

The Americans knew what the answer to this question was. But again, how far were they prepared to go? 'An in-between solution might be the targeting of the jihadis that Turkey and also Saudi Arabia backed in Syria and Iraq. Doing so made total sense. The US couldn't support both the Kurds in the war against Isis, its prime target, and the pro-Turkish jihadis who, together with Jabhat al-Nusra, were fighting both the Kurds and the regime. By the laws of pure symmetry, it had to be one or the other. The US knew it, but its decision-making process was growing slower than grass on parched land.

'If the Americans threw their weight against the Kurds,' Ari said aloud to himself, 'they would lose the only reliable ground forces against Isis. And if they threw their weight against all jihadis, they couldn't take for granted the response of both Turkey and Saudi Arabia, their unreliable, vagarious, untrustworthy partners. The latter option presented another major difficulty. It would meet the strong opposition of many Americans for whom the enemy wasn't Isis but Bashar al-Assad and the Russians behind him. Emboldened by the stalemate in the peace negotiations, these Americans seemed to prefer a military solution to the crisis even at the risk of an outright confrontation with the Russians.

'The US,' Ari concluded, 'has found itself in a no-win situation. Either it backed up its policy by force, facing, as a result, the unequivocal hostility of its Turkish and Saudi allies and an uncontrolled situation on the ground, or it backed out, letting, as a result, Turkey and Saudi Arabia run the show. But the latter option was also full of dangers as the interests of those two Powers considerably diverged from those of the US. The goal of both Turkey and Saudi Arabia was the domination of the Middle East against the opposition of Syria, Iraq and Iran in a way that could lead to new regional wars that could change all regional maps. It was also the creation of another equally dangerous, Sharia-based theocratic state backed by either or both of them. The withdrawal of the US from the scene would further leave the Turks free to pursue their military campaign against the Kurds.

'Deeply divided,' Ari kept thinking, 'the US could easily lose the plot altogether. That is to say, if, finding the bathwater too cold for one finger and too hot for another, it hasn't lost it already.'

The major complications in the wider political scene, together with everything else that was going on in his life, had again crescendoed Ari's anxiety. 'Hell,' he almost shouted when he felt he had reached an impasse. 'I'm not here to solve these sorts of problems. I must focus on what's on my plate.' He was fully aware he needed to calm down. With a little effort he eventually managed to re-focus on the requests for help in front of him and to make a few recommendations, which, he was sure, would not be of much help in the current situation. What had occupied his mind before, the momentous decisions a number of nations had to make, was now indiscernible. Thinking about such issues now looked like a joke.

Then his phone rang. On the line was Thiago, the Spanish NGO representative Ari had met in the lecture given by the German professor.

'Do you fancy dinner in town?'

'What a good idea!'

A good meal with some nice wine in the friendly company of Thiago was just what the doctor had ordered.

They met later in the day. Thiago first suggested they go for a Turkish bath at Nur-al-Din Bath, a place located between the Azem Palace and Straight Street. It was a place for men only. They had a sauna and then a soothing massage, followed by a delicious mint tea. Refreshed, they then walked to a Chinese restaurant, opposite to Café Narcissius, for some Sweet & Sour Chicken Cantonese Style or a Crispy Duck with Pancakes. As they discovered, the chef's wife was back in China to escape the Syrian hell.

Inevitably, their talk almost instantly turned to the on-going war. And unsurprisingly, the Kurds, who had recently come into the picture much more forcefully than before, also invaded their evening.

'These people in Syria, the Kurds,' Thiago said, 'are the most effective fighting force against Isis in Syria and yet they are now being attacked, not only by Isis and al-Qaeda, but also by Turkey. How complicated can the whole situation become?'

'Yet, talking about complications, one must also take into account,' Ari said, 'both the US and the Russian involvement in all this. The US has backed the Kurds against Isis, but it's also, as far as I know, providing intelligence to the Turkish military against them. Ridiculously, on the one hand, it supports the Kurds against Isis, but, on the other, it works against them wherever Turkey so demands.

'Russia, likewise, backs up the Syrian Kurds as long as they don't threaten Bashar al-Assad. But the moment other factors such as the re-positioning of Turkey's foreign policy come into the picture, you don't know what they'll do.'

'True, very true,' said Thiago. 'Nobody, absolutely nobody is committed to the establishment of a Kurdish state. Turkey, Syria, Iraq and Iran oppose it fiercely and the rest of the world doesn't give a damn. The Kurds' contribution to the war against Isis is appreciated by many. But when all this ends, they'll be left to their own devices and to the mercy of their oppressors.'

'If they haven't in the meantime been betrayed by the Russians or the Americans,' Ari added. 'Unless, of course, they've managed to establish facts on the ground.'

The waiter was at their table, ready to take their order. 'We'll have an hors d'oeuvre, won't we?' Ari asked.

'Yes, of course.' They ordered it together with some red wine.

'You know,' Ari said while filling their glasses, 'the Kurds' maltreatment by the world has been disgraceful. They are the fourth-largest ethnic group in the Middle East after the Arabs, Persians and Turks, numbering about 30 million people, and they form a distinctive community, united through race, culture and language. By the way, did you know that their language is recognised only in Armenia as a minority language?'

'No, I didn't,' said Thiago. 'But I know that using their language is viewed as a treacherous activity in some countries.'

'Yet,' Ari carried on, 'all their efforts to set up an independent state have been brutally quashed over the years. Their history is a history of betrayal, oppression, and genocide. Nothing else, absolutely nothing else. But the world doesn't want to know. It's happy to see their struggles being washed away by waves of oppression.'

Thiago moved his head up and down to indicate his sympathy with their predicament and Ari again filled their glasses with some wine. Meanwhile, their hors d'oeuvre had arrived – crispy chicken wings with Thai sauce and sesame prawn on toast. They had a few bites and then Ari carried on.

'They unsuccessfully revolted against the Turks and the Persians in 1880 – mind you, that was long before any of the Arab groups had raised the nationalist flag. And then in 1916 and 1917 they were turned, just like the Armenians, into Turkey's victims of a large scale ethnic cleansing. Seven hundred thousand of them had been forcibly deported by the end of World War I. They revolted, again unsuccessfully, against the Turks in

1925, 1930 and 1938. In response, the Turkish government forcibly relocated more than one million Kurds and banned the use of Kurdish language, dressing and cultural activities.'

'Yes, their ethnic identity was totally denied,' Thiago said. 'They weren't Kurds. They were "Mountain Turks".'

'The situation,' Ari continued, 'didn't improve after World War II, until the Kurds eventually revolted again in Turkey during the 1980s. Since then, more than 40,000 people have been killed and hundreds of thousands displaced.'

The main course had in the meantime arrived, and they both decided to leave politics aside for at least a while. The topic turned to Damascus' night life, which, Thiago, as Ari discovered, had been able to appreciate much more than himself.

'The Damascenes,' he said, 'love a night out. Lots of places, many of them recently opened, are always crammed. The party rolls on despite the crisis. Thoughts of the war are left to daylight hours.'

'Yes, I know,' was Ari's response. They had another glass of wine, saluting the spirit of the Damascenes. The discussion then turned back to the Kurds.

'Similar problems,' Ari continued, 'appeared in Iraq, too. The Kurdish revolt of 1922 – 1924 against British rule, aiming for the establishment of an independent Kurdish state, was suppressed and so was the 1961 Kurdish revolt against the nationalist Iraqi government that emerged after the 1958 revolution. The Iraqis' subsequent "Arabisation" policy, involving the settlement of Arabs in areas with Kurdish majorities, particularly around the oil-rich city of Kirkuk, had led to another failed Kurdish revolt in 1974.

'Much more serious trouble was spelled out for them during the 1980s Iran-Iraq war in which the Iraqi Kurds backed Iran. Saddam Hussein didn't forgive them for that. Nearly 200,000 civilians were killed during his campaign against them, which included chemical attacks, the most infamous of which was the attack on the town of Halabja that instantly killed 5,000 civilians.

'Still, despite everything, another Kurdish rebellion occurred in 1991, after Iraq's invasion of Kuwait and its defeat by the US coalition. It was once again violently suppressed. But the subsequent no-fly zone prompted by the US and its allies gave the Iraqi Kurds a degree of self-rule. That relative independence expanded after the US-led invasion of Iraq in 2003.'

'The Iraqi Kurds,' Thiago said, 'did support the US-led invasion. Didn't they?'

'Yes, they did. But despite the interim settlement achieved after 2003, internal boundaries between the Iraqis and the Kurds are still very hotly disputed, often violently. Hence the 2014 seizure by the Kurds of the city of Kirkuk and many other territories in Northern Iraq, which has infuriated the Iraqis.'

'No end to it at all,' Thiago said before drinking the last of the wine in his glass.

'Likewise,' Ari continued, 'the Iranians have brutally acted against the Kurds, though their violence never matched that of Turkey. Yet, Ayatollah Khomeini, the new religious leader of Iran, declared a jihad against separatism in Iranian Kurdistan in 1979. He even declared that nationalism among minorities is both against the Islamic doctrines and helpful only to those who don't want the Muslim countries united. The 1980 Kurdish revolt was subsequently crushed by the Iranian military. Entire Kurdish villages and towns were destroyed and thousands were sentenced to death. Altogether, more than 10,000 Kurds were killed in the process.

'Even now, as I've heard,' Thiago said, 'clashes between regime forces and Kurdish militants often take place in the north-west of the country. Twenty Kurds were hanged only very recently, weren't they?'

'Thankfully,' Thiago carried on, 'the situation in Syria is not all that bad. Syria's Kurds have, of course, long been crudely suppressed and denied basic rights as when, in the 1960s, some 300,000 of them were denied citizenship. Kurdish land was confiscated and redistributed to Arabs in an attempt to "Arabize" Kurdish regions and Kurds in Syria are still not allowed to use the Kurdish language or publish books and other materials written in Kurdish officially. But, while they faced routine discrimination and harassment by the government, they've at least never been massacred!'

'But the Kurds did of course revolt against Bashar al-Assad,' Ari replied. 'They want their own homeland. Just like the Catalans!'

'Oh, leave the Catalans alone,' Thiago said laughingly.

Having finished their dinner by this time and all set to go, they asked for the bill. But, as they discovered, it was raining outside and they were not prepared for it. 'OK,' they agreed, 'let's have another glass of wine and see how it goes.'

This gave Ari the opportunity to add another few words to what he was saying. 'You see,' he said, 'the Kurds have a right to a home, but when they claim it, they're brutally suppressed. That's been the pattern for more than one hundred years. And when they try to take their fate into their own hands, as the Kurds in Turkey do now, they're branded as "terrorists". That's what the Turks say and that's what the Americans say. On the other hand, the Kurds who've revolted against Bashar al-Assad are the modern day heroes for the Americans.'

'You see,' Thiago said, 'the establishment of a Kurdish state in Syria is utterly objectionable to the Turks. It would represent an existential threat to Turkish territorial integrity. Once such a state is established, nothing can hold back the Turkish Kurds.'

'It's as you say,' Ari replied. 'And this is the reason, or one of the reasons, Turkey is absolutely determined to invade Syria to end their insurrection. And this is also what complicates Turkey's relations with the US and, by extension, the US relations with Russia and indefinitely prolongs the Syrian war.

'But why, I wonder, why does the world so miserably fail to respond to the Kurdish plea? Why, for example, doesn't the UN at least give the Kurds the right to be legally represented within the world body? Why doesn't it campaign for their recognition as an ethnic entity? It's all bloody politics. Nothing right or wrong by definition. Self-interest rules.'

But they knew that the whole issue had less to do with the Kurdish problem and more with the designs of both the theocratic Saudi Arabian regime and the Ottoman fantasies of Turkey that both run in opposition to the US policy in the Middle East.

'I wonder which way Washington will choose to go,' Thiago said. 'And how this will affect its relations with Russia. But...'

He did not finish the sentence as the front door of the restaurant had violently opened and a young Arab had just burst in. He rushed towards the kitchen and, out of breath, he asked the proprietor where the back exit was. His eyes were flooded with fear and his voice demonstrated a disturbed state of mind.

The befuddled gaze of the proprietor, a Chinese in his forties, glowered at him. 'What...?' he managed to ask.

'Where's the back door?' the man screamed at him.

The Chinese man's finger pointed backwards. 'There.'

The man rushed towards it and almost instantly disappeared from view. A minute later, two security men, both out of breath, stormed in. 'Where's he gone?' they asked the proprietor.

'There,' he said, pointing towards the exit.

They rushed towards it and they, too, were out of the restaurant in no time. Frozen in their seats, the customers were looking at each other, puzzled and bewildered. Who knows? Thiago and Ari wondered. It could be anything. But more likely, as they both agreed soon after, the Mukhabarat was in action to catch another 'enemy' of the state. Whatever it was, the incident had unsettled them and ended their wine-soaked conversation.

By this time, the rain had stopped. Ari offered Thiago a lift on his motorbike, which was gratefully accepted, and after taking him to his flat, he drove straight back home. The day had turned out to be longer than he expected.

But so was the night. Half-asleep, Ari heard a noise out in the street in front of his flat – heavy steps moving with some uncertainty. Gradually they drifted away, but soon after they were again penetrating the darkness of the night very close to his flat. He had never before come across anything like this. He walked to the window to take a look. No luck. With the power cuts, the night was pitch black.

He headed back to bed, but Hypnos was not willing to do him any favours.

Chapter 26
In gruesome nakedness

U p early in the morning the next day, Ari got ready for his journey to Eastern Ghouta to meet Khaled. As the winter had taken its toll and the driving rain was drumming on the veranda of his flat, his motorbike was not of any use at the moment. The ground was a quagmire. Arming himself with a heavy jacket, he wondered for a moment how all these people, trapped without heating and of course without food and medical supplies in Eastern Ghouta but also in other districts, were coping. It was difficult even to imagine.

Wael Sharabi, the taxi driver who had collected both Laura and himself from the airport not all that long ago, was in front of his door half an hour after he was called. Instead of saying hello, he addressed Ari with the words lam naraka nhu muddah – long time to see.

'Can you take me to Eastern Ghouta?'

'Of course. Get in.'

They set off for Eastern Ghouta, having to pass through checkpoints everywhere. The capital, one could see, was as heavily fortified as before. Sharabi had not heard of Laura's death. Though very familiar with such atrocities, he was very disturbed upon hearing of it. His body language expressed his feelings with more clarity than his words. He was a Sunni himself, he said, but the atrocities committed by either Isis, al-Qaeda or the Islamic Front were making him sick. The frankness with which he expressed his thoughts was indeed very brave because people, almost as a rule, refrained from expressing an opinion others might take exception to.

Having expressed his condolences, he proceeded to say that he remembered that he had driven Laura to Eastern Ghouta, perhaps the day she was killed or a day or two earlier. He knew she had met with Jaysh al-Islam officials because she was talking in the cab about them and he remembered she had mentioned something about the Saudis. 'They're too involved in your affairs,' she had said.

It was all in tune with what Ari had heard before.

His arrival at the town's half-demolished streets coincided with the ending of the morning's bombardment of the town by the Syrian air force.

Looking for safety, the town's women and children had once again silently moved to surrounding farm fields, as they had been doing daily. But even there, they were not safe. Unsafe and hungry, four out of five residents had already fled Douma, a town which was once a bustling community of around half a million people.

Retaliating, insurgents were using equally indiscriminate tactics by firing their rockets against the Syrian forces.

Following the death of Zahran Alloush, the mood in Douma was very different to what Ari was familiar with. All he could sense by observing the Jaysh al-Islam officials present was disappointment, depression and pessimism. His death had sowed doubts in the garden of their certainties. Silent at their unutterable wretchedness, they were aimlessly moving around, as if this would eject the consciousness of their leaders' death from the body that contained it. They all looked as if they were oddly familiar strangers doing oddly familiar things. The acromegalic features of the situation he found himself in was something he had never seen before.

But the talk behind closed doors was about the Saudis, who in conjunction with Jaysh al-Islam, had failed to carry out successfully the latest attempt on Bashar al-Assad's life. Secrecy was important, but it could not be easily maintained as months' worth of frustration and rage was spilling out into the corridors. All this brought back the information he had received earlier about meetings between the two sides that Laura had for some reason been aware of.

To get a clearer picture, Ari looked around for Khaled, but he could not see him anywhere. He asked another Jaysh al-Islam official if he knew where he was and he was told that Khaled had been killed earlier in the day by a bomb. The bomb had hit one of the rebels' local headquarters and killed half a dozen other officials.

Aghast, Ari stood motionless for a minute. Frozen. His heart rate accelerated, his skin went hot then cold with sweat, his brain jerked to a halt, its engine idling. He wished he smoked for a minute. If he did, a cigarette might have gone a long way to calm himself down. He sat on a bench and, mechanically, took out of his pocket a packet of salted peanuts and had a few without really knowing what he was doing.

The hope that he would eventually unravel the mystery of Laura's death seemed to have completely evaporated. Redefined, reality now demanded radical re-adjustments he would have to embark upon, but only when he had calmed down. For the moment, he had to deal with the disappearance of his unfulfilled hopes. It was then that his eye caught Khaled. Together with a few other Islamists, he was at the moment entering the half-wrecked building. Talking to each other at the same time, they were all looking very animated. Khaled saw him and indicated that he would be with him quite soon. 'Quite soon' turned out to be a bit longer than what Ari had anticipated, but Khaled was at last with him.

He gripped his hand and gave him a hard squeeze. Ari was slightly taken aback by his welcoming him as an old friend not seen for years. Did this indicate a change of his attitude towards him?

'Hi! How are you? I thought you were dead,' Ari started the conversation cheerfully.

Khaled flicked a smile.

'It was somebody else they thought was me,' he answered, rather unsure as to the tone his voice ought to have.

Then he gestured for Ari to follow him to a window table, far from eavesdropping people. Khaled chose to sit on the arm of the chair while Ari took a seat. As others might still be within hearing range, they both traded in small talk for a while. When the small crowd moved away, Ari raised the issue of Laura's movements a day or two before her death.

'I know,' he said, 'that the Saudis were involved in her departure. They felt threatened by her, and I want you to tell me why. What kind of threat did she represent to them?'

More forward this time, the Syrian told him that the story had begun when Zahran Alloush, the head of Jaysh al-Islam, had contacted Bandar bin Sultan, president of the Saudi intelligence, and told him that Laura possessed some highly compromising information.

'What kind of information?' Ari insisted. 'Did it have to do with the Jordanian mafia? I wouldn't have thought so. If that were the case, it would be the Jordanians, not the Saudis, who would have acted.'

Drawing on his fine command of the English language, Khaled said nothing. He had the answer, but he did not seem eager to deliver it. He was probably feeling, Ari thought, that he had already gone too far with his explanations, which had heavily compromised Jaysh al-Islam, his organisation, and he was weighing the merits of any additional information. What he was doing was, in fact, very dangerous but also very brave of him as, Ari was aware, Jaysh al-Islam was never going to forgive him.

'Yes, it was the Saudis who acted,' Khaled eventually said, 'and alarmed, they ordered the force to "take care" of her.'

Ari had something definite in his possession for a change. But the crucial question, which manifested itself in words which Ari did not even have to think about, remained. 'Why did the Saudis want her dead?' Khaled at this point decided to make a move and break the seal of secrecy. In a resigned tone, he explained to Ari that he had passed onto Laura information that the Saudis, though not knowing how Laura had got hold of it, were not prepared to let the West get their hands on.

'What information?' Ari asked again.

'They had planned the assassination of Bashar al-Assad,' Khaled eventually spelt the secret out. 'It was to be carried out in the Presidential Palace by members of the President's own staff.'

'Wow!' Ari gasped. He remembered very well the attempt on Bashar al-Assad's life, something like a couple of days after Laura's death, but the commotion he was going through at the time had parenthesised it.

'But why had Khaled given Laura such a top secret? He must have liked her very much,' was his very first thought. 'Perhaps he had fallen in love with her. And when a man is in love, there's no secret that a woman cannot extract from him in proof of his love. Even Achilles had disclosed to the Trojan Polyxena, whom he loved, the vulnerability of his heel.'

'Though she had never made herself explicitly clear,' Khaled continued, 'Laura had taken a dim view of this plan. "It wouldn't be good for Syria", she had said. She couldn't force the Saudis to abandon it, of course, but she could frustrate its realization by airing it on the BBC. The day that Ahmed Zaman, the head of Jaysh al-Islam's intelligence, and Omar Tawfeek, the head of the Saudi overseas operations, were here, she did make it clear to them that she had heard of their plan and asked for confirmation. They denied its existence of course, but they knew, if aired, the plan would have to be abandoned. They could not go ahead with it.

'The decision to silence her for good was taken only half an hour after she had left.'

Ari was dumbfounded. The truth now stood before him in all its gruesome nakedness. He had not known what to expect from Khaled when pushing him for information. But what he had been told hit him on the head. It was not, of course, the first time that the Saudis had worked on similar plans. Many still remembered the botched attempt by King Saud on Nasser's life back in 1958 for the preparation of which he had spent a vast amount of money.

More importantly, Saudi government officials, including members of the Saudi royal family and the Saudi intelligence, were actively involved in the 9/11 terrorist attack. They had supported the hijackers in every way they could. Were the Americans aware of it? Of course they were, except that they had decided not to activate the smoke alarms and raise public anger at Saudi Arabia, a key ally.

Khaled looked at him and said nothing more.

'I can see what happened next,' Ari said. 'And what happened next is only what one would expect. Afraid that she would pass on the information to the BBC and thereby compromise their plans, they decided to remove her from the picture.'

'God!' Ari exclaimed a minute later. 'And what I had been thinking all along was that her killers were members of the Jordanian mafia. Considering that Laura had enough leads to follow to expose their stealing, this was entirely possible. If aired, the story was bound to make headlines, particularly in the US. But what didn't fit in my version of the story was the information that it was the Saudis rather than the Jordanians who seemed interested in her. It didn't make sense.'

Khaled silently listened and Ari continued, though he was now practically talking to himself. 'What I didn't know was that Laura had in the meantime come across information regarding the plot to kill Bashar al-Assad. That must have happened when I was in Yarmouk.'

If successful, the assassination was bound to cause a major explosion not only in Syria, but in the entire Middle East. Under the circumstances she had no choice but to give this story total priority. Another reason to give it her full attention immediately had been the timing of the Saudi action – in the next few days. Events albeit after her death had just confirmed it.

The attempt on Bashar al-Assad's life had, of course, been thwarted as his would-be assassins had been uncovered and arrested. As a result, two days later came the ill-prepared attempt, unsuccessful again, on the President's life in a Damascus street. Rockets fired from a distance did not even hit their target.

Determined to block the planned assassination by airing it on BBC, Ari was sure that Laura felt that this was the best service she could offer to the Syrian people. Rather than help to end the Syrian crisis, the killing of the President would only make matters worse. There was no viable alternative to his rule. The 'moderate' opposition was in total disarray and, in the greater chaos in which the country would be expected to descend to, the only ones to benefit from his death would be the jihadis.

Ari knew that this was a view not shared by everybody. American but also British officials, strongly disagreeing with the Obama administration, which had primarily targeted Isis in the last few months as opposed to Bashar al-Assad, had been recklessly demanding military strikes against his regime. This, they had been arguing, would not only weaken the Syrian President, but it would also increase the appeal of the opposition. The anticipated change in the military balance would then have a positive effect on the peace talks.

'Was it possible that Hollinger and Kreegan shared their views? Ari wondered. 'Very possible and also likely.'

And this despite the Pentagon officials' fears that Bashar al-Assad's removal from power would only engender total chaos and make Syria easy prey for Islamic militants. Should Hollinger and Kreegan have taken the hardliners' position, their target was not so much Bashar al-Assad himself, but the Russians whose presence in the Mediterranean was guaranteed by the Syrian ruler.

'What we're dealing with here,' Ari thought, 'is the old "Eastern Question" Western diplomacy was obsessed with for much of the 19th Century.'

It was what had caused the Crimean war of the 1850s between Britain and France, who fought to bolster Turkey, and Russia, who planned the carving up of the Ottoman Empire's European parts. It all led to the year-long Anglo-French military campaign in the Crimean peninsula and the defeat of the Russians, but at a very high human cost: 25,000 British and 100,000 French plus up to a million Russians who died, almost all of disease and neglect. The Middle East, for many, presented Europe with 'a new Eastern Question'.

Whatever the arguments in favour of or against the 'Eastern Question' thesis, the arguments against Bashar al-Assad looked to Ari himself, and, as he was sure, to Laura, too, as nothing but quixotic. Targeting Assad's regime with Cruise missiles would ensure the war, along with the anguish of the Syrian people, would be prolonged even further. It would also strengthen the jihadis. Even more alarmingly, it could easily bring the Americans into a direct military conflict with the Russians.

This was not just the view of an outsider. It was also the view of all those Syrian democrats who had five years earlier protested in their thousands in every Syrian town against Bashar al-Assad's authoritarian rule, demanding an end to it. But that was five years ago, when the promise of a better future was still alive and the jihadis had not posed a lethal threat to their rights. All people now wanted was an end to the war and the defeat of the jihadis. That was Maryam's approach, too.

Ari could see Laura judging the options in front of her, dismissing the ideas of the obstinate Saudis and going for the only thing that made sense under the circumstances: the frustration of their plan. Its airing would do it. He was sure she was fully aware of the dangers inherent in the situation, but she had obviously chosen to disregard them.

'The woman,' he thought while his eyes brimmed with pride, 'was the embodiment of a principle, the image of an idea. She had both convictions and guts. To have been a friend of hers was a gift, an honour I value more than anything else.' But this did not reduce the pain her departure had inflicted, herringboning his heart. She personified the sublime beauty of everything he loved and valued.

Khaled's thinking, meanwhile, had been moving along similar tracks. Talking to Ari after he had passed onto him the crucial information he needed, and assuming, Ari was now sure of it, that his life was fast coming to its end, he explained how frustrated he had been with developments in his own country.

'The rebellion against Bashar al-Assad,' the Syrian said almost mournfully, 'has turned into a murderous civil war. On top of this, I can't agree with Jaysh al-Islam's crude ideology and practices. I've been attracted to the Islamist cause, but all I now feel is disillusionment with its connections, policies and more than anything else the elaborate brutality it's been demonstrating in the pursuit of its aims.'

While he was talking, Ari could see that he was being watched by several Jaysh al-Islam rebels at the other end of the conference room. He thanked him from the bottom of his heart for all his help and, giving voice to his apprehension about his future within this organisation, he asked him if there was anything he could do for him. 'If you want,' he suggested, 'I can help you to move from Syria, to England or Greece. Something tells me you're no longer safe here.'

He did not say that he had a premonition that he would never see him again.

Khaled looked at him in a way that clearly manifested his textured pain, but said nothing. He only smiled.

'His last smile?' Ari wondered.

Eventually, Ari moved out and crossed the street that was now fully exposed to the rigorousness of the weather. The feeling that he himself was being shadowed was now ever present. He glanced to the left, then to the right, and occasionally searched the faces in the crowd behind him. But he could not tell if anyone had his eyes on him for certain. No one seemed to pay him any undue attention. In the process, he tried to memorise the features of anyone whose eyes rested on upon him enquiringly even for a few seconds.

His peripheral vision, employed on a full time basis now, was of no help either. But a nagging apprehension, an instinct to beware, an abstract warning made the presence of his fears powerfully felt. Finding no hiding place, they could easily be detected on his face.

Half a dozen kids between the ages of six and fourteen stepped into his path. With some effort, he was out of their way. It was then that his eye caught the figure of a man standing behind him some thirty metres away. He instantly recognised him. He was the man who had looked at him menacingly when he had left the office of Mark Hollinger. His presence, no longer a vision of his tormented mind, represented a threat Ari could not ignore. He wondered what to do for a minute. It was a question to which he could not find an answer. He could not go to him to ask what he was after, as he would be dismissed as an idiot. He imagined the scene.

'Why are you following me?'

'Who's following you?'

'You.'

'You must be out of your mind. Go see your doctor.'

Or the scene could take a different turn.

'Why are you following me?'

'I'll tell you. Come with me.'

'Where?'

'Here.'

'Here' was a cul-de-sac in which the one-eyed man pulled out a knife and cut Ari's throat.

If it was a Hollywood film, where Ari would have all the help he needed from both the scriptwriter and the film director, he would immobilise the jihadi and forcefully extract from him all the answers he wanted. 'But this is not a Hollywood film,' he reminded himself. 'And this isn't a time for fantasies.' The bitter smile that appeared on his face was one of ironical self-dismissal.

The instance nevertheless passed with nothing untoward occurring. But in the same day, he decided that he had to ensure that, if attacked, he would be able to defend himself effectively. He had to get a gun. As a terrorist attack was an ever-present possibility, many Damascenes had already done so – if, that is to say, they could afford it! A Chinese-made Kalashnikov rifle could be bought for $500 on the black market. Its Soviet version was more expensive.

He went to the nearest ATM and got the cash he needed, or he thought he needed for the purpose. His next stop was the crossing to the rebel-held Eastern Ghouta, where Yaman, an army officer he had met a few times, could easily oblige. Government soldiers were known for selling weapons provided to them by the regime at bargain prices. However, he was not there. 'Sorry, he's been killed.'

He accepted it the same way he would have accepted the news that Yaman was not there because he had just taken his annual holiday break. Death had become small change in the Syrian life market for everybody except the dead person's mother. His next stop was at a café frequented by Adnan, the arms trader he knew. He was not there, but Ari managed to trace him and he was in his place soon after.

'Well, well, well! What brings you here?'

'I need a gun.'

'What for?'

'To kill mosquitos. Too many of them.'

Adnan, with his face still buried in a multi-decker sandwich, took him inside his small storage room. AK-47s and RPG launchers were propped against the walls. Rocket-propelled grenades were laid down in rows on the floor next to bayonets and camouflage combat belts. Bullets were spread out on the workbench at the back, opposite a cabinet with small drawers full of other ammunition and ordnance.

He was offered a semi-automatic Browning Hi-Power and a box of cartridges. But he had, of course, to learn how to use it as well as his fork and knife. Obligingly, after he took some time to find his personalised toothpicks he was looking for, the arms trader showed him the essentials.

'If I'm attacked,' he was now sure, 'I'll be able to defend myself.'

It dawned on him that in doing so, he might well have to shoot and kill. The idea had never crossed his mind before. 'Shoot to kill? Kill another human being? I can't even kill a chicken.' Another thought hit him. 'But that's not just me. Most people feel the same. Given that, if we didn't have butchers to do what's necessary, most of us would be vegetarians.'

But he might well have to kill. He did not like it at all and the idea oozed away for a moment. The thought that by doing so, he would only be protecting himself did not offer the comfort he had imagined. But he felt that, if killing an attacker was something impossible to avoid, he would just have to do it. There was no other option. The days of innocence were over. 'Innocence,' he reassured himself, 'is a delusion.'

The thought that he could defend himself instead of turning into a thug's victim was pretty comforting until another one crossed his mind. 'What if rather than being shot at, the jihadists had booby-trapped my motorbike? Or my lavatory?' He would then be instantly transferred to the realm of non-existence without even a chance to say a heartfelt goodbye to the world.

Unsettled and wishing he had a job which would preserve not just his life, but also a few of his illusions, he climbed onto his motorbike and drove to his office. Looking at its mirror, he could see the same Peugeot-207 he had seen before outside Hollinger's office constantly behind him.

'What on earth do they want,' he wondered again. 'If they want to kill me, why don't they go ahead and try? What's holding them back? What do they want to find out before they act?'

The vigour of his mental process shot up as soon as he thought of the part the two intelligence officers, Hollinger and Kreegan, were playing in the story. They had failed to protect Laura and they were now failing to protect him against the mortal threat posed by the jihadis. 'What was the reason behind their inaction? Professional incompetence? Ethical deficiency? A failure of will? And if the latter, what was the reason for it? Whose interests were they protecting?'

He felt waves of anger which knocked down the shield of the calm self-control that marked his professional conduct. Back at his workplace, he went straight to the office of his boss, Richard Samuels, to ask him point blank who Mark Hollinger really was.

Something did not, however, look right. His colleagues, whom he had passed before entering Samuels' office, had their hands down as if they were absorbed by their work, and Samuels himself looked overwhelmed by a white sadness.

'Brigitte,' he said. 'She was badly injured in an explosion in Sayyidah Zaynab.'

'How badly?'

'She's in intensive care.'

The blasts, near Syria's holiest Shi'ite shrine, had hit a bus station and a military headquarters building south of Damascus. Claimed by Isis, it had killed 71 people. The intention behind it was to disrupt the meeting that government and opposition groups had planned in Geneva in a bid to start talks aimed at a political solution to the conflict. Footage showing burning buildings and car wreckage in the neighbourhood where the shrine is located was being broadcast on Syria's state television.

The mosque near the explosions contains, according to Shi'a Muslim tradition the grave of Zaynab, granddaughter of the Prophet Muhhamad. It is a destination of mass pilgrimage by Shi'a Muslims from across the Muslim world. For the Sunnis, Zaynab's tomb lies in the mosque of the same name in Cairo.

Brigitte had joined the UNRWA office in Damascus at about the same time Ari had and the two of them had worked together in Yarmouk, when they had visited it some time ago, and later on in Hama. Ari liked her self-conscious grace, her straightforward attitude and her refreshing approach to issues that kept constantly coming up. She was a noble and selfless person, very committed to the job she had to perform, a breath of fresh air in the ghastly environment they had to live in almost daily.

He could only hope she would recover and fairly soon return to the office to fill the huge gap her absence had created. But something in him was whispering that the doctors were only trying to postpone the arrival of the inevitable. Whatever, the news was very disturbing. Death was once again indiscriminately hitting his world. So many people he knew were no longer around. 'When will Samuels', Garrahan's, Cole's or my own turn will come?' he wondered. It seemed that it was not a question of 'if' but 'when' that was going to happen.

He felt disgusted at the blatant show of human wickedness – bigotry, intolerance, prejudice, greed, stupidity, hatred, misanthropy, injustice. Their true cutting edge was on show all around him. 'But how could one escape all of this? Or, perhaps, the right question is how could one escape human nature?' The thought horrified him.

'You're losing your marbles,' he told himself once again. 'You're becoming a critic of human nature like a cow in an abattoir. Stop it.' He did so as his thoughts could even stop the church clock at the moment. But his heart was bleeding.

At that same moment Garrahan stormed into his office. 'They're dead. They're all dead. Our three colleagues taken hostage by Isis are dead. Slaughtered. On Facebook, a photo displayed their heads for everyone to enjoy.'

Nothing seemed to be bad enough. Something worse was always on the way. Lost in the frozen featurelessness of the moment, they could only hear humanity's voice bleating in the wilderness. Hope had become something like a luggage lost in the world's Futility Square.

'I think,' Garrahan said, 'I'm going back to Ireland to study paleoichthyology.'

Chapter 27
Looking death in the eye

Horrified at the news, Ari abandoned his internal dialogues and decided instead to proceed with what he had in mind when he went to Samuels' office.

'Who's this Hollinger?' he asked him, point blank. No introduction. No explanation. No articulation. Samuels, with the sort of mind that could see round corners, ought to have the answer.

Slightly puzzled, the 'boss' looked up from his computer and smiled. 'This is above my pay grade,' he said. 'But I've heard that he's been in active service for nearly twenty years.'

'Yes?'

'Before he came to Damascus, he'd served as an operational officer in Iraq, investigating the trafficking of arms and looking for weapons of mass destruction.'

'Is Mark Hollinger his real name?' Ari asked.

'I doubt it,' Samuels said. 'But even his real name is probably not his real name.'

The difficult question came last.

'Could Hollinger be involved in a plot to assassinate Bashar al-Assad? If yes,' he added, 'it fits with a pattern. Assassinations aren't, of course, considered to be a good idea by the intelligence agencies. But, on the other hand, they're never off the agenda. For example, as far as I know, MI6 once considered the idea of assassinating Slobodan Milosevic, the president of Serbia, by staging a car crash using a powerful strobe light to blind the driver. Couldn't it be involved in a similar plan against Bashar al-Assad here in Damascus?'

Samuels looked at him with the professional detachment of a sommelier who examines the wine without any intention of drinking it.

'Or,' Ari carried on, 'I could mention the CIA's attempts to assassinate Fidel Castro, or the bozos at MI6 who had been involved in a plot to assassinate Muammar Gaddafi in 1995.'

'I very much doubt it,' Samuels replied, probably with reference to the spirit rather than the letter of the question. The conversation ended there.

Ari could not really expect anything more. He started walking towards the exit, but then, just like Lieutenant Columbo, the Los Angeles homicide detective, he stopped and asked Samuels one more question. 'And Kreegan? Who's Kreegan?'

'A half-Jewish American.'

'Anything more?'

'Sorry, I don't know anything about him.'

'Well,' Ari said, giving up, 'you must at least know which half of him is Jewish. The top or the bottom?'

He walked out while Samuels smiled as if that was his legal obligation.

Meanwhile, the Syrian President's position seemed to be strengthened by the day as the Russian military intervention had changed the balance of power on the ground. A number of Free Syrian Army rebels, those who had not joined Isis, re-joined the Syrian army, while the breakup of Syrian rebel strongholds in and around Damascus accelerated after the killing of Zahran Alloush.

So was the case in Aleppo where government forces were smashing their way through the defences of Jabhat al-Nusra and the other jihadi forces in the area.

But the end of the war was still far away and unlikely to appear in the rear-view window before the forces of destruction had completed their job. Meanwhile, under a UN-sponsored ceasefire, at least 2,000 rebels evacuated part of Yarmouk, the Damascus suburb, while at the same time several thousands of Isis fighters were transported from the Syrian capital to their Syrian headquarters. The Syrian army, backed by Hezbollah forces, had also captured the town of Marj al-Sultan and its airport in Eastern Ghouta, further reinforcing the Damascus international Airport and the road that leads to it.

In a demonstration of the regime's new-found confidence, new posters of the President replaced his previously fading images hanging from the centre of soaring archways that welcome you into Syria. Military checkpoints had been bolstered and brightened by fresh coats of paint in the black, white and red tricolour of Syria's flag. Overall developments were not, however, progressing satisfactorily for the regime.

The plan was for Russian air strikes and missiles to clear the rebels out of one area after another and for the Syrian army ground troops to storm in and take over. But these troops, together with Iranian and Shi'ite militias and also Hezbollah fighters, were proving too slow to press the advantage given to them by the Russians. The latter were, as a result, losing patience with them.

But concurrently, the search for a political solution in Syria had received fresh impetus as the US and Russia were trying to get representatives of both the government and the opposition to attend 'proximity talks' planned to be held in Geneva at the end of January. On the table was a Security Council-endorsed road map for peace, including a ceasefire and a transitional period ending with elections.

Ari welcomed these developments because, as a result, some peace and tranquillity might soon return to most parts of Syria as it actually did when the cessation of hostilities was announced and the fighting was significantly reduced. The elimination of Bashar al-Assad, which according to the CIA would shift the balance of power in favour of the 'moderate' opposition, was no longer on the cards. Among others, the Pentagon opposed it. Washington had gradually given up on the rebels, whose train-and-equip programme it had already terminated, and was ending its war for the replacement of Bashar al-Assad. His removal, it was now aware, would only favour Isis, the murderous ideological offspring of Saudi Arabia.

But the next question was what Bashar al-Assad intended to do, what 'concessions' he was prepared to make in order to reach an agreement with at least some of his opponents. Russia, whose military intervention had bolstered his forces, was not exactly on the same page as him. Its prime concern was not the fulfilment of his ambition to win back militarily all the territory he had lost, but its own interests, which required an end to this war. A Kurdish state in northern Syria would probably suit President Putin as this would administer a heavy blow to the Turkish 'Sultan'. And the end of the war would help the normalisation of Russia's acanthaceous relationship with the West and most of all with Washington.

The possibility of a ceasefire had been welcomed by many Syrians, too. Many had told Ari so, including the three young men, all single, college-educated professionals, he was talking to earlier in the day. They did not like President Bashar al-Assad, they said.

'I was arrested and beaten up,' one of them added in a low voice to make sure he was not overheard, 'because I had drawn a moustache on a poster of the President.'

But if they had to choose between an Islamic fundamentalist takeover and his regime, they would go for the latter without second thoughts. 'Our only desire is to see Syria's return to the stable, secure state it was before the war,' one of them said. 'The last thing that Syria needs is yet more violence.'

'Until then,' another one of them added half-seriously, 'I'm not planning to get married. If I did, nobody would come to my wedding. Most of my friends have left the country.'

The spirit of the 'Arab Spring' had all but gone and people were debilitated by the immense toll the war had exacted. 'The future had lied,' and, exhausted, they had collapsed.

The ceasefire talks were, however, anything but trouble free. Whatever the terms between Bashar al-Assad and the 'moderate' rebels, it could hardly be extended to the Islamists, including, apart from Isis, non-Isis military groups such as Jaysh al-Fatah. The latter, formed in late March 2015, included the al-Qaeda-affiliated Jabhat al-Nusra, the Turkish-backed Ahrar al-Sham and other smaller Salafist jihadi forces. The coalition, without a leader or a unified command, operated around the northern cities of Aleppo, Idlib and Hama. Equally unpalatable were other groups such as Jund al-Aqsa and Jaysh al-Islam.

Islamist but explicitly not jihadi, the latter was gradually being drawn into an armed conflict with Jabhat al-Nusra in Eastern Ghouta that later developed into a full-scale war. The situation was so tense and confused that many people actually believed that there was never going to be a peace deal.

'They all run to the finishing line,' Samuels told Ari when the two of them were discussing matters in his office, 'but as things stand, there's no finishing line. It's almost next to impossible to have a peace deal when the country is split into numerous compartments, each one of them under the control of a different group. This war is not going to finish any time soon.'

'It's as you say,' Ari agreed. 'Nobody,' he added, in an effort to dispel a bit of the bad feeling, 'has served it an eviction notice.'

Soon after, he asked Khaled for another meeting. He was sure that there was more to the story he had told him. They arranged to meet the following morning. A bit more relaxed as he knew that he was gradually getting to the bottom of this hideous affair, he then phoned Garrahan at his home to meet for a drink in town. As his phone was busy, he texted him and Garrahan came back to him in no time.

They met close to the Bab Touma Gate, in the town's Christian quarter, near Bab Touma, an area with a cluster of lively bars with dance floors and DJ beats. Once again, Muslims and Christians were cheerfully mingling with each other outside the steamy hammams and the souks in which their owners were standing behind the same wooden counters their great-grandfathers did. Designed to meet the middle class desires, many shops were displaying the latest in fashion.

'A decade or so ago,' Ari said while looking at one of their windows, 'luxury wasn't something the Damascenes were familiar with. Then, in 2005, Bashar al-Assad took a broader view of his country's interests and started to liberalise its economy steadily. His Association agreement with the EU gradually removed import tariffs on EU goods in exchange for financial and technical support and new massive projects helped the development of many sectors, including the financial services, education and training, healthcare, oil and gas, retail and construction.

'Tourism was the prime benefit of this expansion. New tasteful restaurants and cafés opened, and so did souvenir shops, art galleries and boutique hotels, all happy in their unqualified comfortableness. The exquisite Al Pasha in Harat al-Yahoud, the city's Jewish quarter, which I visited only a few weeks ago, is a fine example of the new trends: a palace of birdsong, rosewood furniture with mother-of-pearl inlay, and the constant, cooling sound of trickling water.'

'I've been there, too,' Garrahan said, rather pleased with himself.

'Yes, it's a beautiful boutique hotel, one of the treasures of the Old City, renovated in 2010 following the conversion of three adjoining, separate 18th Century Damascene homes. The city was at the time blossoming as a tourist destination. But look at it now.'

'Pathetic and sad,' Garrahan agreed before Ari could give his sombre mood an outward form. 'But, at least,' he added, 'the long deserted and neglected Jewish Quarter did receive the attention of the authorities. They restored it and beautified it like the rest of the ancient walled city. The ancient Jewish community is of course no longer there. Yet the Arab neighbours do still remember the families who used to live there. Their synagogues and schools are still there with their Hebrew inscriptions.'

They finished their beer and ordered another one while a group of refugees out in the street seemed to be celebrating something very noisily. The refugees, people who had escaped the hell which fighting in many parts of the country had thrown them into, were everywhere in Damascus, even in its most prosperous districts.

When the time came, the two of them parted and Ari drove back home for a good night's rest. It was not to be as he was being chased by nightmares that reflected his state of mind. Up rather early in the morning, he left his flat, chatted with the shopkeeper next door and, while walking to his motorbike, tried to plan his day's work.

Reaching the place where he had parked, he absent-mindedly took the key out of his pocket only to drop it as soon as he was about to use it. He went down on his knees looking for it. It was then that he discovered that something was sticking out from the top of the back wheel. It was a film, held in place by two pins. He wondered what this might be for a minute. Attached under the mudguard, as he discovered after he checked again, there was a small black parcel, which he had seen before but only on the internet.

'Bloody hell,' he said loudly. 'This can only be a bomb. A victim-operated device.'

His motorbike was booby-trapped. What he should expect to find inside the black box attached under the mudguard was the bomb itself and all it takes to activate it. He stood there motionless, totally bewildered at its detection. A cloud of inchoate feelings buzzed around him in no time and he was in touch with immensity a minute later.

He had no experience whatsoever in this field. He had only discovered the trap thanks to his good luck, his clumsiness, a blessing in disguise. Perhaps he was also guided by some sort of intuition, which many people in Damascus had unconsciously developed. After all, he knew that the hours ahead were pregnant with disaster. He could not, of course, tell how all of this would end. The handwriting of his destiny was indecipherable.

In the meantime, a few people, curious about what was going on, had formed a circle around him, talking agitatedly and loudly. They knew as much as he did that the black box was a killing device. A policeman, who appeared soon, ordered them to keep a safe distance and called someone over his phone. In no time, the area was flooded with police cars. In one of them, there was the bomb disposal expert.

Ari was taken to the police station where he was interrogated by officers eager to discover why he had been targeted. He was not quite sure what he should or should not tell them. But rather than explaining, he asked them to contact Rafiq Shahadah, the head of the Syrian intelligence.

'He'll tell you,' he said confidently, while totally uncertain as to what the man would tell them. But that did not matter. All that mattered was that he would certainly tell them to let him go without answering their questions. Waiting for a response, he looked at the two men with swollen eyes and blood on their faces who had just arrived and stood next to him. Handcuffed, both of them emitted a smell of humidity, blood and sweat, the smell of torture. One of them was a prison officer.

'What have they done?' Ari asked one of the police officers later on as he was about to walk out.

'They used a drone to deliver phones to jihadis inside the Sednaya military prison in Damascus.'

Drones were extensively used by the coalition forces against Isis either for intelligence purposes or to hit various targets and Isis had flooded the Internet with the names and addresses of those involved in such operations. But drones were also used by Isis itself to gather information or to produce videos for propaganda purposes. They were manufactured in several drone factories near Mosul or developed from kits and parts found on the Internet.

It was the first time Ari had heard that drones had been used to distribute phones to prisoners in Syria!

'Am I surprised?' he wondered. 'No! Of course not! Why should I be? Drones are a must-have gadget these days, easily available on the high street.' He wondered for a minute what the technologically streamlined future had in store. 'Not sure we should be looking forward to it,' an old thought re-emerged in his mind with the same force as in the past.

Soon after, the police commander told him that he was free to go and Ari was out on the street in no time. His motorbike, safe now, was waiting for him. He climbed on with some trepidation as he had still not recovered from the shock and stayed there, almost frozen, thinking about what would have happened if he had not discovered the explosives. 'The pieces of my body, assembled together, would be resting in the local mortuary in a bag.' The thought made him feel dizzy.

He started his motorbike and he was back to his flat soon after. He filled his glass with whiskey and emptied it in one gulp. It tasted like dead water. He did not feel good at all. He had, of course, just managed to avoid the empty eternity by chance. But the rent to life he was paying was exorbitant. Besides, death was hiding somewhere very close him. He could sense his presence, smell it, even see the aura of doom his propinquity emanated. Nothing extraordinary about it, as things had turned out.

Perhaps that was the price for his stubbornness, thick-skinned like Churchill's. If he had dropped the search for Laura's killers as Hollinger and Kreegan had advocated, he would certainly not be in this position. But could he? Would he? The answer was again an emphatic 'no'. On the other hand, he was sure he had learnt something from the experience except that at the moment he could not work out what it was.

He just had to carry on and hope for the best even if this reduced the number of suns he was going to see set down to a single figure. What he had arranged with Khaled had, under the new circumstances, to be re-arranged. As soon as this was done, the two of them met in Douma as before. Except that Ari arrived at his appointment with some delay. An unexploded cluster bomb, one of the many obstacles those left in the town of Douma were experiencing on a daily basis, had forced some time-consuming navigation through the city's ruins.

But Khaled was still there, waiting for him. He confirmed that Laura had been killed by his own people following a request made by the Saudi intelligence to this effect. He himself, tired of it all, had decided to withdraw from the Islamist organisation and to return to private life, a life in which 'nobody would be expecting anything of me'. Ari was pleased to hear that.

Interestingly, however, Khaled added that Hollinger had full knowledge of the Saudi plot to assassinate Bashar al-Assad and had given it his blessing. Ari's guess was that Hollinger had not passed on the information to London because he knew that the plot was not in line with the policy his government was following at the time. He wondered what the British would have done if he had passed it on. They certainly would not have informed the Syrian President, but they might have dropped a word of caution to the Saudis.

But did Hollinger know that Jaysh al-Islam had killed Laura in conjunction with the Saudis?

He had no definite answer to this. He did not think that Hollinger knew about the Saudi decision to kill her, but it was very likely that he had been informed that they were the guilty party after her death. Considering his hostility to anything relating to Laura's death he himself had been raising with him, this seemed to be the more likely script. To protect the Saudis, he had done his best to cover up their part in the story. Saudi Arabia was, after all, a 'key ally'.

The next day, Khaled was found dead in Eastern Ghouta, beheaded by the Islamists. A note, reddened from the gush of blood from his ruptured throat, attached to his body informed everyone that he was a traitor. Ari's heart had dried so much by this time that it could not even feel the pain. His capacity for suffering had withered.

Khaled was one of the most decent people he had come across in his life and his loss was a loss for the entire Syrian nation. He was a man willing to stand by his beliefs whatever the cost to himself, and this without the jihadis' expectation of rewards in the afterlife. He was the man the Arabs should turn into a hero. He knew, of course, that this was never going to happen. Khaled's name was going to rest outside history, be forgotten.

But he also knew that his own time had come. The jihadis were after him, too. He was in a state of war. Thinking about it all, particularly during the hours of the night, when he remained sleepless until the stars disappeared in the light of the morning, often gave his stomach a burning sensation.

The next day, though slightly disoriented by some sort of an ill-feeling, he was back in his office. At its front door, where dustbin bags had been ripped off during the night by cats, a woman said 'hello' to him. He could not remember who she was. They must have met somewhere before, except that he did not have a clue as to where this 'somewhere' might be. He belatedly returned her greeting, when he was practically beyond her visual range.

'Who's she?' he wondered again. But he still could not recall. 'My memory has opted for early retirement,' he told himself. He recalled that he still could not remember who had directed 'Battleship Potemkin', the 1925 Soviet silent film. But the moment the name of the film came to his lips again, the director's name, for a day on the tip of his tongue, effortlessly came up. 'Eisenstein,' he said. 'Sergei Eisenstein.' He was pleased with himself.

By the time he had stepped into his office, the thought that he would have to leave Damascus as soon as possible had already been mentally accepted. All that was now necessary was its confirmation by his inner self. He was thinking about it intensely when the unexpected made its appearance in the form of Robin Giles, a *Guardian* journalist.

'I would very much appreciate your thoughts on Laura Heineken's death,' he said over the phone.

'OK. Come over.' 'If I were to die,' Ari thought, 'at least by talking to *The Guardian* man, I would have at least given the world the story it was denied.' He did not believe in coincidences, unless they were of course planned. 'But who could tell?' He gave the issue a bit of consideration. 'Well,' he eventually decided, 'perhaps there's such a thing as coincidences, after all!'

The Guardian man was in his office in no time. He had probably called Ari on his mobile just outside the building that the office was housed in. He was a young man, slightly older than Ari, with a fully-fuelled energy tank. Tall, casual and easy-going, he shook hands with Ari, accepted the espresso he was offered and activated his tape-recorder.

'I hope you don't mind it,' he said, taking the answer he would like to hear for granted.

'No, it's fine,' Ari reassured him.

'OK,' Giles said, 'now tell me what's happened.'

'I will,' Ari answered, 'but you first tell me why you're coming to me to unravel the mystery of Laura's death?'

'I heard about you from Samuels. The issue was accidentally raised when we met and he told me you know the whole story,' Giles replied.

Capturing in painful granularity the hostile political background against which initially Laura and then he himself had to operate, Ari gave him an account of what happened.

'I see,' Giles said at the end. 'Grandiose schemes, murderous plans, never-ending intrigues, betrayed ideals. And blood on everybody's hands.

I was hoping,' he joked, 'you would tell me something that was surprisingly new.'

'Sorry, that's again the same old story,' Ari replied.

'You know, by the way,' Giles added, 'many people in the West, including many *Guardian* readers, would love to see the end of Bashar al-Assad.'

'So would I,' Ari said. 'But not under current circumstances. His going now would benefit only the Islamists, whether Baghdadi funs or "moderates". And this would be disastrous for the Syrians. It would force them to live their lives in tune with the primitive theocratic rules of the religious extremists.'

He recalled a similar discussion with Laura not all that long before she died.

'I don't care,' she had told him, 'what the "majority" in France, Britain or America think about it all. There are no "moderates" in this war. The opponents of Assad are all Islamists of one shade or another. Yet they are backed up by the West for strategic reasons. The West is, however, wrong on two counts. First, an Islamist victory would harm its own strategic interests in the Middle East, and secondly, it's pursued regardless of the interests of the Syrian people themselves. All the latter want right now is the ending of the war and a life free from the Islamist tyranny. I don't therefore care what the manufactured "majority", if it's indeed the majority, thinks. No majorities can force my conscience to accept the unacceptable.'

'I wish, Ari said, 'I could one day put all of this in a book. But the narrative of such a book will have to look like a painting, something that would give a visual quality to the sufferings and the characters in it. But I don't think I've got what it takes to do it justice.'

'You can always try,' was Giles' encouraging response.

The attempt on his life occurred in the evening of the same day, soon after he had dashed out of his office. He had stayed there for a bit longer than usual, as he needed to finish a report. Before leaving, he took a look out of his window to check the weather. The damp January wind carrying in its wings drops of rain was as still as it had been all day: radiantly indifferent as to its impact. The low bruise-black clouds made sure no stars were visible. Nothing to look forward to.

He was soon on his motorbike, driving down the city's practically empty streets. Some threat, which seemed engraved on the body of the night, would not, however, let him relax. There was nothing more to it than a nagging anticipation of something waiting to happen, an admonitory warning, an instinct telling him to keep his antenna in a state of alert. He scanned the street and the adjoining buildings, but nothing drew his attention. Still, the feeling of being watched persisted.

It did not take him long to discover that he was being followed by a car. Its movements were only too easily detectable as the car driver was not interested in concealing his interest in him. The truth instantly penetrated his mind and he accelerated in response. The powerful engine purred beneath him as the speedometer reached its high end. So did his vitality, whose wheels synchronised their movement with those of his engine. Still the car did not move from his rear-view window.

Forced at some point to withdraw to a tangle of malodorous alleys, he saw two men stepping out of the car, and then moving slowly and steadily in his direction. They were not taking any precautions as they were certain that Ari was unarmed. The stab of fear in his gut ensured that he was not hallucinating. So did the smell of stale cabbage that filled the air. In the stillness of the night, he could hear the beatings of his heart. It seemed as if it was going to burst out of his chest.

He ran for cover behind a parked car, removed his helmet and dragged a hand through his hair. He then focused his gaze on the assailants. He could clearly see them. They were certainly not the kind of men who could recite Sophocles' *Oedipus Rex* in Greek. Still, he had to remain calm, control his impetuosity. 'This isn't the time for a wrong move I may not even be able to regret.'

Hidden from view, he remained there for a while. The Jaysh al-Islam gunners vanished from his vision for a moment, and Ari glanced at the moon, which failed to pass on a casual greeting this time. The men then re-materialised. They knew where he was and approached him with knives in their hands. He knew exactly what they intended to do at that point, what was in store for him if he failed to act expeditiously. The bells inside his head instantly turned on piercing his brain, and his breath came out in ragged gasps.

He waited for a while until the two men got quite close. He then caught his bottom lip between his teeth, aimed at them and fired his gun.

He hit both of them. The sound of the shots in the still night was carried all the way to the main road. He did not move. Death might still be around waiting for him. He stared at the bodies on the ground and scanned the main road in which a few cars were moving fast. Satisfied that he was not being watched, he then approached the bodies of the two assailants. One of them had been killed instantly. The second one, also hit by a bullet, was lying down on the wet road, unable to move.

Ari was overwhelmed by a new feeling that he had once again never experienced. He was, on the one hand, greatly relieved that he had just escaped the net of death. The law of self-preservation could never dictate anything different. But, on the other hand, he could not come to terms with what his taking care of his life had necessitated. 'I've just killed someone,' he reflected. 'I've taken this man's life.'

But it was worse than that. 'Yes, I've killed him,' he kept thinking, 'but who knows, I've also left a child without a father, a woman without a husband or a mother without a son.' The ghastly, cruel, monstrous thing he felt he had just done overwhelmed him. 'Yes, it was in self-defence,' another part of him argued. 'But I still killed a man. And I'll have to live with it forever.' Unconsciously, he squeezed his eyes tight as though he could make what he had just gone through disappear.

The only living creature he had killed in his life was an ant and that when he was still a kid. And he still remembered it. He remembered the little creature sauntering in front of him while he was seated in his sunny balcony, his shoe moving over it and crushing it along with the feeling of shame his action had filled him with. 'It was only an ant,' a part of him kept telling himself. 'Yes, but you didn't have to wipe out its life,' another voice was arguing much more convincingly.

He would not be tormented by such thoughts, of course, if he had died instead. 'Once you die, you don't have to think of your actions,' a voice inside him whispered. Death, in front of him, inclined his head, perhaps in agreement with what he was thinking. 'Does that mean that it's easier to die than to kill?'

Whatever, he now had to get away from the scene. He did just that. Taking all precautions, he stepped out of the darkness and, on his motorbike, he ran against the cold blast of the winter. This time, he went straight to the flat of James Garrahan, his colleague, to spend the night.

'What?' Garrahan asked when he opened the door in his pyjamas. 'What's going on? Where've you been? What happened?'

He was genuinely alarmed. Without explaining anything, Ari, with a forced smile on his face, told him that he had a rough night and then asked him if he could spend the night in his flat. 'Of course,' was the obliging response.

'And please do order a pizza.'

Garrahan did just that and then excused himself as he had, he said, to fix his washing machine which had flooded. On his way out, he was swearing at the manufacturers for the planned obsolesce of their products.

The next day, explaining the reasons for it as briefly as he could, Ari told his boss he had to return to London. 'There's no way I can stay here any longer,' he said. 'They'll take me out the very first moment they can.'

Samuels did not argue with him. He could clearly see the picture, in terms of both Ari's predicament and the jihadis' murderous intentions.

'What a terrible situation,' he muttered, probably talking to himself. 'But you've been great in coping with all this. Your determination to get through this awful business is amazing. Your commitment to our values is awe-inspiring. Your courage is truly staggering.'

Silent for a minute, as if this could erase the awkwardness of the occasion, he then proceeded to add a few more words. 'Your contribution to our work here has been fantastic right from the beginning. You've been truly great. I'm really going to miss you.'

Ari was touched by the sincerity and the warmth of Samuels' words. He thanked him and then left for the airport to catch the flight to Beirut a few hours later.

Back in Britain, he visited the BBC's director-general to whom he dextrously explained what he knew about Laura's murder – the story she was after, the interests that had led to her elimination from the scene, the part these 'sincere hypocrites', the British and the American intelligence officers had played. The director-general listened with great interest, and, more importantly, full of empathy. But, as he obviously did not want to commit himself, all he said at the end was 'it doesn't sound right'.

His 'doesn't sound right' was definitely a reference to the Saudis' action. He might have also meant the Western intelligence agencies' action or inaction, though this was much less clear.

Ari heard later that the BBC man had raised the issue with the Military Intelligence Chief Alex Younger and the Foreign Secretary Philip Hammond. With a twinge of displeasure for the BBC's intrusion into their business, they both refused to acknowledge any responsibility. If their response could be summed up in a few words, those words were, 'we don't want to know'.

Moral flexibility was viewed in their quarters as an asset.

The next day, *The Guardian* published Robin Giles' story on its front page.

The day after, Mark Hollinger was recalled back home. He had become a liability.

Lightning Source UK Ltd.
Milton Keynes UK
UKOW06f0205101017
310687UK00003B/63/P